Praise for I Am My Beloveds

"Imagine the propulsive plot ⋯ multidimensional character⋯ The combination is rare and ⋯ nick has pulled it off. I disa⋯ ⋯ every choice that every character made in this audacious (and very sexy) book, and that's exactly what made me keep reading, because Papernick made me care about each person he summoned to life in it. In an era where we dismiss everyone who doesn't think like we do, *I am my Beloveds* offers radical curiosity and empathy."
-- Dara Horn, author of *Eternal Life* and *People Love Dead Jews*

"Part *Le Ronde* and part *Bob and Carol and Ted and Alice*, two very different couples intersect a brave new world through surrogacy, fidelity, pregnancy, aging parents, faith and loss. Raucous, revolutionary and also, so much fun."
— Caroline Leavitt, *New York Times* bestselling author of *Pictures of You* and *Cruel Beautiful World*

"Everyone in *I Am My Beloveds* howls their lungs out at life's inequities, at love's fickleness, and mostly at one another. But if you listen closely, they're also howling up from the pages at you, inviting you to follow them through this poignant, painful story of love found and lost and found again. For anyone who adored Emma Straub's *Modern Lovers*, now there's Jonathan Papernick's *I Am My Beloveds* to spend some time with and ... fall for."
— David Samuel Levinson, author of *Tell Me How This Ends Well*

"*I Am My Beloveds* is a warm, funny, thoughtful, and often heart-wrenching portrait of a modern couple testing the boundaries of their relationship, while exploring the outer limits of their love for each other. It's an engaging and timely read, perfect for a generation of readers much more open to the allure (and pitfalls) of polyamory."
— Lana Harper, author of *Payback's a Witch*

"Jon Papernick's storytelling is always compelling. Enticing, surprising, and provocative all at once."
— Kevin Allison, *Risk!* podcast and MTV's *The State* and *Reno 911*

"*I Am My Beloveds*, Jon Papernick's latest novel, is about many things: love and the lack of it, the passage of time and, most importantly, how we live now. I am full of admiration for this writer and his daring imagination. He is a truly gifted novelist, and this is his finest book."
— Steve Yarbrough, author of *The Unmade World* and *The Realm of Last Chances*

"*I Am My Beloveds* is a compulsive read, at turns heart-wrenching, angry, funny, and sweet, but always smart and vivid. Papernick is a master of growing empathy from the smallest detail, in doing so has crafted a winning protagonist in Ben Seidel, who I was eager to follow, warts and all, wherever his misadventures in open marriage might lead."
— Sara Nović, author of *Girl at War*

I Am My Beloveds

Jonathan Papernick

THE
STORY
PLANT

The Story Plant
1270 Caroline Street
Suite D120-381
Atlanta, GA 30307

Copyright © 2021 by Jonathan Papernick
The Library of Congress Cataloguing-in-Publication Data is available upon request.

Story Plant hardcover ISBN-13: 978-1-61188-319-0
Story Plant e-book ISBN-13: 978-1-945839-57-3
Story Plant paperback ISBN-13: 978-1-61188-349-7

Visit our website at www.TheStoryPlant.com

First Story Plant Paperback Printing: June 2023

Printed in the United States of America
0 9 8 7 6 5 4 3 2 1

Also by Jonathan Papernick

The Book of Stone
There Is No Other
Who by Fire, Who by Blood
The Ascent of Eli Israel
Gallery of the Disappeared Men

For Kim, my beloved

I owe a great debt of gratitude to two amazing people who helped midwife this novel into existence.

Thank you, Michelle Caplan, whose guidance, passion, and insights have always helped to make me the writer I always knew I could be.

Thank you Caroline Leavitt, my literary guardian angel, who loves me even when I feel unworthy of love. Your support means more to me than you can possibly know.

"Nothing in the world is single;
All things by a law divine
In one spirit meet and mingle.
Why not I with thine?"

— from "Love's Philosophy," Percy Bysshe Shelley

1

Ben Seidel's heart was still pounding from his run around frigid Spy Pond when his wife, Shira, swept into their living room wearing a little black dress, flared jauntily at the hem, and a pair of glossy black pumps Ben had never seen before. Ben, in his orange compression tights and sweat-wicking pullover, could not have looked more at odds with his wife of eight years.

"Wow," Ben said. "You look amazing. Where are we going?"

Shira, who was nearly a foot shorter than Ben without her four-inch heels, smiled softly at her husband, squinching her eyebrows together as if she had stepped on a particularly jagged piece of Lego.

"Not we. Me," Shira said. "I'm going out. Sort of a Galentine's Day thing."

"But it's Saturday night." Ben sighed. "It's Valentine's Day."

"That's tomorrow," Shira said, adjusting a twisted bra strap. "We didn't have any plans for tonight. Remember I asked you a couple times?"

Ben did not remember Shira asking if they had plans because they had stopped making plans, spending most Saturday nights in front of the television debating endlessly over what to watch on Netflix and going to bed well before midnight. Ben pulled off his fleece hat and reflexively combed his fingers through his matted, thinning hair. "Maybe I had a surprise," Ben said.

"And you know how much I love surprises," Shira countered. "But you didn't, right?"

Shira was wearing contact lenses for maybe the third time that Ben could recall, rather than her usual thick-framed glasses which the two of them joked about as she labored over her drafting table. *They look like old TV screens!*

Now, her eyes looked bigger somehow, her lashes thicker, almost dangerous; the complex alchemy of women's makeup forever a mystery to Ben.

Ben had forgotten what it felt like to truly desire Shira with the sort of urgent passion they had when they had first met, when he and Shira would spend all weekend in bed discovering each others' secret places. But that had changed even before she got sick, long before the hysterectomy, her body closing up to Ben like a tulip at night. Even when the pain had gone, Ben and Shira had not returned to each other, aside from brief, infrequent encounters in the dark of their bedroom to remind them they were still husband and wife, whether or not they would ever raise a child together.

Shira's eyes glittered and she quirked a single eyebrow. Ben felt an urge to take her in his arms and kiss her. "I'll tell you what. We'll get you a giant ribeye at Davio's tomorrow night, which is *actually* Valentine's Day. I'll even drive."

"It's a Sunday night," Ben said, heart collapsing. Sunday night was reserved for *60 Minutes*, the *New York Times* crossword and early to bed, not romance.

Shira hadn't dressed up for him since forever, and he felt almost embarrassed by his sudden hunger for her, the way a hormonal pre-teen might feel getting hard for his cousin at a family reunion.

"Where are you going tonight?" Ben said as he slipped off one shoe and then the other. He had trouble drawing a full breath, and he was pretty sure it had nothing to do with his regular six-mile loop.

"A party," Shira said.

"With who?" Ben said, more sharply than he intended. He couldn't figure out how to not make it sound like some sort of petty accusation.

"Liz," Shira said, a small smile forming. Her lips were as red as if she had bitten into Ben's jugular. "Remember? The woman I told you about from my life-drawing class."

"The stripper?" Ben said, eyes itching.

"She's a burlesque dancer," Shira said. "And that's just for fun. You know, a sometimes thing. She's an artist, like me."

A hard fist formed in Ben's throat, and he dropped down onto their couch, knees trembling. "That sounds like a date."

Shira's mouth fell open, and she took a step or two backwards, as if she'd been blown by a strong gust of wind. "Ben," she said, her voice small, "it *is* a date. I've been looking for the right words to tell you all week. I fucked up, okay, because I was scared to tell you."

"Why would you be scared?"

"Because I don't want to hurt you and I don't want you to talk me out of it."

Ben turned away from Shira and caught his reflection in the glossy blackness of their living-room

3

window. With his chewed up hairline and spandex tights he looked as unlovable as he felt. He just wanted to escape into the forgiving embrace of a hot shower, but they had to have this conversation now, before Shira did something that might break the two of them forever.

"I didn't know you really, actually meant it," Ben said. "About being open. I thought we were still talking about it. I thought we'd have a discussion first."

"I'm sorry," Shira said. "I thought you understood that *was* the discussion." She paused and flicked some invisible speck off the coffee table. "What about Jane?"

"She's just a friend," Ben said.

Ben had met Jane by chance, running on the Minuteman Trail, and they had started texting about the joys of running, to stretch or not to stretch, the Murakami book. They had begun texting each other so naturally that Ben felt he had to keep it secret or their friendship would disappear. When Shira caught him furtively texting Jane one night she asked Ben if he was cheating on her. He had said of course not, never, but the discussion about opening their marriage had begun.

"You think she's not into you?"

"She's married."

"Don't you find her attractive?"

"Yes, but it doesn't mean I want to fuck her."

"Come on, Ben. You find her attractive but you don't want to sleep with her?"

Ben leapt to his feet. "We were drifting. I felt so far from you, and I needed someone to talk to. I would never cheat. You know I never would."

"But you hid her from me. Who's to say it wouldn't happen eventually?"

"That's not fair. You're projecting because you think I lost interest in you, but you're the one who gave up on me."

"I did *not* give up on you! My body went through major trauma." Shira's voice cracked, and her make-up started to run. "Excuse me if sex was the last thing I wanted. From you or anyone."

Shira followed Ben into the kitchen, and the sound of her clacking heels in pursuit made Ben want to slip on his Asics and run.

"And now you want Liz," Ben said.

"I want to feel the pleasure of being a woman, not just the pain."

"Then why not do it with me? I'm you're husband."

Shira was silent for a long moment, and she wiped her nose with the back of her wrist. "Sometimes," she began, "the thought of sex with you feels like return-ing to the scene of a crime."

"What?" Ben said, and then he had no words, his voice silenced by a sour thickening in his throat.

"Every time I think of sex—I think of us trying—I feel sick and sad and ... hollowed out. There's noth-ing inside me anymore that can create life."

"I'm sorry. I wish you didn't see it that way. You have so much left to create."

"Don't patronize me, Ben."

Shira looked at Ben with her big, wet eyes, and he wanted to take her in his arms.

"Do you still find me attractive?" Ben said.

"Devilishly so. I just need to learn to love my body again."

"Do you still love me?"

"Of course I do, Ben, and I always will." Ben started to interrupt, but Shira held up a hand, signaling she would be heard without his commentary. "But this could be a good thing for both of us. I need some sort of reset. You know, rebooting my relationship with my own body. You're free to explore your desires while we find our way back to each other. No matter what happens, I will always be your soft place to land."

"I don't want to lose you. Am I?" Ben said. "Losing you?"

"Of course not." Shira offered a pinkie for Ben to shake. "I promise."

"You can't know that," Ben said, listlessly hooking his finger in hers.

"This is important for both of us. I know this will help bring us back to each other. You are always my husband."

"Can't we figure this out on our own? What is it I can't give you?"

Shira chewed on her lip and looked away from Ben; she was usually so good at eye contact. "The mystery, the unknown, exploring different parts of myself. That feeling of being wanted. It's like nothing else, that look in their eyes when they just have to have you."

"The look Liz gives you." Ben's shoulders felt so heavy, as if he were carrying a backpack full of his regrets.

"Yes. It's very powerful." Shira expelled a long sigh. "I truly believe this is a way back to ourselves, a way for us to be how we used to be before everything went down."

"In the meantime, I'm competing with a woman."

Shira had been with women as an undergraduate at Smith, and Ben had always been turned on by the prospect of his wife and another woman; he just somehow imagined he'd be a part of it if it happened again.

"Don't be silly. You're not competing with anyone. I come home to you, I live with you and I love you."

Shira threw her arms around Ben and buried her face in his chest. "I love you. Please try and see this as a good thing, a springboard to the next phase of our lives. Together. Me and you."

Ben held Shira as her body shuddered against his chest.

"What now?" Ben asked, after a moment. He and Shira fit so well together, the way she melted into him.

She peeled herself away and wiped her face with a dish towel they'd gotten on a trip to Maine. "I have to go. I'm sorry. I can't be late."

"Okay. Have fun tonight."

"Why don't you send Jane a flirty text, and then take it from there."

Ben looked at Shira doubtfully. "Really?"

Shira smiled and did her best Bogie imitation, "I think it could be the beginning of a beautiful friendship."

Ben felt a stirring in his groin. Maybe Shira was right. Maybe Jane was into him.

"Listen, babe, I've got to run." Shira grabbed her long down coat from the closet. "You don't need to wait up for me. We can catch up in the morning."

"Wait," Ben said, heart thundering in his chest.

Shira did a little half turn, her face in profile over her left shoulder. "What's up?"

"I love you."

"I love you too. I promise you we're going to be all right."

2

One Year Later

Ben sat alone on his and Shira's sensible microfiber couch, laptop propped on his knees, entirely miserable. Shira was out canoodling with her girlfriend again, while Ben scrolled through a dizzying carousel of profile pics on Tinder, leaden heart thudding in his chest.

It was Shira's night with Liz, and the two of them were at a Pi Day party at some down-market rental in Jamaica Plain. Shira had baked a blueberry pie and dressed for the occasion with a handmade symbol stitched to her sweater. No matter how innocently it began, the night would end with Shira in Liz's bed.

Ben thought he had put this nightmare of doubt and longing behind him when he had married Shira and they had started, in earnest, to build a life together. Shira had always been there for Ben when it counted most, offering warmth and comfort and love. He had done the same for Shira, and that finely calibrated construct of falling and catching, falling and catching, felt as if it would carry them through to forever. But this past year had been the hardest of Ben's life since the year his parents died. During those endless nights when Shira was out doing things with Liz Bird he wished not to imagine, it felt as if Shira had spirited away some essential element of himself, and that he was disappearing amid the middle-class trappings of their well-appointed suburban condo. Ethical non-monogamy was supposed to be a good thing for them, but Ben felt as if he had drawn the short blade that cut deeper with every passing day.

Aside from going for another run, the only way Ben knew to fill the emptiness he carried in his chest was to drag himself back to the apps and the confounding wilderness of online dating. He could never quite understand what cis and genderfluid and sapiosexual were supposed to mean, or whether he was ISO a GF or FWB, a LTR or just some basic TLC as he stumbled his way into a world in which size queens took sole measure of worth in inches and girth, in which bondage and domination was considered an asset, even a kindness, and every new human connection was a disposable thing with more, always more and greater possibilities, strutting their stuff just over the digital horizon. The apps were never the magic Sorting Hat Ben wished them to be, but that didn't stop him from returning again and again to the illuminated screen of his phone in search of someone, anyone, who would make him feel less alone. Maybe finding a girlfriend of his own would make Shira realize that he was still a man in full. Not a roommate, but a husband worthy of her attentions in the bed and out.

Over the past month, Ben had sent out no fewer than twenty-seven personalized, grammatically correct messages to various women on Tinder, OkCupid, JDate and even Ashley Madison. His screen name was simply Benarchitect, not Patsfan69, 420guy, or whosyordaddy, so he already had a leg up on some of his competition. That, and the fact that he never began a conversation with a gross come-on line about the awesome ramming power of his monster cock or his desire to go down on her like the *Titanic*, but, rather, with a thoughtful callback to something meaningful from each of their bios. Because he looked non-threatening in his brand-new cobalt-blue polo shirt, fixed smile plastered to his face, he soon found himself juggling several hopeful conversations with KristinOKC, KristinTinder and Jen#4. But these conversations often went nowhere as Ben's charm abandoned him, or the women read deep enough into his profile to figure he was married, and they disappeared.

Ben's smartphone address book was a graveyard of lost hopes: Two Abigails, two Kellys, three Megans, one of whom Ben kissed as a Red Line train roared into Park Street station, and four Jens, punctuated by a solitary Chelsea, Heidi, Kat, Lisa, Millie, Sam, Suzy, Theresa, Violet, Zoey, and a woman who insisted Ben call her Khaleesi, Mother of Dragons. Most depressingly, Jane had blocked Ben months earlier when he told her he and Shira had opened up their marriage and he was looking for someone special *wink* *wink*, telling Ben she was uncomfortable hanging out with him, that the flirting had been fun when it felt safe, and that she cared about him, but she needed to step back both for herself and her husband, who would be freaked out if he knew Ben was willing to cross the line from friendship to sex.

That was why, when Ben's phone lit up with a simple, unexpected text from KristinOKC saying *k, meet you there @9*, Ben's heart, his tiny, battered heart, filled his chest with relief.

Ben stood a fit six-foot-one with a straightish white smile, solid shoulders and a flat stomach. His eyes were a neutral brown, his aquiline nose well proportioned. There was nothing particularly distinguishing about the way he looked—he'd been mistaken more than a few times for *that guy from that place*—but sometimes, from the right angle, with just the right lighting, he believed he looked downright dashing. But he was losing his hair, mousy brown and prone to curling. Not by the handful, but enough he could see his hairline creep back a few millimeters every couple months. Ben still had most of his hair, but he was sure he'd be bald by forty. In his profile pictures he managed to artfully crop himself mid-forehead, rather than relying on the obvious baseball cap to hide his most glaring flaw, so he hoped his receding hairline wasn't a dealbreaker with KristinOKC, as he suspected it had been with some of the others.

KristinOKC, sporting a sleeveless sequin minidress, an auburn side braid tied at the tip with a purple ribbon, and thick-framed librarian glasses, sitting at the crowded mahogany bar of a hip Davis Square nightspot, looked exactly as advertised.

"Heeeeeeeey!" KristinOKC said, spotting Ben approach. She greeted him with a friendly hug and an air kiss which Ben took to be a good sign as he slid into the chair next to her. Ben's lungs ached, as if they were filled with wet sand. As good as KristinOKC looked, she wasn't Shira. He wanted to be with Shira, only Shira. Every date with a new woman followed a familiar pattern: hope, then longing, then sadness. But Ben was determined to do his best to show KristinOKC he was the fun, kind, chill dude he promised in his profile.

"Must be nice to get out of the lab and relax for a while," Ben said, at the very moment he realized he had mistaken her for KristinTinder, the postdoc at MIT, who had surely ghosted him after he seemed to confuse weather and climate during one of their conversations. He knew the difference and had been trying to make a joke that obviously fell flat.

"The lab?"

"Yeah, I mean, isn't the entire world just a great big laboratory?"

"That's a bit of a general statement," KristinOKC said. "But sure."

Alcohol was always best at times like this, so Ben asked KristinOKC what she wanted to drink. "Gin and tonic," she said.

It took a few tries for Ben to flag down the bartender, and when Ben turned his attention back to KristinOKC she was deeply immersed in the glossy screen of her phone. KristenOKC, belying her nickname, was swiping right on Tinder.

"Libations have been ordered," Ben said, forcing cheer into his voice.

"Oh, sorry." KristinOKC turned her phone over on the bar top. "I just swipe right on everyone, see how many matches I can get."

"That's interesting." Ben hoped he wasn't furrowing his brow. He looked like a middle-school assistant principal when he did that.

"Not really. It's part sociological experiment. Hey! I guess you're right about the world being a laboratory." KristinOKC laughed, or, rather, ha-ha'ed. "I know it's crass and gross and shallow, but the other part is pure ego gratification and I can't help it. I'll probably end up in the bad place, but it's just too much fun."

Their drinks arrived and they exchanged the usual. She was from Gray, Maine, received her Masters in Library and Information Science from Simmons College, and worked at a not-for-profit promoting literacy among refugees and new citizens. She had two roommates, preferred cats over dogs, but harp seals over cats! Loved vegan paella, the Brontë sisters, The Lumineers, Richard Linklater and the color purple, both the book and the actual color, lol.

Every time Ben went through the routine of reciting his bio he felt he was only half a man; a degree, a job and not much else. Something important was missing, something that explained him better than reciting his favorite food and color and book, so tonight, rather than skipping over the fact he had a wife until he felt it was safe to do so, he told KristinOKC he was married and then, much to his shame, he appended "sort of," as a feeble explanation. Ben's bio said he was married and in an open relationship, but he was amazed how many women seemed to skim his profile, missing that important detail, as if his marital status had been written in invisible ink.

KristinOKC asked what he meant by sort of, and Ben explained.

"So how does that work?" KristinOKC said, nonplussed.

"To be honest," Ben said, "I'm not sure it does."

"Then why are you doing it?"

KristinOKC seemed genuinely curious and sympathetic, so he said, "Because I love my wife."

"That's sweet, Ben, but do you actually want to be in an open relationship?"

"Yes. Of course! Definitely." He wanted badly to order another drink but the bartender's back was turned. "Kinda sorta."

"Kinda sorta? That's hardly a ringing endorsement. It sounds to me like you're polyamorous under duress. Not cool." KristinOKC shook her head for emphasis. "Not cool."

"It was the best way forward."

"What do you mean?"

There was something in KristinOKC's open expression that told him he could speak honestly. Some women found such candidness to be attractive, alluring even. Ben told KristinOKC about his and Shira's desire to have a child and how sex had been painful for years before they discovered Shira had cancer, and by then it was too late to freeze her eggs.

"Nobody expects cancer in their twenties," Ben said. "We just assumed we'd have a family. Never questioned it. The diagnosis was such a shock, and Shira withdrew, blamed herself. It's hard seeing someone you love hurt, knowing there's nothing you can do to take away the pain."

"Shira's a nice name," KristinOKC said, smiling. "Your wife's better now? She's in remission?"

"She had a full hysterectomy. She's cancer free."

They were silent for a moment, and Ben wondered whether he had said too much, whether he was trying to gain sympathy through Shira's pain.

"I'm sorry," KristinOKC said. "So how did you end up being open?"

"I don't know. We were both destroyed by the whole thing, the entire path of our life that we had planned—you know, kids and family—just gone. It was devastating, and I think we got onto this track of pain and sadness and forgot how to enjoy each other."

KristinOKC nodded along with Ben, focusing her eyes on his. "What about adoption?"

Ben sighed. "We tried a bunch of agencies here and overseas and they were either scammy or too expensive or they flagged Shira's cancer, saying adoptive parents needed a clean bill of health. That just sent Shira spiraling all over again. We just wanted to be parents so badly, and doors kept slamming in our faces."

"What about surrogacy?"

"Expensive. Only one of us was working," Ben said. "And Shira's health."

"That sucks."

"She blamed herself and really withdrew from life. I just hated seeing her shrinking from the things she once cared about."

Ben signed her up for a life-drawing class, and she loved it, seemed to come alive. And as the weeks passed she became more and more the woman Ben had known before all the bad stuff went down. She revived her dormant business, and everything looked as if it was getting better, but she had met someone, a woman, and she was happy and started taking care of herself again.

"I just couldn't say no because I love her, and I thought it was temporary and that we'd find our way back to each other."

"I'm glad your wife's happy," KristinOKC said. "But what about you?"

"It's not that bad." Ben considered how many men would have felt lucky just to be sitting at that bar with KristinOKC. She was smart and beautiful and kind, and she was talking to him when she could have been talking to anyone. "Yes my wife is in love with another woman, and it hurts, but I have the chance to love anyone I want, *and* have Shira too. I'm lucky, actually. I have a lot to be grateful for."

"And how many other women do you love?"

Ben's silence said everything.

KristinOKC said, "This isn't fair. There needs to be balance for this to work. Believe me, I've been open since college. It's not for everyone, and I don't think it's for you."

Ben nodded as he realized he was definitely, definitively, unquestionably, not going to have sex tonight. "Why did you agree to go out with me?"

"Because I wanted to go on a date with you."

"But why?"

KristinOKC lowered her eyes a bit and looked away. "Because you seemed kind."

"Do you still think I'm kind?"

"Go home, Ben. Tell your wife you love her. Tell her you want to nope out and go back to just you and her again."

❦

It was after eleven when Ben returned home. Shira was still out with Liz, and their condo felt empty and forbidding. Ben had convinced himself Shira's affair with Liz was worse than if Shira had been with another man because he could never do with Shira what

17

Liz and she did together. He could never provide whatever it was Liz Bird, with all her crazy tattoos and piercings and punk rock attitude, could provide. Ben wanted only to crawl into bed with Shira and hold her, feel her soothing warmth against his skin, for her to smother his desolation with her familiar body.

Ben remembered his ring, secured behind a lonely, crumpled condom in the tiny change pocket of his jeans, and fished it out with fingers stiff as chopsticks. He held it in his hand for a moment, staring at his warped reflection in the curve of the gold band. He thought back with amazement to his wedding day all those years ago, the feeling of boundless optimism and warmth and safety, the sense that he and Shira were embarking on a great adventure that was theirs and theirs alone. No crystal ball could have envisioned such a sad spectacle as him returning home alone from another failed date and furtively slipping his ring back onto his finger.

Ben poured himself some brandy and wandered out to the sunroom Shira used as her studio, the hub of her burgeoning Judaica business.

A square of beige, textured paper lay in the center of Shira's tilted art desk, her jars of ink and calligraphy pens neatly arranged in their places.

Though Ben could not read the intricate Hebrew script, he knew Shira was working on a baby-naming certificate for her childhood friend Melissa back in Maryland. It seemed Shira had stopped right in the middle of a word, her usually steady hand spidering southward on the document, and Ben could not help but think Shira had been overcome at that moment by the irreversible fact she would never give birth to a baby, never have a child of her own.

The Seidel name Ben's father had passed onto him, whatever in the world it was worth, would end with Ben. Though he tried to inoculate himself against this pain, raising images of soiled diapers and milk vomit, tantrums and meltdowns, the brattiest of snot-nosed children screaming sleeplessly for yet another bedtime story, Ben knew joy and happiness was just on the other side of these trifles, and that he and Shira would have loved and cherished whomever their offspring turned out to be. The children would need their parents to protect them, teach them, build them up, show them the way to make the world a better place, just as Ben and Shira's parents had done for them. Without a child, there was only Shira, would only be Shira, and, on nights like this when Shira was out with Liz, the thought terrified him like nothing else. He wanted to take Shira by the hand and kiss her as they used to and tell her he knew he was far from perfect, but he loved her and wanted to thank her for loving a fallible creature such as himself.

Shira's work hung framed on the wall behind him, mostly ketubahs, intricately designed Jewish marriage contracts, swirls of colorful, entwined flowers and vines, lithe tree branches bending and arching over Shira's beautiful Hebrew calligraphy, stating a man may not divorce a woman against her will. Sometimes there were English phrases as well, and Ben read aloud the iconic phrase from the Song of Songs: *I Am My Beloved's and My Beloved Is Mine.*

All around him, judgment hung on his very own walls; his marriage was a mess. He would never be a father, would never know the safety and comfort and purpose and belonging of family. He was barely a lover to Shira anymore. They did it every few weeks, but the act of union was desultory, obligatory, going through the expected motions of husband and wife. Each of the ketubahs on the wall represented joy and happiness and Jewish continuity, linking one generation to the next, and Ben hungered to be a link in that chain, to be every bit the fully realized, fully grown man his father was, and his father had been before him. It would never happen with Shira, and Ben wondered if they were just running out the clock on their marriage, winding down one tick at a time until they were strangers who couldn't remember why they had chosen each other in the first place.

Ben finished the last of his brandy, a warm starburst forming inside his belly. The alcohol must have hit him harder than he expected because Shira's signature, bearing her maiden name alongside his own last name, struck him like a slap in the face: Shira Seidel-Weismann. Had she been hedging all along with that hyphen? Had she ever intended to give herself fully to him? Ben was prepared to sacrifice his dreams of fatherhood just to be with Shira, she and him and no one else, because Shira was his love, his only love. But *he* was not *her* only love.

The only time Ben was able to fully take possession of himself and make sense out of the senseless was when he ran. For that hour, his heart beating a steady 140 beats a minute, blood cycling through his veins, Ben knew everything would turn out all right.

He slipped into his running shorts, laced up his shoes, and before long he was flying around Spy Pond, light as air. The path was three miles around, give or take, and Ben could have run all night. Alone out there on the trail, taking the hills and dips with ease, a fat moon guiding his way, he might have been the first person in the world, or the last, a solitary late-night runner trying simply to catch up with his best self. Ben wasn't the least bit lonely out there. The rhythmic sounds of his footfalls soothed him, driving him onward. His even breathing filled him with a clean rush of restorative air. He required no one else's permission to receive the unique pleasure of his endorphins blasting on all cylinders, and he wondered why he would ever stop, why he would ever relinquish this power he had over his untamed emotions.

All the confusion of the world seemed to melt away as Ben circled the pond a second time, and he felt a sudden rush of clarity. By the time he returned home dripping sweat in the crisp March evening he knew what he needed to do. KristinOKC was right. His arrangement with Shira was not fair. Stop seeing Liz, stop seeing her now because it is hurting me, it is hurting us. Let's start again, just you and me.

Shira was asleep in bed, breathing easily. She had left the lamp on for Ben, and in its dim glow he studied her serene, almond-shaped face, her long eyelashes, her tender lips curved into a peaceful smile.

This is my wife, Ben thought with amazement, *this is my wife*. Soon she would belong to him again, only him.

He undressed and washed himself in the bathroom sink, his desire for her rekindled. He would have woken her and fucked her all night as he did when she was new to him, an open-hearted junior

21

at Smith College, but he didn't want to disturb her dreams.

How long had it been since he had even deep-kissed her? How long had it been since their kisses had been anything but perfunctory, habitual, polite? How had he ever allowed it to come to this?

Ben clicked off the bedside lamp, pulled the sheets back and slid into bed beside Shira. Her body was warm, alive with possibility. Shira alone had the power to restore Ben's fragile sense of self and piece him back together, one kindhearted kiss at a time. He cuddled up close to her, kissed her softly on the neck, and smelled the distinct patchouli scent of Liz on Shira's skin.

There in the darkness, it was as if there were a third person in bed with them.

3

Ben tried to bring awareness to his breathing, to clear his mind and follow the natural flow of his inhale and exhale, the involuntary miracle of existence measured out breath by neutral breath. But with every cool intake, Ben's mind leapt back to Shira and Liz and all the pornographic possibilities of how they actually pleasured each other—with fingers, tongues, toys? Liz entering Shira with an obscene, neon-colored strap-on fastened to her bony hips? Misery illuminated itself in the darkness like an X-Rated midnight movie: Liz taking his wife from behind, riding her face like a cowgirl, sucking her breasts with those electric red, maraschino lips. The fact he was being replaced by a pierced tongue and a slab of molded latex fired Ben's feelings of inadequacy like nothing he had ever experienced, and he replayed the tape again and again and again, his overtaxed limbic system ablaze like a five-alarm fire. Liz Bird had to go, she absolutely *had* to.

Shira woke up sometime after eight, rolled over and pecked Ben companionably on the lips. Ben barely had a chance to say good morning before she shuffled off to the bathroom. For Shira, it was just another rainy Sunday, and Ben, still groggy, was amazed to see, in the gray light of a late winter morning, that Shira was still Shira.

Shira's electric toothbrush hummed from their adjoining bathroom, and Ben dragged his tired body to face himself in the bathroom mirror.

"Hey!" Shira said, speaking to Ben's reflection, the Day-Glo orange toothbrush still churning in her mouth. "You were out late last night. Hot date?"

"No. Not hot."

Shira offered a foamy "Oh?"

"I went for an extra long run."

Shira clicked off her toothbrush. "At that time of night? Is everything okay?"

"Would you still love me if I was bald?" Ben asked.

"What kind of question is that? Of course I'd love you." Shira adjusted her glasses. "I'd miss you, but I'd still love you."

"That's not funny. I'm really losing my hair."

"No you're not. And, for the record, your father wasn't even a little bit bald."

"Not yet, he wasn't."

Ben imagined his parents side by side on their white-sheeted, king-size bed, together forever, spooning perhaps, still as the grave.

"Benjamin, please stop this. It's not healthy. And you're not balding!"

Ben ran his fingers through his hair, revealing not a forehead, but a five- or six-head. "I must be a genetic anomaly, because I AM balding."

"That's an adult hairline, you goober."

"I hate it."

"Well, I love your hair." She tousled his hair. "It's so soft. You could grow it out like when you were a kid."

"I'd look like a clown with a Jewfro." Ben shook loose of Shira's touch.

"What's bothering you, babe?"

"I don't know. I miss having fun with you."

"We have fun. Don't we?" Shira smiled a small smile, her teeth absently working her lower lip.

In the mirror behind her, Ben could see clearly where Shira had shaved her head at the neck, the new piercings at her ear. She was even starting to look like Liz.

"I want to do something special. Just me and you. Today. Now."

"Sounds great," Shira said, brightly. "I'm open. What do you have in mind?"

Ben hadn't thought that far ahead. "I don't know, maybe go for a hike or something?"

"I don't mean to be contrary, but does hiking around Walden Pond in the freezing rain sound fun to you?"

"I just want to be with you." Ben frowned. "It doesn't matter what we do."

"I'm not saying no!"

Ben regarded his wife. She was nearly a foot shorter than him at five foot two, her little hands and unpainted nails scuffed and ink-stained from laboring at her drafting table. Had Shira's body thickened over the years? Of course it had. Her skin was still smooth, her tanned, oval face unlined. Her strong legs were muscular, her body feminine and round-hipped, just a bit extra at the ass. How he had worshiped that ass once. He recalled asking Shira, back when they were still dating, if he could fuck her in the ass and she had gamely said yes. But Ben had to stop because it hurt too much and they had never tried again. He could never imagine being that bold now. Shira had grown from a girl to a woman in the ten and a half years they had been together. Ben, for his part, had had a full head of thick hair until he was nearly thirty, and looking ahead into the future he wondered whether he would have recognized either of them.

"We can see a movie or go to a gallery," Ben said. "Or maybe we can grab brunch."

"I've got an idea!" Shira's face brightened. "There's this drag queen show and brunch downtown every Sunday. I've been wanting to go forever."

"Drag queens?"

"Save your pearl clutching, Ben. It's brunch and mimosas. I know you'll love it. We can day drink together. Doesn't that sound fun?"

This sounded like precisely the kind of thing Liz and Shira did together when Ben was not around.

"Wouldn't you rather go with Liz?"

"I'm asking you, dummy. Come on." She chucked him on the shoulder.

"I want to do something that's just ours. Something just for us."

"I've never been with her. We've just talked about it. Please, Ben, let's do this. We can make it a new tradition. You and me."

"And a bunch of drag queens," Ben added.

"Yes! This will be so much fun."

Ben wore a moss green L.L. Bean crewneck sweater Shira had given him for Chanukah, a pair of crisp dark-wash blue jeans, and a pair of hiking boots. He had recently, in a moment of rare sartorial inspiration, bought a black pork-pie hat with a luminous feather tucked in the hat band that Shira swore made him look distinguished, so he wore that as well. This was as fashionable as Ben ever got.

Shira looked gorgeous in a yellow flowered dress and strappy heels. Her chin-length hair, cut into an uneven hipster fringe, was swept back from her forehead, slicked down into a hard shell. Her bright red lips were painted the precise color of desire. Ben could have eaten her whole. When Ben leaned close to kiss her she said, "Careful, you'll smudge it."

They found a table near the front and sat down. The tables around them were filled with small, noisy groups: bachelorette parties, gay men clinking champagne flutes and laughing, he and Shira.

"Why don't you wear lipstick more often?" Ben said.

"Like around the house when I'm sketching?"

"I don't know. You look like a model."

Shira laughed. "So many size-eight models. I hate to break this to you, but even real models wear sweats and scrunchies at home."

"Well, you look really, really good."

"You don't look too bad yourself, *jefe*." Shira yanked down the brim of his hat.

The server took their drink orders, and Shira asked if it was possible for the chef to make scrambled eggs for Ben without milk, since the buffet was pretty much off limits for him, aside from the bacon and some pale, fibrous honeydew and cantaloupe. In restaurants, Shira took care of Ben. She was the one to check in with the server to make sure there was no dairy in the food he was going to eat. Ben appreciated Shira taking charge, as he always felt slightly embarrassed, calling attention to the most broken part of himself like the poor, loveless kid at the peanut table in the lunch room. But lately it had come to feel like she was mothering him.

Their cocktails arrived just as the emcee strutted onto the stage in impossibly high platform boots, a micro mini skirt and a whip-like blonde braid that swung all the way to their ass. Ben and Shira clinked glasses, and Ben said, "To us." Shira was already clapping her hands and wolf whistling as Penny Dreadful gyrated their hips to Cher's "Believe."

Ben and Shira tossed crumpled dollar bills to the performers as they danced and sashayed past their table, stuffing their tips into garters, bras, beneath their colored wigs. Every so often Shira brushed hands with Ben or threw him a flirty wink. It was like old times, when they still lived in a crooked-floored triple-decker in Somerville and explored Boston and its environs with excitement and a sense of wonder at what the two of them could discover together.

Ben was feeling pretty good by the third drink. He had just motorboated a massive pair of foam boobs belonging to Stella the Fella, who looked like they could have driven a concrete mixer in their everyday life, when the emcee called for volunteers to come on down and participate in the finale.

Shira's arm shot up in the air.

Penny Dreadful, bewigged now with cherry red bangs and devil's horns, in a black leather corset, acknowledged Shira's raised hand with a "Yass queen, yassss!"

But Shira didn't rise from the table, and when Ben heard Penny Dreadful say, "Are you ready to cum, Mister Pork Pie Hat?" he knew he was a dead man.

Ben stared at Shira, frozen, hoping to confirm some tragic error of understanding. There must have been some amendment in the constitution that forbade such a thing. But Shira was laughing with such joy and happiness, tears pouring from her eyes, that Ben just wanted to take her in his arms and kiss her.

"Go on, baby. It'll be fun."

"For you maybe," Ben said.

"For all of us," Shira said, positively glowing.

Britney Spears' "Toxic" boomed from silver-spangled speakers, and all the dancers fanned out throughout the crowd, whirling and spinning and shaking what God clearly did not give them. They owned their borrowed womanhood in a way Ben could never comfortably own even his own body. It wasn't that Ben was afraid of the drag queens; it was the fact that they were dancing like it was an article of faith, and Ben could not dance. He had convinced Shira to play Leonard Cohen's "Hallelujah" as their wedding song in large part because it was slow and he could hold Shira close and simply sway without risk of losing control and looking foolish.

Shira slid her half-finished drink towards Ben. "Courage. You can do it."

He really had no choice now because Penny Dreadful, towering over him, beckoned dramatically into the microphone. "Let's see you shake your moneymaker."

Penny Dreadful managed to lasso Ben around the shoulders with a pink feather boa as he downed the last of Shira's drink. He had no choice but to follow Penny Dreadful up to the stage, shanghaied and terrified. He had never felt more exposed. All eyes were on him as he walked, simply walked, to the front of the bar, his gait stiff, head forward as if he were trudging to the gallows. Somehow, the basic act of walking felt sour and spoilsporty, and he had to admit he was having fun. So Ben, without thinking about the how of it, or even the where, began to dance. He twisted his hips, shook his ass, waved his arms in the air. With the stage lights in his eyes, Ben could not see Shira and the rest of the crowd, and for a moment he was alone, slipping back in time to his bedroom on Long Island, going crazy before his mirror, secretly dancing to Ace of Base on the radio, hairbrush microphone clutched in his hand. And then he was back, mimicking the moves of Penny Dreadful, Stella the Fella, Queen Merry and Lulu LaStrange, bumping and grinding and camping it up beneath a blizzard of glitter and strobing lights. When it was over, all Ben could think to do was toss his hat into the crowd as the lights went down.

"There's my sexy man," Shira said, throwing her arms around Ben.

"Did I actually just do that?"

"Yes. You. Did!"

She pulled Ben down by the feather boa to her waiting lips and kissed him deeply, passionately, as though something elemental between them had changed. Ben didn't want this kiss to end. It would be too painful to go back to the way things had been the past year.

"Get a room, kids," Penny Dreadful said, smacking Ben on the ass as they passed by. "You were fantastic, darlin'."

"He's mine," Shira said, running her fingers through Ben's sweaty hair. "And I'm not sharing."

Ben didn't remember the last time Shira had wanted him so badly. It was as if they were dating all over again. His stomach swirled with that confusing mixture of joy and sadness, because this moment would pass.

"I've got an idea," Ben said. He couldn't bear the thought of returning to their condo, slipping into their sensible Target pajamas, watching TV all night and going to bed. "Let's get a hotel. A nice one. Five stars."

"Fuck yes!" Shira grabbed Ben by the hand and pulled him towards the exit.

"Wait," Ben said. "I've got to find my hat."

"No you don't. Let's go. Now."

As soon as they keyed into their room on the eighth floor of The Four Seasons Shira pulled her dress over her head in a swift motion as if she was performing a magic trick. She stood before him in matching black lingerie, her olive skin flushed at the neck, breathing heavily. Ben had become used to her usual cotton underwear and practical flesh-colored bra, and stared at her with a sense of wonder, casting his own clothing to the floor as if he were shedding a burial shroud. Ben dropped to his knees before Shira and kissed the pale line of her abdominal scar, tracing the horizontal slash with his lips, his tongue. She had never let him get this close, and now he felt he could finally do his part in healing Shira. But Shira wasn't having it. She tapped Ben on the shoulder and said, "Bed. Now."

They slammed into each other hard and fast and angry, as if each of them were so wound up with grievance there was no room for tenderness. Ben wondered how he had ever survived without the hot animal tang of her fervent kisses, the sweet sting of her nails raking his back, her polished white canines at his chest, his neck. When he thrust himself into Shira, pressed as deeply as he could go, her hips tilted at just such an angle, it was as if Ben might slip his entire body inside her, dissolve completely into Shira and subsume his entire being, as if through the efforts of their lovemaking she could save Ben from himself. Free and wild and fully present, Ben felt like the best version of himself—younger, handsomer, stronger, capable of anything. He just wanted to hold onto that feeling forever.

After they both came, they lay side by side atop the bed's tangled covers in silence, Shira's chest rising and falling, her breasts glistening with perspiration. Shira had never been more naked to Ben before, as if he had rediscovered something precious they had lost. In the dim light, with her lipstick rubbed away, Ben was amazed how narrow her lips looked, like two pink lines drawn by a child's crayon. Her mascara had run, raccooning her eyes. He had looked deeply into her eyes as he had come, and it was as if they were swallowing him. It had been so long since she had allowed herself to be so open with him, giving herself entirely to Ben, losing herself in the act of union. Yes, the sex was amazing, but not simply because of the physical act; something was happening on an emotional level, a vital reconnecting, a fusion of souls, where they simply fucked because they *had* to, ravenously, like starvelings at a feast, and Ben wanted to know if things were good with them now, if this meant Liz could go, if it would be just the two of them again. What would their future together look like now that things had changed? But asking would come off as some sort of anxious interrogation and break the spell of their afterglow. So they lay in silence, sweat cooling on their bodies as their breathing returned to speed.

Finally, Shira spoke. "You just totally had me. That was fucking seismic, Ben."

"It was amazing! What happened?"

"Honestly?" Shira propped herself up on an elbow, the bedsheet toga-ed around her torso. "Seeing you up there dancing today. It was like I was seeing you through the eyes of a stranger, as someone separate from myself. Not Ben as part of Ben and Shira, hubby and wifey, just a handsome, confident man enjoying himself, and that was so sexy to me. It was beguiling, seriously beguiling."

"I love you," Ben said.

"I love you too, baby."

Ben's stomach seized and did a full twist. The moment had come.

"What does Liz give you that I can't?"

"Oh, Ben, let's not do this now."

Though Ben had thought it many times, he had never said the words out loud before. Just seven simple words. "I want you to stop seeing Liz."

Shira reached out a hand and caressed his cheek. "I'm sorry, Ben. I can't."

"You mean you won't. This isn't the way a marriage is supposed to work."

"There is no 'supposed to.' Marriage is a constant evolution, a chance to grow together *and* separately. Why can't you learn to take the crunchy with the smooth?"

"This arrangement is not working out." Ben's throat was so dry. "It's too difficult. Sometimes it just hurts so much. What is it I'm not giving you?"

"Stop," Shira said.

"I just need to understand what I'm doing wrong so I can fix it."

"Don't spoil things. We just had a lovely time together."

Shira stood up, dropped the sheet and started dressing, slipping back into her sheer black underwear. Now they seemed slightly vulgar, an insult to his pain.

"Ben, do you realize how many men would kill to be you right now? You have a still-beautiful wife who really does love you—*I love you dammit*—and trusts you so much you have the freedom to sleep with anyone you want."

"I only want you. There's nobody else I could imagine ever wanting."

Ben felt small and ridiculous lying there naked and exposed as Shira slipped back into the armor of her clothing. He climbed off the bed in search of his boxer shorts.

"I've seen you practically walking on air some nights when you return from a date with someone new you've met. You're living the life, babe."

"I know we agreed to be 'don't ask, don't tell' about all this, but I have to tell you so you know: the last thirteen months and two days while you have been involved with Liz, I have slept, awkwardly, with three women a grand total of five times, received two blowjobs and a depressing hand job in a parking lot in the back of a single mom's mini van."

"You never saw any of them again?" Shira said, quirking her eyebrow. "They were just some randos you met online?"

"They're not randos. If they're randos to me that would make me a rando to them, and I don't want to be somebody's rando. Believe me, every single moment I was with them I wished I was with you."

"That's so sweet." Shira slipped into her dress.

Ben was still naked, pathetically in search of his boxers.

"It's not sweet," Ben said. "It's pure pain because they're not you. I want you. Not some rando who won't even remember my name." Ben's face was so hot with shame, he couldn't bear to look at Shira. "Don't deny my pain. This is too much. Are you going to leave me for Liz?"

"Benjamin Seidel, how many times do I have to tell you I have no intention of leaving you. You are my person. I know this isn't always easy for you, and it's not easy for me either to see you hurting, but this is the life we're in and we're doing our best."

"It's not good enough. I hate being jealous that you're sleeping with her when you should be doing it with me, but I can't help it." Ben paused just long enough to realize this was not the time to ask, before he blurted out, "When was the last time you were tested?"

"Tested? For what?"

"STDs."

Shira met Ben's eyes, the muscles of her jaw tightening as her tone switched to that maddening didactic voice she used when she knew she was right and pity the poor fool who didn't agree. "You mean STIs. You don't want to stigmatize sexually transmitted infections. If you're sexually active you probably have HPV. People get chlamydia. Most people with herpes are never symptomatic and barely infectious."

"That doesn't answer my question. Have you been tested?"

"I don't like this tone, Ben. You sound like a fucking prosecutor. Yes, I've been tested. Every three months. Have you?"

Ben had gotten ahead of himself in the heat of the moment. He had not been tested and his empty expression showed it.

"I'm sorry," Ben said. "I thought I was done worrying about this kind of thing. You used to only have sex with me. I thought that's the way things were always going to be. I just feel like I'm on the outside looking in."

Shira's face softened, her eyes too. "Me and Liz are about way more than just what we do with our lady parts. You have no idea how much Mario Kart the two of us have played. We take walks, we cook, we watch movies, we talk, we snuggle."

"And how is that supposed to make me feel better? I want to do those things with you."

"You think video games are lame."

"I'm not talking about Mario Kart! I'm talking about me and you. I'm jealous, okay, and I hate it."

"Ben, we have the power to get used to anything, and change can take a long time. Jealousy is not an emotion. It's a social construct. It has to do with who you are and how you feel about yourself. Only you can change how you react."

"That sounds like a self-serving excuse. Jealousy is real. Not a social construct. Put yourself in my shoes for a minute and you'll see."

"I love you, Ben. I've loved you my entire adult life, but I can't fix you and I can't leave Liz."

"Why are you blaming me? I don't need fixing. We do. We need to see a therapist and figure this out."

"Don't pathologize what we have. It sounds a lot like shaming. Maybe me and you do need fixing, and I know we will find a way. But I'm not leaving Liz."

"Then you can't possibly love me," Ben said, finally finding his boxers crumpled behind the trash basket.

"Just because I love Liz doesn't mean I don't love you equally. Love isn't finite. There's plenty to go around."

"Wait, you love Liz?"

"Yes. I do."

"Wow." The room seemed to spin around Ben, the ugly watercolors on the walls dripping their pastels like a melted ice-cream cone. Equal wasn't good enough. Ben wanted to be more than equal. Ben wanted to be the only one. He couldn't believe the daughter of a world-renowned cantor and macroeconomist was not only fucking this polyamorous sideshow act, but falling in love with her as well. This was too much.

"Ben, you know I love you."

"I don't know that. What about showing me sometime?"

"What just happened between us in bed?"

"I need you to love me all the time."

"I do. But that doesn't mean I can't love Liz as well."

"How can you possibly love two people? It's impossible."

"Love is not a monopoly."

"You're supposed to love me!"

"I do. I do love you."

"And you love Liz as well."

"Yes," Shira said. "I love Liz too."

Ben's jaw ached and his temples pounded. "Maybe you're clinging to Liz because you don't feel like a whole woman anymore, but it's not true. You're everything I could ever want. Maybe being with Liz makes you forget what we had wanted to do together, but it doesn't matter, as long as we have each other."

But it did matter, and Shira knew it. They had started a college 529 plan not long after Ben landed his first real job. They had Googled elite pre-schools together, bought all the books about what to expect when expecting. They had been so practical and methodical it made him sick to think about it now, the stupid assumptions they had made about something so complex as creating an entirely new human being.

Shira was silent for a long time, body frozen, eyes narrowed. Then Shira's hardened features melted into tears. "That wasn't fair. It's not fair. It wasn't fair to say that. You have no idea how much I hurt."

"We've both lost something," Ben said. "We both hurt."

"I just wanted to be a mother so badly, and now I can't. That's been taken away from me, forever."

"I know that and I'm sorry. Can you at least stop this nonsense with Liz so we can figure ourselves out? Just me and you. We will figure something out. Please."

"I can't. I just can't."

"Why not?"

"Ben, can we not do this now?"

"I want to go home," Ben said. The cyclone-tossed bed behind him served only to mock his desolation. "I can't stay here now."

"Do you want me to come with you tonight?" Shira said, inching closer to Ben, her voice tentative.

"Of course," Ben said. "We belong together."

4

Ben and Shira did belong together. They had always belonged together. Ever since Shira brought Ben home to Bethesda for Passover to meet her family that first time, Ben knew she was his life. Shira's parents had taken Ben in as one of their own, and Shira's father, meaty hand on Ben's shoulder, loved to offer Ben advice on subjects as diverse as automotive care, wine and food pairings, and how to tie a bow tie. Shira had always been open and warm and kind, quirky in a way that made Ben feel he had been invited into a private world he could have never known on his own. With Shira, Ben's life expanded from that of a solitary architecture student to a world of karaoke and spicy margaritas, Star Wars marathons and Women's Day marches. They cooked Shabbat dinners together and fasted once on Yom Kippur until their stomachs overruled and they ordered the biggest Chicago-style pizza they could find, laughing drunk on boxed wine for all they would need to atone for. When Ben was fired from his first job at blue-blooded Brenton Foss, Shira said, "Screw them. Stuck up mofos don't deserve you." And when his stomach ached for countless agonizing, baffling months, it was Shira who insisted he cut dairy entirely out of his diet.

And Ben encouraged Shira to follow her dreams to be a working artist despite her parents' demands she get a Masters in Social Work, supporting her as she honed her craft and built an enviable list of contacts from well-connected rabbis to Judaica shops, from Toronto to Boston to Miami Beach.

Building a family just made so much sense. They worked together, and having kids was never in doubt. Now that there would never be kids, Ben was left to wonder if the presence of Liz was a prelude to an end of his and Shira's life together. If life with Shira meant life without a family to raise, he would take Shira any day of the week.

One night later that week, Shira said, "Hey," as Ben loaded the dishwasher. "What if you find somebody of your own, an inamorata?" Shira said. "Wouldn't that make it easier for you if you had a girlfriend?"

"I don't want a girlfriend. I only want you."

"You have me, Ben. I love you. I've always loved you. And I expect to love you as long as I live."

"I'm just a two-bit talent. I'm nothing special."

"You're you." Shira took Ben's face in her hands. "Nobody else in the world is you, Benjamin David Seidel. And that's what makes you special. I get a front row seat for this ride. This is our adventure, and we're in it together." And then Shira looked Ben squarely in the eyes. "I promise you, I'm not going to leave you."

"But I can't give you what Liz gives you."

"No, you can't. And she can't give me what you give me. It's not fair to expect our partners to be everything at all times: lover, playmate, critic, partner in crime, headshrinker, sounding board, whipping post. I know

I can't be all things to you. That's why a girlfriend might help. Someone to give you what I can't give."

"If you stopped seeing Liz, you'd be able to give me more of yourself."

"That's the thing. I'll never eat pork ribs with you, I don't like the cold pragmatism of the Bauhaus Style, I don't care if I see all the Major League baseball stadiums; frankly one is more than enough for me. But that doesn't matter. Why should we be everything to each other, when there is a whole world of people to share yourself with?"

"Isn't that why we got married?"

"Yes, and no. Yes to be the cornerstone of each other's lives, but not the be-all and end-all. There needs to be some space, some mystery, some separation. But, I swear, you have me, Ben. You have me."

"And you have Liz."

"You're afraid you're missing out, aren't you? That's what's going on, right?"

Ben lowered his eyes, then reached for the detergent bottle and poured some green gel into the dishwasher.

"Can I see your phone?" Shira asked.

"Why?"

Shira finished wiping down the counter with a cloth and slipped it into the fridge handle. "I know you've spent a lot of time cultivating connections with people you've met online. I've seen you off in the corner intently texting away. How about going through your address book and checking in on a few of them? Kick the tires, see what's up?"

Ben threw Shira a skeptical look.

"Timing is everything. Maybe they weren't ready. Maybe they were waiting to hear from you again."

"Nobody is waiting to hear from me."

"How do you know if you don't try? You're a nice guy. You're fit, you're good looking. Baby, you're a catch."

Ben turned on the dishwasher, unlocked his phone and handed it to her with a sigh.

"Who knows?" Shira scrolled through Ben's phone. She arched an eyebrow. "Here, three months ago," she said, face illuminated, "you told Theresa you were going out for a run and she didn't write back, and neither did you. It can't hurt. Just say hi. Let her know you're thinking of her and ask if she wants to get a drink."

"I don't need your help."

"As your best friend, I'm saying you do need my help. You just gave up on her. Who even told you to stop texting her?"

Shira typed something into Ben's phone and showed him the screen: Hey! It's been a while! I just wanted to see how you're doing? Want to grab a drink this weekend? ☺

"It's innocuous," Ben said.

"Exactly. Who knows what might happen with Theresa. Should I send?"

The white noise of the dishwasher hummed like a hundred angry bees in Ben's ears. He moved into the adjoining living room, Shira following close behind. "Fine," Ben said.

Ben had liked Theresa. They had talked about the first time they each ran a marathon. She had thrown up at the twenty-three-mile mark. Ben had slipped in the rain and twisted his knee but he had finished eventually, at a slow jog. Theresa had grown up in Suffolk County on Long Island; him, Nassau County. They both attended the Subway World Series with their fathers as high schoolers, Theresa as a Mets fan, he as a third-generation Yankees fan.

Shira hit send, and right away Theresa's composing bubble appeared on the screen.

"See?" Shira said. That single arched eyebrow again. "She's answering."

They did have a lot in common, and Ben thought maybe he *had* let things go too easily with Theresa. Ben and Theresa had gone out twice and kissed the second time after drinks at a hip oyster bar. They even discussed going running together sometime at the Chestnut Hill Reservoir. Ben had even picked out a hole-in-the-wall taco place to take her to after their run. But something about the whole thing still felt furtive and dishonest, so Ben pumped the brakes, afraid that consummating a relationship with Theresa would hurt Shira. Theresa was taking a long time to respond but he could already envision the two of them laughing over this misunderstanding over drinks. *I should've written again, Ben would say. No, I should've written, Theresa would say.*

The text appeared at last. Who's this? Sorry, I don't recognize the number.

Ben felt as if he had been kneed in the balls.

Shira, unfazed, was ready to respond, fingers poised above the screen.

"What are you doing?" Ben nearly screamed.

"I'm answering her question."

"You can't do that."

"Why?"

"Because she'll know it was me."

"Isn't that what you want? For her to write back: *Hey Ben. Great to hear from you.*"

"Give me my phone." Ben lunged at Shira as she slipped, laughing, out of his reach.

Shira found herself on the other side of their beige microfiber Pottery Barn couch, phone held high like a prize. Ben gauged whether he could leap the thing without injuring himself.

"This is for your own good," Shira said.

"I'm serious."

"Fine." Shira pouted. "I won't write back to her. Even though it costs nothing and might lead to something special between you and her."

Ben practically flew around their sectional couch and snatched his phone back.

"One more thing," Shira said. "I'm not done with you yet."

"I'm not texting any more women from my address book. As a matter of fact, I'm going to erase those numbers right now. It's pointless."

"Let me at least help you fix your Tinder profile," Shira said. "There's nothing wrong with a little ego rubbing every once in a while."

Ben let out a dry laugh. "More like ego punching. I'm going to shut it down. It's a pretty bleak place for a balding thirty-four-year-old married man."

"Jesus Christ, Ben, you're not balding. This is so fucking exasperating. Jason Statham is bald. The Rock is bald. Sean Connery is bald. Jean-Luc Picard, captain of the Starship USS *Enterprise*, is bald."

"So, you agree that I'm bald?"

"That's not what I'm saying! Those men are bald and they are totally hot and you, my sexy man, still have most of your hair."

"Some of it," Ben corrected.

"You're insane. You know that? Let me at least look at your profile. I can guarantee you one thing. If you don't put yourself out there, nothing will happen."

Ben hesitated, and Shira extended her hand, the flat palm upraised, awaiting his phone.

"Fine." He logged onto his profile. "Just go easy on me, please."

Shira smiled and caressed Ben's shoulders, working the muscles with her free hand. "Relax. You have such a lovely smile." Shira paused. "Oh, babe, you've got to up your thirst-trap game."

"What's wrong? These are nice, respectable pictures."

"First of all, no pleated pants."

"Why? Those are my nice pants. I got them on sale at Nordstrom Rack. It's a good, durable pant. Every man needs a good pair of pleated pants."

"No they don't. Please trust me on this one. Stick with jeans or flat-front khakis."

Shira scrolled through the rest of his pictures. "Why aren't you smiling in these pictures?"

"I am smiling."

"That's not a smile. That's a grimace. Show them your adorable dimples."

"I'm not in the mood for this."

"Your whole face lights up when you smile."

"For the last time, I am smiling."

Shira turned the screen to Ben. "You look constipated here. And here. And ... you really do suck at selfies."

"That's it." Ben snatched the phone from Shira.

"I'm just trying to help."

"I don't need your help finding someone else. I just need you."

"I know what you need." Shira led Ben to the bedroom. "Come on."

They slipped off their clothes, Shira kissing him tenderly, urging him along, tongue fluttering in his mouth. There was no place Ben would rather have been, that close to Shira, her body tensing around his, quicksilver beads of perspiration forming on her skin as he moved inside her. This was his wife, this was his love. But she was also Liz's love, and as he shuddered towards completion Ben couldn't help but wonder why he was not enough.

"How was that?" Shira turned her face to Ben. "Feel better? You are not alone. You have me."

"What's it like when you do it with Liz?"

Shira pulled her hand from Ben's and leapt out of bed. Her firm breasts looked like precious untouchable things. "Really? That's what you're thinking now. We just made love and you're obsessing over my girlfriend."

"Sometimes I feel like I'm getting the leftovers."

"Are you serious? What we just did was just table scraps to you?"

"The Four Seasons was —"

"Fuck you, Ben." Shira's eyes blazed. "Fuck you. I'm going to watch Anderson Cooper. Do not follow me. Just go to bed. Maybe tomorrow you won't be such an ass."

Sometime after three, Ben awoke to Shira shaking beside him. She was crying softly into her pillow, trying not to wake him. Ben fumbled for Shira's body in the dark and she pressed her body close to his. Spooning him from behind, Shira continued to sob barely articulated words as if she were speaking another language. This frightened Ben so he reached over and clicked on the bedside lamp.

Shira's damp hair was matted against her cheek. "It's my fault," Shira said. Her big eyes pooled with tears. "It's my fault."

"What's going on?" Ben's heart clenched.

"I had the most terrible dream."

Ben turned to face Shira. Her entire body shook. In all their years together, Ben had never seen Shira like this before.

Shira wiped her nose on the top sheet and cleared her eyes with fisted knuckles. "They came to me. Each of them, alive and dead at the same time. Lily, Zoey, Lilah, Rachel, each of them with their tiny empty-eyed faces reaching out to me saying, *momma, momma, momma*. They were so real, I could almost touch them, feel their skin, smell their breath."

Ben took Shira in his arms and kissed her face. "It was just a dream."

"It was my fault."

"You didn't do anything wrong."

"Yes. I. Did. I made plans. I was arrogant enough to assume it would happen."

"We both made plans. It was both of us, but it's totally reasonable and even responsible to plan."

"As my father likes to remind us," Shira said, "'Man plans, God laughs.' I've wanted to have a girl named Lily since grade school. She was so real I could even imagine the conversations we would have about feminism and art and—" Shira began to cry again. "Stupid. I'm so stupid."

"You're not." Ben took Shira's face in his hands. "You're too hard on yourself."

Shira looked back at Ben, and her glossy brown eyes were so big and round as she regarded him in silence, he thought he had finally broken through.

"I just wanted to be a mother so badly." Shira hiccuped between a new round of tears. "I would've been such a good mother. I just know it. I'll never be able to experience the most important thing a woman can ever do."

Ben took Shira's hand and laced her fingers with his. "Can I kiss you?"

"Of course."

Ben kissed Shira softly on the lips and tasted her salty tears. He pulled her closer and felt her heart, that most baffling of organs, beating in her chest.

"You're the best person I've ever known," Ben said. "You did nothing wrong."

"I've done lots of things wrong. I'm a hooman bean." She was silent for a long time, and when Ben was certain Shira was done speaking, she added, "I'm sorry, Ben. I'm so sorry for everything."

"You're sorry for Liz?"

"I'm sorry for how you feel about Liz." Shira took his hand, massaging the pads of his fingers; thumb, index, middle, ring, pinky. At last she said, "I'll do better to make sure you always know how much I love you."

5

Ben ducked out of work early to meet Shira at the Museum of Fine Arts to see the Goya exhibition. The place was packed, the gallery echoing with a low hum of countless unarticulated voices. Ben had to edge his way through the crowd to keep up with Shira who was eager to see Goya's *Disasters of War* prints up close so she could study how he used light and shade and shadow, to understand how the master could possibly convey such vivid horror without the use of color.

Goya's work was irredeemably grim, the dismembered corpses, the beheadings, the executions turning Ben's stomach sour, and he told Shira he was going to check out the ancient Egyptian gallery. He would catch up with her in an hour. Shira nodded distractedly.

Ben had just turned away from Shira to leave when he saw her: tall and slim and pale-skinned in a red pencil skirt and heels. She stood motionless, near the exit, a forbidding get-back stare on her face, her hair pulled back tightly at her temples, fragile body rigid with a hidden tension. Everything in her manner said to leave her be, but something inside Ben said that she could love him, help ease his loneliness, make him feel like he mattered. He knew instinctively if he spoke to her, his life would never be the same. And he knew he shouldn't do it; it felt wrong with Shira in the gallery behind him. But some signal beyond words said for him to do it, do it, do it, so he slipped his wedding band off and dropped it into his pocket.

Ben sidled up beside the woman, who remained still as if she were made of marble. He wanted to find a way to make her smile, but he could barely draw a breath, heart knocking against his ribs. Her body shifted as if she were about to take leave, and that was when Ben said, "Am I the only one who expected to see cans of beans on display?"

"Excuse me?" the woman said, expression unchanged. Her lips, urgently red, told Ben to STOP.

"Forget it," Ben said. He'd sensed mystic connections with women in the past, certain these feelings would play out as he imagined, and had been wildly, humiliatingly wrong. "Sorry, it was stupid."

He turned to walk away, when she said, "Tell me. Tell me what was stupid."

Her eyes were on Ben, an expectant look on her face, lips parted, a bemused tilt to her head.

"I was just making a joke about Goya canned beans. You know, like if Warhol painted Goya cans instead of Campbells Black Bean Soup."

Her face broke out into a smile. "That was a bad one, but so good. I love Dad jokes. Everyone here is so grim-faced. A little levity is much appreciated."

"That's for sure," Ben said, relieved. "These pictures are giving me PTSD."

"Goya is not my favorite," she said. "And that would be an understatement."

"Then why are you subjecting yourself to this?"

"I was supposed to meet a donor for a late lunch at the cafe in the courtyard, but he flaked at the last minute. So I thought I'd check it out and see if my tastes have evolved since college. I can now decisively say they have not."

"So, who do you like?"

"John Singer Sargent is my all-time favorite. But I like Mary Cassatt a lot as well. What about you?"

"I like Rothko."

"Really?" She squinted. "Why?"

There was something awesome, in the true sense, in Rothko's work, almost frightening, as if the true face of God was hidden somewhere in his massive color fields.

"His work just does something to me. I can't really explain."

"I'm not much for abstract expressionism. I'm old-fashioned, I guess."

"Isn't there a Sargent gallery here?" Ben said, hopefully.

"Of course. The MFA is the Singer Sargent mothership."

"Would you like to accompany me?" The word "accompany" was stiffer and more formal than Ben intended, but the offer was out and a small smile appeared on her face.

"Yes, I would like to accompany you."

Just hearing her utter that single syllable in all of its unbounded yes-ness made Ben's body flush with joy. Her piercing green eyes had softened as she looked at Ben anew.

Ben followed her out of the gallery, a whip-thin vision of pure desire, long-necked and poised in glossy red heels. He glanced back once to see if he could find Shira, dressed in her broken-down work jeans and battered combat boots. She must have disappeared around a corner, immersed in the mechanics of one of Goya's disturbed drawings.

Ben hung back a little, watching her hips shift as she walked. She smelled so good too, just a subtle hint of citrus trailing behind her. In her heels, she was the same height as Ben, which would make her five foot nine, a full seven inches taller than Shira on a good day.

"My name's Ben," Ben said, drawing even with her.

"I'm Pamela." She extended her hand to shake. "Never Pam."

Ben took her hand in his and felt the warmth of her body flowing into his like an offering. The blood pumping through the pulsing veins in her palm came directly from her heart. Holding her hand felt like ... What the hell was he doing? "Sorry," he said, dropping her hand as if he'd touched something hot from the oven.

"It's okay. I shake a lot of hands. I've had every kind of handshake times a hundred. And this was fine."

"Well, fine is all I ever aspired to. My handshakes used to be just okay, and before that adequate —"

"You have nice hands," Pamela said, surprising Ben into silence. "They're strong, but tender. You don't have to prove yourself through brute force."

Could she actually be attracted to him, with his fucked up hair, khakis and standard blue button-down?

"All this handshaking," Ben said. "What are you, some kind of celebrity? Are we going to end up in the gossip pages?"

She laughed, but it was a tight, restrained laugh, as if she was used to laughing for punctuation rather than genuine feeling. "I'm actually Executive Vice President of Major Gifts for a large national not-for-profit."

They found themselves in the Art of the Americas wing, paying little attention to the art, eyes on each other, oblivious to their surroundings. "What do you do? For work."

Ben told her he was an architect at a firm over by Rowes Wharf and that he was helping design a big mixed-use project at the Boston Seaport that had recently broken ground.

"Would I know any of your work?" Pamela squinted her eyes again, a fine dusting of barely noticeable freckles on the wings of her nose and her cheeks.

"Nothing too famous. A third-tier college welcome center in New Hampshire was a big deal for about five minutes. I'm a massive Walter Gropius fanboy. I make a pilgrimage to his house in Lincoln every year. I'd love to work entirely with the clean lines of the International Style, but that won't pay the bills. So I'm kind of a journeyman. I do what I've got to do. I've been lead designer on a few projects here and there."

Ben asked her where she was from, since everyone Ben knew was from somewhere else, and Pamela said she had grown up in Philadelphia and had studied literature at Yale. She had moved to Boston proper, or *proper Boston*, more precisely, after completing a graduate degree from the Heller School at Brandeis University and had been working for the same organization over on State Street since she graduated. Ben was surprised to learn she was a year older than him. He would have figured thirty, thirty-one at the oldest.

She talked rapidly about the terrible roommates she had had, laughing here and there for emphasis as if she had been holding something back for a lifetime and only now felt free to let loose. She talked about the great one-bedroom apartment she was subletting in Beacon Hill and how much she loved to live alone.

Alone was good, Ben thought. Alone meant not married. Ben couldn't say the same for himself, but he had a hall pass from Shira, and for now that was just as good. After a year in the dating wilderness, even a dinner date with Pamela would be a minor miracle, so he didn't concern himself with any problems that might arise later.

"It's weird how Boston is both such a liberal city and such a conservative city," Ben said.

"Exactly." Pamela's eyes sparkled. "The Boston Brahmins are as uptight as the Main Liners. Puritan Boston and Quaker Philadelphia are alive and well."

Pamela's hip bumped against Ben's once as they rounded a corner, and his pulse raced at the realization that Pamela felt his gravitational pull as strongly as he felt hers. He was under her thrall, a serious case of the she's-with-mes, transforming him into the guileless boy he had once been, so fortunate just to be in the company of a beautiful woman.

"And don't even talk to me about dating in Boston."

Ben couldn't imagine she would have trouble dating. She could have picked anyone she wanted.

"Yep," Ben said. "That's no fun."

"Tell me a dating nightmare," Pamela said.

"Why?"

"So I don't feel so alone in my dating misery."

"There was one woman from Beverly," Ben said, "who was into CBT and kept trying to convince me I would like it."

"Cognitive behavioral therapy?"

"That's what I thought, but nooooo. CBT apparently also stands for cock-and-ball torture."

"Ouch."

"Seriously."

Ben's phone buzzed and his heart began to race. He would have talked to Pamela all day and into the night as well, but Shira must have tired of the pressing crowd and was looking for him. "One used hashtags every few sentences; hashtag hungry, hashtag YOLO, hashtag shootmeinthehead. But they're sort of all dispiriting in the same way. They check their phones constantly, sipping complex cocktails and nibbling artisanal nut-based cheese and quince jelly they order to satisfy their vegan diets, not asking any questions about me, personal or otherwise, as if I'm just something to be tolerated until the real thing comes along."

"That sucks," Pamela said.

"Yep. It kind of makes you feel like you don't matter."

"Well, I think you matter."

"Well, thank you. I think you matter, too."

"People don't know how to treat each other anymore," Pamela said. "I mean, some ogling piece of crap Airdropped me a dick pic on the T on my way over."

"I'm sorry. I'd never send you anything inappropriate if you gave me your number."

Pamela smiled. "You're asking for my number?"

"Yes. Is that okay? I'd like to see you again." The words came out of his mouth just like normal words Ben said countless times a day, but inside he felt as if he was on the verge of collapse, his stomach a knotted mess, knees weak with nerves.

"Ask me now. In person. I don't want to just chill or hang out. Ask me on a date, a real date."

"Will you go on a date with me?" The words, to his ears, felt so old fashioned as to be laughable. But Pamela was not laughing.

"Saturday night," she said, extending her hand. Her nails were painted a bright glossy red. At that moment, Pamela's fingernails were the very pinnacle of feminine elegance.

Ben went to shake it again but Pamela said, "Give me your phone. I'll put in my number."

"I can do it." His screen would be filled with alerts from Shira wondering where the hell he was.

He removed his phone from his pocket—it was hot to the touch—and asked Pamela for her number. She gave hers, and Ben gave his in return.

"It was very nice to meet you, Ben."

"It was nice to meet you, Pamela."

Ben watched her walking away, and he wanted to pump his fist and scream out, "Yesssssss," but he had to find Shira right now.

He found her in the gift shop, leafing through a copy of *Make Way for Ducklings*. She was so familiar to him he had forgotten just how small she actually was. Seeing her with her head tilted down, glasses pressed to her face, absorbed in the book, he wanted to take her in his arms and hold her right there in the gift shop.

"There you are," Shira said. "What's that look on your face?"

"I just love you."

"Well that's good to know. I love you too, but you're smiling like a fool," Shira said. "There's something else, right?"

Ben just blurted it out. "I met someone."

"What?" A wrinkle of confusion formed between her eyes.

It felt disloyal to say such a thing to his wife, but not telling Shira would have been worse.

"A woman. I met a woman."

Shira sucked in a deep draught of air. "That's. Wow. I didn't expect—"

"Neither of us like Goya, so we checked out some of the other galleries."

"It's okay." She rearranged her pinched expression into a smile. "It's okay."

"We just sort of met. Just like that."

"Well, congratulations." Shira offered her small hand for Ben to high-five. "What's the story, morning glory?"

"We're going to go on an old-fashioned date."

"And she's okay that you're married?" Shira said, matter-of-factly.

"I didn't get the chance to say. I mean, we just met."

"Ben! You have to tell her right now. She probably assumes you're single."

"I wouldn't presume to know what she assumes."

"This is not right, Ben. We're talking about ethical non-monogamy. You can't deceive her."

"I'm not deceiving anyone. We had a nice conversation. I'll tell her. I promise."

"When?"

"When I see her. On Saturday."

"You need to text her and tell her right now. Remember, no deception, no lies."

"I don't tell you how to be with Liz, so please don't tell me how to be with Pamela. I'll tell her when I see her."

"This is different. We are talking about what is moral, what is right."

"I'll take care of it. But this is my thing, and I need you to let me do it my way."

6

en texted Pamela when he got home from the MFA, and that *so great to meet you!* message began an near constant conversation that carried late into the night, continuing through the week, punctuating their workdays with debates about the superiority of fleece over flannel, the relative merits of vitamin supplements, juice fasts and organic produce. They mocked Mark Wahlberg's fake Boston accent, commiserated over the death of record stores, video stores and John Lennon, the greatest Beatle of all. They agreed the advent of the smart phone was simultaneously the best and worst invention ever. Pamela sent Ben a snapshot of a dead squirrel she found on the Boston Common with a handwritten sign beside it saying: *Free Squirrel.* They laughed over that for days exchanging texts about other free things nobody would ever want—free mattress, used; free cat hair; free chopped liver smoothies; free amateur poetry.

But they talked about more than just minutiae and cultural detritus. As the week progressed they shared more and more about themselves. Pamela had an older sister, Penny, with whom she didn't speak, a cousin serving as a federal judge in Washington state, and an innate sense that somewhere down the strands of her DNA she would find a great woman warrior. She had no desire to have children, and sometimes wished she lived in another, more simple era.

Like before vaccines and penicillin? Ben asked.

Yes, Pamela joked. I strongly believe I'm a consumptive at heart. I'd be right at home on a fainting couch.

Ben told Pamela he grew up a nice Jewish boy on suburban Long Island with all the advantages one could ask for, experienced an ordinary late-century childhood with baseball and bike riding and video games, state school in Binghamton, girlfriends in a minor key, and no major trauma. That came later, and Ben never talked about what happened to his parents, except to Shira, who had so completely been there to put him back together.

He did not tell Pamela he was married because he was afraid she would disappear on him, and now that he had found her he couldn't bear the thought of losing her. Her texts were already becoming a sort of lifeline, giving his days a sense of meaning. Ben worried he was driving into a cul-de-sac, with Pamela riding shotgun at his side, lights off, engine racing towards an inevitable crash, and he wished their was some way he could make Pamela understand how much he cared for her, how much she had come to mean to him in such a short time, and to please, please, please not leave him when he told her he was married.

Pamela confided how much she hated her freckles, which came on strong in the summer, and how the asshole boys at school in the suburbs of Philadelphia had relentlessly called her a "speckled trout";

and how she had, as an overwrought teenager, threatened to drown herself in the Schuylkill River just to prove she was not a coldblooded fish. Ben wished he could have been there to tell her how awesome she was and protect her from all the needless hurt and disappointment.

Do you think we would have been friends in high school? Ben texted Pamela one night, while Shira undressed for bed.

I'm glad you didn't know me then. I was moody, sullen, kinda sour. All I wanted was to be left alone so I could read another book. I read a book a day for years.

Ben found a picture of himself from eleventh grade in gym shorts and a white T-shirt and fired it off to Pamela.

Oh my god, you were such a dork. I love it! Look at your hair!

Ben hoped she would send back a picture of her own, but when she didn't, he asked: *Would you have been friends with him?*

Sorry no lol, Pamela said. *Am I terrible?*

You like me now, Ben said. *That's what really matters.*

What can I say? Timing is everything.

Ben was still absorbed in texting Pamela when Shira returned from her Friday night with Liz, exchanging intimate bits of him for her, her for him. It was late, and Shira dropped her shoes and backpack to the ground, signaling she wanted his attention. It was pouring outside, and Shira was drenched, her hair matted to her face, glasses fogged. Ben knew Pamela would be checking out soon anyway to prepare for bed so he texted good night and fired off the 🌝 emoji.

Pamela returned a 🖤 and Ben's stomach flipped.

"You're like a teenager with that phone. Have you been texting all night?"

"Yep," Ben said.

"You really like her." Shira wiped her lenses on a towel.

"I do."

Shira smiled a soft, guarded smile. This was new ground for Shira, and it was clear she was working to support Ben and his new relationship. "I want to see you happy. I really do."

Shira wriggled out of her jeans and yanked her sweater over her head, dropping them onto the floor beside their bed. "Maybe it's time me and you and Liz spend some time together. If you're comfortable."

The pictures of Liz Bird Ben had seen on Facebook with her bottle-blonde hair and frightening tattoos and piercings raised a sort of snobbish revulsion in Ben: Shira's over-the-top rebellion against the mean. The idea of meeting Liz felt more a punishment than anything else, a reminder of his shortcomings as a husband, so he had always told Shira no when she had asked about them meeting.

"It's important to me," Shira said. "It's important the people I love know each other. Once you meet her, you'll see she is really a great person."

"I'm sure she is. I'm just not comfortable."

"But you have Pamela. Doesn't that make it easier?"

"I don't *have* anyone. Do you know how scared I am she'll run as fast and far as she can when I tell her I'm married?"

Shira offered Ben a hug in her mismatched bra and panties. "If she likes you now, and it seems like she does, a lot, I think she'll roll with it. Relationships are always complicated." Shira's body was a furnace against Ben's chest. He rested his chin on top of her head. "I can write you a note." Her words vibrated up through Ben's jaw. "So she knows you have permission."

"Thanks, Mom. That wouldn't be awkward at all."

"People do it. Not like notarized, but a nice hand-written note saying everything is open and above-board."

"Somehow I don't think that's a good idea."

Shira pulled back from their embrace and looked Ben in the eye. "How about dinner with Liz? She is your metamour."

"You know I hate that word."

"I'm trying to be inclusive, Ben. You're part of this."

"I'm really so not part of this."

"You can be part of this. Maybe the three of us can try and play sometime. You know?"

"Play? What are we, six?"

"Just an idea" Shira said, and then, making her voice gruff: "Metamours be with you. Handle this, you can. Alone, you are not."

Ben hated to say no to Shira, particularly considering how understanding and open she was about Pamela. He would have to meet Liz at some point if Shira insisted on it, and he was about to offer a solid maybe. But he was never, ever going to sleep with her, especially as long as Pamela was around. Then Ben saw on Shira's bare arms what looked like multitracked rope marks, cross-hatched patterns etched into her wrists like a bracelet. She had bright pink indentations at her ankles as well.

"What is that?" Ben said. "Didn't we always agree, no marks?"

Ben and Shira had tried some light bondage early in their marriage with fuzzy pink handcuffs, feathers and blindfolds, her calling Ben "Commander," saying she was a bad girl and needed to be punished. But it had felt silly and artificial and they had not pursued things further. Still, the thought that Shira was exploring without him felt like a whole other level of desolation.

"Forget it," Shira said. "It's nothing."

"It's not nothing. I don't need this paraded in front of me like a trophy."

"It's not like that, Ben."

"How would you like it if I came home with a massive hickey on my neck?"

"I wouldn't like it, but I'd deal with it."

"So you think I should just deal with it? Is that it? I can't be near you right now." Ben grabbed his pillow and the extra blanket off the end of their bed and left his and Shira's bedroom without saying goodnight.

"Ben," Shira called. "Come on. Don't go to sleep mad."

"I won't be able to sleep. Thanks for that."

Ben made up the couch and pulled out his phone. He knew Pamela was asleep but he wanted to text her and tell her how much he had come to care about her, but he resisted the temptation. Instead he scrolled back through the past few days of messages, starting at the very beginning, and read them over and over again in the dark until he finally, mercifully, fell asleep.

Waking up to a text from Pamela was like waking up to a kiss, starting his day off full of good feelings and happiness, no matter how tired he was, but there was no text from Pamela when he awoke. Ben was nervous and distracted all Saturday morning, afraid anything he might say might cause Pamela to call off their dinner date. So he didn't text when he awoke or even after his long run out to Concord on the Minuteman Trail. It was unusual for either of them to go more than a waking hour without checking in on the other, but this morning, nothing. Finally, at 12:02, on the verge of hyperventilating, heart pounding wildly, Ben fired off a simple: *Hello??*

A moment later Pamela texted back. *Hey I was wondering what happened to you. Everything ok?*

Yes, Ben said. *Yes. Everything's great. All systems go for tonight.*

Great, see you at seven.

Ben arrived early at the restaurant, a little spot in the North End, known for its handmade pasta and delicious Neapolitan pizza. He loved their pizza marinara but agonized over the menu in case Pamela was open to sharing.

Ben's phone buzzed with a message from Shira offering a quick text wishing him well. *You'll be great tonight. Just be you.*

He thanked Shira and went back to tearing strips out of the paper table cloth and shredding them into a small pile.

Pamela arrived not long after. Ben rose to greet her and Pamela offered him a quick kiss—on the lips! This was a good start, and Ben's labored breathing instantly eased. She was beautiful, of course, lips painted bright red, shiny black bob caressing her bare shoulders.

"Look at you," Pamela said. "Wearing a jacket and everything. This *is* a date."

"You look amazing," Ben said. "Sleeveless in April is a bold move."

"I may not look it, but I'm made of sturdy stuff," Pamela said.

Pamela's pale neck was longer than Ben recalled, her rhythmic pulse palpable beneath her skin. She wore a small silver pendant that rested above her breastbone and rings on three of her long fingers. Her green eyes were soft, unguarded, as she sized him up entirely without judgment. They had shared so much this past week through the cold medium of text, so much about their pasts and where they had come from, and now they sat close enough to touch. They were no longer strangers, but they had never shared an experience together aside from their brief meeting at the museum. He hadn't even thought to ask Pamela her last name. How easy it would be for them to return to being strangers, leaving barely an impression on each other's lives, erased from memory like a single day among a countless march of days. Ben's heart revved as Shira's voice in his head urged him to do the right thing. He had to tell her he was married before he lost his nerve.

The waiter appeared and asked if they'd like a bottle of wine. Ben looked to Pamela and said "A bottle of red? A bottle of white?"

Pamela laughed. "Scenes from an Italian Restaurant?"

"Yep," Ben said.

"You are so Long Island," Pamela said, rolling her eyes. "Are you all required to take the Pledge of Allegiance to Billy Joel?"

"Pretty much." Ben laughed.

"How about a nice red? A cabernet maybe?"

"Perfect," Ben said, telling the waiter they'd be ready to order when he returned with the wine.

"You never told me your last name," Ben said, turning his eyes back to Pamela.

"You never asked."

"I'm asking now."

"It's Whitney."

"Very classy. Any relation to the Whitney Museum Whitneys?"

"Goodness no." Pamela laughed. "Not even poor country cousins."

"Well, it's nice to make your acquaintance, Pamela Whitney."

"I don't know your last name either, which means I couldn't Google you and find out if you are a serial killer, or, worse, a Republican."

Anyone with a smart phone could figure out in a couple clicks he was married to Shira. "It's Seidel of the North Hempstead Seidels. Ben Seidel, last of his name but first in his class."

"Ben Seidel," Pamela said, smiling. "Now I know everything. And first in your class! I'm impressed."

"Well," Ben said. "Maybe I was stretching the truth there a bit for dramatic effect. To be honest, I was fair to middling."

"One thing I like about you is your commitment to honesty."

Ben's blood chilled. He had to tell her right now, but couldn't bear the thought of ruining everything, just as they were getting started.

"I have to say—" Ben's stomach lurched. "And hear me out because it's not as bad as it sounds, but I'm sort of, technically, kind of married."

Pamela's skin paled to a translucent ghostly white, a deep crease forming between her eyes. "You're going through a divorce?"

"No, not a divorce," Ben said, searching for the right words. "My wife ... We have this sort of arrangement, you know, where she can see whomever she wants and I can—"

"Your *wife* says it's okay?" Pamela said. "I can't fucking believe this."

"I didn't know when to tell you," Ben pleaded. "I wanted to tell you in person."

"Well, thank you so much for that courtesy," Pamela said, her words clipped, lips thin with rage. "I'm going to leave now and we're not going to speak anymore."

"Let me explain. Please."

"There's nothing you can possibly say. You lied to me." Pamela rose from the table at the exact instant the waiter arrived with their bottle of wine.

"I didn't lie," Ben said. "I told you the truth."

"It's too late, Ben. Your truth doesn't match mine. Goodbye."

And then Pamela was gone, leaving Ben alone in the crowded dinner-hour restaurant with two untouched glasses of Cabernet sitting before him. It would have been a mistake to go after her, so Ben did the next best thing and downed his glass of wine in a single, annihilating gulp.

If he hadn't told Pamela he was married, he and Pamela would be having a lovely evening right now, laughing and flirting and who knows what. He had no choice but to tell her. To not do so would be cruel and heartless and selfish. He just wished he could have been selfish long enough that he could have kissed her, really kissed her, held her in his arms, just once.

Ben finished his second glass of wine when the waiter appeared and asked him if he wanted to hear about the evening's specials. "No thanks," he responded. "Just the check."

Ben's phone buzzed on the table.

Hey.

It was Pamela.

I'm sorry I walked out on you. That wasn't very nice. Would you like to come over and talk?

Ben sprinted all the way to Pamela's apartment—a red-brick Federal style townhouse at the top of Beacon Hill—in record time, the comeback kid, ready for redemption. He stood in the cramped vestibule catching his breath before pressing a trembling finger to the buzzer.

Pamela rang him in, and Ben took the stairs two at a time, breath ragged and raw from his sprint up Beacon Hill. Pamela opened the door with a sheepish look on her face and invited Ben inside.

Pamela's apartment was simply decorated, with tasteful modern touches on a black-and-white pallet. A low cream-colored couch and a chrome-and-glass coffee table sat centered on a diamond-patterned Moroccan trellis area rug. Quiet jazz music played somewhere.

Pamela invited Ben to take a seat and asked if he would like a drink and Ben said, "Definitely."

Ben couldn't believe he was sitting in Pamela's apartment, when just a few minutes earlier he was dead to her. Ice cubes clinked into glasses in the galley kitchen out of Ben's sight.

"I'm really sorry," Ben called out. "I didn't know how best to tell you. I was just so anxious—"

Pamela appeared in the living room through the opposite end of the galley kitchen, surprising him. "Just shut up and drink." Pamela placed a lime-rimmed glass before Ben and took a seat beside him on the couch. They clinked glasses and drank: vodka tonic.

"I wanted to apologize," Pamela said, turning to face him. "You didn't lie to me. You told the truth, five minutes into our first date. A lot of men might never have said anything at all, hidden the truth for years."

Ben opened his mouth to explain himself, but Pamela cut him off. "It wasn't easy to hear—it sucked, actually—but you were honest with me, and I appreciate that."

"It wasn't easy to say."

"Look, we haven't even had one full date yet. After tonight we could end up hating each other. I don't mean to be a Cassandra, but whatever we have together will end. Relationships crash and burn in tears, or fade away out of boredom, but they end. You can almost count on that. The thing is," Pamela said, sweeping her hair out of her eyes, "I like you. I feel safe with you. And I trust you. Even more now that you had the guts to tell me about your situation."

The way she looked at him made Ben feel like the most special person on earth.

"Then I should tell you, in the name of transparency," Ben said. "I love my wife."

"I'm glad." Pamela looked away, jaw tightening. "You deserve to be happy."

"Who said I was happy?" Ben said, and they both laughed.

"Hey," Pamela said. "At the museum, did you feel a sort of zap or zing in your stomach, like an electrical thing, like a shock?"

"Maybe more of a pow or—"

"Kiss me," Pamela said. "Stop talking, and kiss me now."

Her soft lips set Ben alight, his entire body a raw nerve ending, aflame with desire. At some point, Pamela stopped Ben, red lipstick smeared. "It's not like we're looking to get married, or be boyfriend and girlfriend. This can just be fun, right? Two people who really like each other?"

"Of course," Ben said breathlessly, pulling her slim body close to him and breathing in the citrusy scent of her hair. Ben wanted to tell her how lucky she made him feel, but Pamela took his hand and led him into her bedroom.

They lay in the bed afterward, Pamela's head resting on Ben's chest, her ear so close to his face, like a small swirling seashell, that Ben just wanted to kiss her there and whisper that she was special and that he would always be good to her. But he knew how foolish it would be to say such a thing so soon, and doing so would only seem like a juvenile ruse for reciprocation.

"That was amazing," Ben said, at last.

"Nothing in the world is single," Pamela said, turning her face to his, locution performance-perfect. "All things by a law divine / In one spirit meet and mingle. / Why not I with thine?"

"I like it," Ben said. "Shakespeare?" Because it was always Shakespeare.

"Shelley," Pamela said, softly. "It's like our bodies already knew each other."

Ben was amazed by the moment Pamela's expression shifted from the tightly guarded public face she showed the world to the private, deeply personal invocation of pleasure; how her muscles slackened in ecstasy, inhibitions cast aside, gasping while he moved inside her, nothing between them, breath hitching towards orgasm. Ben traced a finger over Pamela's skin, from delicate clavicle to sternum, caressing the shallow dip between her small breasts. His cock stirred and he needed her again, right then, to recapture that closeness, to possess and be possessed, to feel that letting go, the release of self. Ben slipped his finger between Pamela's legs, and pressed a kiss to her lips. "Yes," she said. "Yes."

Later, after they had dressed, Ben said, "I want to see you again."

"I want to see you too." Pamela had washed the makeup off her face and she looked younger, as if she had wound back time, showcasing an earlier version of herself. Ben wished he had known her all that time, going back to her first summer camp kiss, her first movie matinee date, her first awkward fuck in a Camden, NJ motel. He could never be her first anything now, but he wanted to be her last. This was more than one night, more than just a fling. This was real, Ben convinced himself, and he imagined a future in which he could have both Shira and Pamela, because life without either one meant a loss he wasn't willing to abide.

"I mean I really, really want to see you again," Ben said.

"That's good, because I really, really want to see you again too."

7

Ben and Pamela fell into a rhythm in which they saw each other several times a week and texted constantly. Ben moved through his days with a fresh spring in his step, because Pamela went everywhere he did: her fun anecdotes about the sleeping man-spreaders on the T, her discovery of a coconut-milk-based ice-cream shop in Allston, a poignant essay from "Modern Love," a quick *miss you* and *want you*, all residing inside Ben's phone. He loved getting her surprise selfies, her luminous face suddenly appearing in his phone while he labored at work or busied himself around the house. In a few short weeks Ben had gathered an expansive gallery of Pamela's many looks, from ironic duck face to windblown dismay to tired hausfrau to steel-eyed minx. He wanted her. He wanted her in all the ways.

One morning, Pamela was so present in Ben's mind that he texted her, needing to know. *I'm totally smitten by you. Am I mistaken that you feel the same?*

No, Pamela texted. *This is special.*

Ben and Pamela spent Patriots Day watching the Boston Marathon on Pamela's plasma TV, devouring nearly a whole Costco-sized tub of Twizzlers, which made Ben promise he would run the marathon next year to melt away all those empty calories. Eventually, they wandered down to Boylston Street to cheer on stragglers as they neared the finish line. "You can do it," Pamela shouted, hoarsely. "You can do it."

It felt good to be out exploring Boston again, and Ben took in his surroundings with the wonder of a wide-eyed tourist. He'd never ridden a Swan Boat in the Public Garden or made out in the Old North Church. A whole new life had opened up for Ben with Pamela at his side, a parallel life for sure, but a life he never knew he had been missing.

It bothered Ben less now when Shira ran off to see Liz in Jamaica Plain, but Shira was always sure to include a vigorous "I love you" with her leave-taking as if to assure him that this arrangement was all okay. It didn't feel like he was cheating with Pamela, but sometimes, Ben had to admit, it did feel like he was cheating with Shira. When Ben and Shira were together, cooking a meal or watching TV, Ben's phone was always close at hand, and sometimes, mid-conversation with Shira, he reached for his phone and began to absently type a quick message to Pamela.

Ben had always wanted to visit the Mapparium, but Shira had been so against Christian Science and their teachings that she refused to set foot on any of their properties, despite Ben's touting the majesty of the three-story stained-glass globe, housed at the Mary Baker Eddy Library. He just wanted to stand inside its belly and wonder at the entire colorful world frozen as if in amber, as it had been in 1935. Pamela marveled, squint-eyed, at the illuminated jigsaw puzzle pieces that were once Siam, Ceylon, The Belgian Congo, French West Africa, long defunct spice-scented lands of monsoons and monkeys; the white man's burden on full display.

The two of them stood in the middle of the glass bridge running through the center of the globe, the world spread out above and below them. Ben held Pamela's hand in his, the bright reds and oranges and greens of nation states surrounded by a soothing aquamarine— no "here be dragons," no sea monsters—calming Ben's blood, even though he knew what he needed to do and how everything rested upon Pamela's response.

"Close your eyes."

"Why?"

"Because," Ben said, "I asked you to."

Pamela's lips turned up at the corners as if she were stifling a smile and allowed Ben to lead her to the end of the bridge, weaving around tourists gawking at the inside-out globe. "Now wait here."

"With my eyes closed?"

"Yes," Ben said. "Trust me."

The Mapparium was also famous for its acoustics. The curved glass walls didn't absorb sound so much as reflect sound waves back, creating a whispering gallery in which Ben was able, beneath his pounding heart, to whisper to Pamela from the opposite side of the bridge. From thirty feet away Pamela must have heard his words with crystalline clarity, the most intimate of words whispered across a crowded expanse of public space.

He knew once he said it he couldn't take it back, but he had to say it, because once it was out in the world, it was real, a shared thing, not just an urgent abstraction knocking around in his brain.

"I love you."

Pamela's eyes flew open, and her mouth dropped open and she whispered, "I love you too."

Afterward, out in the street, Pamela, in her dark Audrey Hepburn sunglasses, was quiet and withdrawn, her expression blank. This should have been Ben's moment of triumph, the achievement of love, an absolute good. One plus one adding up to one. Pamela had never looked so pretty as in her light summer dress, but something was wrong. She walked a step or two ahead of Ben, hips swinging defiantly, and when he placed a hand on her shoulder, asking her to slow down, she flinched, her shoulder flicking Ben's hand away.

"Is everything okay?"

Pamela stopped at a red light. "Everything's fine."

"Did I do something wrong?"

Pamela's eyes shifted from Ben to the walk signal on the opposite side of the street. "I just want to go look at books. Okay?"

"Sure." Ben reached for Pamela's hand. She took it in hers, limply.

They walked in silence for a stretch, Ben wondering if it was something he'd said.

"I loved the Mapparium. Wasn't that amazing?"

"If colonialism is your thing," Pamela said, tossing her head derisively. "Why not raise a statue to King Leopold II while you're at it?"

"That's not why I brought you there. It's an architectural wonder. I think it's magical."

"Do you know how much blood was shed conquering those lands? How the native peoples were treated?"

"I see a beautiful globe, and you see a holocaust."

"Basically."

"Forget it. It was a mistake to take you there. I didn't know you'd hate it."

"I didn't. I'm just—" Pamela's voice wavered. "Nothing. It's nothing."

After a moment, Pamela took Ben's hand anew, gripped it in her own, caressed his fingers. "Sorry. It was lovely. It was romantic."

Ben wanted to tell her again he loved her, but instead he said, "I just like to be with you."

Pamela's mood had brightened by the time they reached the Brattle Bookshop, fueled by a caramel swirl iced coffee and a keyed-up young busker on the Boston Common belting out Chumbawumba's "Tub-thumping."

Ben found himself browsing old paperbacks in a cluttered corner of the shop, sinuses tickling at the musty pages, when Pamela snuck up behind him and stage whispered, "*I admire the fine proportions of my darling.*" She slid her hands around to Ben's crotch, feeling his contours. "*As evidenced by the large bunch of keys you always seem to have in your pocket, whose burning thrusts would unlock any virgin cabinet.*"

"What is that?" Ben laughed. He loved how Pamela lit up when she read to him. Usually it was Keats, Donne or Dickinson, but this was something completely different.

Pamela flashed Ben a book of Victorian erotica.

"Shall I continue to caress your lordly priapus?"

"I don't know what that means, but I'm going to say yes."

"Let's get out of here," Pamela said. "I'm buying this."

Back at her apartment Pamela, said, "I'm going to read to you some letters from Lady Beatrice Poking-ham, a poor consumptive on the verge of the grave."

Ben was still fully clothed, having mixed drinks for the two of them while Pamela changed into some elaborate lingerie, a push-up corset and garters. Pamela lay back against her plush pillows, legs slightly, teasingly apart, and ordered Ben to stand, fully clothed, at the end of the bed and listen like a proper gentleman.

Pamela licked her finger and turned the page with a flourish. She read in her stagy, mannered voice about the orphaned daughter of the Marquis of Pokingham; an indulgent school mistress; a cruel governess; some filthy, impudent drawings and a beautiful, fair girl who took a fancy to a young Lady Pokingham, who covered her in burning kisses, groping the most private parts of her person. "'*What are you afraid of? You may feel me all over too; it is so nice. Put your tongue in my mouth, it is a great inducement to love and I do want to love you so, dear. Rub your finger on my crack, just there.' So she initiated me into the art of frigging in the most tender loving manner. 'Ah! Oh! Rub harder, harder—quicker,' she gasped, as she stiffened her limbs out with a kind of spasmodic shudder, and I felt my finger all wet with something warm and creamy.*"

Pamela read on about the pouting lips of Lucy's cunny, her mons veneris covered in a profusion of curly black hair. There was fucking and there was sucking and there was licking, and Pamela read on, voice teasing. Ben climbed onto the bed and peeled out of his clothes, a throbbing nerve, wanting, needing Pamela now, that very instant. Pamela kept reading, "*Ah; you rogue. I don't care if we're caught. I must have it.*"

He yanked Pamela's panties off as she continued to read unabated. She was clean shaven, her pink folds wet with desire. Ben slipped a finger inside her, then sucked the juice from it. Pamela kept on reading, not even breaking into a smile of acknowledgment. *"I couldn't help giving the darling a good suck after the exquisite pleasure he afforded me."*

Ben took this as a challenge, burying his face between her legs, swirling his tongue over her clit. Her thighs clenched around Ben's head but she read on. This was the place Ben belonged, right here, forever. Her hips arched against his eager mouth, pressing Ben in deeper, deeper, but she kept reading. Ben couldn't make out the words, ears squeezed tightly between Pamela's thighs. Ben's entire face was glazed with Pamela as she thrust her hips against him, fucking his fingers, fucking his face, drenching him with her juices. An earthquake gathered somewhere in Pamela's depths, a flaming bolus of pent up energy, her body shuddering as she continued to gasp out the luxurious adventures of Lady Pokingham. Ben slid his free hand over the sheer material of Pamela's corset, finding her left breast, squeezing her nipple as she bucked against Ben, exploding into a riotous orgasm.

"Fuck me, Ben. Fuck me now. Just get inside me."

The book lay splayed on Pamela's chest and he crushed it between them, slipping himself easily into her. They fucked until they each came and Ben collapsed onto Pamela. Heart pounding against hers, he whispered, "I love you."

"I know."

In the exultant silence that followed, Ben traced a finger along the contours of Pamela's cheekbones, marveling at their perfection, the smoothness of her translucent skin, along the bridge of her nose and across her Cupid's bow of her lips, bee-stung from the intensity of their kisses. She bit his finger playfully. "You're so worshipful."

"Is that weird?" Ben said.

"I'm just not used to it."

"Is that a good thing?"

"You make me feel special."

"Because you are."

Ben and Pamela's relationship had taken several giant leaps forward that day and now, lying in Pamela's arms, Ben allowed himself to sketch out a future that would have been unthinkable just a few short weeks ago. He wanted to do so much with Pamela.

"I've got to pee." Pamela untangled herself from Ben and strode naked to the en suite bathroom, her delicate shoulder blades spring-loaded like tiny vestigial wings. Through the echoey acoustic chamber of the tiny bathroom, Pamela called out, "You're still oozing out of me."

"Sorry," Ben called. "Is it gross?"

"It makes me feel closer to you."

"I can never get close enough."

"Wanna bet?"

Pamela stepped out of the bathroom wrapped in her red silk kimono. She climbed onto the bed and rested her head on Ben, her breathing slowing. Ben thought Pamela had drifted off to sleep when she said, "Tell me something you've never told anyone before," her words muffled by Ben's rising chest.

"Like the time I shoplifted Mike and Ikes from Duane Reade when I was eight?"

Pamela raised her head and looked Ben square in the eyes. "Tell me something that explains you, Ben Seidel. You never talk about your parents."

"I never talk about Derek Jeter either, and he was my childhood hero."

"You're really not going to tell me about your parents?"

Ben was silent, remembering the phone call that snowy February morning. Shira was there with him at his apartment in Amherst and, though they had only been dating a couple of weeks, she held Ben and promised she'd be with him every step of the way. Shira skipped class for a week to join Ben on Long Island for the funerals, and sat shiva with Ben until the last of the mourners had left, and the two of them had been together ever since.

"They were my parents," Ben said. "What's there to say?"

"Were?" A deep frown crumpled her soft features. "Why didn't you tell me?"

"There's nothing to say." He brushed a finger across her lower lip, then took her chin in his hands and kissed her.

"Please, Ben. Don't lock me out. You can tell me anything."

"Are you hungry?" Ben said. "I'm starving."

"Please, go on. I want to know."

"There's nothing to know."

"What happened?"

"It was a long time ago."

"You're really not going to tell me about your parents?"

"I don't see how it's relevant to me and you."

Pamela was silent for a long time and then her eyes filled with tears. "I wasn't supposed to fall in love with you. It's such a helpless feeling. I hate it."

"Why?"

"Are you serious? Ben, you're married. You have someone else to share yourself with."

"But you knew that. I've been honest with you."

"Your doctor says you have six months to live because cancer. That's honest. Honesty doesn't absolve you. Pain is pain."

"This is far from cancer. We love each other."

"We do, but the thought that I'll never really know the true you kills me."

"You know me as well as anybody."

"I won't call that a lie, but it's false and you know it." Pamela turned away from Ben. "When you leave me, you go home to your wife, climb into bed with your wife, fall asleep with your wife, wake up with your wife. And me, I'm alone."

"You're not alone. I love you."

"Your love for me is just a pretty movie with the sad parts cut out. You only know half the story. Do you know what it's like when I'm here and you're off living your life?"

"It's not that interesting. I promise."

"You don't get it, do you? I'm thirty-five years old and I'm alone."

"You're not alone. We're connected. I'm always here."

"A text inside this fucking phone is not the same thing as being with you. I want to *be* with you. I want to make plans with you. I want to know you'll be here with me when it counts."

"I'll do whatever I can to make that happen," Ben said. "Whatever it takes. We can make plans, fill our calendars with a hundred dates right now."

"Will you please stop with your empty, childish words. I've been asking you to spend the night for weeks. Just one night. This shouldn't be so hard. I don't know how much longer I can do this."

"Do what?"

"This. Everything. Us."

"You are the love of my life." The words slipped from Ben's mouth because there was nothing else to say that would show Pamela just how much she meant to him. In that moment she was the only person who had ever mattered.

"And Shira's not?"

Ben had no words that wouldn't represent a complete betrayal of his marriage vows.

"Then leave her," Pamela said. "Leave Shira. She already has somebody. Problem solved."

"I can't do that." Ben paused just long enough to know how bad his words sounded. "You're both the love of my life. Shira and you."

"Get out," Pamela screamed. "Go home, Ben. Go home now."

A familiar itching raked at the base of Ben's skull as he tried to protest. He told Pamela he loved her as much as he could love anyone in the world, more even; he would always be there for her, night or day, but Pamela cut him off and said, "You have to know, this thing we have together isn't easy for me."

"What's going to happen now?" Ben pleaded.

"I don't know, Ben. Maybe you should figure it out, because you're running out of time."

"I love you."

"Go home," Pamela said, her eyes raw and red-rimmed. "Your wife is waiting for you."

8

Shira's yellow Beetle, Buttercup, sat in the driveway and Ben was grateful, in his desolation, that Shira was home. Ben opened the front door of his and Shira's condo to find Shira pacing barefoot back-and-forth across their living room, phone in hand, her father's booming God-voice filling the space. Shira's tight jaw and knuckled expression said she and her father had been going at it for a while. She raised her eyebrows at Ben and raked her fingers exasperatedly through her hair.

"Daddy, you need to wear it. This is your health we're talking about."

"Health *shmealth*," Cantor Weissmann said. "I'm as healthy as a horse. We're talking about my voice, and I can't risk hurting that."

"Sleep apnea is not a joke."

"Your *noodge* mother has given me that PSA a gazillion times. Suddenly snoring's a disease? People lived for thousands of years without CPAP machines."

"People died," Shira pleaded.

"People have always died and they will keep on dying, C-CRAP machine or no. You're a good daughter. You've said your piece and I hear you. But I won't use it. You want your father to look like Darth Vader?

Most importantly, the forced air dries out my throat. That I can't have. You know my voice is my bread and butter."

"Daddy, please."

"I have to go."

"Wait! Ben's here."

"Hullo, Ben!"

"Hi, Joel. Double ditto on whatever Shira said." Ben always felt he should call his father-in-law Cantor Weissmann like the rest of the known world, but the cantor had insisted Ben call him Dad. But that felt wrong to Ben in so many ways, so he settled on Joel.

"Joel, you know how much Shira cares about you. Please listen to her. Your daughter learned her smarts from the best."

"I know, I know. She's such a pain. And now she's all yours. Listen," Cantor Weissmann said, "I've really got to go now. I appreciate your concern, kids, I really do, but I'm fine. I'm fine. I love you, my little songbird."

The call disconnected and Shira screamed, "Fuck! He can be so stubborn."

She dropped down onto the couch and buried her head in her hands. "I don't know why I even bother talking to him."

Shira's small, rounded shoulders trembled above her bowed head. Ben wedged himself in beside Shira and rubbed her back in firm sweeping circles—wax on, wax off—as her rigid body softened and she melted into him. The soft curves of her body against his soothed Ben like so many countless times before. Ben looked into Shira's gentle, apologetic eyes and said, "I love you," three simple words no different than what he had said to Pamela. But, coming from Ben's mouth now, the words felt almost like a different language, familiar, smooth in his mouth, tested by time and a shared history.

"I love you too," Shira said back, her soft words muffled by Ben's shoulder.

Shira had no illusions about Ben. She loved him with all his faults.

"Your father knows what he's doing. He'll be fine. I promise."

"My mother says he wakes up gasping for air every night."

"Yet, he says he rides fifty miles a day on his racing bike. I'm sure he knows his own body better than we do. If things get out of hand, he'll take care of it. Remember he's personal friends with all the top doctors at Johns Hopkins."

"How could I forget?" Shira laughed, mocking her father's unshakable sense of self. Shira lowered her voice and pridefully raised her chin. "A Whiffenpoof at fifteen, graduated from Yale before my neighborhood friends could even drive. I could have excelled in any field. My friends at Johns Hopkins say I could have been a terrific surgeon. But like Lenny Bernstein said: your voice is a gift to both the world and the heavens."

They both broke out laughing at the larger than life father-figure who never failed to find a way to aggrandize himself.

"I've missed you," Shira said, running her fingers through Ben's hair. "Our schedules haven't matched up well lately. Kinda sucks, don'tcha think?"

"I'm here now."

"You know what I'm saying, silly. It's just nice being here, the two of us in for the night with nowhere to go. It's been too long."

It had been a long time, but it was hard to regret too much when he had been spending time falling in love with Pamela.

"What's the matter?" Shira turned her big brown eyes to Ben. "Something happen with Pamela?"

There was no handbook for how to do this, so Ben simply said, "I told Pamela I love her."

Shira was silent for a long moment. "And do you? Love her?"

"It feels like love. Yes. I just feel happy when I'm with her."

"Wow!" Shira stiffened, fingers fanned out across her chest. "This is tough. I didn't expect that."

Ben wasn't sure what sort of response he had hoped for but he hadn't anticipated Shira's drooping shoulders, her trembling voice, that look of shock. He had thought she had sort of known all along, as if it were to be expected as a matter of course.

"I mean, I'd gamed it all out, convinced myself it wouldn't hurt when it finally happened, but it does."

"I'm sorry. I don't want to hurt you."

"It's okay."

"It's not okay." He should never have told her.

"You have nothing to be sorry about." She stroked Ben's cheek. "I told you it would happen. You're a catch, baby. And this is our deal. I've found Liz, and you've found Pamela, but me and you, we always have each other."

Ben flashed Shira a doubtful look.

Shira closed her eyes and took in a long, calming breath. "We do, baby." And Ben couldn't tell whether Shira was trying to make him feel better or trying to convince herself.

It was hard for Ben to accept that he could always have anyone. The thought that he and Pamela might be through threatened to sink his entire life into darkness, and a return to the pendulum swing of Shira and Ben, Shira and Liz felt like nothing less than utter defeat.

"Well," Ben said. "I may have lost Pamela."

"What do you mean?"

"She kicked me out of her apartment."

"You know it's not all going to be wine and roses. Relationships ebb and flow. These things happen."

"I don't know if she'll give me another chance. I made her cry. I just hate that."

"Tears happen. Because she cares. If she didn't cry, I'd be more inclined to worry."

Shira propped herself against the big embroidered throw pillow beside Ben, knees to her chest, eyebrow arched, her heart-to-heart face on.

"Are you sure it's love? Like for real? I mean, it's pretty new."

"Why wouldn't it be? You and Liz happened pretty fast."

"I know, but new relationship energy can be all consuming. It feels like love, it looks like love, it hurts like love—"

"You wish me and Pamela were over, don't you?"

"Not at all! I just want to make sure you remember that you're married to me and that we're a couple."

"And yet there's you and Liz."

"We need to make more time for us. I miss you."

"When you say us you mean me, you and Liz. You think that's a better deal than me and Pamela."

"At least me and you would be together more, rather than running around with this woman you say you love."

"It's love," Ben said. "It is. I haven't felt this way—" Ben paused and took in his wife, every version of Shira's evolution from optimistic college Junior to that very moment, layered one on top of another. "Since I met you." The fine lines around Shira's eyes told Ben how far they had come.

"Wow," Shira said, face flushed. She was rarely at a loss for words. "I need a minute." She exhaled a long breath, then another, and finally said, "Really?" Her voice cracked when she said it and Ben's heart hurt to hear it.

"I'm sorry," Shira said. "I want to get old and weird with you. I really do."

"Even if that means we'll never be parents together?"

"You're my person, always have been. We will find a way. I know the two of us together can do what we need to do to make each other happy, however we get there. I promise I'll do better by you, okay?"

"Thank you. When I met Pamela, the pain of missing you just sort of lifted like a weight from my heart. I felt worthy of love again."

Shira pouted her lips. "I'm sorry, Ben. You have to know I always love you, even when I'm with Liz. I'll try to be more aware of your feelings. I guess I can be a selfish bitch sometimes."

"You're not a bitch."

"What do you need from me to make things easier with Pamela? I want to be fair to you the way you've been to me. Let's find a solution together."

Ben knew the answer right away, and he imagined he and Pamela staying up late in her cozy Beacon Hill apartment, making dinner, watching movies and fucking with no timer ticking down to his premature leave-taking. They could sleep in, find a farmers market and go for a walk on the Esplanade. They could do so much. They could do everything. But this would mean more time away from Shira, and that was not a good thing. How did he square his desire for both women, when being away from one risked opening a chasm with the other?

"I'd like to stay over at Pamela's sometimes. Maybe once a week."

Shira chewed her lower lip, working it with a pearly canine, as she pondered Ben's request.

"That's a pretty big change to our agreement. If I do the same with Liz we risk becoming strangers in our own house, and I want us to spend more time together, not less."

"Never more than once a week," Ben said, animated. "I promise. Strict rules. No negotiation."

"And we schedule time for just the two of us every week. A proper date. A real adventure. But, I've got an ask for you in return." Shira wore a small mischievous smile on her face.

"Liz?" Ben said.

"I don't want us to compartmentalize our lives like this. Maybe I'm just greedy, but I want my two loves to know each other and like each other. Is that too much to ask? We can start with a dinner. Simple. No pressure."

"Why do you want us to meet so badly now, after all this time?"

Shira's mouth tilted up just a bit at the corners as if she knew something Ben did not. "I think you'll really like her."

"All right," Ben said. A meal was a small obligation in return for regular nights with Pamela. "We'll have Liz over for dinner, but I make no promises about liking her."

"I'm sure you'll be a perfect gentleman." Shira threw herself into Ben's arms and kissed him. "Come on, kiss me like you mean it."

Ben closed his eyes and kissed Shira, but all he could see was Pamela. He wanted to text her that very second and tell her the good news.

Shira rose from the couch, hand extended to Ben, a come-hither look on her flushed face.

When Ben hesitated, Shira grabbed the pillow and hit Ben with it. "Jesus Christ, Ben. Grow up. I know what's going on. You've known Pamela for like two months and suddenly your wife of eight years is forbidden fruit?"

Biology always wins out when faced with the flimsy justification of ethics and morality, and Ben's need was a fungible thing which he was powerless to resist. In what world could it possibly be wrong to give in to his wife, anyway?

It was moments like these Ben wondered how he could ever want someone else when he could be this close to his best friend in the world. They snuggled for a long time afterwards, Shira teasing Ben that he looked so serious when he fucked her and that it looked painful when he came.

"Have you seen your face?" Shira laughed, contorting her own face to mimic his.

"You're mocking me."

"Maybe a little. But I do it with love."

"Let's do it again. I'll turn out the lights so you don't have to see my ridiculous face."

"I love your face, but I'm bushed."

She clicked off the bedside lamp.

"So, sleep?" Ben said.

"It's late," Shira said.

"Okay," Ben said. "Goodnight."

After Shira's breathing slowed and she had drifted off to sleep, Ben grabbed hesitantly for his phone. Still drunk on the magical cocktail of adrenaline, dopamine and oxytocin, Ben couldn't sleep, mind racing between Shira and Pamela and all the erotic possibilities the two of them contained. His black screen came to life beneath the protective tent of Ben and Shira's top-sheet to reveal no new notifications. Why would Pamela want him when he was sleeping with Shira, his wife of nearly a decade? A sinister emptiness pressed in all around Ben and he had to place a hand on Shira's sleeping hip to remind himself he was not alone. He was losing Pamela, he was really losing her. He knew he had one last chance to make his case; a night together, a full night together. If only he could get Pamela to agree to a sleepover at her place, he knew she would see that what they had was special and worth keeping. Ben opened the composing box on his phone and typed:

My dear Lady Pokingham, I am writing to inform you that your paramour, I, Benjamin Seidel of House Seidel, has accepted your invitation for a scandalous overnight of trysting and rutting at your domicile on Beacon Hill. Your prompt affirmative response is breathlessly awaited. Yours affectionately, Lord Benjamin Seidel.

9

In the bleary light of day Ben's playful text looked like nothing more than an embarrassing, desperate ruse, full of false confidence and dopey, juvenile bravado. Of course Pamela didn't respond, and a pit opened in Ben's stomach. Shira was already up, working in her studio, Lady Gaga playing from her Bluetooth speaker, so Ben lay back on his and Shira's bed, wracking his brain for just the right combination of words to get Pamela to respond. Finally, after typing and erasing a full manifesto on his love for Pamela, he settled on *Goof morning, beautiful,* only to realize too late that autocorrect existed to personally mock him. He quickly typed, *Lol, good morning, beautiful,* knowing there was no way such a foolish, transparent text deserved a response.

Ben was so sick with worry he could barely get his breakfast down. He needed a change of environment, to slip out of his saggy boxers and oversized Battle-Green 5K race T-shirt, to dress like the man he wanted to be. Ben threw on a pair of pressed khakis and a shirt and tie, phone never leaving his line of vision, like a time bomb set to ignite. He called out a quick goodbye to Shira so as not to interrupt her work, and left the house without even showering.

By the time he arrived at his office at Rowe's Wharf, Ben had convinced himself Pamela was lost to him. Ghosting was for Tinder kids, no-consequence losers, and broken people who didn't give a flying fuck who they hurt. That wasn't Pamela. But Pamela's indifference was such a shock to the system that it threatened to occupy Ben's mind all day and beyond. He needed to hear from Pamela, and he needed it now, even if it meant beclowning himself further. Clearly, texting was a dead end.

Ben was sweating as he rode the frigid elevator up the seven floors to Pamela's office, mopping his face with the tails of his shirt.

Pamela's door was open and she was on the phone talking animatedly. For a moment, Ben could only stare, thinking how lucky he was to know her, just going about her business in a gray sleeveless dress and heels while Ben watched. She saw Ben in her doorway and made a sour face. After an endless moment in which Ben stood stiffly in the doorway, his sweat-soaked shirt chilling his skin, he heard Pamela say, "I'll have to call you back."

She hung up the phone and Ben's heart roared in his ears. "You're out of your mind," Pamela said. "What are you doing here?"

"You didn't respond to my texts," Ben said flatly.

Pamela stood up from her desk and frowned. Without a word, she brushed past him and closed her office door. "Ben, this is not okay."

"You don't even have the courtesy to respond to my texts."

Pamela was silent for a long time, her jaw clenched. "I can't give you what you want."

"That's not true. You give me everything I could ever want. When we're together, nothing can touch us."

"It's not enough."

Ben leaned in to kiss her, hoping the touch of his lips against hers would reset things between them.

"Not here," she said.

She wore an earthy red lipstick and just a touch of eyeliner. She was close enough Ben smelled a hint of coffee on her breath.

"I want to give you what you need."

"You can't give me what I need," Pamela said.

"I spoke to Shira and she agreed I can stay over. Once a week even."

"Do you even hear yourself? I can't live my life depending on whether your *wife* gives you the okay."

"I thought you'd be excited. When I texted you last night I thought you'd—"

"I was on a date," Pamela interrupted. "A trustee from the BSO. We'd been messaging for a couple weeks and he texted after you left, so I went to meet him."

Ben's mouth actually fell open and his breath hitched. "I don't understand."

"There are lots of men out there who could make me happy besides a married man."

"Are you and him dating now?" Ben's voice was barely a whisper.

"Definitely not," Pamela said, animating for the first time since he arrived in her office. "He showed up at the restaurant wearing those salmon-colored Nantucket red pants with the little lobsters on them, a bow tie and boat shoes. He spent most of the night talking about himself. A total dud."

"Then why didn't you text me back?"

"I didn't want to speak to you."

"But I wanted to speak to you."

"I'm a single, independent woman. I can't be at your beck and call."

"You're not a single woman. You're my girlfriend."

"And you're married," Pamela countered. "Sometimes I think I'm better off alone, but I do love you. I really, stupidly, do."

A heavy boot of despair pressed on Ben's chest but he managed to say, "What happens now?"

Pamela shrugged and Ben's face fell.

"What can I do to convince you to say yes? I'll do whatever you want. Two sleepovers a week, maybe a third every third Thursday. Flowers. I can send flowers. Dozens of them. FaceTime whenever you want. We will always be in touch. Whenever you need. I just love you. Please."

"First of all, you can stop this little-boy routine."

"What are you talking about?"

"Look at yourself, Ben."

"I don't want to lose you. We can just enjoy each other. Have fun together."

"We've moved way beyond that, Ben, and you know it."

A chill ran through Ben and he reached for Pamela's hand for what might have been the last time. *"I have drunken deep of joy."* Ben's voice cracked with the memorized words. *"And I will taste no other wine tonight."*

Pamela tilted her head, green eyes widening. "You've been reading Shelley without me?"

A flock of fluttering birds filled Ben's belly as he recited from some deep reservoir of memory Shelley's words Pamela had recited for him during that first intoxicating get-to-know you week in which they discovered so much more than each other's bodies. "*The sunlight clasps the earth / And the moonbeams kiss the sea: / What are all these kisses worth / If you don't kiss me?*"

"Thou," Pamela said. "'*If thou kiss me not.*'"

"Sorry." Ben's heart hammered in his chest. "Wilt thou kiss me?"

Pamela's lips turned up into a small smile. "Do you still want to do that sleepover? I will kiss thee then."

"Yes. Yes, I do. How about tonight?"

"It's a school night. Don't you have more poetry to memorize?" Pamela said, laughing. "And anyway, I have plans."

"Another date?"

"Ben, please stop with this. Isn't it enough that I love you?"

"I want you."

"You can't always get what you want," Pamela said. Then softening, "Saturday night, my place?"

"Yes to Saturday!" She may have been dating other men, but Pamela loved him and was trying with him, and he was getting a sleepover and not Mr. Nantucket Red. "Definitely yes. Thank you."

But what if Pamela's next date was a better match? The men she would meet wouldn't all be self-centered washouts like the BSO trustee. What if he was more available than Ben? What if he was richer or funnier or had a better car or knew how to play guitar? He'd have flowing locks of hair, a devilish smile, a rapier wit. He would quote the romantics back to Pamela, rather than listen in slack-jawed awe like Ben as she recited "Auguries of Innocence" in its entirety. He'd be an Ivy Leaguer like Pamela, not some state-school wannabe who couldn't tell a sonnet from a sestina. These thoughts and more followed Ben wherever he went during that very long week, in which every minute Pamela did not text him back he assumed she was in the arms of another man. She rarely initiated contact beyond "just checking in to see how you are," but Pamela responded as normal, nothing in her tone suggesting a rift. But Ben couldn't help wondering if she was furtively messaging him as her lover lay in bed beside her. The fact that Ben couldn't know for certain what Pamela was up to ate at him, haunted his dreams, caused him to doubt himself in entirely new ways. He must have looked so ridiculous when he came. Nothing, in fact, could be less attractive than the horrifying convulsions that overtook his face during that most intimate of moments. How could he let Pamela see him like that? Were his legs too hairy? Was his nose too big? Did he ever forget to flush? And how mortifying it was the time he belched after polishing off a plate of Pad Thai? He'd been eating like a pig, hadn't he? Why would an elegant woman like Pamela want a man like him, a married man like him.

When Shira asked Ben if he was up for bowling one night that week, Ben jumped at the chance, if only to get himself out of his head. It was date night, and though there was nothing romantic about borrowed shoes and bowling balls, he was with Shira.

Shira bowled granny-style, bending low to the ground and two-handing the ball down the lane. The ball rolled ever so slowly, and Shira corkscrewed and contorted her body to coax the ball from going into the gutter. She wore a pair of faded jeans and a black T-shirt, her hair playfully twisted into pigtails. Shira laughed every time she messed up, and high-fived Ben whenever he got a strike or a spare.

Not long ago, this would have been a fun night, the two of them drinking cold beer out of brown bottles and speculating idly about the sex lives of the players in the adjacent lane: Walrus Mustache does it with the lights off and Barry White on; Britney or Tracee in the pink Red Sox hat can't cum but fakes it because she's afraid she's broken. Tonight Ben could only think of Pamela.

"What's the matter, babe?" Shira said. "I mean, you're destroying me and you're not even rubbing it in."

"Just thinking."

"I forbid you to think," Shira said, smiling. She touched Ben lightly on the arm. "It's okay. You're good. This is our night. Let's enjoy it."

Shira held a blue-swirled ball in both hands as if she were cradling the entire world.

"Will it ever be just the two of us again?" Shira put the ball down and threw her arms around Ben as he continued. "Are you and Liz a forever thing?

"If I said it wasn't, I'd be lying. If I said it was, I'd be lying too."

"Then what's going to happen?"

"I don't know," Shira said, and Ben thought he heard a tremor in her voice.

"It's my fault."

"It's no one's fault. It just is."

"You are so beautiful," Ben said.

103

Shira blushed, embarrassed. "Why do you say that?"

"You just are. Sometimes it just amazes me."

"Are you fishing for a compliment, my handsome man?"

"Nope, just showing my appreciation."

"Well, thank you. It's always nice to hear."

Shira picked up the ball and did her thing, rolling the ball, eventually, into the gutter.

"I think meeting Liz will be a good thing. For all of us."

Ben still felt a stab at his heart when Shira said her name. "I'm nervous," he said.

"Don't be. Would I invite a monster into our home?" Shira bared her teeth and curled her tiny hands into claws. "I'd like you to come to love her too. She's going to be important in all of our lives."

Ben didn't know what Shira meant, until suddenly, and blindingly, he did. Shira was talking about the three of them as a thrupple, together as one. She was building an off-ramp for Ben, where he wouldn't have to return to those lonely nights on the apps after Pamela was gone. She loved him and this was her way of proving it.

Ben knew that Pamela would never tolerate him and Shira and Liz being together, but their clock was winding down; it was only a matter of time until Pamela found someone else. Poetry had saved him this time; he didn't know what he'd do the next time Pamela tried to leave.

The thought of losing Pamela only made Ben desire her more.

❧

Saturday night arrived and Pamela answered the door wearing only her glossy black Louboutins, sheer thigh-highs, and a lace demi cup bra, her face made up for battle, black eyeliner fiercely applied, deadly red lipstick, a hint of citrus at her throat. She appeared like a fever dream, framed between doorpost and lintel, beautiful, terrifying.

"Damn, you look good," Ben said.

Pamela took his hand, led him wordlessly to her bedroom, and ordered him to strip. Ben complied. He couldn't believe he was actually going to have sex with this beautiful woman, though he had done so dozens of times before. He stood before Pamela with his foolish erection announcing his readiness. Ben felt clumsy, awkward, standing before Pamela with his hairy man body with all its sharp angles and sandpaper skin. Pamela positively glowed in the dim-lit room.

"What are you going to do now?" Pamela said.

"I'm going to have sex with you." Ben's heart whirred in his chest.

"Then do it!" Pamela ordered.

Ben had never had trouble performing with Pamela or Shira or anybody else, but now he felt he was auditioning for his own relationship, trying to prove he could give Pamela something no one else could. He tried porny contortions, uttered absurd, embarrassing phrases meant to turn Pamela on, but he just couldn't stop thinking about somebody else doing all this to her and more. When Ben finally rolled over, frustrated and ashamed, Pamela touched him softly on the shoulder and asked what was the matter.

"I've never had this happen before."

"Don't worry. We can try again later. We have all night together."

Ben lay on his back with his head resting on one of Pamela's feather pillows, staring at the ceiling. "Why do you need other men?"

"Dammit, Ben. Let's not do this now."

"We need to talk about this."

"You're such a processor. Why can't you just enjoy the moment without analyzing every word and gesture for meaning?"

"Do you have any other dates lined up?"

"Ben, stop."

"So you do."

Pamela stiffened and rolled off Ben's chest and clutched a pillow in his stead.

"You're going to Maine with your wife for the Fourth of July weekend. What do you want me to do? Sit home in sackcloth and ashes missing you, wishing it was me with you instead of her?"

"This trip was planned before we even met. What do you want me to do?"

"The question is, what do you want to do? Be a grownup." Pamela jumped out of bed.

"I can't stand the thought of you with another man."

"I don't exist for your pleasure alone."

"That's not what I'm saying—"

"How do you think I feel every single day knowing you're sleeping in another woman's bed?"

Silhouetted against the drawn blinds of her bedroom window, Pamela look like a Balinese shadow puppet, as if she had slipped from the third dimension into the second, the dimension of infinite imagination. A hundred future scenarios played out in Ben's head and none of them involved him and Pamela.

"What if you met Shira? Would that make things better? She's not some monster who hates you and wishes you ill. Just meet her, and you'll see she's very accepting and that you have nothing to fear," Ben said, echoing Shira's placating words about Liz. "We're having dinner next Friday, before we go to Maine. It'll be awkward for me too since Shira's girlfriend is going to be there too. What do you think? We can do this together. The two of us. Like a double date." Ben forced a smile onto his face.

Pamela stared at Ben, dumbstruck. "Are you out of your mind? I'm not your emotional support pet. I don't want to be part of this psychodrama. I only want you."

"If you only want me, don't date anyone else. I'll make it up to you. I promise."

"Don't you dare, Ben. This is the twenty-first century. I won't be a kept woman. If you think you can buy me off with a nice dinner and a sleepover, just forget the whole thing because you don't understand me at all."

"What do you want?"

"I want you, Ben."

"You have me."

"I don't."

"There has to be another way," Ben said. "There's got to be a solution."

"There isn't, okay?"

Ben climbed out of bed to comfort Pamela.

"Don't touch me. I think you should leave. Get dressed and go home to your wife."

"Stop. Tonight's our night. We can order in, watch Netflix—"

"You stop. I don't think you understand how much I'm hurting here."

"I love you," Ben said.

"Words, always words! Honestly, sometimes I wish you hated me. It would be that much easier to walk away."

"Don't do this. Please," Ben pleaded.

"Go home. Have a perfect postcard weekend in Maine with your wife. I don't want to hear from you until you're back."

10

Ben did not hear from Pamela all week. No matter what he texted or how he phrased his words, Ben could not convince Pamela to respond. He sent flowers to her work and to her apartment, hoping to shake loose some stream of empathy. But Ben knew Pamela wasn't avoiding him to hurt him, but rather to protect herself from pain. There had to be a way that Ben could fix that pain, for both of them.

Every man Ben saw on the street was a rival, someone better suited to Pamela's needs, taller, handsomer, better dressed. Ben imagined one of his colleagues ravishing Pamela on her king-sized bed when he recalled she and Steve were suddenly mutual Facebook friends, and that he too was from Philadelphia. How had they met? How long had they known each other? Were they old friends, a high school crush perhaps? Or had they just met on some dating site, connecting over their shared experiences about growing up in the City of Brotherly love? At work, Ben scrutinized Steve, picturing Steve and Pamela doing all the intimate things he and Pamela had done. He wasn't married, and he was better looking than Ben, with his cleft chin and easy smile. He would be a perfect match for Pamela.

Ben asked Steve what he was doing after work, certain he had plans with Pamela. "Wanna grab a beer?" He recalled how they had drunk beer and talked about baseball and eaten wings after work once, several years back. It was fun to drink beer and talk about baseball and eat wings, and now Ben wanted nothing more than to drink beer and talk about baseball and eat wings with Steve.

"I've got plans, bro."

Of course he had plans, and Ben's heart flipped in his chest.

"Gotta date?" Ben asked. Small talk was death for him. He must have looked like some crazed paranoiac, the way his wheedling voice rose in accusation.

"No," Steve said. "I don't 'got' a date."

"Okay," Ben said, relieved. "Let's grab a drink sometime. You like wings, right?"

"I'm done with that Atkins shit," he said. "I'm vegan now."

Every day after work Ben ran, pushing himself farther and farther, hoping to clear Pamela from his mind, but he felt as if he had already lost her. Had Pamela broken up with him? He tried to convince himself that life without Pamela would go on as before. He had Shira, and he was finally ready to meet Liz, and maybe one door had closed to open up another. But Liz wasn't Pamela, and Liz could never be someone Ben shared fresh intimacies with. No matter what Shira and Liz did to welcome him, Ben would always be the interloper, the newbie, the latecomer.

Shira was chipper all week, excited about the calendar project she had proposed to a small Jewish publisher. The editor had loved her watercolor paintings in the style of medieval illuminated manuscripts and wanted her to do a mockup of the Hebrew alphabet for a children's book they were considering as well. Ben did his best not to yuck Shira's yum, dumping all his fears and insecurities onto her, but he had no one else to talk to, no one else besides Pamela.

"Do you think me and Pamela are done for good?" Ben said.

Shira sat on a low stool in the middle of her studio sorting through a pile of newsprint sketches, setting aside some, crumpling others into balls and tossing them into the trash. The good ones usually got transferred to expensive vellum paper, while the remainder went down the memory hole. Shira looked up at Ben. The late afternoon sunlight shone through the tempered glass of her studio's picture window, making Shira's skin glow like honey.

"Ben," Shira said, continuing her sorting, "I just don't have the bandwidth for this right now. I'm sorry. I really am." She peeled off three sketches, crumpled them up and tossed them towards the bin, missing with all three.

Ben bent over to retrieve the balled-up sketches. Curious, he uncrumpled one and saw something that looked like an alien, with a central trunk and a pair of appendages stretching out from the top. These tentacles curved down, adorned with ovoid balls at the end. This was not a Tree of Life or a menorah or like anything Shira had ever drawn before. She liked science fiction but had never, as far as Ben knew, drawn aliens or monsters. Perhaps she was sketching out a tattoo for Liz. That had to be it. The Illustrated Woman would put anything on her body, apparently. Ben spread out the other two sketches on Shira's drafting table, this weird crustacean staring back at him. Those balls had to be eyes.

"I'm trying to clean up here," Shira said, irritated. "Can you stop messing with my stuff?"

"What is this?" Ben held up one of the sketches for Shira.

Shira looked up and immediately her eyes filled with tears. "They're my hysterectomy. They're my fucking hysterectomy."

"I'm sorry." An endless silence passed before he spoke again. "That's what you've been working on?"

"It just kills me that they couldn't extract my eggs first. Every day I think I should have insisted they do the injection."

Ben remembered the risks involved and how the two of them had to make a quick decision that would change their futures forever. "But the doctors said that kind of hyper-stimulation could have fueled the cancer and further put you at risk."

"Could have," Shira said. "Could have! Now I definitely can't have a child ever. There's no doubt about that. It would have been worth the risk, if it gave me even a minuscule chance of using my own eggs later on."

"We made a choice and now we have to live with it," Ben said.

"You think I don't know that? Like Sophie's fucking choice; save my eggs and risk cancer, save me and lose all hope of being a mother. Sometimes I hate you for not talking me out of it. That's why I withdrew from you. I couldn't stand the thought of you touching me after what you did."

"What did I do?"

"It was your job to look out for me. And you, Ben Seidel, my husband and life partner, let me down."

"What? We made the decision together."

"It was your job to tell me I was wrong. It was your job to stand in my way. I wanted nothing more than to be a mother. I could give a fuck if those injections spread the cancer. All I ever wanted was to be a mother." Shira sobbed into a tightly clenched fist. "You said we could adopt. How did that work out? There are countless healthy women out there lining up to adopt, and me with everything required to make life ripped out of my body."

"Stop," Ben said. "We can still make it happen. There are so many agencies we haven't tried, so many countries."

"No, no, no, no, no," Shira screamed. "Getting rejected by some social worker or agency drone in China is like being told all over again that you're never going to have a baby, and I can't put myself through that anymore. And even if it does happen, it can take years and years and more money than we could ever scrape together. The entire process is just cruel. It's cruel. I would rather have cancer than run that gauntlet again."

"You don't mean that," Ben said, stroking Shira's hair.

"Just stop, Ben. I want to be alone. Please."

❦

Friday arrived and Shira buzzed around the kitchen preparing challah and her grandmother's old world recipe for chicken and roast potatoes, aimlessly singing the chorus of "Tradition," from *Fiddler on the Roof*. It made Ben's heart melt watching Shira focused so intently on making the perfect dinner. She had apologized to Ben after their blow up and she said of course she didn't blame him. Sometimes it was just too much to hold all the pain inside, and Ben was in the right place to receive her fire.

The kitchen smelled of garlic and paprika and the friendly smell of Shira's braided challah rising in the oven. She wore an apron and an old bandanna on her head like a pirate. She looked adorable, her lips pursed in intense concentration. Ben ached for her and he pressed a tender kiss onto the back of Shira's neck.

"Not now, please," she said, slipping out of Ben's arms.

Ben watched the poetry of Shira's movements, the determined way she bent over to look into the oven, the way she scratched her nose with one of those silly lobster claw oven mitts. God, he wanted her.

"Aren't you worried about tonight?" Ben said.

Shira stopped what she was doing, untied her apron and let it drop to the floor. She took off her glasses and placed them on the kitchen counter beside the cutting board. Her deep brown eyes were still red from chopping onions. "Come here," she said, opening her arms. "I'm nervous too, but I really believe tonight is going to be special for all of us."

"I don't know what to expect," Ben said.

"Just be open to whatever comes."

Despite their differences in height, their bodies fit together perfectly, Shira's soft cheek warm against Ben's chest, his heart beating in her ear. When she hugged him, really hugged him, Shira held on tightly, entirely present, holding on long enough for their bodies to reacquaint themselves with each other, long enough for their brains to release the magic neurotransmitter oxytocin, flooding Ben with a deep, satisfying sense of contentment. When they were done, Shira booped Ben on the nose. "Why don't you go set the table."

Liz Bird arrived exactly when expected, and Ben greeted her at the door with a suitable smile. Liz wore a little black dress and heels, her garishly tattooed arms covered in a complex mess of skulls and vines and flowers on full display.

"Here," Liz said, jamming a magnum of wine into Ben's arms. "Molotov!"

Ben wasn't sure if Liz was making a joke or whether she had meant to say "Mazal tov."

She extended her hand to shake Ben's and they touched for the first time. Even her knuckles were tattooed with Gothic lettering he could not decipher. It was a firm handshake, not unfriendly, just awkward, her palm a little damp, as if she too were nervous about what lay ahead.

She had a goofy space between her two front teeth that signaled she never had the financial advantages of orthodontia. Her white-blond hair reached halfway down her back, the ends dyed a bright cotton candy pink; her head was shaved on one side. Each ear was pierced in nearly a dozen places.

"Shira's still getting dressed."

Ben knew Shira well enough to recognize she had done this by design, her idea of exposure therapy, so he and Liz would have a chance to acquaint themselves first, without her getting in the way.

"Noice place," Liz said, surveying the layout of the condo: the polished hardwood floors, the simple, unobtrusive art on the walls blending seamlessly with inherited Judaica, the Pottery Barn couch and coffee table with matching brass candelabra. "So this is where it all happens." Watching Liz take inventory made Ben feel middle class to a fault. He imagined Liz and Shira fucking on a frameless futon in a Jamaica Plain rental surrounded by incense and feral cats and wondered how his and Shira's condo could ever be a love nest for the three of them.

Ben told her they only owned the first floor but the upstairs neighbors were nice and usually didn't make much noise. They were both associate professors at MIT. Funny story, when David and Ivy first moved in ...

Liz did not respond, her attention wandering towards the sun room, Shira's studio.

"Do you like music?" Ben said, trailing behind her, acutely aware of her patchouli scent tickling his nose. "We have lots of music."

"Sure."

"How's Miles Davis? *Kind of Blue*."

"K." Liz said.

Ben put the CD on and followed Liz into the studio where she was studying Shira's work. Liz moved about carefully in her heels, as if she were afraid she might break something. She was curvier than Ben imagined, her breasts larger, her body firm and fit. He'd always pictured a sort of Millennial lassitude when he thought of Liz, a mid-twenties "I'm going to live forever" casualness to the way she treated her body, a feral canvas and not much more. But she took care of herself, and for the first time Ben felt a stirring of desire. Bent at the hips, blue eyes intently focused on Shira's brightly colored Hand of Miriam—a densely ornamented open hand filled with swirls and arabesques, a giant all-seeing eye fastened in the center intended to ward off evil—Liz looked kinder, softer, than the image Ben had conjured over the many months of her affair with his wife. She studied Shira's work, his wife's work, with a careful appraising eye, admiring Shira's lines, her obsessive attention to detail, humming softly under her breath.

"Shira is really good," Liz said.

"The best," Ben responded.

Shira entered the sunroom with a flourish. "Whassup, girlfriend?"

Liz turned her face to Shira, a wide smile breaking out across her face. "Shir, so good to see your studio. Great stuff, incredible calligraphy. And you, you look gorgeous."

They hugged briefly, a warm friendly hug. Then Shira kissed Ben decisively on the lips, holding it for a two-count, then whispering, "Thank you."

Shira had replaced her glasses with contact lenses and she wore a bright sundress and leather sandals, her toenails painted for the occasion. She wore a velvet choker at her neck with a red glass heart pendant Ben had bought her one Valentine's Day. She hadn't worn it in years, but she was wearing it now. The heart matched her shade of lipstick.

"Okay, who wants some vino?" Ben said, snapping his fingers along with Miles Davis, determined to show Liz and Shira a good time.

"I can always use a drink," Liz said. "Anytime, anyplace."

They moved into the dining room, and Shira asked Ben to say the blessing over the wine. Ben chanted the prayer as best he could, and then, still channeling his great uncle Maury back on Long Island, added the toast: "*L'chaim*."

"*Nostarovia*," Shira responded, downing her glass in a swift gulp.

"*Chai-yo!*" Liz said, adding a toast of her own.

Ben's entire body went ice cold, then burning hot. This had been a tradition between Ben and Shira since their box-wine dating days in Western Mass., exchanging colorful toasts before tipping back their glasses, and here was Liz, smiling and offering her own as if it were the most natural thing to do. Ben could not believe Shira had shared this tradition with Liz, something he thought belonged to them and them alone. Ben felt gut-punched at this betrayal, but knew better than to say anything. Tonight it was Ben's job to be open, to find a way to get along with Liz, to be game for anything that came his way, and to even like her because he loved Shira.

Because he loved Shira.

There was only one thing for Ben to do, and that was to get shitfaced drunk.

By the time they finished the two bottles of wine and started in on the magnum of Shiraz Liz had playfully brought in honor of Shira, Ben was having a good time.

Ben sat at the head of the table with Shira at his right and Liz at his left. They found common ground discussing their favorite fonts and typefaces; Ben, the architect choosing the clean lines and readability of Helvetica as his ideal font.

"Come on," Liz protested, "you can do better than that. That's like saying tap water is your favorite drink. It's practically invisible."

"That's right," Ben said. "Helvetica works because it's so universal you don't even notice you're looking at a typeface designed by a human being. In an urban landscape, Helvetica is as natural as a tree in a forest."

"But it's so boring," Liz said, twisting her face. "No identifying serifs, no personality, no history. Shira, help me out here. Tell me this isn't true, that this is all a big joke."

Shira smiled, and winked at Ben. "He also eats his cereal dry."

"That explains everything." Liz laughed.

"Don't persecute me because I'm lactose intolerant," Ben insisted. "Can you imagine how exhausting life would be if we had to work to read basic street signs because someone decided to use Victor Hammer's American Uncial on all public signage? How about Comic Sans? There's some personality for you. Vulgar, but all in good fun. Listen, if Helvetica offends your tender sensibilities, I'll go with Verdana."

"You know your shit," Liz said, smiling a gap-toothed smile. "Of course, your taste is shit too." Liz laughed and so did Ben. "Of all the gorgeous, eye-fucking fonts in the world you choose Helvetica, the font of public works projects and middle management. You're just so practical."

"Oh, lay off him," Shira said. "Ben's not always practical. He'll even dare to wear his Yankees cap out into the streets of Boston. He'll never give up on his team no matter where he lives; so respect, right?"

Liz nodded, her eyes sparkling.

Ben asked Liz to name her favorite font, enjoying the mental jousting, the light ribbing. There was almost something sexual in the back and forth between them and this connection now would help overcome some of the awkwardness later.

"Blackletter, obviously," Liz said. "It's hella old, but it's the opposite of a sterile mid-century neutral typeface that refuses to make a statement. Can you imagine Motörhead written in anything but Blackletter Metal?"

"You're talking about novelty fonts, gimmicks with very little practical use," Ben said.

"I get it," Shira said. "I like something with a little more personality as well. I'm kind of in love with Garamond and its classic design. But Blackletter, I mean it works for newspaper mastheads, but could you imagine the entire newspaper written in that font?"

"Exactly," Liz said, as if Shira had just proven her point. "Gothic script was the basic script used across Europe for nearly five hundred years going back to the twelfth century and illuminated manuscripts."

"And that's exactly why no one knew how to read." Ben laughed.

"Touché," Shira said, clinking glasses with Ben.

The Shabbat candles flickered down between them and Liz talked candidly about her childhood growing up in rural Connecticut and of her drug and alcohol addiction, starting in the eighth grade, and how she had run away at sixteen and traveled the world learning tribal designs from the Middle East to Tibet to New Zealand, which convinced her she could make a career as a tattoo artist.

Everything had taken on a soft edge as the sun had set, and the dark windows reflected warped images of the three of them laughing and talking animatedly. Liz poured another round and raised her glass. "May the road rise to meet you."

"How many tattoos do you have?" Ben asked, transfixed by this illustrated woman. He was able to make out the words *Demi* and *Monde* inked in black across her knuckles.

"I honestly don't know," Liz said, draining a glass of wine. "Thirty five, maybe forty."

"Do you regret any of them?" Ben asked. He always thought tattoos to be distasteful, low class, and he imagined what Liz would look like in thirty years.

"Regrets?" Liz said. "No. Because they're all part of me. But, if I had to say something, it would be the life-sized Colt .45s on my hips. I guess they are kind of stupid since I'm totally against the Second Amendment." She laughed, or rather snorted adorably. "But I don't regret them. That would be like regretting a freckle or a scar."

Shira poured them each another glass of wine. "If I were to get a tattoo—"

"You are not getting a tattoo," Ben said.

"I can get one if I want, but I said 'if,'" Shira continued. "*If* I were to get a tattoo I would get the Hebrew word for 'breathe' tattooed on the inside of my wrist, so that I remember to always breathe."

Liz made a dramatic chef's kiss and said, "That's perfect, babe."

Shira and Liz turned their attention to Ben.

"I wouldn't get one," Ben said. "No offense, Shira, but I want to have a Jewish burial."

"Shit, does that ever bring the conversation down," Liz said, laughing. She turned to Shira. "Is he always this morbid?" Then to Ben she said, "God's not going to come down from the mountaintop and strike you dead just for answering the question."

"Fine," Ben said. "I would get 'Shira' tattooed in bold letters right here above my heart. That way you'd always be near me."

"Awww," Liz said. "That's so sweet."

"Well I've got news for you, kid," Shira said, poking Ben in the ribs. "You can say goodbye to your Jewish burial."

"I guess I'm dead anyway, so it doesn't matter. As long as we're together, that's what really counts."

11

Things were going so well with Shira and Liz by the time they moved to the couch in the living room for dessert, Ben figured it was time for one of them to make a move. Alcohol made the whole world seem brave and open and exciting and Shira and Liz had just danced together to Salt-N-Pepa's "Push It," as if they were performing a mating ritual right there in his own living room. Ben realized he had the capacity to love the entire world and that he was, quite possibly, the richest man in the world. Liz finished another glass of wine and arched her back in a theatrical yawn, and Ben made some flirty remark about the size of her mouth. With her arms in the air, hips raised slightly, Liz was, in the parlance of animal biologists, presenting. Ben, as an average instinctual mammal following the phero-mone trail of countless predecessors across the animal kingdom, was hardwired to recognize such a signal. "So," Ben said, wine-fueled bravado driving his words, "should we get started?"

Shira and Liz, sitting together on the microfi-ber love seat across from Ben, suddenly looked ner-vous, both their faces blank, eyes wide with fear. With his words, their body language had changed so profoundly that Ben's erection turtled and dis-appeared.

"I'm ready for this," Ben said. "Aren't you ready for this? Because I am ready for this and I'm good and ready."

"Oh shit," Shira said. "He's plastered."

"I'm not plastered," Ben said. "I'm happy, goddammit. Let's do this."

"I know you guys have been going through a difficult time," Liz said, leaning forward, exposing her cleavage, the gap between her teeth. "Shira wants so badly to be a mother, and we both think you would make a wonderful father." Shira clutched Liz's hand, her lips pressed tightly together as if she were trying to stifle a scream. "I'd like to carry your child for you and Shira."

This was not what Ben was expecting. They had just been dancing for him, grinding even; the only thing that was missing was a pole and a clutch of sweaty dollar bills.

"You would be the sperm donor, and I would be the surrogate mother."

"Benj," Shira said, "we tried so hard, and look at all the pain it has caused us. Liz is offering us a second chance to have a family."

Ben couldn't imagine Liz as the mother of his child; any child for that matter. Ben was about to respond with an "I don't know what to say," but the screen of his phone lit up suddenly, flooding Ben with a hot panic. Pamela hadn't texted all week, and she chose that moment of all moments to text, his phone buzzing on the table. "I have to get this," he said, reaching for his phone.

"Dammit, Ben. Not now," Shira said, glaring at him.

"I need to get this," Ben said. His skin itched and he realized how thirsty he was. He could check his phone quickly when he reached for his wine glass.

"Turn it off," Shira said. "This is more important."

Ben turned off his phone, wanting so badly to just take a peek at Pamela's text, but it was impossible. He placed his phone on the coffee table, imagining Pamela waiting for his response, and receiving none.

Shira and Liz stared at Ben in smeary-eyed silence, waiting for some sort of response.

"Well?" Shira said.

It occurred to Ben that Shira and Liz had spoken about Liz carrying their child, set this evening up, and dropped this bombshell on him without even consulting him. Wasn't he supposed to be Shira's primary partner, Liz a secondary? First the ritual of the toast, and now this? Why were Shira and Liz discussing major life decisions like this behind his back? Why didn't Shira talk to Ben before approaching Liz?

"Ben," Liz said. "Are you okay?"

He regarded her and her pink-dyed hair and pierced tongue and thought: *Do I want this troubled high school dropout, this free-loving, tatted-up burlesque dancer to carry my child?* Sure the child would have half of Ben's DNA, but none of Shira's, not a scintilla of her cantor father's world-famous voice, not a spot of gray matter coming from Shira's mother, the economics professor.

"I'm fine," Ben said.

"We didn't mean to ambush you like this," Shira said. "It's just something we've been talking about."

"Well, don't you think you should've talked to me first? I'm your husband, your life partner, and that still means something to me."

"I'm sorry," Shira said. "We didn't exclude you on purpose, and we're coming to you now. You want a child as much as I do."

Shira came over to Ben and sat in his lap, caressing his hair, kissing his face softly. Up close he smelled for the first time a new perfume on Shira's skin, subtle, fruity, with a heart note of spice warm in Ben's nose.

"Come on, Ben. Whattya say?"

"This isn't fair," he said. "With her sitting there."

Liz looked up a little sharply.

"You know what?" Liz said. "I'm going to go freshen up. Take your time. I'll leave you guys alone."

When Liz was gone and the bathroom door had clicked shut behind her, Shira said, "This is what you want, isn't it?"

"I wanted a child with you, only you."

"What could be better than bringing up a child surrounded by so much love? You know, it takes a village?"

"Why didn't you talk to me about this?" Ben said.

"It's been a process to get this far, Liz carrying our baby. This isn't an easy decision for her either. This is about bringing another life into the world. I'm sorry I kept you out of the discussion, but I couldn't think of any other way. The discussions were so fragile. But now that you and Liz know each other."

"We don't know each other. We had dinner and a few laughs."

"Isn't it enough that I want to do this?" Shira said.

Ben had always felt that true love meant aligning one's desires and hopes and dreams with those of one's beloved, but now, faced with this question, he did not know how to answer.

"The child won't be Jewish. The mother is not Jewish. I know how important that is to you."

Shira had clearly been waiting for this response from Ben and she was prepared. "As Reform Jews, according to the 1983 Resolution of Patrilineal Descent, the child will be considered Jewish if the father is Jewish and the child is raised in a Jewish home. But, you need to know, Liz is prepared to have the child convert so there are no doubts that our child is Jewish."

"What about your father?" Ben said. "Does he know about Liz? How will he feel?"

"I'm his only daughter. It may be difficult at first, but whatever I want, he will want for me too." Shira paused, her face flushed. "Benji, I love you. I really, really, do, but she's here and she's not going anywhere. We can make this work. Me and you and Liz. The three of us. I know we can."

Fathering a child with his wife's lover would certainly mean the end of his relationship with Pamela, who already wanted more than he could give; but she may have already been lost to him.

Saying no would mean the end of Ben and Shira.

Shira offered a crooked pinkie for Ben to shake. "Everything is going to be all right."

"I need to think about this," Ben said, ignoring Shira's finger. "And I need to pee."

The bathroom door was closed, and Ben tapped three tentative knocks. Liz opened up right away. She had cleaned herself up, washed her face, reapplied makeup, fixed her hair. She looked pretty, and vulnerable for the first time—waiting for Ben's approval.

"I guess I should apologize," Liz said. "For not thinking about how you would take this. I thought

I was giving the two of you a gift, a really intimate and personal gift. I didn't know it was more than just about me and my body."

Ben watched her red lips move, that adorable space between her teeth, the silver ball flashing from the center of her pink tongue, and that was when he grabbed her and pulled her close, kissing her on the mouth, madly, deeply, like a starving man. Liz kissed back for a heartbeat, maybe two, and then extracted herself from Ben's arms.

"Don't do that," she said.

"What do you mean?"

"Don't."

"But, I thought you wanted to have my baby."

"Stop," Liz said. "Oh my god. Please, just stop."

And with those words she brushed past Ben and into the hallway. Her high-heeled footsteps tapped along the hardwood floor away from Ben, towards Shira. Ben's scalp tightened over his skull in utter humiliation.

"Shir," Liz said, brightly, "I think it's time I call an Uber."

12

Ben woke with a booming hangover and reached for his phone. It wasn't in its usual place, and he scanned the bedroom in search of it.

"Hey, boozehound," Shira said, fresh-faced. She wore cut-off shorts and a green tank top, hair tied back with a green elastic she'd snatched from Whole Foods. Shira had already packed for their weekend in Maine while Ben slept. He couldn't figure out how she could be so chipper. He was pretty sure she and Liz had matched him drink for drink. *Oh my god, did I try and kiss Liz?* Ben just wanted to burrow back under the sheets. Liz wants to carry our baby, Ben thought. How would that even work? For a moment Ben wasn't certain the events of the previous night had actually occurred, but then he recalled Pamela had texted him several times and he, for the first time ever, had not responded. She had wanted him, and, like an idiot, he had turned off his phone, fearing Shira's wrath.

"I'll get your breakfast," Shira said. "Two eggs or three?"

"Where's my phone?"

Pamela was there now, inside his phone, waiting for him.

"Brush your teeth, Ben. I'll get it."

Ben climbed out of bed, took a moment to gather his legs and looked in the mirror, his hair porcupined, face greasy from the cocooned labor of dreams. Shira handed him his phone and he took it, chest pounding.

"I put three eggs in the pan in case you're hungry. We need to get going soon. Traffic on 95 is going to be a nightmare."

Ben thanked Shira and turned on his phone. It whirred to life, the glossy black screen filling with alerts from Pamela: seventeen texts, five missed calls and two voicemails. Ben's heart wheezed. Pamela had never phoned him before, not once, even when they had been texting constantly. She was avowedly not a phone person. Something had to be wrong. Ben opened his phone with an icy dread, his entire body pocked with goosebumps. He did his best to draw a full breath and read.

Pamela's texts started with a cordial: *hey what are you up to* and *i ate too much* increasing in intensity as the hours passed to: *Where are you??* and then: *Why are you ignoring me!*, and, at 12:42 *Are you really this petty?* At 2:47 Pamela wrote: *Did you ever care about anyone besides yourself?* A pair of final 4:12 a.m. messages read: *I can't say this over text I just can't* and then: *It's ok—have a nice life.*

Ben couldn't bring himself to listen to her voicemails. He threw on a pair of pants and pulled a T-shirt over his head. It was amazing how just a few simple words fired off into cyberspace could change his physiology, the sound of her voice alone possessing the power to break him down to his component parts. Sweat coated his entire body, his mouth was dry and he was afraid if he didn't see Pamela now, he might collapse in grief.

"Breakfast is ready," Shira called from the kitchen. "Hurry up. We've got to beat traffic."

"You're going to kill me," Ben said, "but I'm not hungry."

"You need to eat something. We've got a long drive ahead."

"My stomach does not agree. Sorry."

Shira twisted her face in sympathetic acknowledgment. She grabbed a Tupperware from the cabinet and slid the eggs in, before popping them into the fridge. Ben rocked from left foot to right foot and back trying to figure how to do this. He hated to lie, but he had to see Pamela now and lying was his only option.

"Let's go, let's go, let's go." Shira clapped her hands to motivate Ben.

"The thing is," Ben said, "something happened on the site last night, and the foreman needs me to come down there right now. It's a structural thing but it shouldn't take long."

"It's a long weekend."

"I know, but this is an emergency. I need to take care of it now. I'm really, really sorry."

"Okay," Shira said, rolling with his story; a small problem with an easy solution. "We can swing by and take 93 to 95. It shouldn't add too much time."

Ben knew if he told Shira where he was going, Shira was going to bar his way. It could wait. This was their weekend and theirs alone. Since Liz came along, Shira scrupulously kept to their husband and wife time, scheduling it like an event, even if the two of them were just going out for a walk down Mass Ave. for a coffee. Shira didn't even text Liz when Ben and she were spending time together.

"I have to go now," Ben said.

"I'll just be a minute. We can go in together."

"Listen," Ben said, suddenly struck by the fact that Shira still awaited Ben's answer about Liz carrying their child. "The drive alone will give me some time to think about what we talked about last night."

"Yes," Shira said, nodding her head up and down. "Yes, good. Just try and be quick please because I don't want to lose a day to traffic."

Ben thanked Shira, kissed her on the lips and was out the door.

Ben rang Pamela's buzzer several times with no answer. There were six apartments in the slim, Federal-era row house, and Pamela occupied one half of the upper floor. Pamela was up there punishing Ben with her silence. If he couldn't find a way to resolve this now, his mind would never be at peace, his weekend with Shira would be spoiled. The intercom speaker crackled to life, and Pamela's voice, like a validation of their entire relationship said, "Are you still sulking in the lobby?"

"It's not a lobby," Ben said. "It's barely a vestibule."

She buzzed him in and he took the stairs at a full run.

Pamela took her time unlocking the door and opened it only a crack so Ben had to squeeze himself in. She wore a black silk kimono dotted with red flowers and stood with her arms crossed in the unlit hallway before him. Her hair was a mess.

Ben made a move to embrace Pamela, but she languidly twirled around and walked away. He followed her to the bedroom. The bed was unmade, her laptop open on her pillow, playing something moody by Lana Del Rey.

"I wish I had a cigarette."

"What's the matter?" Ben said.

"Are you serious?" she said. "You honestly don't know what's going on?"

Ben told her he had no idea. He had drunk too much and his phone was off and he passed out without checking it.

"See?" she said. "I needed you." She hesitated, picked some lint off the front of her kimono and continued, "But you weren't there."

"I'm here now."

"You weren't here last night. That's when I needed you."

Ben took a step forward to hold her in his arms, but Pamela said, "I can't stand the thought of you touching me right now."

Ben felt so lonely standing that close to Pamela, that close to the bed where they had so many times been intimate with each other, the ecstatic phantom forms of their past selves making love right there before them as if to mock this entire pathetic moment.

"Do you even respect me just a little bit? Or am I just a convenient diversion from your failing marriage?"

"That's not fair," Ben said.

"What do you know about fair?" Pamela's voice dropped, and she said in a flat monotone, "I'm pregnant, Ben. I'm fucking pregnant."

His throat tightened, gripped by an invisible hand. "What?" Somehow Ben did not anticipate this, had never considered that such a thing could happen with Pamela.

"I took three different tests last night and each one said I'm pregnant. I missed my period."

"Are you sure it's mine?" Ben said, stupidly.

"Yes, it's yours!" Pamela said, punching Ben on the shoulder with a half-closed fist. "This may come as news to you. But I haven't slept with anyone else. Just you, Ben."

As if reading his mind Pamela said, "Dating is a horrible ritual and I wouldn't wish it on anybody. It's enough to turn anyone against the human race. I haven't found anyone who didn't depress me with their predictability."

"I thought you had plans all weekend. I thought you met somebody."

"I was up puking at 6:17. And then again at 7:04. Alone."

"I'm sorry," Ben said.

"Not as sorry as I am," Pamela said, narrowing her swollen eyes. "Sometimes I wish I liked you more."

Pamela's words stung, but Ben was still trying to integrate the idea that Pamela was pregnant with his child, the humble foot soldiers of his immortal DNA hitting their mark. A child, containing multitudes, equal parts Pamela and Ben, who was in turn equal parts each of his parents, now stirred inside Pamela, an entire world waiting to happen. Ben's father's athletic build and warm brown eyes, his dimples, his mother's fierce sense of right and wrong, her lactose intolerance had all been passed down to Ben. What parts of his parents would have a chance to live again? Would his and Pamela's daughter carry the soft timbre of his mother's voice, their son his father's riotous laugh?

"That time at the MFA, Ben, talking to you. That was the biggest mistake I ever made."

"Stop. Please," Ben said. "You don't mean that."

"I don't know what I mean anymore. I've never been to your stupid condo, never seen where you live. I don't know what your bedroom looks like, your kitchen. Do you leave your underwear lying around, your dishes in the sink? Are you a slob? Do you make your wife pick up after you? You always try so hard to be on your best behavior when you're with me, but that's not really you, is it? I can't imagine what you're like when we're not together. It's just you and me and this apartment. Don't get me wrong. It's a lot of fun, but sometimes I feel like a dirty secret in your life, and I deserve better than that."

"I'm giving you everything I can."

"Exactly." Pamela shook her head. "That's the problem." Pamela squeezed Ben's hand in hers; her red nail polish looked to have been picked or chewed off. "I had five shitty dates this week, thinking I could find a way to erase you, but I can't. I just can't. I love you, Benjamin Seidel, and I hate myself for it."

She opened her kimono, revealing her soft, pale skin. Ben tracked a constellation of her freckles with his eyes, that intimate game of connect-the-dots, wanting only to place the palm of his hand on the flat of her belly, thrilled and terrified by the life within. He was going to be a father. He pulled Pamela close enough that her belly met his and he kissed her. He felt a delicate tremor pulsing in her neck, but Pamela received Ben's kiss halfheartedly. This only inflamed Ben's desire more and he pressed on, pushing his tongue deeper into Pamela's mouth. He'd kissed her so often he felt entitled to those soft lips, the acrobatic tongue and everything that would naturally follow.

"No," she said, drawing away. "I'm not going to do this."

Ben immediately thought she meant abortion and he was simultaneously relieved and saddened, because this was his child, his child and not Shira's. But Pamela's rigid body and crossed arms meant she wasn't going to end up in bed with him where all the trouble started.

"I'm going to be a mother to a married man's child. How trashy is that?"

"I thought you didn't want kids."

"I lied, Ben. I fucking lied." Pamela's face crumpled. "Because I didn't think it would ever happen. Because I didn't think it would ever happen."

"Aren't you on the pill?"

"You're going to blame me now? When you refuse to wear a condom because you want to be 'closer' to me? Maybe I forgot once or twice, okay?"

Pamela spun away from Ben, talking to the empty room as much as him. "I'm going to be a single mother. How do you like that?"

"You're not single."

"The crumbs you offer hurt more than they help. Weekly sleepovers? What a joke."

"I love and support you, no matter what you choose to do."

"Oh please. Cut the Mr. Nice Guy act. There's nothing to choose. I'm thirty-five years old and this might be my last chance. Sure you hear stories about women in their forties having babies, but I don't want to be a senior citizen when she goes off to college, retired when he gets married. A child needs its mother, no matter how old he or she is."

Pamela paused and flashed Ben a knowing look. If only his parents were still alive, he knew they could help him get through the chaos he had caused. They always seemed to have answers that eluded him; without them, he was lost. Ben suddenly missed both his parents so badly that he knew he would do anything to help Pamela bring this child to term.

"I'm keeping this baby."

Ben was silent, so many contrasting thoughts tumbling through his mind. He was going to be a father, and that meant everything he knew in life was going to change. Shira would leave him and hate him forever, but he was going to give her a child too, so maybe there was some way everyone could get what they needed.

"Say something, goddammit. Say something, please. Just tell me everything is going to be okay, that you are truly going to be there for me."

"I promise I will be there. I'm here now." Part of Ben was inside Pamela right now. This curled up shrimp of a thing gestating in her belly would bond the two of them together forever.

"Then hold me," Pamela said, falling into his arms.

She was so thin, it was hard to imagine a life springing from such a delicate body. Pamela folded into Ben's arms and held on tight. "I'm scared."

Ben said he was scared too.

"Is it weird how much I want it? I want it, I want it, I want it."

Ben had wanted to be a father for so long, but had always thought it would be with Shira.

His phone rang, vibrating against not just his thigh, but Pamela's too, as if Shira could sense a disturbance in The Force.

"Are you going to get that?"

"No. It can wait."

Pamela threw herself at Ben with such unexpected fervor it was almost frightening how she held him so bruisingly tight, pressing herself into him, whispering how she loved him, needed him, and Ben, reverently caressing her body, said he loved her and needed her too, afraid this child would mean the end of him and Shira. Losing Shira would be the worst thing that could happen to Ben. But he wanted, needed, Pamela as well, because she was the key to a part of Ben that had been dormant for far too long. He was a man in full with both Shira and Pamela; without Shira, he was nothing, without Pamela he was miserable. Afterwards, Ben and Pamela lay naked on the bed together, Ben running his hands over Pamela's flat belly, tracing the fragile contours of her rib cage with the lightest feather touch he could muster. Shira's belly would never hold life, a future that would outlive the both of them, but Pamela was having Ben's natural-born child. Pamela's pale body was so different from Shira's, his safe harbor for so many years.

Ben slipped out of bed in search of his clothes.

"I have to go. I'm sorry. I have to get back to Shira."

Pamela seemed to ignore Ben's words and then said, "I miss my brother."

At first Ben thought he had misheard her. "Your brother?"

"I miss him. I just want to speak to him now, tell him what's happened to me."

Was it possible that Ben's efforts to compose his texts just right had caused him to miss a fact as important as Pamela having a brother? Was he really that clueless?

"Why don't you give him a call?" Ben said.

"What do you mean?" Pamela said, thin face expressionless. "He's dead."

Ben froze in place as if he were filled with ice.

"His name is, was, Charlie."

"What happened? I had no idea."

Pamela took a long, deep breath as Ben sat down beside her on the bed, a reassuring hand on her thigh.

"I was fourteen years old, playing hooky with my friend Grace and her older sister and a couple of her friends who were Juniors at Germantown Friends. It was the first sweltering day of June and we were going to swim at the Delaware Water Gap, show off our bikini bodies to the sun god. Charlie found out we were going and begged to come. He was just twelve, and there was room in Grace's sister's van, so we said yes, laughing all the way there as our lame schoolmates sweated through social studies. This was my first true act of rebellion and it was going to be great, the freedom to swim and splash and ditch school for once."

Pamela burst out crying, in deep wracking sobs. Ben threw his arms around her, holding her tight, kissing away her tears.

"It's okay," Ben said.

"Charlie just wanted to show he belonged with the big kids, and I told him to go away, go swim or something. We were so busy smoking menthol cigarettes, passing around a bottle of Olde English and talking about sex like we knew anything about it, and Charlie, showing off, just swam out, shouting in a voice meant to sound like William Wallace from *Braveheart*, 'They'll never take our FREEDOM,' before he was swept away by the current."

Pamela's heart pounded against Ben's chest, thumping at him like a fist.

"It was my fault," Pamela said, regaining her composure. "I brought him there, I ignored him, my best friend, my brother. It was my job to take care of him and I failed."

"I'm so sorry," Ben said. "I had no idea. I am so, so sorry. It's not your fault. It was a mistake. You were young. You were a child."

Pamela was silent for a long while, pale knees pulled to her chest. "I've never told anyone before. Nobody ever. My parents and I don't even talk about him. Every photograph of him ever is just gone, his stuff boxed up and disappeared. It's like he never existed, and that kills me."

Ben took Pamela's hand in his and felt the blood racing through her veins.

"You're the first person I've ever felt safe enough to share this with. I don't know why. Maybe it's the guileless way you move through life, like a young boy who doesn't know how powerful he really is simply because of his Y chromosome. You're kind to me, you don't judge. You're living a charmed life and don't even know it."

If only Pamela knew the fears that clung so fervently to Ben, that feeling that everything you love and care about can be snatched away in an instant. One moment you have a family, the next you are alone, orphaned at twenty-four. Ben had never told Pamela about his parents because this was something he and Shira alone shared, the most traumatic event in his life, that would color all future relationships and encounters, that, somehow, against long odds, managed to bind them together. Shira had loved Ben and held him as he mourned, though they had only been dating a few weeks. It would have been so easy for her to move on and find someone else, someone free of such fresh grief. What did Ben have to offer at the time anyway besides tears and rumination and sleepless nights? Shira was just a Junior at Smith College, untouched by tragedy, surrounded by privilege, and yet she had chosen Ben. When she had invited Ben to her family's home in Bethesda for Passover just a few short weeks later, Ben had been embraced and welcomed, and Shira and he had been family ever since.

"It's not so charmed as you think," Ben said. "I've suffered too."

"Your parents?" Pamela said.

Ben nodded.

"Do you want to tell me what happened?" Pamela's green eyes had taken on a special intensity.

Now that Ben was going to be a father, it only felt right to share what had happened with his parents, not only as an exchange of intimacies between he and Pamela but also as acknowledgment that they had lived and loved and were not, in fact, lost forever. His parents, gone from this world, were going to be grandparents to his and Pamela's child. Just thinking about it knocked the breath out of Ben and he took a long moment to gather himself.

"It was February and there was a massive blizzard on Long Island, more than a foot of snow with wind-chills dropping below zero. I was in Amherst too busy falling in love with Shira to consider what was going on back home. I usually spoke to my parents every few days but hadn't thought to call them before the storm."

At some point the power had gone out for a large swath of Nassau and Suffolk counties, and Ben imagined his humble postwar bungalow covered in snow. His father would have gone out to the attached garage and turned on the generator, assuring Ben's mother that they wouldn't miss a minute of *Nightline*. They usually fell asleep with the TV on, but this time they wouldn't wake, wouldn't feel the headaches, the weakness, the nausea or the confusion, because sometime in the night the carbon dioxide overtook them in their bed. The snow drifts would have been too high for Ben's father to drag the old hulk into the yard, but he had left the garage door open believing there would be sufficient ventilation.

"Oh," Pamela said, covering Ben with kisses. "I'm so sorry."

"They will never know their grandchild."

"No, but their grandchild will know you."

Ben began to cry, softly at first like an engine idling, then his body shook, tremoring with the force of his grief, a long low moan escaping his throat, acknowledging as much as anything that the risk of losing Shira forever was as real now as it had ever been. How could he do such a thing as become a father without her? How could he hurt so much the one he loved?

Ben reflexively reached for his phone and saw the texts from Shira asking when he would be home; they had to hit the road, stat.

"I have to go," Ben said. "I'm sorry. I have to."

"I know." Pamela wiped Ben's tears with the sleeve of her kimono. "Thank you for sharing. I really feel we can do this. I know we're going to find a way to raise a happy child. Are you going to leave Shira?"

Ben didn't respond, except to kiss Pamela softly on the forehead, the way his mother did for him when she tried to soothe his worries. The towering joys and ecstatic pleasures of the past few months were behind them. Everything was going to be difficult from now on. The logistical minefield itself would be impossible to navigate; never mind the emotional risks of sharing the news of Pamela's child with Shira, or burying it in a dark hole never to be found. The lie would be as bad as the truth, and both could be fatal for him and Shira. Ben owed Shira the truth, but the truth would rock her world like nothing the two of them had ever been through. Ben couldn't imagine how he could raise a happy child when he needed both Shira and Pamela in his life to make him happy.

13

The drive up to Portland passed with companionable small talk about anything but the night before with Liz, Ben's voice wavering whenever he tried to speak, his Adam's apple thick in his throat. When Shira found an NPR documentary on the radio, Ben was relieved he could tune out his worries about Pamela and her pregnancy and mercifully focus on someone else's problems.

Ben and Shira checked into their bed-and-breakfast, an elaborate Victorian mansion in the heart of downtown Portland, a little after two o'clock. Shira climbed out of the car, stretched her arms in the air, tilted her head up at an adorable angle, eyes glimmering with a familiar mischief.

"Look at that widow's watch. Imagine doing it up there, with the whole city alive below us, not knowing a thing."

Shira had chosen this particular inn because of its historical widow's watch, a charming glass-enclosed jewel box boasting a stunning view of Casco Bay and Portland's many islands. It was supposed to be romantic, a return to the pinnacle of their erotic connection that afternoon at The Four Seasons. Shira had labeled their Portland weekend; *Fuckfest Part Deux*, after booking the room, but sex was the farthest thing from Ben's mind, tormented by a gnawing sense of guilt at what he had done.

The Chamberlain Suite featured a king-size bed stacked high at the head with plush white pillows smelling faintly of fresh lavender. Shira kicked off her sandals, flopped into the center of the bed, arms and legs inscribing snow angels onto the duvet. "This bed is so huge. We've come a long way from lumpy futons. I need to feel close to you. We need to be close to each other."

Shira began to undress but all Ben could think about was Pamela and what their child would mean for him and Shira. How could this child exist without blowing up his life with Shira?

"You're freaked out by last night," Shira said, squinting at Ben with her 20/80 vision. "Aren't you?"

Ben's florid agony was on full display, face red, eyes bouncing from one thing to another, settling on anything but Shira. He was sweating though the room was practically an ice box.

"Benji, say something. Please," Shira said, her imploring tone hushed by her growing worry. "I'll accept whichever answer you give and I promise I'll never bring it up again. I just so extravagantly want a child, and I thought maybe this was the best way."

Ben wanted to give Shira what she wanted because he loved her and wanted to build a family with her that would carry them off into eternity. How cruel would it be to deny her now? Saying no would open a gulf between him and Shira that would never be bridged. Shira would always resent Ben, and Liz would still be there for her, a vacancy sign hanging conveniently outside her womb.

"Yes," Ben said, perfectly miserable. "Yes, let's do it."

"Really?" Shira's eyes were wide, wet, glistening with joy. "Really? We're going to do this? Really, really?"

"Yes." Ben's voice was hoarse, throaty.

"Then get over here and fuck me, Ben."

Ben climbed onto the bed and took Shira in his arms and kissed her hard on the mouth. But her lips were closed, not prepared to receive him, and Ben felt Shira's body stiffen in his arms.

"I need to call Liz," Shira said, pulling back. "She's going to freak out."

Shira grabbed her phone from the nightstand and told it to call Liz.

There would always be that third person between them; Liz would always be a part of their life, a neon-colored wedge between him and Shira, biologically, undeniably, part of their family. There was no graceful way out now, and he rolled over, pulled his knees to his chest and did what he could to regulate his breathing.

"Heyyy, babe," Shira said into the phone, a huge bright smile spread across her face. "Uh huh." She nodded her head as if Liz, a hundred or so miles away, could actually see her excitement. "He said yes! We're going to do this!"

Liz shrieked with joy on the other end of the line and Ben was overcome by a quick, deflating desolation, his arms and legs suddenly heavy, weighed down by the sour thudding of his heart.

The pregnancy would only bring Liz and Shira closer, and where would that leave Ben while the two of them cooed over Liz's growing belly?

"Benji." Shira nudged Ben out of his ruminations. "Liz wants to speak to you."

Ben sat up on the bed and pressed the phone to his ear.

"How's the proud papa?"

Ben had never spoken to Liz on the phone before, and her voice was surprisingly warm, intimate, as she added, "Isn't this exciting? We're actually going to do this."

"I'm looking forward to it." Ben imagined that adorable gap between her teeth and kissing those pink lips, the silver ball implanted in the center of her tongue swirling in his mouth, setting him alight.

"Me too. You're so awesome, Ben."

Ben was going to be a father with two different women, neither of them his wife.

"Hey, can you put Shira back on?"

"Sure," Ben said.

"Laters."

Shira took the phone, her entire body vibrating with excitement, her legs juddering nervously against the mattress. "I know! Isn't this crazy?"

Shira had not looked so happy in years. "Okay, gotta go, babe." Shira's reluctance seemed to have melted away, and Ben felt her releasing months of built up tension. "Love ya. Call you when I'm back."

There was something almost mournful about their sex, as Ben mechanically went about his business, simply fulfilling a duty he was in no state of mind to fulfill. He had put a baby in Pamela, and he was going to put a baby in Liz. But no matter how he and Shira made love, no matter how hard he came, he would never be able to do that with Shira.

Ben and Shira rented a tandem kayak and splashed around in the calm waters of Casco Bay in search of Portland's historic lighthouses. Ben was just a few feet behind her at the stern, Shira in the bow, her posture ballet-dancer straight, singing in a high, warbling voice, "I Wanna Marry a Lighthouse Keeper." Ben did not sing along but he marveled at how happy, how free her voice sounded now that he had agreed to have Liz carry their child, and Ben closed his eyes to etch that pure, unburdened moment of Shira aglow in his mind forever.

They reached the rocky shores of Cape Elizabeth, and the oldest lighthouse in the state of Maine, its whitewashed conical tower set in proud relief against the pale blue sky. The aquamarine waves foamed in angry knots and dissolved at the craggy shoreline as seabirds chattered a dissonant chorus above, the salt air bracing, fresh as the first day on earth. Ben wondered how many sailors had been safely guided to port by that beacon standing sentry on the narrow headland facing the cold Atlantic, and how many lost and lonely men had, in search of love, bet their entire lives on a dead reckoning of the heart, and won.

"Well, isn't that the coolest thing ever," Shira marveled, hands cupped over her eyes, surveying the endless expanse of the Atlantic beyond Portland Head Lighthouse. "What do you think, *jefe*? Should we buy it?"

"Why not?" Ben said. "Our closest neighbors would be several thousand nautical miles across the sea." Maybe Ben and Shira and Liz and Pamela and their two babies could all live together in that lighthouse at the edge of the world.

Shira laughed. "Perfect! No more neighbors walking on the ceiling, no creaking bedsprings, no late-night washing machines. Just this. Pure peace and quiet."

One day Ben would be nostalgic for this moment—just he and Shira out on the water, content together. Before long Shira would turn her attentions to the joys and challenges of motherhood, and Ben understood with a hint of sadness that they would never really be alone again.

"Hey," Ben said, resting his paddle before him. "Look at me. I want to see your face."

Shira turned her head slowly, her lovely face in profile, aglow over her yellow life vest, an eyebrow arched slightly for effect. "How's this?" Shira said. "Can you see enough of my face?"

"Never," Ben said, reaching for his phone to snap a picture.

"Well," Shira said. "Never is a long time."

"It's a good thing we have a long time," Ben said, but he couldn't help wondering how long they really had now. There was a text from Pamela saying she loved him, and Ben dropped the phone back into the hull of the kayak as if he had touched a burning coal.

Ben and Shira left the rest of their day in the hands of serendipity, wandering the charming little city from the cobblestone streets and lobster shops of the Old Port up through quiet residential neighborhoods with their sturdy gingerbread brownstones and wrought-iron fences. They found a craft market in Deering Oaks Park, lit up theatrically by the warm streamers of the setting sun. Ben told Shira she looked beautiful. She thanked him and said she felt beautiful.

Amid the breakdown of stalls and tables, macramé and batik, hand-blown glass and home-brewed kombucha, a young couple, just embarking on their great adventure together, beckoned Shira and Ben to take a look at their wares. The man was tall and slim and wore suspenders over a plaid shirt, cut off at the shoulders. His thick Van Dyke beard and wax-tipped mustache made him look as if he were playacting. She wore a vintage-looking Holly Hobbie dress, a small bump at her belly, black Doc Marten boots and thick black-framed glasses. Van Dyke announced in a nasal voice that didn't match his bearing that all their infant and toddler clothing was hand stitched and made of eco-friendly, one-hundred-percent organic, soft, brushed cotton.

Shira stopped at the table, hesitantly, and squeezed Ben's hand. She lifted an adorable pink-and-white-striped bodysuit from the table. She marveled, eyes glistening. "Look at how small she's going to be. Her little body. Imagine her hands, her fingers, her perfect, precious feet, her toes."

"Just so you know," Van Dyke said, "our pink is gender neutral. And our dyes are ethically sourced and completely non-toxic, so your baby will—"

"My baby," Shira said, her voice thin, expression blank. "My baby." She dropped the onesie back onto the table as if it were a soiled diaper and gripped Ben's hand in a vise-grip that told him everything he needed to know.

"FYI," Van Dyke added, "we take Square and Apple Pay and we donate five percent of all proceeds to UNICEF."

"Thanks," Ben said. "We're good."

"I need to eat something," Shira said in a flat monotone. She forced a smile onto her face, but her shoulders drooped and her chin trembled as she stalked away from the table.

"Hey," Ben said, brushing a strand of hair from her face. "You okay?"

"I'm fine."

"Let me buy you a pair of earrings. Or a necklace. They have some lovely pieces over there." He tugged her in the direction of the jewelry stand, but Shira slipped from his grip and rummaged through her bag until she found a chrome cylinder of red lipstick and a compact mirror.

She applied her lipstick in silence, a neutral, emptied-out expression on her face. She regarded herself in the mirror, smacked her lips for punctuation and said, "Nah, I don't need anything here. Let's just get really drunk."

They found a noisy, falling down fishing shack at the end of a crooked street in the Old Port district and ordered cold pints of golden craft beer and a dozen Blue Point oysters, a dozen Malpeques and a dozen briny Belon oysters. The wood-paneled floors were slanted and scattered with peanut shells. The walls were crowded with ragged nets, battered buoys, ancient lobster traps and a ship's wheel with a clock in the center, intended to make the place feel authentic. An old tube television suspended behind the bar showed a Red Sox game.

"*Salud*," Ben said, clinking Shira's glass with his.

"Up your bum!" Shira responded, her face bright, open.

"Feeling better?"

They sat in the corner at a cramped zinc table, their knees touching.

"Yes. Yes." She leaned close and kissed him. "And thank you."

"For what?"

"For agreeing to make this happen. I know I have asked a lot of you. But this is good. This will be good." Shira sipped her beer, a soft expression on her face.

The oysters arrived and they had to hold their beers to allow room for the aluminum trays piled with shredded diamonds of ice and oysters on the half shell.

"I didn't know how hungry I was," Shira said, slurping down a full-bodied Malpeque, and then another.

Ben squirted some lemon on his and sucked it into his mouth. It was sweet and salty in perfect measure. "So, I was thinking." He hoped to gain Shira's attention, but she was busy devouring another oyster, sucking it out of the half shell, her lips slick with brine.

"These are so good they oughta be illegal," Shira said.

"Well, they sort of are. They're not exactly kosher."

"That they're not." Shira laughed. "Hey, we'd better enjoy them now since we won't be having any *treif* in the house once the baby is born. No shellfish, no pork—a nice Jewish home."

Ben did not recall discussing whether they would be keeping a kosher home. *How is this going to work?* he thought. A kosher home with Shira and a regular home with Pamela? Would Ben go back and forth between the two homes? And where would Liz live? Would she sleep in bed with him and Shira? And if so, how would Pamela feel about that? Pamela would not be happy about Liz, and though the thought of losing Pamela threw Ben into a momentary panic, the prospect of having sex with Liz and redeeming his failed kiss with her excited Ben in that beer-fueled moment, so he just opened his mouth and said, "How's this going to happen? Me and Liz. Do you want the two of us just to set up some dates to rendezvous, you know, when she's fertile?"

Shira froze, dropped a shell into the melting ice. "Rendezvous?"

"To meet up." Ben felt foolish for having used language straight from a paperback bodice-ripper. "You know, to do it? Have sex, do the deed."

"I don't understand." Shira's brow wrinkled with concern. She adjusted her glasses and looked at Ben in a way that made his stomach drop like an elevator in freefall. "Ben, how do you think this is going to happen?"

If the table had been larger Ben would have hidden under it, but instead he gulped down the rest of his Allagash White.

Shira took Ben's hand in hers. "You didn't think you were going to sleep with her? Did you?"

"Of course not."

"Are you sure? Because it sounded like you think you're going to have sex with Liz."

"I didn't say that."

"What did you say, then?"

"Nothing. I'm not even attracted to her. Come on. Too many tattoos."

Shira pursed her lips as if she were measuring the size and impact of her next words. "And the kiss last night? What was that all about?"

"Liz told you?" Ben's temples throbbed wildly. A stroke, Ben thought, or, better yet, an aneurism, quick and painless and bury me at sea.

"She tells me everything. That's how couples work."

"But we are a couple," Ben snapped. "We are even married according to the Commonwealth of Massachusetts, and, for good measure, we are bound by the laws of Moses and Israel and the Jewish people."

"Ben. Don't," Shira pleaded. "Please."

"It's bewildering that you didn't tell me you wanted Liz to carry our child, a living human that will remain with us until the end of our days. Don't you think you should have told me?"

"Come on," Shira said, eyes averted, a small half-stifled smile on her face. "I do tell you everything."

"Except this." Ben thunked his pint glass down. "What's her role going to be after the child is born? Is she going to be a third parent, make contributions to the child's college fund, become a full member of our happy household? This isn't fair and you know it. You should have talked to me first."

"Let's not fight."

"I'm not fighting." Ben drew a slow breath through his nostrils. "What I'm saying is, I feel like you're leading the way and I'm just expected to follow. It's like I have no agency in this marriage."

"Oh, Ben," Shira said, her brow creased with concern. "You do want this, don't you?"

"I want us to have a family. Of course I do. I just want to feel that I matter. I really thought I was about to be part of things with you and Liz, the three of us together, but now I feel incidental, unimportant."

Shira reached out and touched Ben's cheek with the tips of her fingers. "You are important. You are worth so much to me. You are worth everything." She kissed him softly on the cheek. "You know how painful this has been. But we found a creative solution. Not a perfect one, I admit."

"A turkey baster." Ben shook his head. "Am I that unattractive to Liz?"

"Of course not! It's just, can you imagine how complicated things would get if you were to sleep with her?"

Ben didn't know how he could ever explain this to Pamela, but Ben instinctively knew that wasn't what Shira was getting at. "What's that supposed to mean?"

"You know. You get attached so easily."

Ben had to unclench his jaw to sip his beer.

"You know what I'm talking about."

"No, I don't."

"You get clingy."

"I cling to you because I love you."

"I know, babe, but it's not just me. The ups and downs of your online adventures. It's like you've lost perspective. Pamela doesn't text you and your day is ruined. I've seen it with my own eyes."

"Stop," Ben said. "You don't know what's going on there. You're not being fair."

"There's nothing wrong with needing someone."

"You make it sound like it's a bad thing to need you."

"Not at all. It's just sometimes I feel like I'm dealing with, I don't know, you can be so—"

"Don't say it. It's emasculating."

"I'm not judging. It's okay to be needy. I'm just stating a fact."

Ben froze and placed his pint glass calmly on a perspiring ring near the edge of the brushed zinc table, his desolate, knuckled heart thudding with false bravado. Even before the words came out of his mouth, he knew he had hit back too hard, invoking the marital equivalent of mutually assured destruction. "I may be needy, but at least I was good enough to get Pamela pregnant the old-fashioned way."

Shira's breath hitched and she said, "What?" her small hand flying to her mouth.

"That's right." Ben was positively on fire. "Pamela is going to have my baby."

That afternoon, as they had wandered the city of Portland, Ben had mused how beautiful Shira looked with her skin tanned a golden Levantine brown. Now, beneath the bare, incandescent bulbs of this erstwhile fishing shack, Shira's skin had taken on a deathly pallor, the living color drained from her in an instant.

"I don't feel good," Shira said. "I want to go."

"No. Let's talk about this. I'm sorry. I'm sorry!"

"I really can't do this right now." Shira pushed back her chair and headed for the exit.

She slipped through a crowd of hungry patrons clustered by the entryway without so much as turning around, and was gone.

Ben fumbled through his wallet, tore out a fold of bills and tossed it onto the table.

In all their years together, Ben could not recall a single time Shira had walked out on him like this. She took pride in her ability to be an effective communicator, never allowing resentments to build and boil. She was the reasonable one. She was supposed to be the bridge builder, the understander.

Ben left the fishing shack, passing a couple line cooks in spattered aprons smoking cigarettes on opposite sides of the nautical-themed entryway. They nodded at him as if in sympathy. "She went that way," one of the cooks called after Ben, and he spun around in time to see Shira, in the glow of a flickering streetlamp, turning a corner onto an adjacent street.

It was nearly nine o clock, the dark sky alight here and there with the first stray bursts of fireworks.

"Go after her, man," the younger, blond-bearded cook called. "If you love her, run!"

Ben ran because he loved her, because he was stupid, because it jolted his sagging heart, because running always made sense. But mostly he ran because his life wouldn't mean a thing without Shira in it, and her abrupt leave-taking reminded him that every ending begins somewhere.

Ben caught sight of Shira again a block ahead of him, moving quickly down the sidewalk, arms swinging with determination.

"Shira!" Ben called. "Wait!"

"Don't say anything. I don't want to hear it."

"Just let me explain."

"What is there to explain? You broke our most intimate trust. You were supposed to be careful."

"I *was* careful."

"Just stop. Please just stop talking. I don't want to hear your voice or look at your face."

She clutched her stomach and Ben asked if she was okay.

"No," Shira said.

"Should I call us a taxi?"

Shira did not respond and carried on walking, only slower now, gingerly.

By the time they reached their bed-and-breakfast, Shira was doubled over in pain, her stomach kicking back at her in rebellion. Her drawn skin was clammy, greenish in the moth-whipped light of the front porch. When Ben tried to embrace her, she pushed him away as if she believed that Ben was incapable of ever comforting her again.

Shira rushed up the wide, carpeted staircase and locked herself inside the bathroom. Ben found himself dumbly outside the door, poised to knock, asking to be let in. He could hear Shira throwing up into the toilet.

"You okay?" he asked.

"Leave me alone," Shira responded, before starting up again.

It could have been a few funky oysters or the pounding of the hot July sun that set her stomach to ruin, but Ben knew she was ill solely because of the foolish manner in which he had told her about Pamela and her pregnancy. Pamela had spent the early morning hours in the throes of morning sickness and Ben had not been there to help. And now he stood just five feet away from his wife, separated by a locked door, and again he could do nothing to help.

Ben marveled at the nauseating symmetry of this day and wondered what exactly he could provide these women aside from confusion, upset and misery?

His phone lay on the dresser nearest his bed and Ben picked it up with a sense of awe. It took everything Ben had to resist calling Pamela right then, just to hear her voice, but Shira was retching quietly into the toilet bowl, and he imagined with an ache her hair pasted to her damp, flushed cheeks, her brown eyes glittering with tears, and he didn't know what to do.

"Please let me in," Ben pleaded.

"No."

"Do you want me to call the doctor?"

"No."

"Should I call Liz and tell her you're not feeling well?"

"Leave. Me. Alone."

The entire city of Portland was alight with brightly colored bursts of celebratory fireworks. The historic widow's watch was empty, and Ben sat on one of the cushioned wooden benches that lined the four sides of the enclosed cupola. Watching the light dancing joyously in the sky, he felt as if he were encased in museum glass, cut off from happiness, his misery on display for the world. That afternoon, Ben had imagined he and Shira making love on one of those padded benches, the voyeuristic thrill of doing it in a public place that even the Boston Globe had seen fit to highlight in its travel section, all the cardinal directions open, exposed, distant lascivious eyes everywhere, but it would never happen.

Ben snapped up his phone to call Pamela, and hit her number. Out the windows, the blazing pageantry of lights played across the sky. Ben wanted so badly to enjoy this perfect evening with someone, to share the beauty of this glorious night on earth.

Pamela's phone went right to voicemail, and Ben hung up without leaving a message. She could have been anywhere at that moment, with anyone at that moment, and Ben was humbled to think that a microscopic piece of himself was growing inside her, and that he had no idea where she was.

Red, white and blue fireworks burst across the sky in a crescendo of light and sound, and Ben dialed Pamela's number again, praying for her to pick up. A final volley of golden sparks sprayed into the sky. Ben fixed his eyes on the deep canvas of the darkening sky, wishing he had someone with whom to share this moment, wishing he didn't have to be alone.

14

Shira was still asleep, curled up on the far side of the king-size bed, when Ben awoke early the next morning. With its excess of pillows and cushions, Ben felt he had been walled off from his wife, banished to the hinterlands of this thousand-thread count floating cloud. He reached over and touched the back of his hand to Shira's forehead. It was cool, her skin clear, eyelids fluttering softly. Whatever sickness had taken hold of her seemed to have passed. Shira must have sensed Ben was watching her because she stirred, opened a single eye and told Ben she wanted to go home.

"How are you feeling?" Ben asked, stroking her hair.

She recoiled at his touch. "Home. Now."

They had planned a full day of activities, meant to include brunch at the Portland Museum of Art, a ride on the narrow gauge railroad and a beer garden lobster fest featuring a half dozen local bands. But Ben knew better than to press Shira, so he began packing their things, his blood racing, brain ablur with re-crimination.

"Ben, tell me one thing," Shira said, climbing out of bed. "How do you think this is even going to work? It's hard enough just raising one child. Have you figured out how you will find the time and energy to be present for our child and not leave the other one fatherless?"

"I don't know. I honestly don't know."

"That's your answer? 'I don't know.' This is the rest of our lives we're talking about. You need to do better than that."

"I'm doing the best I can."

"No you're not," Shira said, her voice sharp, eyes narrowed.

Ben took a step back, averting his eyes so as not to suffer the heartbreaking steel of her frigid stare. "You're mad at me."

"Mad?" Shira screamed. "I'm furious with you. I'm enraged. I'm way past mad. I've been desperate for a child of my own, and you go and knock up your mistress."

"Hey, you're the one who asked your girlfriend to carry my child. You didn't even consult me first."

"Fuck off! Pamela would have been pregnant even if we hadn't discussed Liz carrying our baby. That's still on you."

"Did you get involved with Liz because you loved her, or because you saw her as a way to get that child you want so badly?"

"Stop."

"Does Liz know you're using her—"

"Stop right now. Just stop, stop, stop." Shira was crying now. "You're being an asshole. I'm not using anyone. I love Liz. I do. I love her."

"I'm sorry."

"Too late for sorry. What are you going to do to fix this problem?"

"I'll do whatever you want me to do to make this right."

"She has to get rid of it. Pamela needs to get rid of that thing growing in her belly."

"I can't do that. She wants to keep it." On an elemental level, Ben wanted to keep it too, but he couldn't let on to Shira or she would leave him in an instant. "We don't even know if the baby is going to be viable."

"That's not good enough. I need assurances that your mistress won't be having your baby."

There had to be a solution. Ben cleared his throat to speak.

"Whatever you are planning on saying, don't bother," Shira said. "I don't want to hear it."

She turned her back on Ben and began packing her bag.

"How can I ask her to get rid of it? You know it's not my place or anyone's place to tell Pamela what to do with her body. You'd be the first to come to her defense if this were anyone else."

"I know that, Ben," Shira said, with her back still facing him. "I didn't say I'm proud of feeling this way. But it's the only way, isn't it?"

Shira's voice rose just a touch at the end of her defense, and Ben saw this as a small opening through which he could talk her down.

"There are other ways."

"I'm listening."

The next words Ben spoke would be the most consequential he had uttered since he asked Shira to marry him. "You have to know," he said. "No matter what happens, I will always love you."

"I wish I could say the same." Shira's voice was flat, emotionless.

"You don't mean that."

"Would you like to test that theory?"

Ben stood on the edge of a dangerous precipice, his heart bellowing in his chest.

"It's still early." He didn't want to imagine this possibility, and his stomach lurched as the words crawled up his throat, but he could think of no other way to appease Shira. "Think of how many pregnancies don't make it through the first trimester. Maybe—"

"I don't want maybe, Benjamin, I want certainty. Whatever happens with that child affects my life and my ability to live it to its fullest, and having my husband's child running around town makes me hate the very idea of you."

Ben shivered, even though the room was warm. "All right," Ben said, breath hitching. "Here's a solution that might make everyone happy." He and Shira and Pamela and the baby. Three caring hearts instead of two. But Shira cut him off before he could voice his plan, which he knew was a dubious moonshot at best, but what else did he have to offer?

"No, no, no." Shira waved her hands as if to scrub Ben's words out of the air. "You don't understand. I don't want a solution that makes everyone happy. I don't care if she's happy. This is not a time to compromise. I just want there not to be a baby. She can't have this baby. She just can't. I'll lose my fucking mind."

"Even if Liz carries my child for you?" Ben countered. "You'll have your own baby to love and care about. You won't have time to think about anything else. The rest of the stuff, finances, custody, we can figure that out, I'm sure."

"I need you to understand, after all the years of me standing behind you, when you were sick, when you were out of work, catching you whenever you fell, I need to know that you're behind me, that you will catch me. This is the moment I need you. I've never asked for much. I don't ask a lot. Just this, Ben. Just this."

Shira's eyes were raw and glazed with tears, her mouth turned down into a sorrowful frown.

"Your baby, the one we were supposed to have together, is inside another woman. Please, Ben," Shira said, her voice approaching a whisper. "Please."

The drive home took half the time as the trip up to Portland, but with the heavy silence wearing on him, it felt as if it would never end. Ben just wanted to hear Shira laugh, to see her face break out into a bright smile, to hear her sing along to one of those cheesy songs on the radio she liked so much. But she just sat, staring out the passenger window, chewing on her fingernails.

When they arrived home, Shira told Ben she was going to Jamaica Plain to see Liz. Ben expected precisely this outcome, but he still felt hot bands of irritation tightening in his chest. Ben just wanted her to stay and talk to him, to give him a chance to soothe her, to make her feel better.

He needed to know they were going to be okay, so he called after her and asked for a hug.

"Okey dokey," she said approaching him, arms tentatively open to receive him.

"I love you," Ben said. "And I'm sorry for everything."

When Pamela opened the door to her apartment she smiled and said, "You're back early."

"I needed to see you," Ben said, palming sweat off his forehead.

"And you know how sexy need is to a woman." Pamela laughed.

"I'm serious," Ben said, eyes still, searching Pamela's.

Pamela stared at Ben in silence, perfectly miserable, lips formed to a frown, restless fingers picking the remaining polish off her lacquered nails. She wore a red silk kimono tied firmly at her waist, neck open in a deep V, her pale skin exposed from her delicate clavicle to the subtle curve of her cleavage.

Ben took Pamela by the hips and kissed her hungrily on the neck, saying he loved her, he loved her so much he didn't know what to do with himself. He felt both intensely sad and desperately happy at the same moment as those absurdly edged words issued from his mouth. Pamela let out a soft breath that felt so intimate it told Ben everything he needed to know.

Ben and Pamela generally subscribed to the dictum "fuck first," and with the warm sunlight filling her apartment, the sharp smell of fresh-brewed espresso redolent in the air, they barely made it to Pamela's bed. Afterwards, as they lay side by side, ragged breath in sync, Ben wondered whether he had done something to hurt the baby, whether he needed to take greater care. This thing inside her, barely the size of a wet lentil, was so fragile, poised as it was on the cusp of existence, that Ben was overcome by a sudden desire to know everything.

"What does it feel like?" Ben asked. "To have a brand new person growing inside you?"

Pamela was silent for a long moment, and Ben thought she had chosen not to answer when she said, "My nipples—they ache."

Pamela's nipples did seem to protrude more than Ben was used to, pink and firm, and he made a move to caress her, but Pamela slapped his hand away. "My high beams are on all the time now. It's a special agony you'll never understand." She sighed and blew some hair out of her face. "I'm going to be a milking machine. How do you like that, Mr. Lactose Intolerant?"

"I think you're beautiful."

"Of course you do. But you're not living in my body. Would you believe what I need right now? A pack of Choward's Violet candy—you know, that old-fashioned candy that tastes like hand soap. My grandparents in Gettysburg used to give it to me when I visited them as a girl. I haven't had it in years and I don't think I ever liked it, but right now I just want a pack of Violet candy, and if you could just go to the store right now and get a pack for me, I think I'd be the happiest woman in the world."

Ben asked Pamela if she wanted him to run out and get her some, a whole carton even, to keep her in Violet candy until the cravings subsided.

"That's sweet. I don't even think they sell it in Boston. When it comes to nostalgic old candy, this is a Necco town."

"Well, what can I do for you?"

"Just be here for me when I need you."

"And when is that?"

"When I need you."

"Are you sure you're ready for this?"

"What's that supposed to mean?"

"It's just this is a huge thing. A baby. A new life. I mean, how is this going to work, on a practical level?"

"What are you suggesting?"

"Nothing."

"You wouldn't presume to tell me what to do with my body."

"Of course not. I would never—"

"That's what all the cowards say. A sensitive liberal like you only needs to a plant a seed of doubt and let the woman's paranoid tendencies take over."

"It's not like that. I want this baby. I really do. But—"

"I know where this is going. A single mother, family out of state. A serious full-time career with no reliable childcare."

"Stop it."

"Before you know it Planned Parenthood is knocking at my door looking like the savior of my lost dreams." Pamela's jaw tightened before she added, "Did she put you up to this?"

"Put me up to what?"

"The barren woman you're married to. She told you to talk me out of having a baby. What's next, bribes, threats?"

This was the wrong time to tell Pamela that he and Shira and Liz were planning on having a baby of their own.

"Be nice," Ben said, chest aching. "Please. Shira doesn't know yet."

That small lie seemed to ease Pamela's anger.

"I'm not suggesting you get rid of the baby. I'm in this. I want it. I want this baby."

"What then?"

"We need to think about the logistics of the thing."

"Logistics?" Pamela laughed a quick, dry laugh. "You sound like some corporate HR hack. What's next? Financial and emotional sustainability? Wellness quotients? Postpartum work/life balance?" Pamela found a terry cloth robe in her closet behind her and slipped it on so it covered her body entirely from neck to kneecaps. "You should leave."

"I'm not leaving."

"Please, just leave me alone."

"You're having my baby," Ben said, his voice thick with emotion.

Pamela softened and offered a restrained half-smile. "I am," she mused.

Ben asked if he could hug her, and he held her in his arms long enough to feel Pamela's heartbeat slow its rhythm.

"There's a two-bedroom garden apartment in Watertown available soon," Pamela said, her breath warm in Ben's ear. "I found it online at like three in the morning. The landlord already emailed me. It's closer to you, it's got lots of sunlight and it's $700 cheaper than this place. I mean, I won't be able to walk to work anymore but I can use the extra money. The second bedroom could be a nursery."

Ben's stomach jolted. "Don't you think it's bad luck to talk about it before it's born?"

"I'm a grown woman. I need to plan, and this place meets so many needs. I can't just chill and go with the flow and hope things turn out okay."

"That's not what I'm suggesting." Ben thought of Shira. He couldn't help it. She'd cried enough tears. He would never be able to think otherwise again, despite the fact that his logical brain said NO in all capital letters. "There's a Jewish tradition," Ben said, "that says talking about a baby before it's born invites the evil eye, and terrible things happen, miscarriage, death, birth defects; all sorts of terrible things."

"I'd be a lot more afraid of mercury in my sushi or e-coli in my spinach," Pamela said, pulling out of Ben's embrace. "If the evil eye were to mean anything, it wouldn't affect my baby since he's not even Jewish."

"Well, what is the child going to be?" Ben asked.

"A human being, I guess," Pamela said. "Unless the evil eye turns him into a three-toed sloth," she added, laughing.

"Stop. You know what I mean. What about church and Christmas and Jesus? You grew up with Jesus, right? I can't do Jesus. I just can't."

"Ben, there's no need to get worked up. I'm nothing, all right. There's no need to worry. The child is going to be nothing."

A cold wave of sadness swept over Ben, his body chilled by the fact that this baby, inching ever so gradually towards being, was already nothing, cut off from wisdom and tradition Ben himself had chosen again and again to ignore. He had made a choice. This child would have no such choice.

"So will you come look at that apartment with me?"

Ben wasn't prepared for Pamela switching gears so quickly, and said, "When?"

"Now, now, very now," Pamela said, breathlessly. "You don't mind driving, do you?"

The apartment was bright and spacious and was owned by a fifty-something Armenian Christian from Syria named Sarafyan who agreed to rent the place to Pamela for a good price on a two-year lease. He assumed Ben was the husband as he directed all monetary and financial questions to Ben rather than Pamela, called him Mr. Whitney, which was such a gentile name for Ben it was almost laughable. But Ben didn't mind since Pamela would be living much closer to him, cutting the distance and travel time in half come August first. And there would be parking, glorious parking.

After Ben dropped Pamela off at her Beacon Hill apartment, he went out in search of a gift to celebrate her upcoming move. He rang her buzzer several minutes later and took the steps two at a time.

"Close your eyes," Ben said.

"Come on, Ben, you're embarrassing yourself," Pamela said. "Just give it to me. I'm not closing my eyes."

"Fine." Ben produced a bouquet of flowers from behind his back. "Violets. Couldn't find Violet candy anywhere."

"I told you." Pamela flashed a real and true smile.

"Look." Ben peeled back the crinkling cellophane. "The leaves are heart-shaped, and, if you desire, both the leaves and the flowers are edible."

"Aww, Ben."

"I ate one in the street. It tastes like someone sprinkled pepper on a rain storm."

"Thank you. That's a thoughtful gift. What am I going to do with you?"

"You can kiss me."

Pamela kissed him, deeper than usual, holding him in her arms. They lay together on her bed, the bouquet of flowers between them.

"Today was sort of a big deal," Pamela said. "I'll be living a lot closer to you. Do you think you can handle me being around more?"

Pamela had a tiny, almost invisible scar on the underside of her chin where some reckless kid's mini golf club had nicked her one long-ago summer at the Jersey Shore. Her hand flew unconsciously to that scar now, worrying it with the tips of her fingers. "You do want to have this child?" She began to cry, a deep sob escaping her lips, and then, as quickly as it began, the crying stopped.

"What?" Ben said. "Are you okay? What's going on?

"I just want this baby. I need this baby. I have to have this baby. I just can't imagine what I'd do if something went wrong."

15

Ben was surprised to find Shira's car parked in the driveway outside their condo. He was sure she would have stayed the night in Jamaica Plain, pouring her misery into Liz Bird's sympathetic ears, comforted by the ministrations of her caressing arms, not returning home until she could stand to look Ben in the face once again. But now, just several hours later, Shira was already home, Buttercup's idle engine still ticking in the afternoon heat.

The front door of their condo opened, and Shira poked her head out. "I thought I heard you."

"Hi," Ben said, uncertainly.

"Come inside," she said, a contrite half-smile on her face.

Ben obeyed, and closed the door behind him once he stepped inside. The living room was stifling hot; they had turned off the air conditioning before heading out for the long weekend, and Shira hadn't switched it back on yet.

Shira sat on the couch, where she had sat with Liz just two days prior, expression downcast, pensive, the tender cords of her pale neck pulsing softly. She tapped the space next to her on the couch and asked Ben to sit.

"Ben," she said, taking both of his hands in hers. "I want to apologize. I was out of line and I put you in an impossible situation."

"I didn't do it," Ben said. "I couldn't."

"Of course you couldn't. I was a terrible hypocrite. My behavior was ugly. I let my emotions get the best of me and I just reacted. I'm sorry."

"I'm sorry too." Ben squeezed Shira's hand for emphasis. "How did things get so messed up between us?"

"Life. It happens to everyone."

"What happened?"

"Liz told me I was being a dick and I had to stop feeling sorry for myself. We sort of had a fight and, in the end, I realized I still want to have a baby with you, and maybe the price I have to pay is to accept that life doesn't always go the way you want it to."

"Liz called you a dick?"

"Actually, she called me a whiny, entitled dick."

Both Ben and Shira laughed in the hot box of their living room, sweat pouring down their faces.

Shira kissed Ben softly on the lips and it meant so much more than just a simple kiss. It was Shira's way of sealing the deal, putting the ugliness behind them so they could forge a path forward together.

"So, now what?" Ben asked. "How is this going to work?"

"I have no earthly idea, and it may be a total mess. But I can't think about it today. I just can't. It's still a long weekend and you owe me some fun." Shira offered up a sheepish smile. "There's this sort of barbecue, picnic thing at a state park in Hopkinton tomorrow. Liz invited us since we're back early from Maine."

"Us?" Ben said, surprised.

"Yes us. We're more of an us than we have ever been."

Ben wasn't sure how true that was. After all, Liz had rebuffed him, and he had made a fool of himself, assuming Liz was going to sleep with him.

"Whose barbecue whatever is this?"

"NETS is putting it on. It's an annual thing."

"Who or what is NETS?"

"Don't get mad," Shira said. "It's New England Thorns Society. It's not a big deal." Ben's blank expression told Shira she needed to explain. "It's a regional BDSM organization. I've been to a couple things with Liz."

Ben's heart jumped and then dropped in the same instant. His sinuses hurt, eyes watering. He recalled his horror at seeing the rope marks on Shira's arms and legs. "That's not my thing."

"It's not like that. And I'm not deep into the lifestyle. I mean, barely. Kink is not some disorder. These are normal people and the event is a family barbecue, so it will be vanilla, no costumes, no toys, just another All-American Independence Day barbecue."

Ben never understood how vanilla had become pejorative for boring, bland, unworthy. "I think vanilla is delicious. I'd take vanilla ice cream over chocolate any day of the week."

"And then you'd have a stomach ache." Shira laughed. "Don't feel threatened, Ben. It'll be a nice day in the sun with hot dogs and chips and a few beers and maybe, if you're lucky, some Tofutti."

"But Liz will be there. Won't you be occupied with her?"

"It's not like that, Ben. And you have to know she invited you as well, specifically asked for you to come. She really did."

Shira made sympathetic eyes at Ben, but he didn't feel comforted.

"Anyway, she'll be busy with her triad partners. Jeanne and Jim are both on the NETS advisory board. Come on. It'll be an adventure. I promise."

Shira offered up her pinky finger for Ben to shake.

Ben agreed reluctantly, because he needed to start sharing experiences with Shira again or risk losing her to Liz.

Shira was in the bathroom washing up for bed when a text from Pamela lit up Ben's phone.

What r u up to tomorrow?

Ben texted back instantly. *What's up?*

I thought we might go for a walk on the Esplanade since you're back early ☺

I can't

Oh

You'll never guess what I'm doing

...

Give up?

Just tell me

Going to a picnic with Shira and her girlfriend. A BDSM barbecue out in the sticks.

You're into that?

Dunno, Ben texted. *I'm open, I guess.*

Pamela did not respond, and a moment later Ben texted, *I mean, I'll try anything once.*

When she didn't respond to that, he wrote, *You know it's not a big deal. I'm not going to do anything if you're worried about that.*

Shira stepped out of the bathroom, a cucumber moisturizing mask smeared on her face, her hair knotted in a sloppy bun. "Your turn, *jefe*."

Ben was so distracted waiting for Pamela to respond he didn't even acknowledge Shira, who climbed onto the bed and leafed through a paperback novel until she found her dog-eared page.

I love you, Ben typed.

And then: *I miss you*.

Pamela did not respond, and Ben's chest tightened, an effervescent fist bubbling in his throat. He just wished there was a way to make both Shira and Pamela happy.

"Why don't you go wash up?" Shira said. "It's been a long day."

"Sure," Ben said listlessly, before typing, *Goodnight??*

❧

Shira was in a chipper mood on the drive out to Hopkinton, singing along to the songs on the radio, as was her habit. She wore a pair of fitted, camo capri pants, a scoop-neck Pixies T-shirt, and chunky wedge sandals, no makeup on her pretty face. She looked so natural and at ease, and Ben, who had settled on jeans and a plain black T-shirt with an old pair of blue Chuck Taylors, wished he could allow himself to relax, if just for a moment. Driving a steady sixty-five, Ben turned to Shira and asked, "What if there's someone I know there, like from work or the community?"

"Don't worry about it," Shira said. "If you see someone you know, you have to remember they are there too. But a lot of people use different names, to separate their vanilla life from their scene life."

"Do you have a scene name?"

"You know how I am about concocting names."

It dawned on Ben that nobody ever really knows anybody, and that intimacy was a transactional thing, a currency exchanged for comfort to fill ourselves with the feeling that we really are not all alone in the world, that fusing person-to-person as one is in fact possible. But Ben realized that he and Shira were falling backwards, and that he knew less and less about her all the time.

"It's Juliette," Shira said, turning down the radio. "Do you like it?"

"Sure," Ben said, eyes forward, jaw tight.

"Don't get like that, Ben. It's just a fun thing. It's nice to pretend to be someone else every once in a while, isn't it?"

"What about pretending to be my wife every once in a while?"

"Whoa. Where did that come from? We were having a nice time."

"Can't you see? At the rate we're going we will be complete strangers a year from now."

"Benji, we're going to have a baby together."

"Do you think that will save us? Bonding over diaper changes and vaccinations. You still believe in vaccinations, don't you?"

"Why are you being like this? What did I do wrong?"

"I just never imagined I would ever be in a marriage like this."

Shira was silent for a moment, then said, "What do you want?"

"I want you. I just want you."

"And Pamela?" Shira responded. "Don't you want her too?"

"I want you. That's what matters."

"And not Pamela? Is she just a side piece or something more?"

"Stop. You're being unkind."

"You love her."

"And you love Liz."

"This isn't about her," Shira said. "Do you love Pamela because you truly love her on a soul-deep level, or because you need to love someone for balance because I'm in love with someone else?"

Ben didn't have a chance to answer as his GPS, which had been silent since they got on the turnpike, informed them that their exit was approaching.

16

Ben crossed the broad, green lawn several steps behind Shira, as if he were trudging towards his own execution. Several barbecues fired smoke signals in a clearing at the edge of a thick forest, a vague clutch of people gathered around the tables under the shade of an open, slant-roofed structure. Shira stopped short before Ben, turned around and said, "I love you. Don't ever doubt that." She took his hand in hers and added, "Try and have fun. Pretty please."

A Day-Glo Frisbee overshot its mark and Ben picked it up and tossed it back to a shirtless man with pierced nipples and a topknot.

"Thanks, man. Want to join us?"

Ben politely declined and squeezed Shira's hand.

"It's okay," she said. "These are just people."

Ben may have felt miserable, but he knew he would never see these people again, and that freed him, set loose a sort of ironic detachment that allowed the observer in him to note the absurd contradictions in style and manner, how a fifty-something professorial-looking man in round owlish glasses and with a prominent Adams apple bobbing above his fully buttoned Oxford shirt held court in his crisp London accent about the beautiful tradition of shibari and other forms of Japanese bondage. Shira stood beside Ben, listening thoughtfully.

"It's really quite lovely how kinbaku stimulates Ki and facilitates energy flow, releasing endorphins and a veritable profusion of countless, remarkable hormones. The bottom, or model, if that designation is your preference, becomes quite intoxicated, falling into a dewy trance-like state that I've heard feels something like floating inside a mother's womb. And don't we all want to return to the cosseted comfort of the womb and fill that lacuna in our soul, if just for a few moments?"

To the three or four young women hanging on every word, he was an expert in an ancient tradition, describing Hojo-Jutsu, the martial art once used by the samurai to restrain prisoners, but Ben sensed in the man's slight stutter, his show-offy locution, his insistence on calling the Japanese people "Nihonese," a deep insecurity that revealed a desperate bullshit artist whom, he guessed, rarely got laid before discovering his apparent expertise was as much an aphrodisiac as a chiseled chin and bursting biceps. Ben turned to Shira, about to say, "Can you believe this guy?" but she had disappeared into the mob of picnickers.

"I am a particular proponent, *and* practitioner, of shinju," the professor continued. "I believe the aesthetics of a well-made karada, or rope dress, approach the divine. Of course, to those who are either unskilled or ignorant, a simple corset will have to suffice."

Ben could not listen anymore and went in search of Shira, wading past a couple dressed in the steampunk style, top hatted and dressed all in black with tinted goggles, industrial gears fastened to their costumes. The woman was telling her partner she wanted "The Rains of Castamere" to be their wedding song. The fiancé's canines seemed to have been altered in some way to resemble those of a vampire.

But most of the people, Ben observed, looked just like anyone he might come across on the streets of downtown Boston, ranging in age from early twenties to mid-seventies. He sensed no overarching style or ideal—all body types, fat, thin, fit, seemed to be welcome. Maybe he had been wrong feeling scandalized. For the most part, they seemed just like everybody else, and, hey, who didn't need a spanking every once in a while?

A stocky man wearing shorts, flip-flops and a backwards Red Sox cap nodded at Ben as he approached and said hey. He had the beginnings of a goatee and the Irish tricolor tattooed on his right shoulder, the Italian flag inked on his left. He held an uneaten hotdog in his hand and gestured to it as if the hotdog were Exhibit A in a court trial. A slim, blonde woman with bangs, wearing a colorful sundress, who Ben thought he recognized from the Starbucks near his office downtown, nodded her head knowingly.

"The problem with sounding is it's hard to find somebody who knows what they're doing. I mean, people will say anything, and this so-called domme I met last year in Providence, I don't even think she sterilized the equipment before inserting it. I got this wicked ass bladder infection that cost me three rounds of antibiotics."

The man in the Red Sox cap grabbed a ketchup bottle off the picnic table beside him and squirted a line of ketchup down the length of the hot dog.

"You should have seen the blood. I nearly passed out."

"You need to use distilled water and antibacterial soap. And boil the water before cleaning. Even if the equipment is brand-new," the barista said evenly, as if she were reciting the ubiquitous EMPLOYEES MUST WASH HANDS BEFORE RETURNING TO WORK credo found at all food service jobs.

"I hope you don't mind my asking," Ben interjected, "but what is sounding?"

"Of course I don't mind," the barista said, no sign of recognition in her blue eyes. "Sounding is when a device of varying widths, either a specially designed implement or catheter or a medical device, is inserted into the penis, sometimes just partway into the glans, sometimes much deeper, into the bladder."

Ben's stomach jumped, his own penis turtling into himself.

"I like to call it cock stuffing," the man in the Red Sox cap said. "It's not for everybody, that's for sure. But it can be addictive, and explosive too. The orgasm is out of this world. But the Holy of Holies is the prostate. Nothing can tickle the prostate like a good deep urethra penetration."

Ben caught sight of Shira out of the corner of his eye and politely excused himself. "My wife—"

"Hey, do you want this?" the cock stuffer asked, extending the hotdog towards Ben. "I'm totally full."

I'll bet you are, Ben thought, before saying, "No thanks."

Ben grabbed onto Shira as if she were a flotation device in the middle of a roaring sea.

"I can't find Liz anywhere." Shira chewed nervously on her bottom lip. Ben understood her trepidation. Shira had never met Liz's triad partners before and didn't know what to expect. It annoyed Ben that Liz had a pair of other partners when she already had his wife. That sort of erotic collecting was greedy, slightly unseemly, especially with Shira factored into the equation. Shira would have been enough for Ben, and yet Ben needed Pamela, and now he couldn't imagine giving up either one. He marveled at his smug hypocrisy and wondered whether anybody could ever be enough for anyone. Ben was about to ask Shira's turned back if she was ready to go when a voice behind Ben said, "You're new, aren't you?"

Ben turned around with forced casualness and said he was.

"I try and meet all the newbies. I'm Genevieve."

"My name's Ben."

Genevieve smiled, her pale blue eyes taking him in. She was tall and slim, with the hard look of a fit woman in her late forties. She had straight shoulder-length hair and severe bangs, rinsed a dark wine red, her narrow face open in anticipation. She wore sporty workout clothes that likely cost a fortune at a place like Lululemon, and Ben imagined her like countless middle-aged mothers rolling up to the local yoga studio in her brand-new Lexus.

"Tell me something about yourself, Ben."

Ordinarily this line of questioning would have felt like a sort of interrogation, but Ben was so relieved, with Shira off in search of Liz, that someone was interested in him he just let it out. "I'm here with my wife, who is here with her girlfriend, who is here with her triad partners. So basically I'm sort of lost."

Genevieve smiled. "We're a very accepting bunch, but it sounds like you don't know what your role is with these people."

"Not really," Ben said. "To be honest, I'm not sure I understand anything about how I'm supposed to be."

"I guess the question is how do you want to be?"

"I don't know."

"If you don't know, how do you plan on getting there?"

"I put a lot of faith in love. I love my wife and she loves me."

"I've seen love destroy more people than it has saved. The only thing you can count on is that love will end."

Ben felt as if he had been kneed in the stomach. "But love is unselfish. It's giving of yourself."

"It is *totally* selfish and it is all about taking, sucking the marrow out of your partner until they're are emptied out."

"What do you believe in?" Ben said.

"I believe in power. I believe in control, in finding our darkness and owning it."

"That sounds pretty harsh,"

"Not at all. I'm talking greater intimacy, transcending the everyday. The sorcery of this sort of power exchange opens the most surprising doors."

"I think I've experienced enough suffering that I don't need to seek it out."

Genevieve smiled a tight smile and looked him over with narrowed eyes. "BDSM is not about real punishment or abuse, but rather a deep form of love, however fleeting. If I choke you, or flog you, it's because on some elemental level you need it to be the most fully actualized version of yourself."

"Pain is still pain," Ben said.

"Not at all. If you trust someone to control your pain and pleasure, you open yourself up completely. It's very freeing."

"That sounds like a stretch to me."

Genevieve regarded him with a sly smile. "Call me Mistress Genevieve."

"Mistress Genevieve?"

"Say it like you mean it. 'I submit to you, Mistress Genevieve.'"

"I don't understand," Ben said, eyes scanning the crowd for Shira.

"Say, 'I submit to you Mistress Genevieve.'"

Genevieve's expression was so stern and serious she looked both brittle and mildly constipated, and Ben couldn't help but laugh. "I can't," he managed to say. "I just can't."

Mistress Genevieve took Ben's hand in hers. "Well bless your heart. You're not a natural-born sub, and you sure as sugar aren't a dom either. If I had my way with you, I would put you over my knee."

"You know," Ben said, "I think my wife is looking for me."

Ben eventually found Shira and Liz and her triad partners spread out on a Navajo blanket not far from the barbecue pits. Even with her back turned to him, Ben knew Shira was upset by the way she sat so straight, as if she were forcing herself not to collapse.

"There he is," Liz called. She smiled a broad, welcoming smile and bade Ben to join them. Ben had expected to be mortified upon seeing Liz after the disaster of their dinner party and his clueless assumptions. But Ben saw in Liz someone familiar, almost comforting among this crowd of strangers; they had broken bread together, laughed and discussed something as intimate as carrying his child.

Ben dropped down next to Shira, and she reached out her hand for his as if by instinct. Shira was separated from Liz and her partners by a complex arrangement of plates, bottles, containers and plasticware congregated around the physical barrier of a Coleman cooler.

Liz wore oversized blackout glasses, and her hair was braided into jaunty pigtails. Her lips were painted bright red. "This is Juliette's husband," Liz said, gesturing to a bearded lumberjack of a man and a ginger-haired woman with shoulder-length coils of curls. "This is Jeanne and Jim."

Ben shook Jim's massive hand and introduced himself as Lord Benjamin.

"Really?" Shira said flatly. "My husband is a lord now?"

"Ben is fine," Ben said, shaking Jeanne's hand.

Neither Jeanne nor Jim were very attractive, and Ben was thankful for that. Liz sat crosslegged between them, pink hotpants revealing a large mermaid tattoo on her inner thigh. Jim's hand rested across the mermaid's luminescent midriff. Jeanne caressed Liz's neck with delicate stroking motions.

Ben could have been walking on the Esplanade with Pamela, holding her hand, kissing her before the Arthur Fiedler Statue as sailboats glided past on the Charles River. It was a perfect, cloudless day; it would have been a perfect day.

Ben turned to Shira, and she looked away. She was in crisis, and Ben understood exactly how she felt. Maybe it was time they went home.

"Jim was going to tell us about his dream," Liz said.

"Oh, it's not worth repeating," Jim said, forking some potato salad into his mouth. "Just the usual Jungian nonsense."

"Where's the bathroom?" Shira said, voice flat.

"There's a stand of Porto-Potties over by the parking lot," Jeanne said.

Shira slipped on her sandals, jumped to her feet and headed off across the lawn. Ben excused himself, saying he had to go as well, and followed after Shira. Her arms flailed at her sides as she tried to put as much distance as she could between her and the three lovers laughing together on the Navajo blanket.

Ben caught up with her and grabbed her shoulder. Shira spun away, and Ben stepped in front of her. Shira's eyes were raw with tears. "I'm feeling really stabby right now. Please leave me alone." She tried to look away, but Ben took her face in his hands and kissed her softly, holding her until her ragged breathing eased.

"Why don't they just put a fucking collar on her?" Shira wiped her eyes with a knotted little fist. "The whole thing just squicks me out."

"You knew they were going to be here," Ben said.

"I did. And I was stupid to come. I can't love on a schedule, turn my feelings on and off when it's not my day. I can't sit there and feel like I don't matter."

"You know that's not true," Ben said.

"It is today."

"I'm sure Liz is not trying to hurt you."

"She's not trying at all. She belongs to them today. She is their plaything." Shira was full-on crying now. "Why does it have to be so hard?"

"What?"

"Everything. Why is there so much pain in love?"

"Because it is the only thing that matters."

Shira looked up at Ben with her big, damp eyes, and she looked so pretty, blinking away a final tear, that Ben wanted to give her everything. The only way he could help fix her was if she faced Liz and worked things out. Ben smiled at Shira—at least he thought he did—and said, "Let's get you cleaned up and head back to the barbecue. I still haven't eaten a thing."

Ben took Shira's hand in his, their fingers perfectly interlaced, like two jigsaw pieces clicking into place. The urgency of Shira's breathing had subsided, the blood pumping through her veins in sync with Ben's. He wondered whether Shira really understood that the way she felt right now about Liz and her triad partners was how he had felt about her and Liz for the entire year and two months of their relationship.

"You know what you've always told me about jealousy," Ben said. "It's a societal construct. It's something we can unlearn. If we choose not to validate it, it loses its power entirely."

Shira went silent for a moment, eyes closed, lips firm. "I'm sorry, Ben. I lied. I lied because it was easier for me to believe it was up to you to control your jealousy about me and Liz. I was selfish and I'm sorry."

"You're sorry?"

189

"It wasn't fair to put that burden back on you. You have no idea how guilty I felt leaving you alone while I ran off to see Liz. But the heart wants what it wants, and making believe jealousy was your responsibility made the guilt so much easier to bear. You should have seen your face every time I walked out the door. Do you know how many times I sat in our driveway, key in the ignition, upset because I knew how badly I was hurting you? And still I turned the key and drove to Jamaica Plain. I couldn't help myself. I just had to."

Shira's eyes misted over with a sympathetic sheen of tears.

"Thank you. Thank you for telling me that."

"I'm a coward," Shira said. "I'm a hypocrite."

"No. You're a human being, and you are my love. You are my love forever."

Shira kissed Ben and said, "*Ani LeDodi VeDodi Li.*"

I am my Beloved's and my Beloved is mine.

As soon as Ben and Shira situated themselves on the Navajo blanket, Liz slid over beside Shira and said, "You were gone a long time. We were going to start without you."

Jim's pile of crushed Narragansett ale cans spread out on the Navajo blanket had multiplied from two to three.

"Start what?" Ben asked.

"Just an old-fashioned game of Kill, Fuck, Marry," Jim said, picking his teeth with the tines of a plastic fork. Then he swigged back a long draught of beer. "So, we will start with Moses, Jesus and Buddha."

Ben and Shira could have left, just kept walking on to the parking lot, gotten in their car and driven anywhere they wanted, but it was too late now.

"Oh God," Liz said.

"You can say that again," Shira said.

"Nothing is sacred to Jim," Jeanne added. "He's a lapsed everything."

"So, I was an altar boy," Jim said. "But that was a long, long time ago. Now, who wants to go first?"

"I'll go." Liz untangled herself from Shira. Her sunglasses sat perched on top of her head, and her blue eyes glittered. "I'd kill Jesus, because we all know he's coming back to life."

"Praise the Lord, we have a believer," Jim said in a rough approximation of a Southern preacher's voice.

"I'd fuck Moses because he's got an angry God behind him, and I'd marry Buddha because he'd let me be what I need to be."

"Bravo!" Jim clapped his meaty hands together.

"That was really good," Shira said, kissing Liz.

Ben reached out a hand for Shira and she took it in hers. He didn't need her to kiss him too, but he needed something more, and his mind flipped over to all the things he and Pamela could be doing at that moment. He loved the way she kissed, how she teased him, her glittering green eyes so intent on him, only him.

"All right, I'll go next," Jim said. "I'd kill Moses because Charlton Heston wants me to pry his gun from his cold, dead hands."

"Yes," Jeanne cheered. "Fuck the NRA."

"Um," Liz said. "He said kill, not fuck."

"You're a clever one," Jeanne responded.

"I'd marry Jesus because of Christians and their never-ending hard on against gay marriage. And I'd fuck Buddha tantrically, until I attain Buddha-hood or the next best thing."

Ben hated everything about Jim—his arrogance, his swaggering confidence, his smug leering eyes. What could Jeanne and Liz possibly see in him? Ben felt himself shrinking in the presence of this giant of a man who, even as he pontificated, had slobbish crumbs of food in his beard.

Shira said she would marry Moses because he was a nice Jewish boy, and that without him there would be no Jewish people. She said she would fuck Jesus because she had seen him practically naked, portrayed in countless paintings through the ages as a sinewy, blue-eyed, bearded rock star, part God, part man, all passion. And, unlike most men, who cum only once, he's supposed to come again.

"Hallelujah," Liz said. "Praise the man who doesn't roll over and go to sleep after he comes."

"And why would you marry Buddha?" Jim pressed, leaning forward in anticipation.

"Because Leonard Cohen is an ordained Buddhist monk, and anybody who wouldn't marry Leonard Cohen is out of their fucking mind."

"Damn, he's still hot," Liz said. "I don't care that he's dead. I'd still jump his bones."

Leonard Cohen had sung Ben and Shira's wedding song, the slow, spiritual "Hallelujah." At the time Ben knew that song would be his and Shira's forever. Shira's joking answer now about marrying Leonard Cohen corrupted that memory, a moment Ben had held close and cherished for nearly ten years. Their life together was no longer just theirs but something cheap to be put on public display for simple shits and giggles.

Jeanne went next. She said she would have Jesus, Moses and Buddha all marry each other in the name of world peace. Their ecstatic, divine fucking would move mountains, shake the very foundations of the earth and obliterate the need for anyone to ever kill again.

"The answer to all strife and chaos," Ben asked, "is polyamorous polytheism?"

"Damn straight it is," Jim said. "Jeanne is a true believer."

"But, isn't love difficult for everyone?" Ben responded.

"I feel sorry for you that you see love that way. Love is not a confrontation to be endured; true love is the termination of doubt, the end of suffering, not the beginning."

"That just sounds horribly naive. That may be a beautiful theory, but it's not the way things work in the real world." How was this all going to work with him and Pamela and Shira and Liz? Two children, one father, three mothers, and wildly differing needs. Now this bloviating fool at the far end of the Ben/Shira/Liz Venn diagram was feeling sorry for Ben. This was too much, too fucking much. The chain of love was long enough already without having to endure Jim's preaching.

"Just let it rest," Liz interjected. "It's just a game. It doesn't matter."

"It's way more than just a game. He's out of touch with his true feelings. He's afraid to let go of his fears and really love."

"Don't talk about me like I'm not here," Ben said. "I'm really not your concern."

Shira filled the space at his side, her soft voice in his ear. "It's all right. We all know he's being a jerk," she whispered. "Just know that I love you."

Ben had felt intimidated by Jim from the moment he laid eyes on his ostentatious hipster beard, from the bone-crushing handshake to his savage wit and otherworldly self-assurance. And why wouldn't he trust in himself when he was fucking two of the three women arrayed on the blanket around him?

"I want to hear what he has to say about Moses, Jesus and Buddha," Jim said, finishing his can of Narragansett and starting in on a new can.

Ben shook his head no.

"Come on, let's hear from Lord Benjamin the Silent."

"Stop," Shira said. "You're being—"

"Let's play something else," Liz interjected.

"It's his turn," Jim said. "He's got a mouth, he should use it."

"No," Ben said. "I don't feel like it."

"And you always follow your feelings? Don't you have any say in the matter?"

"I just don't want to," Ben said.

"Oh ho." Jim laughed. "You're going to take your ball and go home. Is that it?"

"Enough with the dick swinging, Jim."

It was Liz speaking. And though he felt Shira's hand caressing the small of his back, Liz's words made Ben feel there was nothing wrong with him and that Jim's words were just the barbed words of a bully, not an indictment of self.

"It's the Fourth of July weekend and we are having a grand old American time, and he is spoiling our fun because your girlfriend's husband is too sensitive to play a simple party game."

"No," Liz said. "You're spoiling it. And he's not just my girlfriend's husband. I'm going to carry his child."

"What?" Jim said, his face slack with shock, eyes narrowed as he took in Ben anew. "You're going to have a baby? His baby?"

"Yup."

"And you didn't tell us?"

"I'm telling you now."

"Wow," Jeanne said, a hesitant half-smile on her face. "That's wonderful."

"And what about us?" Jim asked, arms crossed over his broad chest in a defensive gesture.

"What about you?"

"What if me and Jeanne want to have a baby?"

"I'm pretty sure you know how that works."

"And if I wanted you to have my baby?"

"I would tell you no."

Jeanne filled the silence, asking if anybody wanted a ripe plum. "They're washed," she added.

"Birdy, come on," Jim said, his voice throaty and vulnerable for the first time. "I thought you were our bitch."

"I'm not anyone's bitch. What I am in the bedroom is what I am in the bedroom, that's it."

A long moment passed before Jim spoke again, the cold can of beer perspiring in his hand.

"I know that. I do."

"We both love you so much," Jeanne said. "You're the light of our lives."

"You know there's no shape stronger than a triangle. We need you."

"Really?" Liz said. "And my having a baby threatens you how?"

Jim's bearing had entirely altered, eyes downcast, voice small. "We just want you."

"I'm sure we have room for your baby," Jeanne said.

"You're never going to meet my baby," Ben said. "That is a firm boundary."

Jim looked at Liz with eyes that seemed to ask *is this true?*

Liz nodded her head.

"I love you both, but having a baby has nothing to do with you or how I feel about you. What I do with my other partners is entirely my own concern. I'm sorry if this inconveniences you, I really am."

"I can't dom you if you're pregnant. What if something happens?" Jim said.

"Then don't," Liz said. "If that's the way it has to be."

"I just wish—"

"Wish what?" Liz said. "That I was just a body, an object?"

"You know it's not that way, sweetie," Jeanne said.

Shira leapt to her feet. "I think we need to be heading back now."

Ben immediately followed Shira's lead, his vision narrowing to a star-spun pinprick before resolving into a woozy lightheadedness. He needed to eat something.

"Oh," Jeanne said. "You're not going to stick around for the raffle? The grand prize is a double ended dildo or an evening in Mistress Genevieve's dungeon."

Shira flashed Liz a knowing look saying *now or never*. "I'm good on the dildo. And we want to beat traffic."

Liz sat frozen, tattooed hands fumbling in her lap, surrounded by her lovers.

"Oh, that's too bad," Jeanne said with surprising sincerity. "It was nice to meet you both. And congratulations."

Jim stared at Liz, an icy, hurt look in his glazed eyes.

Ben could feel Shira cringe as she squeezed his hand, pulling him with Olympian strength towards the parking lot.

"Can you believe the chutzpah?" Shira said, when they were out of earshot. "It's like they think Liz cares about them the same way Liz cares about me."

Ben understood that misapprehension well.

They had reached the middle of the lawn, and Shira had not stopped seething that Liz had stayed behind with Jeanne and Jim.

"Can you believe her?" Shira said. "She should be here with us now."

"Maybe I just want to be with you. That's all I ever wanted before all this craziness began."

"Please, Ben. Can't you see I'm hurting?"

"I'm sorry. I need to know you love me."

"Of course I do, Ben."

"Then say it for me. I need you to say it now."

Shira threw her hands in the air, exasperated. "I love you, I love you, I love you, I love you, I love you, I love you. Got it? I fucking love you."

"If you could marry Liz, would you?"

"I'm married to you, Ben."

"That doesn't answer my question. Do you love Liz as much as you love me?"

"What kind of question is that? Do you love Pamela as much as you love me?"

There beneath the hot sun, Ben knew there was only one answer, only one thing he could say that would elicit the response he needed. "Of course not. I love you. I always have and I always will."

Shira smiled wistfully and opened her mouth to respond when they heard Liz calling from the far end of the lawn, "Hey, wait up!"

Liz ran towards them at a surprisingly quick clip, arms pumping at her sides. "Can I catch a ride back with you?"

17

Pamela texted Ben three days later, breezily asking him to come over. She had not responded to any of his messages since the BDSM picnic, and Ben knew she was upset. But Pamela was calling now, so Ben jumped in his car, picked up a dozen roses and drove to Beacon Hill.

Pamela opened her apartment door wearing a light summer dress. It had only been a few days since they had seen each other but there was something different about Pamela. Ben could just make out a vague strawberry patch around the wings of her nose where Pamela had tried to cover up a subtle burst of rosacea with one of her expensive masking creams.

"I've been spotting," Pamela said, a husky rasp to her voice.

Ben's whole body went ice cold and he dropped the flowers, gathering Pamela into an embrace. "What?"

"Just some blood in my underwear. The Internet machine says it's not a big deal. Otherwise it's cancer, but it's always cancer."

"What do you mean, it's not a big deal? This could be a huge deal."

"Stop, Ben. I'm freaking out, okay? I need you to be strong for me."

"What's your doctor's number? I'll call right now."

"It's just a light flow, nothing like menstrual blood. It's pretty common during the first trimester. It should go away in a few days, but in the meantime I am really goddamned scared and there's always, 'What if it gets worse?' I can't lose this baby."

"Of course not. What do you need me to do?"

"Just stay with me a while. Be with me. I'm scared. I can't do this alone. I hate to say this, but I need you, Ben, I need you."

Ben followed Pamela to her bedroom and lay beside her on the bed. She rested her head on his chest, sighing deeply. "What am I going to do?"

"You're going to have this baby."

"Yes, but then what? When it comes down to it, I really am alone."

Ben sucked in a deep breath and gritted his teeth. "You're upset I went to the picnic. I get it. Believe me, there's nothing I would've rather done then spend the day with you."

"Those words don't mean anything. Don't you understand? You didn't respond to my text. I was trying to show you how much I love you even though I was sad you went to the picnic. I was trying to be an adult, trying to be accepting, trying to show you I understand that you're free to do things without me, and you just left me hanging."

"Which text? I always answer your texts."

"Keats' letter to Fanny Brawne."

Ben had no idea what she was talking about.

Pamela spoke now in that formal Ivy League English major tone, almost stagy in its crispness. "I almost wish we were butterflies and liv'd but three summer days—three such days with you I could fill with more delight than 50 common years could ever contain."

"I saw it and it was lovely, and I responded as soon as I could," Ben said. "I was driving back from the picnic."

Shira was in the passenger seat beside him, Liz in the backseat, the three of them deconstructing the mess of that afternoon through a whirl of accusations, apologies and promises to be more mindful moving forward.

"*Home now. Tired* is not a response. I was trying to be loving and you dismissed me. You need to do better than that if I'm going to be carrying your child. Much better. I refuse to do this alone."

After Ben had dropped off Liz in Jamaica Plain, he and Shira had gone home and made love, palliatively, almost regretfully, as if to acknowledge that the state of their relationship had passed beyond their control.

"I'm sorry," Ben said. "I messed up. What can I do right now to make things right?"

"Just kiss me. I need to be close to you."

They kissed and their teeth clacked together, and Ben gathered Pamela into his arms, heart pounding as if they were kissing for the first time. He brushed some hair from her eyes and kissed her face, fingers tracing along the pulsing vein in her neck, hands sweeping in slow concentric circles around her breasts, lightly pinching her left nipple.

"Ouch," Pamela said.

"Sorry," Ben said. "I forgot."

"It's okay." Pamela rolled onto her back. "I'm hating my body right now."

"Don't do that. What you're doing right now is a beautiful—"

"Just stop with that. I don't need a lecture right now on the wonders of motherhood."

They lay in silence together, and Ben tensed up again, wondering what he was supposed to do. He knew Pamela wanted him to give her pleasure but he didn't know how. He slid his hand down between her legs, and Pamela gripped his wrist. He stopped, shifting his arms stiffly to his sides.

"What's it like to kiss Shira?"

"It's nice," Ben said, doubtfully.

"Nice how?"

"Do you really want me to tell you? I like it. I don't know, it just feels like kissing."

Pamela squirmed up onto one elbow, scrutinizing him with a soft expression on her face.

"What magic does she have that I don't have? Is it just that you've known her a long time? Is that it? She's an old habit you can't kick?"

"That's not fair."

"Please, please, please, please don't tell me about fair."

"I'm sorry, but you asked."

"I'm the double caramel ice-cream sundae in your life. I'm that sweet treat you get to look forward to when your life gets you down."

"That's not it. You know that's not it."

"Everything I get from you is secondhand, your kisses, your tried and true techniques. Was it Shira who taught you to focus on the clit when you go down on me? Was she the one who set your rhythm when you make love? I want something that's just for me, something you've never done with Shira. Just for me. Just for me." Pamela's voice trailed off.

"All right," Ben said. "I want to give myself to you. I don't want to hold anything back."

Pamela's eyes lit up. "Thank you. I want to give you an experience you've never had before. I want us to explore together. You went to that picnic and I asked myself why I was being so timid with you. Why I didn't just come out and ask you. Because I know you will enjoy this."

Pamela reached behind her and opened her dresser drawer, producing a glossy black oblong box roughly the size of a hardcover book. "I used to do this with Dane and he loved it. It just totally made him go off."

Dane had been Pamela's boyfriend for three years after graduate school. They had tried living together in a sort of engaged-to-be-engaged situation, which broke down not long after Pamela realized he was an inveterate slob who was unable to respect her need for an orderly living space. But he had been her longest-lasting boyfriend, so it was only natural they had tasted more at the sexual buffet table than she and Ben could have in their brief time together.

"So, yes?" Pamela said. "I need you to trust me."

"I do trust you."

Pamela lifted the top off the box and produced a pink rubbery item that resembled a moderate-sized rubber penis about the size of his own. Ben was pretty sure he knew what Pamela wanted to do with it, and his butt cheeks clenched protectively.

"You like it when I stick my finger in your ass. Don't you, Ben?"

"In the moment, I guess I do, but this is—"

"No different. Maybe a little bigger, but it will feel so good. I promise you."

"I believe you. I'm open to trying it for you."

"Not just for me. For you."

Pamela reached into her dresser drawer and removed a small plastic tube. She unscrewed the cap, squeezed, and applied the clear jelly to the dildo.

"Take your clothes off. Let's do this."

"Now?"

"Strip," Pamela ordered, and began salaciously humming the tune of "The Stripper."

Ben reluctantly climbed off the bed. He hated to be on display. He had definitely never done this with Shira, but if he wanted to keep Pamela there needed to be a healthy give-and-take. Only this time, he had to meet her more than halfway. He slipped off his pants joylessly and Pamela cheered him on. "Come on, you sexy man."

Ben had never felt less sexy. He stood naked before Pamela, his penis flapping dismally against his thigh. Pamela climbed down off the bed, sank to her knees and began working him with her mouth. It wasn't long before he was rock hard and ready to go.

"Up on the bed," Pamela said. "On your hands and knees."

Pamela remained fully dressed, and something about this imbalance, his nakedness against the armor of her clothing, stirred something in him.

"I'll start with one finger," Pamela said. "I know you like that."

"Wait," Ben said.

"I'll take it slow, I promise. Just know that I love you and we are doing this together, for each other."

Ben could never imagine himself allowing Shira to do this to him, but she had seen him on the toilet in the morning more than once, and that removed any mystery there may have been about what went on back there.

At first, Ben felt a sharp pain as it entered. He cried out and considered telling Pamela to stop.

"Shhhhh," Pamela soothed. "The pain will pass."

Pamela held it in place, just the tip, as his muscles relaxed and the toy slipped all the way inside him.

"Let's just hold it there for a moment," Pamela said. "Nice and easy. You're doing a great job."

Ben had to pee and was afraid he might lose control of his bladder with all this pressure building in him, but it was a temporary sensation, replaced quickly by something close to pleasure. Pamela pushed it farther in, and Ben felt a terrible pang in his belly, shifting his innards. It was inside him now, all the way.

"Feel good?" Pamela asked. "So many raw nerve endings."

"Yes. I just feel sort of filled up,"

"You see? This is good. I knew you could handle this. Now I'm going to fuck your ass until you beg me to stop."

Ben's temples were sweating now, his mouth dry as Pamela slowly slid the toy back and forth, her rhythm increasing with each stroke. Pamela's body was pressed up behind Ben's, encircling his torso, his hips, fingers caressing his clammy skin. Pamela rested her head against the warmth of Ben's back so he could feel her breath tickling his shoulder blade.

She whispered, "You like this?"

"Yes," Ben said. "Yes, yes, yes, yes, yes."

Her motions sped up, and she was pounding Ben the way he pounded her, and he belonged to Pamela, he belonged to her like he had never belonged to anyone before. Ben took himself in hand and stroked himself as Pamela fucked his ass, until he came, emptying himself of all his worries, fears and doubts, collapsing in a warm puddle of sweat and funk, the most intense wave of love washing over him. Pamela had taken him to a place he had never been before, never even imagined possible.

"You want to know how much I love you?" Pamela said. "That's how much I love you."

18

Shira's parents were in town for a performance her father was giving that week at Temple Israel and insisted Shira and Ben join them for dinner at Smith & Wollensky. Ben wasn't looking forward to another lecture on *terroir* and the robust grapes of the Bordeaux region, but Shira was excited to see them for the first time since they'd visited them in Bethesda for Chanukah.

"We can tell them in person we're going to be having a baby," Shira said, carefully applying earth-tone lipstick to her parted lips.

Something ominous stirred in Ben's gut, like a shark circling.

When he did not respond quickly enough, Shira caught his eye in the reflection in the bathroom mirror. "What?" she said, flatly.

"Shouldn't we wait until this is an actual? You know, until we're farther along?"

"Why should we wait until the High Holidays or Thanksgiving when nothing would make my parents happier than knowing right now that we are on our way to starting our family? This is a good thing, Ben. Let's not be stingy with it."

"I hear you." Ben tightened the half Windsor at his neck and said, "I'll drive."

The restaurant was in the Back Bay Castle across from the Park Plaza where Shira's parents stayed whenever they were in town. Shira's parents stood to greet Ben and Shira with a firm handshake from Cantor Weissmann, and a whispered air kiss from Shira's mother, Barbara Sachs-Weissmann.

"You kids look great," Cantor Weissmann said, his voice deep and resonant. He slid back into the leather banquette, gesturing expansively. "Sit, please sit."

Shira's father was about five foot eight and solidly built, with a broad chest and strong shoulders. He wore a tailored navy three-piece pinstripe suit with a conservative blue tie. Cantor Weissmann nodded his great leonine head with satisfaction from the sumptuous comfort of the banquette as his children arranged themselves across from him and his wife. Ben pulled his chair close to Shira and reached for her hand. But Shira didn't even wait for the waiter to take their orders before she said, "There's something we want to tell you."

"Really?" Barbara raised an eyebrow uncertainly. She was taller than her husband, elegant and severe and whip-fit, in a scoop-neck black dress, a simple silver brooch pinned above her heart. "What is it, darling?"

"Listen," Cantor Weissmann said, "why don't we order some wine and take our time with whatever it is you want to tell us. This isn't a drive-through on the interstate."

"You just think people are tedious and dull," Shira said, "without a glass of wine in your hand."

"You said it, not I." Cantor Weissmann laughed, his florid silver-goateed face full of life. He grabbed a waiter passing by and said in a stage voice, "Send us your sommelier."

"Right away, sir."

Cantor Weissmann turned his attention back to Ben and Shira and said, "I'm inclined towards a nervy red tonight, maybe a Chilean Malbec. But you are our guests, so why don't you tell me what you're in the mood for."

"As long as it's got alcohol," Shira said.

"Come on," Cantor Weissmann said, rapping his thick knuckles on the white tablecloth, his gold signet ring glistening. "Indulge an old man. Ben, what say you?"

"I wouldn't exactly say you're old; more of a certain vintage."

Cantor Weissmann laughed, but prodded Ben for an answer, waving his powerful hand to go on, tell him what he was in the mood for.

"Joel," Barbara Sachs-Weissmann said, "believe it or not, not everyone shares your passion. Even after all these years I'd still prefer a strong gin and tonic. Maybe the kids might want to order for themselves."

"Wine is my weakness," Cantor Weissmann said. "You can hardly blame me for that."

"Wine is fine," Shira said. "Red, white, blue, it doesn't matter."

"All right then. I'll choose something friendly and accessible we can all enjoy."

"So, the concert tomorrow night?" Ben asked. "What are you going to be singing?"

Cantor Weissmann jutted his jaw out just a bit. "This showcase will be entirely different than anything you've seen me do before. The songs will not be from liturgy or scripture, but from the Jewish-American songbook."

"Joel's agent thinks he has a chance to go mainstream, taking on the standards with that voice. He's proposing a CD and a national tour."

"Barbara, please," Cantor Weissmann said. "*Kein ayin hora.*" Then he turned his thick neck away from the table, mock spitting, "*Tfu, tfu, tfu.*"

"Daddy, that's great news," Shira said. "Who's on the playlist? Please say Adam Lambert. Oooh, or Adam Levine!"

"Everything begins with George and Ira Gershwin and Irving Berlin. Then Rogers and Hart, Jerome Kern, Sondheim, of course, then, for the youngsters, Neil Diamond, Carole King, Paul Simon—"

The wine steward, an attractive young black woman with short-cropped hair, in a shirt and tie and apron, appeared before them. "So nice to see you again, Cantor Weissmann."

He turned his head to the woman and said, without returning her greeting, "Did you ever track down the 2011 Domaine Armand Rousseau?"

"I can check into that," she said.

"Some clown at Morton's in Manhattan tried to sneak a 2012 past me. Everyone knows 2012 was too hot to produce a credible Pinot Noir."

"I'll tell you what," she said, with a sassy toss of her head. "I'll surprise you. You won't be disappointed. I promise."

Shira's cheeks were flushed after she downed her first glass of wine and Ben reached for her hand under the table—*slow down*—but she batted it away.

"So," Shira said, leaning forward. "Daddy? Mom?"

That got Shira's parents' attention. Barbara sat up just a little straighter, unconsciously fixing her hair. Cantor Weissmann said, "If I have Orelie pour you another glass would you promise not to guzzle it like a cup of punch at a sorority mixer?"

"We're going to have a baby!" Shira said.

"That's wonderful," Barbara said, her face positively glowing, as if a lightbulb had just flicked on. "I just knew it."

"How," Cantor Weissmann said, choosing his words carefully, "is this going to happen?"

"We have found the perfect surrogate who is going to carry our child," Shira said.

"Going to?" Cantor Weissmann said, twisting his signet ring on his pinky finger.

"Daddy, I thought you'd be happy. You're going to be a *zayde*."

"You're okay with this, using a stranger's eggs? There won't even be any part of you or me or your mother in this child. You have no idea what you might end up with."

"Jesus fucking Christ, Daddy. Can't you just be happy for me and Ben? This is what we want."

Ben had been afraid of such a reaction from his father-in-law, who questioned everything like the Grand Inquisitor and made everything somehow about him and his good name. He could be so exhausting, and Ben just wanted to take the heat down a bit so Shira could have her moment. He hated to have to bring this up in public, in front of his in-laws. "Joel, we will be using my sperm." The waiter had just stopped by their table, but quickly wheeled away. "And we, me and your daughter, will be raising this child. All of Shira's values and beliefs will be passed on to the child, everything she ever learned from you and Barbara."

"The Torah recounts the story of Hagar and Abraham and Sarai," Cantor Weissmann said.

"You're not actually going to bring up Ishmael, are you?" Shira said, her voice rising so the corporate blue shirts at the next table turned their heads. "So much for pluralism and free will and the belief that I can actually raise this child—"

"I'm sure the surrogate has been carefully screened," Barbara said, placing a calming hand atop her husband's. "I'm sure the surrogate has passed a psychological screening and that she is healthy physically. There's usually a very rigorous process. Of course, she's already given birth to at least one healthy baby, so the surrogate will be an old hand at this. And there will be a contract so the surrogate doesn't try and make a claim ex post facto on the child as her own."

Shira looked defiantly at her parents. "I don't think I'm hungry." She moved to get up but her knees hit the table, jostling the wineglasses and the silverware.

"Simmer down, Shira. You're not going anywhere," Cantor Weissmann said, trying to reel her back in. "It's my job as your father to make sure you see this from all angles and think about what sorts of problems you might run into. This is no time to be a Pollyanna."

"Can't you just be happy for me, for us?"

"What will my being happy for you do for the baby? Happiness is an emotion that blinds reason. What you are considering—"

"We are not *considering*," Shira interrupted. "We are *doing* it. The considering part is over."

"All right," Cantor Weissmann said. "What you are *doing* will have consequences that will echo down the generations."

"Oh please," Shira said. "Save me the sermon."

"I'm sure," Ben said, "you will love this child and care about it as much as if it came from Shira's own womb."

There was a long silence. Barbara sat frozen, her delicate hands resting stiffly on the white tablecloth. Cantor Weissmann's left eyelid fluttered involuntarily as he stared hard at Ben, worrying his lower lip with his ashy incisors.

"Of course, Barbara and I will love our first grandchild and he or she will be a blessing to you and your parents' memory," Cantor Weissmann said.

"Thank you," Ben said, his throat thickening. If only his parents had been alive for this conversation.

"There should be no doubt in your minds that we will treat this child as our own."

Barbara smiled a grateful smile. She could be really quite pretty when she allowed her severe demeanor to melt away, and Ben saw something in her face that reminded him why he loved Shira. But Cantor Weissmann, who had many thoughts and opinions to share about everything, was not done.

"The problem is the fact that we are, as of now, committed to loving this creature who comes into the world not tabula rasa, but with flaws and deficiencies and tendencies of the surrogate who provides the eggs. Who knows what traps are hidden in her DNA?"

"I think we'd better stop talking right now and order some food," Shira said sharply, "before I say how that sounds suspiciously like eugenics to me, and how ironic it is that a man whose parents escaped the Third Reich would rely on a racist, debunked theory rather than just wish me and Ben well as we begin our journey as parents."

Cantor Weissmann flushed, stunned as he stammered out, "Shira Tziporah, my songbird, you have to know that's not what I meant."

"Fine," Shira said. "I want a big steak. And I want it bloody."

The rest of the dinner passed without incident. Cantor Weissmann recovered sufficiently to recount the time he sang the national anthem at Camden Yards with a case of laryngitis. "It was during Cal Ripken Junior's last season, and the stadium was packed to say farewell to a hometown legend, and I had no voice. It was comical to hear, wasn't it Barbara?"

"I begged you to postpone, to reschedule."

"This was my chance to meet the most durable player in the history of baseball. You think I'd cancel after all the injuries he played through? I tried apple cider vinegar, gargled warm salt water, peroxide, honey, lemon juice, even onion syrup, of all the fakakta things. And something in that magical combination kicked in not five minutes before I was due on the field and I belted out the Star-Spangled Banner like I've never done before. It was a tremendous performance. Cal Ripken signed a baseball for me that said: *To the Man with the Big voice. Best #8.*"

In the end, they all ate and drank and had a fairly good time, hearing every detail of Shira's parents' recent mission to Israel, augmented by a lengthy iPhone slideshow. They never did return to the subject of their prospective child, and that was probably for the best, Ben thought. They said their goodbyes in the street, hugs all around, and Cantor Weissmann said, "We will see you tomorrow night. Just give your names at the door—say you're my special guests."

Shira's face dropped as soon as they had crossed the street. "Fuck," she said. "Fuck, fuck, fuck. I don't know what I expected. I don't even know why I wanted his approval."

"Because he's your father. Just be grateful he's in your life. He doesn't disapprove. He's just being cautious."

"Crap," she said. "Just crap."

Ben pulled Shira into an embrace, resting his chin on the top of her head, and she briefly melted into him. "Liz wants to meet us for drinks at Lolita Cocina." Ben wasn't ready to drive and was going to suggest a walk around the Public Garden until he sobered up, but he was curious to see how Shira delivered the news to Liz.

Liz sat in the elbow of an L-shaped couch in a dark corner, sipping a frozen margarita out of a salt-rimmed glass. Her hair was down, the pink ends freshly dyed, thick black eyeliner at her eyes, her lips a glossy shade of coral. She wore a tank top with a picture of The Powerpuff Girls on it and a knee-length tube skirt, hiked up enough to see the octopus tattoo on her right thigh.

"Hey, you," she called, raising a beringed hand in the air and gesturing for them to hurry up and sit the fuck down. "I couldn't wait," she said, kissing Shira, who sat between them, and then, more awkwardly,

Ben. "So, I started without you. I'm three drinks in. Who's up for mezcal shots? I ordered one for each of us."

Ben said he had to drive, so seltzer was good for him, but Shira said she'd drink Ben's shot for him.

"Oh no," Liz said, putting on a pouty face. "What happened?"

"He just doesn't get it. It's like he holds me personally responsible for my hysterectomy."

"What happened?" Liz said, hand on Shira's thigh. Ben mirrored her gesture and placed his own hand on Shira's other thigh.

"Was it me?" Liz said. "He didn't approve of me, did he? Like I'm just some queer, tatted *shiksa*."

Shira leaned in to kiss Liz, but Liz pressed Shira, "What did he say?"

"I didn't mention you," Shira said, after an agonizing stretch of time.

"Wait, what?" Liz said, visibly stunned, her eyes wide, mouth slightly agape, the silver ball in her tongue visible.

"It never came up."

"What exactly did you tell your parents?"

The mezcal shots appeared, and Shira snatched hers up and drank it down without even squeezing the lime slice into it.

"I'm sorry, babe. I fucked up," Shira said.

Liz flung Shira's hand off her thigh and just stared at her, unblinking as she gathered herself. "I don't even know what to say. I feel like I've just been kicked in the balls."

"Shira's father is not the easiest person," Ben said.

"Let me get this straight," Liz said. "You met your parents for dinner to tell them about the surrogacy and you didn't even bother to tell them about me, your fucking girlfriend, who, by the way has been taking estrogen and progesterone for weeks to prepare my uterus for your baby. I mean, fuck that noise."

Liz had been taking hormones for weeks? Ben suddenly felt ill.

"What exactly did you tell them?" Liz pressed, chewing on the end of an acrylic nail. "Tell me what you said to them."

"I told them," Shira said, "we had found a surrogate willing to carry our child."

"And?"

"And he started bombarding me with all these questions. I'm sorry. I never had the chance to mention you."

"Oh," Liz said. "That's better. It just slipped your mind. You forgot your girlfriend offered up her fucking uterus because she loves you so god damn much she'd do anything short of murder for you."

"I'm sorry," Shira said, crying sloppy, drunken tears; her face a smear of anguish. "What do you want me to do?"

"I know adulting is hard, but you need to make this right," Liz said, her voice steady. "Or else I walk. I mean it."

Shira's eyes grew big and she sniffled, she actually sniffled.

"That means no baby and that means no me. It's over. You'll never see these fine tits again. I'll just bolt. For real."

In that moment Ben wanted nothing more than for Shira and Liz to split, so he could have Shira all to himself, the way things were supposed to be. He'd wished for this moment so many heartsick times, and now it was playing out before his eyes; a careless response, a misunderstood gesture, and it was over; it was that close to happening. The energy crackling around the three of them had changed so profoundly that Ben could envision in precise detail a future without Liz Bird in it, and he understood, as if struck by summer lightning, that if Liz left Shira, really walked away for good, Shira would be alone with no chance for a child, a crucial filament of connection between Ben and Shira severed, while he and Pamela grew closer as Pamela bore his child. In a logical world, there would be nothing holding Ben back from giving himself to Pamela, to raise their child together. How could he justify not giving himself full-time to Pamela and her baby? It would be the right thing to do. But he loved Shira so much his heart hurt, and Ben could imagine nothing more cruel, more devastating to Shira than for her to lose this chance at having a child while Ben moved on with Pamela and his child.

"We'll work this out," Ben said, trying to keep his voice calm. "Nobody's leaving anybody. You love each other. There's a solution to every problem."

"All right," Liz said. "Your move, Shira."

Shira blew her nose into a napkin, straightened herself up and said, "Well, there's only one thing to do, and that's for you to meet my parents."

19

Ben almost told Liz she cleaned up nicely when she showed up at his and Shira's front door the following evening wearing a simple black dress and nude stockings with a string of pearls, no cleavage, a pair of simple earrings in each ear, but he knew he would sound like some smug suburban jerk, so he just said, "Wow."

Her hair was swept into a complex updo, face clean, natural, barely made up—a modest red lipstick on her lips.

"Hey, Ben," Liz said, leaning in for a hug. Liz smelled of Shalimar, a perfume Ben's own mother used to wear on special occasions, and Ben, transported to another era, held onto the hug longer than he might otherwise have. Ben told Liz Shira was trying on a third outfit and promised not to come out until she had everything perfect for tonight.

"Well, I look forward to the reveal," Liz said, wandering into the living room in her modest black pumps. Ben asked Liz if she wanted a drink and Liz said yes please, please, please. "I'm so wigged out about tonight. You know what I mean?"

"It'll be fine," Ben said, trying to convince himself by vocalizing those words. "Cantor Weissmann loves his daughter, so he will love you."

Liz raised a skeptical eyebrow. How did Liz and Shira do that? *Black magic*, Ben thought, twitching his facial muscles to little effect.

"Does he love you?"

Liz's question caught Ben off guard and he stumbled. "I know he likes me. I mean I'm pretty sure he doesn't mind me."

"Make that a double," Liz said, laughing nervously.

"Don't worry, I'm like the son he never had." Ben poured two fingers of his best single malt, some twenty-five-year-old whiskey he could not pronounce.

"You're not going to join me?" Liz asked, fingering the glass. She had repainted her bubblegum pink nails a soft rose color. "A lady never drinks alone."

Ben laughed, wondering whether Liz should be drinking at all considering what she was trying to accomplish, but under the evening's circumstances he understood the urge. "I'm the designated driver, but I'd hate to scandalize. Pellegrino and lime is all right?"

"As long as you've got a glass to clink."

They raised their glasses and Ben, surprising himself, said, "To many wonderful years," because anything less would break Shira's heart.

"Aw, that was sweet," Liz said. She tossed back her glass and said, "Sláinte."

The bubbles of the sparkling water snapped in Ben's sinuses. "Can I ask you something?"

"Sure."

"Is there anything else I need to know? You and Shira. My place with you and Shira. I don't know," Ben said. "Other things, beyond hormone therapy, beyond—"

"I'm sorry, Ben," Liz said, face softening. "It's not Shira's fault. I started the hormone therapy on my own to show Shira how serious I was, to show her how much I love her."

"But she never told me. This is all happening behind my back."

"It's not nearly as sinister as it sounds. Shira knows how important being a father is to you. She hated the idea of letting you down. We wanted to make sure we were far enough along in the process before involving you, in case it didn't—I don't know—in case it didn't happen, so you wouldn't get your hopes up for nothing."

"You said we. Shira and me used to be a we. Now I'm an I and you're a we, and where does that leave me?"

Liz laughed or rather snorted, bright, quick and adorable. "You sound like Dr. Seuss."

Ben poured himself some brandy. "I'm afraid I'm losing her. Death by a thousand cuts."

"You're not losing her," Liz said. "Me and Shira work precisely because of you and her. Without you, we collapse."

"Why is that?"

"Because she loves you, because you are so much a part of her life. Because she'd be lost without you."

"That's not true. She seems fine without me."

"That's because you're there, because you have her back, because she trusts you with her life, no matter what happens. Don't ever forget that."

Ben sipped his brandy. "And without you, me and Shira collapse." Ben paused, considering. "Because of Pamela. And the baby."

"If that's the new math, I'd need a PhD to sort that one out." Liz's eyes looked so big. "But one thing I know is that we need each other. The three of us. And we need to be good to each other."

"I've been more than good to you," Ben said, his raspy voice run through with melancholy. "I've given space for my wife to love you."

"I know. What I mean is, I need to be good to you, to never leave you out of life decisions again." And now Liz crossed herself comically. "Cross my little black heart."

"You mean it?"

"Yes. I promise to be as good to you as you promise to be good to Shira."

Ben finished his drink and sank back into the couch.

"You can talk to me," Liz added. "You can ask me things. I'll be honest with you. I have nothing to hide, I promise."

The brandy was warm in Ben's belly, and his thoughts coalesced around Pamela and the package she had sent to his office that afternoon.

"I hope this doesn't offend you." Ben hesitated a long time, not sure he wanted to invite Liz further into his private world, but he knew he couldn't, shouldn't, share this sort of thing with Shira. It had been a long time since Ben had a friend to confide in. "You're sort of a sex person. You know, like in the scene, and I don't know—"

"Go ahead," Liz said. "Shoot."

Ben began in hushed tones, his voice so guarded Liz had to lean in closer. "The other night at Pamela's we tried something new, something, well, something

I never thought I'd do." Ben paused, half hoping he wouldn't have to say more, that he was being clear enough for Liz to respond accordingly. "Do you want another drink?"

"I'm not letting you off the hook that easy. I'm long past the days I could be bought for a drink or two. But yes, I want a damn drink."

"I shouldn't have said anything. Forget it."

"You're such a tease. Now go on. I won't judge. I promise."

"But Shira—" They could hear Shira behind the bedroom door singing Beyoncé's "Single Ladies." She most definitely did not have her father's voice.

"You know how long she takes to get ready." And they both laughed because Shira sometimes spent more time getting ready for an event than she did at the actual event.

"Pamela had this pink dildo thing and she wanted to put it in my, you know, and said it would make me feel good." Ben couldn't believe he was saying this out loud. "I had honestly never thought about doing such a thing."

"I get it," Liz said. "A lot of guys think it's gay for some reason, even though there's no actual dick involved, no other man in the room."

"Yeah, well, it was just the two of us." Ben had replayed that evening again and again through his mind, amazed by the sudden realization that he could receive sexual pleasure through more than just his dick.

"And? Did you do it?" Liz offered a warm anticipatory smile, the gap between her teeth prominent.

"Yeah." Ben smiled. "It felt good, like nothing I've ever experienced. But I feel strange because I did this amazing thing without Shira, and I don't even want her to know about it. I don't know what to do. I always thought we were supposed to share everything. We'd never do anything like this. It just feels … I don't know."

"Just because you're sharing a life together, doesn't mean you have to share everything," Liz said. "It's important for you to have some things just for you. It's important there's some mystery your partner will never know. It's not deception, it's human nature. If Shira knows every thought and feeling and experience you have, what incentive is there for her to keep trying to know you? The fact that parts of us are unknowable is what elevates love to the erotic."

"You're not going to tell her, are you?"

"Of course not, Ben. You shared this with me in confidence." Liz sipped her drink, decorously. "Believe it or not, I care about you."

"You do?" Ben was shocked to hear those words issue from his wife's lover's mouth. "Really?"

"You do know I'm going to be carrying your child, right?"

Ben looked at Liz, all dolled up on his and Shira's couch, pregaming to steel herself for meeting Shira's parents, and was suddenly overcome by laughter, his shoulders shaking, doubled over, tears flooding his eyes. "This is really happening, isn't it? This is my life!"

"It's our life now," Liz said, laughing.

"I never thought it would come to this."

"Aren't you glad it did? We're doing this together. I mean, what an adventure for us to share."

Together. Ben liked that word. Us. We.

"So, Pamela sent me a package yesterday. To my office. Can I show you?"

"Sure."

Ben opened the lid of a low wooden bench he and Shira had bought one Black Friday at Pier One. He fumbled through a tangle of woolen hats and scarves and produced a Gore-Tex glove nobody ever wore and slipped out a small beginners' butt plug he had hidden as soon as he got home. It was fire engine red, smooth in texture and tapered at one end, with a broad flange at its base. He quickly handed it to Liz as if he were passing off a baton in a relay race. "There was a note that said, *So I can be with you when I'm not with you. To be worn at my request.*"

Liz smiled softly as she turned the toy in her hands.

"She wants me to wear it tonight, to the concert."

"So." Liz leaned forward, tilting her head to the side. "Do you want to wear it or not?"

"I don't know. Isn't it kind of—" He paused, looking for the right word. "Unseemly?"

"I think it's fucking hot."

"In synagogue with my wife and her parents present?"

"Especially," Liz said. "This woman loves you and wants to be with you, but she can't be with you the way she wants to be, and this gives her power, a feeling of control. This is a way for her to participate in your life when she's not there, to expand the erotic boundaries beyond her bedroom. The question is, do you want to please her? Do you want to make her happy?"

"Of course I do."

"You know what would really make her happy? Send her a text and let her know you put it in."

"You two look like you're getting along."

Ben's heart seized, and he managed to stuff the butt plug between the sofa cushions.

Shira appeared before them and she was a knockout, in a fitted floral summer dress, strappy sandals and her hair pulled back from her face. She'd done some magic trick with her makeup that made her eyes look huge. Something with her cheekbones too.

"Damn, girl. You look gorgeous," Liz said, crossing the room to kiss her on her cherry red lips.

"And look at you!" Shira responded.

"I'm speechless," Ben said. "My wife is a runway model."

"And my handsome husband is too kind."

"I call it like I see it."

"Yeah, well you're biased," Shira said, turning to Liz for a more discerning perspective. "How's my décolletage look?"

"Perfect."

"Yay! We've got to run or we're going to be late."

"I think Ben said he had to go to the bathroom first," Liz said, taking Shira by the elbow. "Why don't we wait out in the car."

"I'll just be a minute or two," Ben said.

"Okay," Shira said. "Then get your ass moving."

20

Shira sat between Ben and Liz, her damp hands nail-clutching both Ben's and Liz's as the lights went down. They were seated third row center for the performance, and Shira was more nervous than Ben had ever seen her. He was so uncomfortable with that silicone thing jammed up his ass, he couldn't assemble the words to soothe her. Every inhale and exhale seemed to shift the toy, causing an uncomfortable friction. Ben's ass throbbed like he was sitting on his heart. His stomach felt seasick and he was about to escape to the bathroom to extract the thing when Shira exclaimed, "Oh my God, there's my mother. She sees me. She sees us!"

"Wave hello," Liz said, releasing Shira's hand. Her mother, hair swept back into a severe, silvering helmet, smiled a brittle, wondering smile and waved back.

Ben waved as well, and he forced something like a smile to his face. Wearing the butt plug didn't feel sexy or forbidden, just stupid and slightly embarrassing. He would have taken it out right then, but the house lights dimmed and the buzzing crowd hushed. Ben shifted in his seat and Shira squeezed his knee sympathetically and whispered, "Looks like you've got *shpilkes* too."

The temple's president appeared and introduced Shira's father with a lengthy, eye-roll-worthy, superlative-filled salutatory. You would think Cantor Joel Weissmann was the second coming of Al Jolson, Pavarotti and Frank Sinatra the way that Morris Lookstein carried on.

"He's got a voice," Shira said, "but this is ridiculous. This will do his towering ego no good."

Liz laughed and shushed Shira.

Ben tried to relax into the discomfort as Shira's father took center stage. Ben recognized many of the songs and was surprised how much he enjoyed himself. This material was much better than the liturgical stuff Ben had been forced to sit through over the years, and he saw his father-in-law in a new light, his polymath skills on full display. The show ended with a rousing rendition of Neil Diamond's "America," in which Cantor Weissmann was joined on stage by a family of Syrian refugees the Women's League had sponsored to resettle in Boston.

After a lengthy ovation, Liz turned to Shira and said, "Did I see your dad do a thing with his hips up there? Or am I crazy?" Liz laughed, thrusting out her own hips.

"He can be so mortifying," Shira said.

"But he's good!" Liz said. "I got all weepy-eyed during his 'Sound of Silence' duet."

It was a feel-good show, and Ben had almost forgotten the true purpose of the evening until he saw Shira's expression darken as her mother made her way over, sidestepping an elderly couple with an unmistakable look of determination on her face. Shira's entire body stiffened.

"It'll be fine," Liz said, touching her lightly on the hip.

Ben told Shira someone must have slipped some cheese into his lunch salad and his stomach was upset and that he had to go to the bathroom that instant.

"I'll run interference while you gather yourself," Ben said, kissing Shira and striding forward with his arms spread wide for an embrace.

How could Ben hug his mother-in-law with that piece of hardware inside him? "Wonderful show tonight. Joel has some major-league pipes."

Shira's mother briskly agreed and told Ben to meet them in the green room for a celebratory drink with the cantor, his agent and the fawning Morris Lookstein.

Ben waded through the crowd, legs bowed, desperate to find the bathroom and get the thing out of him. Shira called after him, "Ben, don't be long. Please."

There was someone in the one stall, so Ben had to wait. He texted Shira: *Don't start without me. I'll be right there x*

Then, to Pamela: *Are you sure you're not trying to torture me?*

She responded right away: *You didn't like it??*

Um, no. Ben texted, before amending. *Sorry.*

It's ok. You were a good sport.

The man in the stall ripped out a cannonading blast, just as Ben typed, *I try.*

When the man had finally done his business, Ben locked the door and dropped his pants, peering through the slit in the stall to make sure no one, not even God, could see what he was about to do. A couple of older men exchanged pleasantries at the sink. He found the flange at the end of the silicone plug and paused, thinking slow-and-easy or one firm, brutal tug? He flushed the toilet to cover any embarrassing cry of pain and yanked it out in one motion. And, oh my God, did it hurt! He felt that he had been donkey-kicked, his rectum a burning star exploding into a supernova as the toy flew out of his ass. He stared down at the red butt plug. It looked harmless enough in his hand, and, to be honest, it wasn't even that big. He wrapped it in toilet paper and unlocked the stall door just as a large, bearded man in a loose gray suit entered.

"What a terrific performance," the shambling stranger said.

Wasn't there supposed to be some sort of code about speaking to another man in the bathroom? Ben slipped the thing behind his back.

"What was your favorite?" the man pressed.

Ben's phone buzzed in his pocket.

"'I Got Rhythm' was tremendous," the man said. "But I'm a sucker for 'My Funny Valentine.' Cantor Weissmann is just a top-notch performer all the way. Have you seen him perform before?"

Ben told him the cantor was his father-in-law.

"Well, *mazal tov*. Let me shake your hand."

Ben nearly dropped the butt plug to the floor. He gestured to the stall and said, "I need to wash."

"Oh, of course, of course. You are a lucky man. Please say *yasher koach* to the cantor on my behalf."

"Absolutely," Ben said.

"I'm Barry Fingrut from Sharon. He might remember me from a thing a million years ago."

When Barry Fingrut had finally turned his back Ben rinsed his hands and dropped the butt plug into the garbage, making sure to cover it with paper towels. He had done what Pamela had asked of him and now it was time to retire the thing forever. He tossed it and hoped no one sifted through the trash. But his DNA would be all over the thing and, for a queasy moment, Ben considered retrieving it to dispose of elsewhere, but his phone buzzed again.

There was a text from Liz: *Where the fuck are you? It's happening!!!*

Ben left the butt plug where he'd haplessly hidden it and flew out of the bathroom in search of his wife, her girlfriend and his in-laws. He managed to find the Family Suite, a sterile living room facsimile earmarked for mourners to gather in privacy after funerals that Barbara had pretentiously called the green room, and heard Cantor Weissmann's voice before he even opened the door. "I feel like Spencer Tracy in *Guess Who's Coming to Dinner*. What the hell is going on here?"

Shira's father stood in the middle of the room, thick-framed eyeglasses on his face, tie loosened, nervous fingers combing through his hair. Shira and Liz stood before him, hands woven together in unity. Shira just stared at her father, wordless, foot tapping on the carpet.

"Ben, you want to help me out here?" Cantor Weissmann said, turning to Ben. His face was flushed, his eyes wild, shifting from Shira to Liz and back to Ben. "This is a joke. We're on *Candid Camera*, right? This was supposed to be my night. This has got to be a gag, Jeff," he said, turning to his agent for confirmation.

Jeff, a slick-haired shark in his late thirties or early forties, shook his head and said, "You know what. I've gotta make a few calls. We can circle back later about the show." And he excused himself.

He was followed by a sheepish Morris Lookstein who offered a mumbled, "Great show tonight," and nodded his head meaningfully at the Cantor before clicking the door shut.

Shira's mother sat alone on the couch now, purse clutched on her knees. "Joel, why don't you try and use a more productive tone."

"What tone?" Cantor Weissmann snapped. "I'm not using any tone."

"Daddy," Shira said. "I love Liz. What can be wrong with that?"

"But you're married to Ben. Ben is still your husband, right?"

"Yes," Ben said. "I am Shira's husband and she is my wife."

"I don't understand," Cantor Weissmann said. "Is this some sort of hippie commune orgy thing?"

"Relationships change, evolve," Shira said.

"So, this is evolution then?" Cantor Weissmann said. "Not a betrayal of your marriage vows? This sounds like irresponsibility of the highest order. Barbara?" Shira's father said, seeking backup from his wife.

"I say nothing." Barbara twisted her lips and locked them with an invisible key.

"There's nothing wrong with you being a lesbian. I accept that. I'm all for experimentation, but I thought you'd be over that by now."

"This is not a phase," Shira said. "This is me."

"So, you're going to leave your husband now for—" He paused. "That?"

"Nobody's leaving anybody. We are polyamorous and we all respect and care for each other."

"Absurd," Cantor Weissmann said. "This sounds like nothing more than hedonism, selfishness and irresponsibility."

This conversation was rapidly getting out of control, and Ben couldn't stand by and let Shira's father attack her and her lifestyle when she needed his support the most. "Can I say something? Please."

Shira's father nodded his head and everyone in the room turned their attention to Ben.

"What we have is the furthest thing from selfish. How can all this love and caring be anything but a good thing when Liz has our baby? A child needs love and it will be surrounded by love."

The room fell silent, and Shira went pale.

"What did you say?" Cantor Weissmann said, his massive fists clenching. "The illustrated girl is having whose baby?"

"Is this true?" Barbara said, leaning forward with interest.

Of all the stupid, thoughtless things Ben had ever said, this might have been the worst. He and Shira and Liz had driven together to a place called Fertility Solutions on Route 128 where Ben had been locked in a fluorescent-lit room with a stack of porn DVDs and magazines and a plastic cup which he was ordered to fill and leave for the nurse. After analysis, Ben's semen showed high motility, excellent concentration, perfect pH balance and beautiful sperm morphology, with sixteen percent of his little guys looking like perfect oval-headed tadpoles ready to strike. Liz, at twenty-seven years of age, was nearing the end of her fertile prime but still had a robust ovarian reserve that would be the envy of any woman hoping to conceive. Ben was going to get Liz pregnant and soon.

Ben just naturally assumed Shira and Liz had told Shira's parents about the baby while Ben was in the bathroom, and now he just wished he had kept his mouth shut. Ben crossed the room and took his place beside Shira, grasping her free hand in his.

"Yes," he said. "It's true. Shira and I want a child and this is the best way for us to do this. We're a family." He paused, measuring his words. "A twenty-first-century modern family."

Shira gave Ben's hand a supportive squeeze and whispered, "Thank you."

"I'm stunned," Shira's father said. "I'm actually speechless. What do you expect me to say to this?"

"For starters, you can say I love and support you."

"Don't try and pull that," Barbara said. "You know we love you no matter what. It doesn't mean we have to approve of everything you do. I can assure you your father and I love you even when you make mistakes."

"You're saying this is a mistake? Having a child with a woman I love? Do you know how many times you told me you wished you could be a grandmother? Too many to count. Do you know how difficult the hysterectomy has been for me? But I refuse to let it define me. And now you're going to give us shit about this?"

"No need to get riled up," Shira's father said. "We're not 'giving you shit,'" Shira's father said, throwing air quotes. "We just want to interrogate this because the consequences of this decision will affect more than just you and your little ménage."

"Oh, come on," Shira said. "Don't start with that patronizing bullshit."

"Darling," Shira's mother said, "if we didn't question your choices, we wouldn't be doing our job as your parents."

"Well, that's where we disagree. I need your support, not your ... What even is this? Disapproval? I don't even know what you're getting at."

"Have you thought about the logistics?" Barbara said. "How is this going to work when the child is here?"

"You know, I'd rather not talk about this right now."

"You need to, Shira," Cantor Weissmann said, his voice firm and authoritative. "What are people going to say?"

"So, that's what it's all about?" Shira pulled her hands from Ben and Liz and stepped forward so she was nearly nose to nose with her father. "It's all about you, isn't it? I know why you didn't want us to adopt, why you wouldn't front us the money, why the whole adoption thing caused you so much discomfort and hand-wringing. Because you, Mr. East Coast Liberal Cantor, were afraid you'd end up with a black grandchild. Or a slant-eyed Asian baby."

"Shira!" Barbara said.

"How dare you," Cantor Weissmann said, his red-hued face afire. "I idolized Michael Schwerner and Andrew Goodman. I marched on Washington and heard Doctor King speak live when I was just thirteen. I have spoken up for racial equality all my life."

"Stop!" Liz shouted. "Everybody just stop. I need to say something, and you all need to listen."

Shira's father crossed his arms at his chest, his eye bags an ashy, unhealthy hue. Shira's mother tilted her head, an inquisitive look on her face. She narrowed her eyes in concentration.

"You don't have to do this," Shira said. "I can defend myself."

"I know," Liz said, "but this isn't just about you anymore."

Liz loosened her updo so her bottle blonde hair fell down her back, the bright pink tips visible now. "I came here this evening wanting to impress you, wanting you to like me, because it's important to Shira and our future together. But there's something else you might want to consider: whether you impress me, whether I like you. I'm going to carry Ben and Shira's and my child. You can choose to accept reality for what it is and be part of the life of the child who can never have too much love, or you can fight us and make yourself irrelevant. The choice is yours. There's nothing you can do to change our minds. We are a package deal. You get us or you don't get us in your lives."

"Shira?" Cantor Weissmann questioned after an endless silence. "Do you agree with this?"

Shira nodded her head solemnly and slipped an arm around Liz's waist.

"But we don't even know her—" Shira's father said.

"It doesn't matter," Shira said. "This is my life. Are you in it or not?"

"Of course we are, darling," Shira's mother said. "But—"

"No but," Shira said. "Yes or no."

"May I speak?" Cantor Weissmann said. "Without getting everyone all, what do they say now? Triggered?"

"Fine," Shira said.

"Good. Dialogue is a good thing and it should not be seen, out of hand, as a threat or disapproval. These revelations just hit us when we least expected it. In the name of fairness let me speak my mind without threats of emotional blackmail."

"Emotions are high," Barbara said. "And perhaps some things were said—"

"Don't try and minimize," Shira said.

Cantor Weissmann twisted the signet ring on his finger and cleared his throat, which, Ben noticed, was raw and edgy after a night of belting out the Jewish-American songbook.

"I have a number of concerns about the situation. Believe me, if I didn't have questions, I'd be derelict, not just as your father, but as a community leader. You have no idea how difficult parenting is even under normal circumstances."

"Normal?" Shira said.

"Let me *speak*," Cantor Weissmann said. "You have no idea the world of confusion in which you'll be raising this child. You know I'm a supporter of same-sex marriage, and it was a process for me to get there, but I always end up in the correct place." Cantor Weissmann's certainty was astounding. "You wouldn't buy a car without asking a hundred questions, or make a reservation at a new restaurant without asking a question or two."

"What makes you think I haven't asked a million questions, haven't thought through every possibility?"

"Answer me this then: Will the child be raised Jewish?"

"That's your first concern?" Barbara said.

"If the child is not raised as a Jew, I have failed as a father."

"Goddammit, this is not about you," Shira shouted. "Can't you just think about someone else's perspective for once? I'm not your chattel."

"You're not going to turn your back on your heritage—"

"I am a thirty-one-year-old woman. And yes, we're going to raise the child Jewish. Liz is willing to convert, but I would never insist. But I resent how you're trying to bigfoot me here with the power of five thousand years of history on your side. I know what I'm doing."

"So, the child will grow up in a Jewish home?" Cantor Weissmann asked, shoulders relaxing.

"I'm still the same person I've always been. My values haven't suddenly changed because I've fallen in love with Liz."

Cantor Weissmann seemed to have aged twenty years in the past few minutes, shoulders slumped, voice strained. "Shira, I love you and I want to support you. But this is a lot for me to digest all at once. I'm going to need some time to process. Will you give me that time? Please?"

"Yes," Shira said, smiling a small smile. "Of course. But don't take too long. You're going to be a grandpa, like it or not."

Cantor Weissmann smiled and embraced his daughter, holding Shira in his arms for a long time, exhaling softly into her hair. He let go of his daughter, then squeezed her shoulders, looking her directly in the eye. "It's a child's job to make a parent crazy, and a parent's job is to love that child regardless. You'll learn that soon enough."

He kissed her on the cheek, then spun to shake Ben's hand in a crushing compensatory handshake. He shook Liz's hand as well. "You're a tough one, aren't you?"

"You have no idea," Liz said. And then, "My father was never in my life in any real way. Shira needs you in hers."

"I know," he said, and then fled the room without another word.

Shira's mom hugged Shira and said, "Don't worry. I'll work on him."

"I know you will, Mom. Thanks.

21

A couple weeks later, Shira received a handwritten letter from her father saying he would never fully understand her, but it was not his place to presume he could or even should. Joel Weissmann's life had not always made sense to his own father, a staunch Bundist and atheist who believed God could not possibly exist in a world where monsters tortured children and fed them into ovens at Auschwitz-Birkenau.

Cantor Weissmann finished his letter with his most heartfelt words:

> Shira, you are the most important song of my life. Just like I cannot control where my words and notes travel once they leave my throat, you are as free as those songs to go where they may, where they must.
>
> Wherever you go, whatever you do, you're always in my heart.
>
> I could not be prouder to have you as a daughter.

Love,

Your stubborn, hard-headed, arrogant, know-it-all, ever-loving father.

Shira finished reading the letter to Ben, expelling a huge sigh of relief. She murmured something under her breath that Ben could not make out and then said, "This is going to happen. We're really going to be parents."

Ben folded Shira into a tight embrace and kissed her on the top of the head, but his heart pounded in his chest as if he had just completed a 10 km run. Ben's father had always been present in Ben's life, a constant, steady voice of encouragement playing in the background like a subtle soundtrack. From the first frigid Little League game in April to the last crack of the bat, his father had been there in the stands calling out, "Good eye," or "Nice grab," or "You'll get 'em next time." He'd shown Ben how to break in his glove and how to grip a curveball and how to ice his arm after a game. His father had been there when Trisha Smith rejected Ben in sixth grade, telling him the poor girl didn't know what she was missing and taking him for barbecue to forget his sorrows. He'd shown Ben how to tie a perfect Double Windsor and taught him to look a person in the eye when he spoke, urging Ben to practice on the counter girl at McDonalds when he ordered his Big Mac, small fries and Coke with no ice. He reminded Ben to always be prepared, leaving a three-pack of Trojans on his pillow years before he ever needed one. His father had been the one to teach Ben how to drive stick in the early morning parking lot of The Gallery mall. He'd been fourteen at the time, and Ben was worried he would crash his father's Jeep, but his father had said, "I believe in you." His father had encouraged Ben to run his first marathon, and had been there cheering with Ben's mother at the finish line. Ben was hard pressed to think of a time when his father had not been available, until suddenly he was gone, completely gone.

And now, after all this time, Ben realized he could not recall the sound of his father's voice.

It had been low and full-bodied with a flavor of the streets of Flatbush sprinkled here and there. But Ben could not recreate that voice in his head, could only conjure a faint echo like a facsimile of a faded facsimile. They had spoken on the phone not long before his parents died, and Ben had told his father he had met a woman he really liked. Even then, Ben had known Shira was his life. Just the way she looked at him with those soft brown eyes, as if Ben were the only thing that mattered in the world.

Ben's father had said, "Well I wish you and Shira a wonderful life together."

They had only been dating for two weeks, and Ben could not recall if there was laughter in his father's voice, teasing his son for getting ahead of himself, or whether on some deep level his father knew this was his last chance to offer his blessing to his only son and his future wife.

"We're going to be parents," Ben said. He wished so badly he could speak to his father. He would find some way to sort out the mess Ben had made. Ben could not be present for both children the way his father had been present for him, and he worried he would let both children down.

"I miss my dad," Ben said. "I miss my parents. I wish they could be here to be part of this."

"I know." Shira stroked Ben's hair. "This is a major life-event. But you're not alone. You have me."

"How is this all going to work? I want to be the best parent I can possibly be, but it's just so complicated." Ben needed to know how he could do this with Shira and with Pamela. He just wanted some form of guidance that would show him the way, but Shira thought Ben was talking about Liz.

"I'm putting together a contract for Liz to sign. It will protect us in the event Liz decides not to relinquish the child."

"Do you really think that might happen?" Just the thought of Liz raising Ben's biological child without his involvement knocked the breath out of him.

"I don't know," Shira said, flapping her hands with agitation. "Liz has been talking about our baby as if it's her own."

"But she's not even pregnant yet."

"That's what worries me." Shira paced around their living room. "I'm afraid once she sees the baby she won't want to give it up. You've heard of Mary Beth Whitehead. We could be in court for years. I mean, I could never imagine carrying a child and then just handing it over to someone else to raise."

"What does Liz think is going to happen? Have you discussed this with her?"

"Kind of, but just in this fuzzy, idealistic way. It's so empowering to think we can accomplish anything we desire, but it's so much more than that. I mean, me and Liz are in different places in our lives."

Ben was silent as Shira's voice echoed off the walls, her words landing with a thud at Ben's feet. "Have you told Liz?"

"I'm afraid to." Shira's voice rose to a thin upper register. "I don't want her to change her mind." She took to pacing the room again, working her lower lip between her teeth, raking her fingers through her hair. "We can pay her. We have money in savings. Ten thousand? Fifteen? She can do a lot with that money."

"How do you think that will go over?"

"Not well. She'll freak the fuck out."

Ben took Shira in his arms. Her body was warm and emitted a faint sour smell. Shira's heart pounded against Ben's chest. "Whatever happens," Ben said, "we'll work it out together."

Shira eked out a small smile, the tender skin around her eyes crinkling. "I love you, you know that?"

"Can I get that in writing?" Ben said. "In triplicate."

Shira laughed and punched him lightly on the shoulder. "Doofus."

"If you had to choose," Ben said, "would you choose the baby or Liz?"

Tears glazed Shira's eyes. "Why is life so fucking difficult? Why can't we just have it all?"

Ben understood that sentiment well but said, "You'll always have me. No matter what."

Shira's body stiffened. "Another woman is having your child. What do you think is going to happen? You can't be a successful part-time parent. It's a full-time job with overtime and shit pay, but we do it because there's nothing more important than nurturing a child and giving it everything it needs." Shira paused and took a deep, audible breath. "I know you love this woman and I've accepted that fact, but our child needs to be your priority. Not your number one priority, but your *only* priority. You can't be a parent to our child and to her child and expect you'll make anyone anything other than miserable."

"Do you think I don't know that? I should be the happiest man alive. I have two women who love me, and my dream of becoming a father is going to come true times two. But I'm just so worried I'm going to let everyone down."

"You think you can please everybody," Shira said, her earnest face softening. Her hair had fallen in front of her eyes, and she brushed the messy strands away with a small ink-stained hand. Her eyes were bright and expressive, full of that deep intangible spark that made Ben love her so much. "You're a good person; you want to be a good person. You have such an ability to care, and you want to please. But you'll never be father of the year if you don't make a choice."

Ben's heart dipped as if it had fallen through a trapdoor. His sinuses tingled and his eyes burned. "I wish my dad were here."

Shira threw her arms around Ben, squeezing him firmly at the waist. "I know. I know."

"He would have been a grandfather. My mother would have been a grandmother. This child would be my gift to them."

"It still can be. You can pass on the lessons they each taught you. How to be compassionate and caring and ... good. Benjamin Seidel, I don't tell you this often enough, but you are a good man. You don't have a cruel bone in your body. You don't want to hurt anyone."

"No." Ben sniffed. "I don't. But I am hurting people. I'm hurting you and I'm hurting Pamela and I'm afraid both these children will grow to resent me if I'm not a father the way I need to be."

Shira squeezed her eyes shut and took a deep, thoughtful breath, expelling it slowly as she gathered her words. Her left eyelid fluttered the way it did when she was nervous. "Ben, I hate to say this, but I think you know deep down you have to make a choice. I won't tell you what to do. I can't do that. But you need to think about the future. What do you think is going to happen?"

"*Never make predictions*," Ben said, his father's voice filling his mind so clearly it nearly knocked him over. "*Especially about the future*."

Shira gave Ben a puzzled look, her head tilting slightly.

"A great philosopher once said that. My father loved Casey Stengel, who at one time managed the Brooklyn Dodgers, the New York Yankees and the Mets. My father had an autographed baseball signed by 'The Old Perfesser.' It was his most cherished object and he guarded it jealously. It was sort of his Magic 8-Ball. Whenever he had a problem he would bring out the baseball and hold it with both hands until the answer came to him. He never let me touch it, but said that one day it would be mine." Ben's voice trailed off, and he had to swallow hard to clear the lump of emotions that had gathered. "When we went to my parents' house to clean it out after they died I looked everywhere for that baseball, in drawers and closets, in the basement crawl space, in the attic, the garage, but I couldn't find it. It was just gone."

Shira squeezed Ben's arm. "Why didn't you tell me this? I could have helped you look."

"I thought maybe it was a sign, that he'd somehow managed to take it with him wherever he was going. Stupid, right?"

"No. It's not stupid. I think it's sweet."

"I just wish I had it right now."

"I know." Shira kissed Ben softly on the lips. "But I believe everything you need to know you already know."

22

Pamela moved from her third-story walk-up on Beacon Hill to Mr. Sarafyan's bright garden apartment on August first. Ben spent Pamela's first evening at her new place hanging pictures, filling bookshelves, rolling out rugs, moving her couch and coffee table back and forth across the living room in various configurations until they found their rightful places. They did so with a quiet determination, exchanging little more than brief comments and instructions. This was something more than just playing house. Ben and Pamela were almost, in a sense, family. But he had never met her own family, or even her friends, as if he were a dirty secret, and he wished to know if they even knew he existed. Of course Ben had never introduced Pamela to Shira or Liz, hadn't even told her they were still trying to have a child of their own, and that lie by omission ate him up whenever he thought of it.

Ben felt as if he were standing over the shoulder of another Benjamin Seidel, on the verge of a new life that did not include the Ben he knew. He imagined their child filling the space with so much life, doing "tummy time" in a honeyed square of sunlight, crawling across the polished hardwood floor, taking its first steps to cheers and smiles, but this future did not, could not, include Shira, and he closed his eyes and sat down on Pamela's couch before he was overcome by a vertiginous swell of panic. This state of suspended animation, in which he had a foot planted firmly in two lives, could not last much longer. Ben had arranged to stay over that first night and they made love in Pamela's newly painted blue bedroom slowly, softly, as if there was a time bomb beneath the bed they were afraid would go off.

Afterwards Pamela gestured to her midsection with her long, delicate fingers. She pressed Ben's hand to her belly, fanning out his fingers. "Do you want to say something? He's in there."

"He?" Ben said, a quick rush of adrenaline racing through his body.

"Just a feeling," Pamela said, in that gauzy after-sex voice that Ben liked so much; her voice husky and warm and so alluring because it was just for him. "I'll know in a couple weeks when I have my ultrasound."

"Wow!" The miracle of conception still amazed Ben, especially considering his and Shira's struggles. "Do you think he knows what we just did? I mean, it wasn't exactly X-rated, but still not appropriate for the under-eighteen crowd."

"Say something to your child, Ben."

"Does it, he, she, even have ears yet?"

"He may not respond now, but he can feel your vibrations."

Pamela began to sing one of William Blake's *Songs of Innocence*, her voice soft and pure and free of her familiar world weariness.

Sweet dreams, form a shade
O'er my lovely infant's head
Sweet dreams of pleasant streams
Be happy, silent, moony beams

Sweet sleep, with soft down
Weave the brows an infant crown
Sweet sleep, Angel mild
Hover o'er my happy child

"That was lovely," Ben said, his throat catching. He was touched by the maternal transformation in Pamela. It had only been a few weeks since she had ordered him to wear a butt-plug up his ass.

"You try now. Sing him a song, so he knows your voice."

"I can't sing."

"Not with that attitude. If you want to sing, you sing. You want to be a father, you be a father. No one is asking you to be perfect."

Ben began to sing a song he remembered his mother singing to him. Tentative, quietly at first, he sang "Alligators All Around," his lips close to Pamela's belly, hands cupped around his mouth to amplify his voice. His mother had sung that song to him and so many others from *Free to Be You and Me*. Ben had not thought of those songs since his own childhood, and he understood now that the process of being a parent was like stepping into a time machine in which his past replayed itself, only this time he would be the parent, moving along familiar tracks overlaid with the wisdom of generations.

"See, you can do it!" Pamela said. "And he likes it." She pressed Ben's hand to the warmth of her midsection. "Feel that."

Ben couldn't really feel anything, imagining Pamela's pulse as a minnow flicking past in a summer stream, the beginnings of his child. It may have been imagined, but to Ben there *was* something, because biology didn't lie, and that knowledge was enough to fill Ben with an explosive shock of euphoria. Some long dormant neurotransmitters fired a twenty-one-gun salute, and Ben's heart felt full and brave, and then, as if cutting a string, he fell back to earth, the blackest grief encompassing him as he drifted off to sleep beside a woman who was not Shira.

A newborn baby lay before Ben, bathed in glowing light emanating from an unseen source. The baby was covered entirely in tattoos, tiny, fragile words scrimshawed in black Gothic lettering onto the soft doe-like skin. Ben knew the words were some kind of warning, a key to his future, if only he could read what was inked onto the infant's skin. But the writing was so small and intricate he needed to take a closer look. Ben reached out to gather the child up into his arms, and its skin was cold like marble.

❦

Morning brought an unblemished blue-skied summer day, flawless in its cloudless majesty. Ben and Pamela were out for a walk, exploring her new neighborhood. Ben had always loved the quiet grace of Mount Auburn Cemetery with its classical monuments and narrow bucolic paths winding through the tree-shaded hills, and he wanted to introduce Pamela to her new neighbor, Henry Wadsworth Longfellow, one of her favorite Romantic poets. It was impossible to feel morbid on such a perfect day, and Pamela walked with a buoyant spring in her step.

"How did you know he was here?" Pamela asked. She wore a light summer dress patterned with red bursts of flowers, and the bright petals against her pale skin made her look positively luminous.

"Charles Bullfinch is buried here," Ben said. And when Pamela twisted her face with confusion, he went on, "He was the first true American-born architect. He designed the State House. I come here every once in a while on an-out-and-back run. This is my turnaround spot, and sometimes I just wander while I get my lungs back. I found he's in good company. This place really is a who's who of nineteenth-century all-stars. Twentieth century too."

"Imagine the cocktail conversations they'd all have. I love this place!" Pamela said. "Thank you for bringing me here." She kissed him. "What's the story with that tower over there? It looks like a giant chess piece."

"Wanna go see?"

"Yes I do."

Ben and Pamela climbed the spiral granite staircase to the top of Washington Tower. Little more than a mile from Pamela's apartment, it stood atop the highest point in Mount Auburn Cemetery, with its grim battlements and Gothic windows shining like mirrors, reflecting the heavens and the earth in equal measure. From the rooftop gallery they could see all the way to Bullfinch's glittering gold state-house dome and the summit of Wachusett Mountain, dozens of miles to the west. It was a perfect, breezeless day with almost no humidity, the Charles River below leisurely snaking its way towards Boston Harbor and the ever-cold Atlantic. Ben slipped his arms around Pamela's waist and planted a tender kiss on her neck, her high SPF sunscreen tingling on his lips. Pamela's pulse still throbbed from the exertion of climbing the six-story tower, and she sank back into Ben, expelling a deep sigh. Ben encircled her rigid body with his arms, his heart thumping against her back.

"You okay?" Ben asked.

"I'm just having such a nice time with you."

"That's good, right?"

"It is." Pamela craned her neck around. She wore her dark, Audrey Hepburn sunglasses, and though Ben couldn't see her eyes behind them, he knew they told a story her words did not. "I like having you around, but you always have to leave, and—"

The beautiful day hung before them like an Old Master's painting—squint your eyes and the centuries peeled away to a simpler time, long before the go-go energy and constant anxiety of the Post Industrial Age—and Ben saw the whole image crumbling before his eyes. Whatever Pamela was about to say set Ben's heart revving like a tired old engine.

"I want to be with you."

"You are with me," Ben said.

"I'm not. The more I see you the harder it is when you're not around."

"But I'm around more. I'm doing my very best."

"Maybe, but I'm still getting the leftovers and it's just not enough. I want to *be* with you. Don't you understand?"

"I do understand. I can stay over more. We can set a firm schedule."

"I don't want a schedule. I don't want to share you. I just want you." Pamela threw her arms around Ben and buried her face in his neck. It was wet with tears. "I don't cry. This isn't me."

"There's nothing wrong with crying." Shira had regular weekly cries going all the way back to their early days. It was a tonic, she said, a cleaning of the emotional pipes. "Crying can be a good thing."

When Pamela pulled away, a patch of her skin had been scraped raw from Ben's two-day scruff. "I'm sick of platitudes, Ben. What am I doing here, renting an apartment in a town in which I know nobody, not a single living soul? What am I doing with my life? I don't want to look back a year from now, five years from now, and realize I'm in the wrong life, that I've given into my weakness and my need to be loved. I'm in deep with you and I'm terrified. I dated a lot of losers before I got to you. A lot. Maybe they wore me down, warped my sense of self. This whole thing is just so humiliating. I'm pregnant with your child and you're married to another woman. You will never leave her."

Ben's stomach dropped like an acid-filled balloon. "I promise we will work something out."

"You don't get it. I can't live my life just waiting for you. I've been dwelling in possibility for too long. Why are you even with Shira? I'm the one who is having your child, not her. Why isn't that enough?"

"It's complicated."

"Laments from a bifurcated life. I don't want complicated. I want simple and easy and—" Pamela's voice broke. "Normal. Why can't we just have something normal? I just want to have what everyone else has."

"Our lives are all a work-in-progress," Ben began. "And what is normal anyway?"

"Don't"—Pamela said, jaw tight, pointing a long, stiff finger in his face—"bullshit me."

"Okay. I'm sorry."

"Do you really love me? Not as some abstract concept, but really love me? That means hard work, sacrifices, it means ... commitment, being there when it counts."

"I'm with you because I love you."

"Stop it. You're not with me. Don't you get it? I can't do this anymore."

Pamela's voice was raised, and Ben imagined it taking wing and floating across Mount Auburn Cemetery, above the tombs and crypts and graves of so many thousands who had left this world without knowing love like he and Pamela shared. If he were to die now, this very moment, Ben knew he at least had experienced two great loves in his life.

"Tell me now. Why are you even with Shira? What does she have over you? I'm having your child, not her."

Ben had to choose his words carefully, but there was no perfect combination of words—even Henry Wadsworth Longfellow would have been hard pressed to massage Ben's next statement into something that would not drive Pamela away forever. He loved Shira and he was not prepared to give her up, because she was as much a part of Ben as water was part of the ocean. Then the words he had been holding in for weeks just boiled out of Ben all at once. He had no choice but to tell the truth, knowing that if he told Pamela he could lose her, just as easily as he could lose her by not telling her. "Me and Shira are having a baby. I provided the sperm. Liz is our surrogate. But I never touched her, not once. But I promise you, I promise you with all my heart, I will be there for you and our child."

As the words left Ben's mouth he realized he may as well have thrown a punch at Pamela as she staggered back and her face resolved into a bloodless grimace. "My child," Pamela roared, "not yours." She spun on her heels. Ben reached out for her, but she slipped out of his grasp, plunging into the cool, echoey stairwell of the tower.

"I love you," Ben said, his words amplified like a cornball voiceover to his own personal drama. "I love you so much."

"Stop it. You use the word like currency. It's worthless, Ben. It means nothing that you love me if you're with her."

"Careful." Ben tried to keep up with Pamela. She was surprisingly fast in her descent, the tapping of her feet on the granite steps setting a brisk pace.

"Too late for that."

Pamela stopped at the first landing, arms crossed at her chest, illuminated in a bright square of sunlight. She had never looked more certain, or more beautiful, the way her lank auburn hair framed her narrow face, her eyes as hard as stones. "Don't follow me."

Ben called after Pamela and her receding foot-steps, but she did not respond. By the time he burst into the sunlight she was already flying down the hillside steps to Mountain Ave., where three or four cars sat parked along the curb. They had arrived at Washington Tower noting the charming names of the paths they took as they wound their way towards the tower—Hazel Path, Myrtle Path, Oleander Path, Rose Path, Sweetbriar Path, Bellflower Path—but she was running now at a quick clip, something Ben had never seen her do. She was a spin class and Pilates person, but she was fast. Ben sprinted after Pamela, calling for her to wait, but she kept running. She could not outrun him, but the idea of chasing her felt grotesque, terrible in its optics.

Pamela stopped to catch her breath, and Ben slowed to a jog, then a walk.

"Don't come closer," Pamela said.

"Please, just hear me out. Please."

A small funeral was underway fifty yards beyond Pamela, the mourners dressed in customary black. "Your life will go on without me."

"I don't want that."

"Look at those people." Pamela gestured towards the gathering. "Do you think they want to be without their loved one?"

"No, of course not."

"You know what that's like," Pamela said, glaring over the top of her sunglasses. "Their lives will go on too."

"Are you saying what I think you're saying?"

"I'm saying exactly what you think I'm saying. Your parents died and here you are; my brother died and I go on. It's life and it sucks."

"Stop! Are you purposely trying to hurt me?"

"Yes! I want you to go away and never come back because I can't take this yo-yo of he loves me, he loves me not."

"I love you all the time," Ben pressed.

"If you really loved me, you'd be with me. All the time. Period."

All at once Ben felt himself coming apart, knees buckling, throat thick with grief, eyes hot with tears. His life had never been the same after the loss of his parents; some important part of him died with them, and he hated to imagine what would have become of him if Shira had not been there to keep him together. Now he was going to lose Pamela, and the thought of that door shutting forever, the double loss of her and their child and everything that came with it, slammed into him with the force of a hurricane.

"I'm sorry," Pamela said. "I wish this could have turned out otherwise. But it can't. Goodbye."

"Wait!"

"I have been waiting. I'm done."

She was only three or four feet away from Ben, but the distance may as well have been the entire circumference of the globe, because Ben would never touch Pamela again.

23

Ben found Shira at work in her studio, hair pulled into a loose pony tail, a graphite pencil tucked behind her ear. As soon as he entered, Shira, noticing a change in the room's energy, turned to Ben and said, "What's wrong?"

For a moment, Ben was afraid to tell Shira. He needed his pain to be validated, and Shira's reaction meant everything. This was no moment for triumph in her response.

"Pamela left me."

In an instant Shira was up out of her chair, arms around Ben. "I'm sorry."

Ben buried his face in Shira's hair that smelled fresh from the shower, the sturdiness of her strong body so different from Pamela's willowy figure. The contrast was startling, and Ben pulled out of Shira's embrace, eyes raw and stinging with the precursor of tears he refused to shed. How did people go about their days and get things done when they missed someone as much as he missed Pamela?

"What?" Shira said, her eyes behind her thick lenses oversized and out of proportion to the delicate contours of her face. "What's the matter?"

"I don't want you to mother me. I need you to be my wife."

"Okay," Shira said, doubtfully. "But I am your wife. What am I doing that's different?"

"I don't know."

"Do you need sex?"

"I don't know."

They stood face to face, Shira looking up at Ben with a worried expression. Her hand rose to brush something off his shoulder, and then she caught herself and settled her hand in place against her thigh. "Do you want to talk?"

"I just feel kind of lost right now."

"I'm sure. Losing someone does that."

Ben wanted to say he was losing more than just Pamela, but he knew how much it hurt Shira to know that Pamela was carrying his child. "Are we just going to be parents from now on?"

"What do you mean? Isn't that what you want?"

"Yes, but I don't want to lose us and just be parents raising our child together. I rarely saw my parents as anything but parents."

"Because they were *your* parents. But they had rich lives, doing things that had nothing to do with raising you."

"I'm never going to know the child Pamela is carrying. The child is never going to know its father."

"You don't know that, Ben."

"Can you imagine never knowing your father? How different your life would have been?"

"No, I can't imagine." With her wrinkled brow and downturned mouth, Ben could see Cantor Weissmann in his daughter.

"That's what hurts the most, the fact that my child will never know me."

"This just happened. Emotions cool with time."

"It's not like I'm going to take Pamela to court."

"No. Not now, at least. Maybe things will change."

"They won't change," Ben said, voice raised more than he was comfortable with. "Pamela wants me to be with her. Just her."

Ben's words rang in the air for a moment, and then Shira said, "Do you want to be with her? Is that why you're so … What are you trying to say?"

"I want to be with you. I've always wanted to be with you, but I'm hurting so badly. People have breakups. I get it. It happens all the time. She loved me, she validated me, she made me feel that I was—I don't know—special."

"I'm sorry. I know I could have done better. Do you still want to be with her?"

"Yes, and no, because yes means no you."

"I love you, Ben. I've always loved you. We've built a life based on that love."

"I know. I'm so grateful for you, but there's is a part of me that always wants more. And though it seems impossible right now that I'll ever stop missing Pamela, I know that time eases the pain, right?"

"Time is an amazing healer." Shira nodded.

"But the child, my child."

And here Shira winced. Ben knew it wasn't easy for her to hear about the child she couldn't have with him. "How do I get over that? I'll never know this child."

"Ben," Shira said, "please try and focus on what's good with us. We, me and you, are having a child."

"She's not even pregnant and we're already making plans. We've been here before."

"Don't do this. Please don't do this."

"And Liz. Liz will always come between us."

Shira bowed her head and then looked up at Ben, her eyes glittering with tears. "I showed her the agreement. It was just a standard surrogacy contract. She kind of wigged out." Shira paused to take a breath. "Well, not kind of, it was a full blown freak out."

"What do you mean?"

"She ripped it up, called it an insult, said I couldn't tell her what to eat, what to drink, what to do, that I was trying to control her life. She kicked me out of her place and told me to go back to the suburbs."

Ben swallowed hard and then cleared his throat. "What does this mean?"

"I had to accept her at her word." Shira looked so small with her shoulders slumped, her teeth nervously working her lower lip. "Liz sees the contract as an issue of trust."

"What happens if she won't give up the child?"

Shira rubbed both her temples as if trying to stifle an oncoming headache. "I did manage to get her to agree that me and you have to be present for the birth of the baby, and that she would relinquish any rights to the child upon its birth." Shira laughed, but it was mirthless. "I even offered to compensate her. But she looked so insulted and said she wasn't a fucking charity case."

"So, what does all this mean?"

"It means I have to be good to her. And to you." Shira took Ben's phone from his hand and set it down beside hers on her desk. "Let's get some fresh air. Just me and you."

She took Ben's hand in hers.

One night Shira insisted Ben join her and Liz for trivia night at a bar in Jamaica Plain. Ben would have preferred to stay home and watch the Yankees-Sox game on TV, but Shira promised it would be fun. "You have to get out of the house. I'll even drive."

Things had been calm between Shira and Liz since the blow-up over the contract, and Ben agreed to go because everyone needed to get along if Liz was going to carry their child to term and then hand it over to Shira and Ben to raise.

Shira wanted to call their trivia team "I am Smarticus," and Liz, spit-taking her lime seltzer, seemed to agree. Ben wasn't in the mood for puns and failed to offer so much as a smile. The glossy black screen of his phone lay silently before him. He had been sending Pamela sentimental songs from Spotify, and links from *The Globe* and *The Times*, and he still held an ardent hope that she would respond.

"Come on, baby," Shira said, squeezing his shoulders. "I want you to have fun."

"Barkeep," Liz called down the bar. "Get this man a drink. A double."

"I'm not in the mood," Ben said.

"You name our team," Shira said. "Whatever you want, that's us."

Shira pulled a silly face, urging Ben to smile. Liz offered pouty red lips and big, lashy eyes, imploring Ben to play along.

"Fine," he said. "Misery Loves Company."

After a couple rounds and a gin and tonic, Ben was able to put Pamela out of his mind, the empty pit of his stomach fuzzing over with an optimistic warmth, even bravado. Liz brought a silly infectious energy, throwing her entire body into answering the questions, and, Ben had to admit, he enjoyed her company.

Seventh planet from the sun?

"Uranus," Ben and Liz said at the exact instant.

"Your anus," Liz said, winking at Ben. All he could think to say in response was, "No, yours."

Shira and Ben knew the Sea of Tranquility was on the moon, while Liz argued it sounded like something from an Ursula K LeGuin novel. All three knew what Lorem ipsum was—Liz happened to have it tattooed on her wrist—while Liz knew the color of the Himalayan poppy—blue—and that a group of pugs is called a grumble, Freddy Mercury died in 1991, and Otto Mesmer drew Felix the Cat. Ben knew Frank Robinson was the first African American manager in baseball's American League, Friedrich Engels co-wrote the Communist Manifesto, and that Monaco was the most densely populated country in the world. Shira knew Wookiees came from the planet Kashyyyk, that actor Albert Brooks' real name was Albert Einstein, and that uranium was the heaviest naturally occurring element.

By Ben's second gin and tonic they were all speaking in questionably believable British accents, Liz calling Ben a bloody wanker when he flubbed a question on the breed of Queen Elizabeth's dogs.

"It's corgis, you twit! The best dogs in the entire world."

"I disagree vehemently," Shira said. "Labs are the best. Loving, perfect, loyal, and so damn cute."

"Lay offa my corgis," Liz said. "Them's fighting words."

The next question froze Ben in place: "Which Romantic Poet wrote 'Ode to a Nightingale'?"

And then, as if she had just sauntered into the bar for a cold one, Pamela stood before Ben, reciting John Keats' words that so perfectly encompassed the way Ben felt at that moment: *"My heart aches / and a drowsy numbness pains My sense / as though of hemlock I had drunk."* The entire bar disappeared with its flashing TV screens and laughing patrons, and Ben was alone with Pamela, his head throbbing with a quick rush of blood. She was showing, her rounded belly cradled in her hands. Pamela opened her mouth to speak, her red lips like a slash of blood. "It's your child, Ben. Yours."

"Ben. Are you okay?" Shira was at Ben's shoulder, her breath warm in his ear.

Ben blinked his eyes hard to clear the static from his brain and he was back in the room. Both Shira and Liz stared at him, identical expressions of concern coloring their faces. "Yeah, I'm fine." Pamela seemed so real he could smell her, almost touch her. "No. I'm not okay. I'm kind of—"

Shira folded Ben into a hug and asked if he wanted to go home. "It's okay," she said, lowering his face to hers and kissing him dryly on the mouth. "I'll drive."

Liz nodded her head in assent and, feeling snappish, Ben wanted to say, "What does this have to do with you?" It wasn't right for him to spoil the fun, to drag everyone else down with him—and they had been having a good time until Ben was reminded of Pamela.

"No, it's okay. I'll just go watch the game." There was an empty seat at the other end of the bar with a perfect view of the Yankees-Sox game. "You two play without me."

"Are you sure?" Shira said. "We can go. It's not a problem."

"Hey, you always say I should make some male friends." Ben climbed off the stool, ran his hands over the front of his pants, flattening out the creases. "I'm going to bro it out for a while."

"Okay," Shira said, smiling. "But let me know if you want to leave."

Ben slid onto the backless stool beside a thirty-something man in a Red Sox cap. He had a stubbled goatee and large, battered hands knuckling nervously on the bar top. A half-drunk pint of Blue Moon sat before him on a damp circular coaster.

Ben greeted the man with a "Hey," and turned his eyes to the TV. The Yankees were losing 1-0 in the fifth inning. Ben had been a Yankees fan as long as he could remember. His father had bought him a Yankees rattle when he was born and taken him to his first game at the old Yankee Stadium when he was barely one. He had always found something soothing about baseball and the languid pace of the game, the interludes between action allowing space to spin stories of legends of the past. Baseball was, in a sense, Ben's home turf, and he could speak comfortably on any era of baseball going back to the Deadball Era.

"Pretty good game," Ben ventured. "I like a pitcher's duel. This kid looks like a keeper." The Red Sox pitcher on TV was a large right-hander with a high leg kick that reminded Ben of Juan Marichal.

The goateed man turned to Ben and said, "His BABIP over the last five starts is flukishly low. I'd expect serious regression as the season goes on."

"He's spinning a shutout," Ben said. "And he's coming back from Tommy John surgery. I think that's pretty impressive." Ben had read in the paper of the prize prospect's setbacks as he rehabbed his arm throughout the spring. He had been back on the mound just over a month.

"He's maybe a 2 WAR player, maybe 2.5," the man said, sipping his beer. "But his xFIP looks gaudy. His FB% is too high to sustain."

Shira and Liz were laughing together at the other end of the bar, and Ben just wanted to cry. They were having such a good time together. Why did they even need a wet blanket like him? He wanted nothing more than to raise a family with Shira, but with Liz always horning in he would feel like a guest in his own life. He craved Shira, wanted just to be alone with her, but whenever he found himself in her arms now, a freighted afterimage of Pamela was there too, out of sync and out of reach.

The man next to Ben was talking about how the Red Sox scored their lone run back in the third inning. "The exit velocity was 117.3 miles an hour with a launch angle of 27.3 degrees. That's a 454 foot blast. He's an ISO beast."

Ben's phone buzzed on the bar top and his mouth filled with bile. He had so conditioned himself for it to be Pamela that every time his phone vibrated his body went through a physiological freakout, ranging in reaction from ice-cold tremors to something resembling a small-scale myocardial infarction. He took a deep breath and looked at his phone's screen. It was Shira.

We need a Lifeline: Who played T.E. Lawrence in Lawrence of Arabia?

Ben just stared at his phone, wondering whether Pamela would ever respond to his texts.

The man beside Ben nudged him in the ribs. "Those two babes over there are looking at you."

Ben looked up and Shira blew Ben a kiss. "That's my wife," Ben said.

"Damn," the man said. "Then what are you doing sitting here with me?"

❦

When they returned home, Ben told Shira he needed to go for a run.

"Can't it wait till morning? It's late."

"I just need to burn off some steam." Ben reached for his new pair of Asics on the shoe mat.

"I can think of better ways to do that," Shira said.

She canted her hips in a way that was meant to be sexy, but Ben was not in the mood. He was still in mourning, and having sex with Shira felt unseemly, dishonoring what he and Pamela had shared together. Sleeping with Shira right then would only amplify his loss of Pamela. He missed her physically. The way his body reacted to her skin against his made him feel like he had sloughed off his usual skin to become, ever so briefly, someone else altogether, braver, more adventurous, desired. He realized now that part of that thrill was due to the fact that there was always something forbidden about Pamela, something ephemeral in their interactions. The intensity of his feelings towards Pamela were due in large part to the impermanence of what they shared together. But she was having his child, and nothing could be more enduring than that.

"Okay," Shira said, kissing Ben lightly. "But please promise to be safe."

It was a cool September evening, and Ben ran faster than he had run in a long time, with the thick heat of summer giving way to the crispness of the coming autumn. He made it to Mount Auburn Street in record time, but rather than turning left toward the cemetery, Ben made a right in the direction of Pamela's apartment. He had thought of running by her place a dozen times, but doing so would make him some sort of stalker and he didn't want that. But Ben couldn't get Pamela to acknowledge any of his texts or phone calls. The right thing to do would be to leave her alone, and he didn't want to cause Pamela any more pain than he had already caused her with his blithe belief that everything would somehow work out because she loved him.

Ben paused to take a breath at the end of her street, thinking about how happy they had both been about her moving closer, and then Pamela realizing her mistake, living in a strange town surrounded by strangers. And now Ben was becoming a stranger to Pamela, left alone with a growing belly, and no one to help her raise the child. Ben couldn't see far enough up the street to figure out whether Pamela's lights were on or not, but he'd made up his mind to go no further and he turned on his heels and ran back home.

24

Liz arrived unannounced at Ben and Shira's condo one evening a couple weeks after Labor Day, screaming, "I did a thing!" as soon as Ben opened the door. Shira had been reading on the couch and leapt to her feet just as Liz raised a plastic pregnancy test aloft like a torch in victory.

"I'm pregnaaaaaaant!," Liz sang. "I'm gon-na be a ma-ma bear."

"Are you 100% sure?" Shira said, wrapping an arm around the curve of Liz's waist as she escorted Liz into the condo. Ben had come running from the kitchen where he was hand-drying an omelet pan from dinner when he heard the frantic ding-donging of their doorbell. He still clutched the damp towel in his hand.

"Of course I'm sure." Liz's blue eyes were bright and expressive with a euphoric energy. "This is so fucking rad. I'm growing a whole new person inside of me."

Ben absorbed Liz's words the way one might receive a slap in the face to rouse one from a stupor. He was wide-awake now, alert and ready for anything, heart tremoring somewhere low on the Richter scale; a sledgehammer thump, but not hard enough for Shira and Liz to notice. He had known Liz was probably going to be pregnant some day soon, but the fact that she actually was pregnant, right now, as she stood before Ben, concentrated his mind on the fact that the next phase of their life had moved from speculation to reality. Liz would be now and forever part of his life, his family.

Liz whipped two more pregnancy tests out of her pants' pocket and handed one to Shira and one to Ben as if she was passing out celebratory cigars. "Two vertical lines means pregnant. Two lines! Look." Liz wasn't wearing any makeup at all, and Ben was amazed how natural, and almost sweet, Liz looked, even with her scary tattoos and pierced septum.

With halting breath, Shira read, "Two lines. That means pregnant." Then she turned to Ben. "Do you have two too?"

"Yep," Ben said. "I have two too."

Shira let out a small, uncharacteristically girlish shriek and, with superhuman force, threw her arms around Ben, her body slamming hard into his. "Oh my God, oh my God, oh my God." Then her voice, low and husky, words meant just for Ben. "This is really happening, Ben. We're really having a baby. Can you believe this?"

Shira looked so happy in that moment, as if the fact of Liz's pregnancy were a giant eraser, rubbing out all of Shira's pain and longing. If Ben had asked Shira whether she believed everything would be good from now on, she would have declared a definitive "yes."

"You may want to wash your hands since those things are covered in my stanky pee."

"I don't care about that," Shira screamed. "We're going to be a mother."

Ben asked if he could hug Liz again, and Liz said, "Of course you can."

Her body was hot like a furnace, and though she smelled of her usual peppery patchouli she felt like a different person, not some tatted-up stranger, but someone familiar, and Ben suddenly understood how Liz carrying their baby was an act of love, not just for Shira, but for him as well.

"Let's have a drink," Shira said. "I've been saving a bottle of Veuve Cliquot since ... Shit, I hope it's still good."

"I'll have to pass," Liz said. "I've got precious cargo in me."

"Yeah, you do," Shira said. "No champagne for you!"

Shira knelt down before Liz and starfished her palm on Liz's flat belly. Liz would have to take out the elaborate piercing before that belly popped. "Hey there, sweetie. It's mama number two."

"Fuck hierarchy," Liz said. "I'll be mom and you be mama. Coequal all the way."

"I like that," Shira said.

Shira whispered something into Liz's belly that Ben could not hear, but he could never participate in something as intimate as what Shira was doing, her soft lips so close to Liz's belly.

"Ben, would you like to feel?" Liz said, smiling so the adorable space between her pearly incisors was on full display.

Ben had never touched Liz's belly before, and he placed a clammy palm to her warm midriff between the life-size Colt .45 tattoos and felt a wave of sadness wash over him. When he had first touched Pamela's belly he believed he had reached the pinnacle of his life, *creating* life, like making fire by rubbing two sticks together, the very elements of creation bursting into existence from the void. With Liz everything had been so clinical, worked out in a lab and not through the physical act of love. They shared no moment of conception, no lovestruck creation myth, as if Ben had not been involved at all. He was a donor, not a participant. He could remember with precise detail what Pamela had looked like the night their child was conceived, what she wore, how they held each other, and he tried to imagine what Pamela was doing at that moment, knowing she would hate him all the more for the fact that he was touching another woman who was carrying his child. There was no going back now.

Shira reappeared in the living room with the bottle of champagne. She asked Ben if he'd like to do the honors. Ben took the bottle and popped the cork, and fragrant silver foam sprayed all over the living room floor.

"Don't worry, we'll get it later." Shira took the bottle from Ben and, holding it out like an offering, she muttered a prayer in Hebrew and took a long, sloppy draw on the bottle so the champagne ran down her chin.

"What was that?" Liz asked.

"The Shehecheyanu." Shira was positively buoyant, and took another slug from the bottle before handing it to Ben.

"The shehewhaaaa?" Liz said.

"It's a prayer Jews say on happy occasions. It's in the Talmud," Shira said, every bit the cantor's daughter. "We've been saying it for over two thousand years. It's like tradition."

"That's so cool. I love that your great, great, great, great etcetera etcetera grandmother back in Europe could be saying the exact same words you just said."

Ben never knew his assimilated parents to utter a single word in Hebrew, but his great uncle Maury, keeper of the flame, surely would have echoed Shira's words upon hearing Ben's mother was pregnant with him.

"What say we FaceTime my folks?" Shira said. "They're going to flip."

"Sure," Liz said. "Just let me fix my face first."

"Your face is perfect," Shira said, heading to her studio to get her iPad. "You are perfect."

"Wow," Ben said, "this is all happening so fast." His heart was still pounding, and he took a swig of the champagne and the carbonation tickled his sinuses.

"I know," Liz said. "It's crazy. This time next year we'll be knee-deep in diapers."

"Shit," Ben said. "We will."

"You can say that again."

Shira appeared in the living room, holding the iPad at arm's length, camera facing Ben and Liz, who had settled onto the couch. Ben's parents would have thought the iPad with FaceTime was something out of science fiction, as futuristic as flying cars and Mars colonies. He wished he could see their faces now.

"Mazal tov!" Shira's parents chimed in unison.

"Thank you." Shira squeezed in beside Ben and Liz, turning the screen so the three of them were all in frame together. "Oh my God, we're so excited."

Shira's parents each had their reading glasses affixed to their glowing faces, their smiles bursting with pure happiness.

Barbara's eyes were scrimmed with tears of joy. "I'm going to be a grandma. Or safta. Yes, that's it. I'm going to be Safta Barbara."

"I don't care what the baby calls me, as long as it's healthy and happy and can carry a tune."

"Be honest, Joel. You want your grandchild to call you Cantor Weissmann."

"Would you stop?" Cantor Weissmann waved a hand dismissively. "I'm having a moment, Barbara. I'm over the moon right now."

Ben could not recall seeing either one of his in-laws ever looking so happy.

"So, Ben, how does it feel? You're going to be a father."

"It feels like," and then Ben lost whatever he was trying to say and broke out laughing. "Wow," he said. "Just wow. I kind of can't believe it."

How many nights had he held Shira in his arms as she wept about a future together with no children. But they had found a way to make it happen and they had done it together. It felt so good to be surrounded on all sides by so much joy. Ben could feel it radiating off Shira and Liz, and it warmed him like a blanket.

"Your body is in for some big changes," Barbara said, looking down her nose to see better through her lenses, eyes trained on Liz. "You may not believe it, but I was as big as a house with that one."

Shira laughed. "Oh, come on. You were stunning. I've seen the pictures."

"To be honest," Liz said. "I'm kind of looking forward to the cravings—ice cream, cookies, pizza—just giving in to my desires and eating whatever the fuck I want for once." Liz's eyes went wide, and then she blinked them shut with a regretful shake of the head. "Sorry. I mean—"

"Don't fucking worry about it," Cantor Weissmann said. "We're all adults, and the baby can't hear yet."

This is what family feels like, Ben thought, and he suddenly realized that everything was going to work out well; it may be messy at times, but they were all going to pull together and do their part in raising this child.

"Listen," Cantor Weissmann said. "I want you to go see Doctor Abramovich at Mount Auburn Hospital. He's the head of Obstetrics and is one of the top OB/GYNs in the country. He's been around forever and has delivered more healthy babies than you can count."

"Oh, yes," Barbara said. "And Doctor Abramovich is such a nice man."

"I'll make a call and get you in to see him right away."

Ben felt Liz's body go stiff beside him. She had a distant look in her eyes, and when Ben tried to catch her attention she looked away.

"Yay," Shira said. "Thank you, Daddy. That's really kind of you."

"Liz," Cantor Weissmann said, "you can trust Doctor Abramovich as much as anybody in the world. I couldn't imagine anybody better qualified to deal with your child's prenatal care. Mount Auburn

Hospital is a Harvard-affiliated teaching hospital and provides some of the best care in the country, in the world even. We are talking about top-level care for your baby."

Liz stood up abruptly and announced she had to pee.

"Okay," Cantor Weissmann said, reading the room. "I'll leave you kids to celebrate. This is very exciting."

"It is," Shira said. "So exciting. Love you both."

"Goodnight Joel," Ben said. "Goodnight Barbara."

"And Goodnight Moon!" Barbara said, laughing.

The screen went black and Shira sank back into the couch with a big sigh, a soft smile playing across her lips. "Ben, I love you so much for helping make this happen. I know it's an unusual arrangement, but we are going to be fine. I just know it." She kissed Ben and tousled his hair. "You're going to be a dad."

"And you're going to be a mom."

Liz appeared in the living room but didn't rejoin Ben and Shira on the couch. Shira patted the cushion beside her. "What's up, babe?"

"You know I'm not going to see your father's fancy doctor."

"Why?" Shira said.

"Because," Liz said. She rocked side to side as if she were measuring what to say or do next.

"But Doctor Abramovich is such a good OB/GYN," Shira said. "I've met him. He's really good. *Boston Magazine* has featured him as a top doc on more than a few occasions."

"Do you even hear yourself?" Liz said. "Do you want me to read his Yelp reviews too?"

Shira stood up, a deep crease forming between her eyes. "What's going on?"

"What's going on is I have an OB/GYN who I know and trust and like."

"I know," Shira said. "But this is about our baby now. Don't you want the best for our baby?"

Liz's body went rigid. Her eyes, which had been so warm and full of joy not long before, had iced over. "You have a problem that I go to a clinic and not some fancy gold-plated hospital."

"That's not it," Shira said. "Just go see Doctor Abramovich for a consultation. If you don't like him, you don't have to see him."

"Oh, thank you very much. You think it's up to you who has access to my vagina."

"That's not fair and you know it. It's not about your vagina. It's about our child's prenatal care."

"Oh, fuck off. My body, my choice. There's nothing wrong with Doctor Quan, and a women's community health clinic is plenty good enough for me and the baby."

"But you can do better. Why take the risk?"

"Okay, I see, so a women's clinic is fine for the unwashed masses, and you write your checks to Planned Parenthood because it makes you a woke sister, but when it comes down to my health it's not good enough for Princess Shira."

"Stop," Shira said, her voice breaking. "Is that really how you see me?"

Ben placed a hand on Shira's knee, signaling he had something to say. Liz glared at the two of them. "Oh no. You're not going to double team me. I'm not having some creepy old man all up in my cervix. No fucking way."

"So that's it," Shira said. "It's because he's a man."

"Yes. And no. I have a doctor I like. A doctor who knows my body. A doctor I feel safe with. Get it?"

"Everyone just calm down for a minute," Ben said.

"Don't tell me to calm down. I'm not being talked out of this."

"Let's just hear Ben out," Shira said. She clutched a rumpled throw pillow to her chest. "He is the father, after all."

Liz paused for a second and crossed her arms. Ben asked Liz to join them on the couch. "Just sit down. Come on."

"Nope," Liz said. "I'm fine right where I am."

"Okay," Ben said. "I think we can both acknowledge this was a kind offer from Cantor Weissmann and that he only means well."

"That's right," Shira said.

"That's your idea of kind? Forcing someone to see a gyno they don't want to see."

"No one is forcing anyone," Ben said. "Shira's parents are trying to help and we should all be grateful for that. But you're carrying this baby, so of course you should see whichever doctor you feel most comfortable with. I get it."

A raw groan leapt out of Shira's throat. "What?" Shira tossed the pillow aside. "One of the best hospitals in the country. Why wouldn't you want this?"

"It's not like we're in Arkansas or Mississippi. There are lots of good doctors in Boston."

"That's right," Liz said. "And I'll still be having the baby in a hospital. One that's not a forty dollar Uber ride. You're not going to shit on Brigham and Women's now, are you?"

"No," Shira said, but she was clearly upset.

Ben briefly imagined Liz going into labor in the back of an Uber. No, this was not how he expected the birth of his child to come about, but he and Shira had made so many plans, so many assumptions before her hysterectomy that had all died on the vine, so he was learning the hard way not to wish-cast too much and to let things happen the way they needed to happen.

"So. I'm sticking with Doctor Quan. She wants me in for an ultrasound at six weeks. End of next week. Are you coming with me?"

"Of course I'm coming with you," Shira said. "And Ben too. We're in this together."

Shira stood up and went to Liz. "Gimme a hug. I'm sorry. I just get freaked out sometimes. What's happening—this—is huge."

"True dat," Liz said. "And soon I'm gonna be huge."

Liz folded Shira into her arms and then said, "Ben. Get over here and join us."

Ben threw his arms around Shira and Liz and thought of Pamela home alone with his baby in her belly. Who would hold her when she needed someone to show they cared? It occurred to Ben that he had never asked Pamela who her doctor was and where she was planning on delivering the baby.

After Liz left, Shira's fixed "see you soon" smile broke and she began to cry. "Why did you do that, Ben? Why did you take her side?"

"I didn't take her side. There are no sides here. But Liz wasn't wrong, and I'm sure her doctor is more than adequate."

"More than adequate is not good enough for our baby. We should have the best, so that nothing goes wrong." Shira stalked into their bedroom and Ben followed close behind. "I just don't get it. You're my husband. You're supposed to have my back."

"I do have your back. Just remember, this pregnancy is going to last nine months, give or take. Do you really want to fight over every little thing?"

"This isn't just a little thing. A clinic, when she can have her pick of any doctor."

"I think Liz has made her pick." Ben brushed a strand of hair out of Shira's eyes and said, "It sounds like you don't trust Liz's judgment."

Shira was quiet for a long time, her face expressionless. "No, that's not true. It's just she isn't doing things the way I would do them, and I feel so helpless because Liz is having the baby and I'm not. It's hard. Really hard. I mean, is this baby really going to be my baby?"

"Of course! It's going to be our baby."

"Then why do I feel like I don't have a place right now?"

"Because it's new and it's scary and because we don't know what's going to happen. But we have to trust the process. We're in this now. It's happening."

"Then why do I feel so crappy?"

"Because it matters so much. And it's out of your hands."

"That's why Doctor Abramovich was so important. I was doing something to help. It was going to be my contribution."

"There will be lots of ways for you to contribute before this is all over."

"You think?"

"I know." Ben raised Shira's chin with his knuckle. "Look at me." Shira did so, eyes sharp, focused on Ben. "That's right. Now take a deep breath."

They both took five or six deep breaths together, looking each other in the eyes, then Ben closed his eyes, signaling for Shira to do the same, and before long Ben could feel his cortisol levels lowering, his heart beat slowing, and he knew the same was happening for Shira when she broke off finally and said, "Thank you, baby, I needed that."

"We both did. It's been a pretty intense evening."

Shira disappeared into their walk-in closet, and Ben assumed she was getting changed for bed, but she came back out with a small box wrapped in festive wrapping paper. "I was saving this. I figure now is as good a time as any to give it to you."

Ben held the box in his hands, expecting it to be heavier than it was. But it weighed just a few ounces. "Is it safe to shake it?"

"Why don't you just open it and see."

Ben tore off the wrapping paper and lifted the lid on the cardboard box to find a baseball cupped in plastic casing, nested in foam peanuts.

"Take it out," Shira said, a huge smile on her face. "It's signed."

Ben extracted the baseball from the box carefully so as not to shed the foam peanuts all over the floor.

At first Ben couldn't believe what he was seeing and his mouth dropped open as he stared wide-eyed at the baseball. The leather of the ball had yellowed with the years, but Ben could easily make out the signature scrawled between the tight red seams of the baseball. Shira's upturned, smiling face reminded Ben of a flower taking in sun. "It's signed by Casey Stengel."

"I know," Shira said, nibbling on her lower lip. "Do you like it?"

"Like it?" Ben stammered. "I love it. It's the most thoughtful gift anyone has ever given me."

"I got it on eBay and it should be certified." Shira sifted through the box, setting loose a hailstorm of packing peanuts until she found the documentation of authenticity. "See. It's real."

The baseball felt so small in Ben's hands. Casey Stengel, the Old Perfesser, had held this ball in his wizened old hands in 1962, the Mets inaugural year in which they had lost three out of every four games and played before nearly a million fans at the Polo Grounds. Ben's father had been one of those fans, a baseball crazy thirteen-year-old who loved their diminutive catcher Choo-Choo Coleman, who could barely hit and couldn't catch either, but the name ... The name was a Hall of Fame name if ever there was one. Ben gripped the ball as if he were about to throw a four-seam fastball and mimed a pitch to home plate, flashes of his father nearly knocking Ben off his feet as if he had just appeared in the room. "You know, my father, my parents, would have loved you."

"I know, Ben. I know."

25

The clinic was a nondescript storefront on a busy commercial thoroughfare in Jamaica Plain. Ben drove the three of them in the Subaru with Liz uncharacteristically silent in the back seat, while Ben and Shira chatted idly about anything but the child Liz was carrying. It was a crisp sunny day, and Ben felt lucky to be alive in that unique way in which autumn felt like a season of renewal. He found a parking spot a block away in front of a rundown bodega and jumped out of the car before Liz had a chance to get out on her own. He offered Liz his hand and Liz took it.

"You're so corny," Liz said, with a smile. "But thanks."

"This is it," Shira said. "It's happening."

Though Liz had never been the least bit fragile, Ben felt the irrational need to protect her as she walked down the sidewalk. She was dressed in red high top Chuck Taylors, a pair of ripped jeans and a black hoodie, dark sunglasses on her face. But to Ben, Liz may as well have been wearing the most delicate silk, tottering on five-inch stilettos over broken glass. He made sure to walk ahead of Liz and Shira, kicking a crushed beer can out of the way, barring Liz and Shira's progression with a stiff-armed stop signal as a stream of cars crawled past.

"I guess this is Ben's idea of chivalry." Liz laughed.

"Ben will hate me for saying this," Shira said, "but he's more old fashioned than he'd like to admit."

"Don't make fun," Ben said. "I'm trying to help."

"And I appreciate that," Liz said. "But I'm not a porcelain doll. I know you mean well, but come on, I can walk a block without a chaperone."

"Sorry." Ben flushed as traffic opened up and the three of them crossed. "I didn't mean to."

"It's okay." Liz squeezed his hand. "It's kind of sweet in a pre-feminist sort of way."

The clinic's waiting room was a standard sterile doctor's office waiting room with worn upholstered chairs lining the walls beneath the fluorescent lights. Soothing pastel watercolors were punctuated by aspirational photographs of women kayaking, jogging, gardening, jubilant atop a mountain peak.

Liz approached the reception window, rapping on the glass with the back of her knuckles.

Shira squeezed Ben's hand, her short nails leaving half-moon impressions of her worry.

"This isn't so bad," Ben said. "It feels like a doctor's office to me."

"I'm just so nervous," Shira said. "We're going to see our baby for the first time. What if something is wrong?"

"Nothing is going to go wrong," Ben assured. "You're okay with this place?"

"Yes. Sometimes I just get set in my ways and, well, you know. I can really be a bit of a snob. A little outside perspective is always good."

When the doctor called Liz in for her appointment, Liz told Shira to join them, but not Ben.

"Dr. Quan will be looking at my lady parts. No speculum show for you."

"Ben's going to join us for the ultrasound, right?" Shira said.

"Of course," Liz said. "But first things first. Don't worry. We're all going to see it together."

Ben dropped heavily into the chair and picked up an outdated copy of *Ms.* magazine.

"I'll call you when we're ready, hun."

And then they were gone behind a heavy door that locked from the inside.

Ben couldn't concentrate to read. Surely Pamela had visited the OB/GYN for several prenatal visits by now. He should have been there beside her, caring for her so she wouldn't have to do it alone.

It didn't take long for Shira to poke her head out the door and say, "Come on, Ben. It's time."

Liz lay on the table, tilted to a 30° angle, her glam David Bowie T-shirt lifted to display her flat tattooed abdomen and pierced belly button.

"Don't you have to take out the ring?"

"That's what you're thinking now?" Shira said.

"I mean, won't it affect the ultrasound?"

"I see you haven't done any googling on the subject," Liz said. "When my belly pops, I'll take it out, but for now it's all good."

Dr. Quan, a pretty Asian woman who looked to be in her early thirties, with her hair pulled back in a severe ponytail, smiled at Ben. "I know you must have a lot of worries as a first-time father, but Liz is young and healthy, and she's in good hands."

"Yep," Shira said.

"And," Liz interjected, "Dr. Quan is a graduate of Harvard Medical School."

"Um, yep." Shira smiled a sheepish smile.

"We like to do an ultrasound at the first visit to assure the baby is in the uterus and has a heartbeat. We won't be able to tell you much beyond that except a better idea of due date."

The technician applied the ultrasound gel to Liz's belly.

"That shit is cold!" Liz said. Shira took Liz's hand and stared at the monitor.

Dr. Quan turned to Ben. "Basically we will be measuring the amniotic sac and gauging how many beats per minute. The heart should look like a blinking or flickering on the screen. That will be your baby. Ready?"

A moment later the screen filled with a disorienting gray swirl against a black background that reminded Ben of the scrambled porn he so eagerly watched on his bedroom TV as a horny teenager on Long Island. The technician slid the wand over Liz's belly in search of the baby.

Dr. Quan pointed at the screen. "This is the uterus. This is the gestational sack. This—" Dr. Quan paused, her fingers circling a blobby peanut-shaped ghost pulsing in a pool of blackness "—is the heartbeat. Do you see it?"

"Oh my God," Shira shrieked, crushing Ben's hand. "Oh my God. It's the most beautiful thing I've ever seen."

"Hardly." Liz wore a huge smile on her face. "It looks just like Necronom IV. Thank you HR Giger for spoiling my pregnancy."

"What's the matter?" Shira said, her eyes anxiously alternating between Liz and the image on the screen.

Liz laughed. "Just an Alien joke. I guess a Xenomorph XX121 isn't that funny right about now."

Ben squinted his eyes and saw something happening on the screen as the image pulsed *hello, goodbye, hello, goodbye, hello, goodbye.* It sounded like a horse galloping across a darkened plain, and Ben just wanted it to slow down long enough for him to wrap his arms around it.

Shira was crying now, overcome with emotion. She dropped Ben's hand and stepped closer to the monitor, eyes fixated on the screen.

"Ben, that's our baby. I can't believe I'm looking at our baby."

"Believe it," Liz said.

"At 5.7 mm, it is growing as expected," Dr. Quan said. "That puts us at just over six weeks."

"This is a miracle," Shira said. "Our baby is growing." She paused and turned to Liz, asking, "May I?" before placing her hand on Liz's abdomen. "Our baby is in there."

"I never thought I'd ever be a mother," Liz said. "But here we are, and it's pretty fucking awesome." Then, raising her voice in a battle cry, "I am a goddess! I make people out of my own stuff."

Shira froze for an instant, barely a second, but it was long enough for Ben to notice and fully comprehend that this was not Shira's baby, not of her flesh and blood, and that she knew she would always be on the outside with this child, no matter how openhearted she and Liz promised to be.

It was Ben's child, but not Shira's, and the reality of that pulsing thumbprint on the monitor's screen only underscored the fact of Shira's inability to carry a child. Shira continued to fawn over the screen and Liz's magic belly, but it was clear now Shira was being brave. This was not her child. This was a terrible compromise, and time would tell whether it was the worst mistake of her life or the best decision she ever made.

The examination room felt suddenly very small, and Ben's legs began to itch. He needed to get outside, alone, to sort out the tumult of feelings boiling inside him.

Dr. Quan continued, "The heart rate is 126 bpm, which is excellent. Precisely where we want to be right now."

The walls seemed to be leaning in, pressing the air out of Ben's lungs. Ben excused himself, claiming he needed some fresh air. *I put a baby in the wrong woman,* Ben thought. *I put a baby in the wrong woman.* It should have been Shira carrying his baby.

Out on the street, Ben could not let go of the thought that his wife, Shira, who so badly wanted a baby of her own, was watching the beating heart of a six-week fetus clicking away inside the uterus of another woman, while Pamela, too, carried another of Ben's would-be children, and Shira, barren, desolate, ever hopeful, had to sit by and smile.

Ben had to be the worst person in the entire history of the world.

Ben slipped his phone out of his pocket, fingers poised to text Pamela that he wanted to see his child, that he wished he had never met her, that he was sorry for everything, that he had every right to be in his child's life. His fingers hovered dumbly over the keyboard, mute and impotent. There was nothing he could say that had not already been said. Pamela knew better than anyone that words were just words, and that Ben had exhausted every last one, so he clicked off his phone and began to pace back and forth along the grimy sidewalk, echoing countless men of generations past perched on the cusp of fatherhood and helpless to do anything about it.

A few minutes later an exhilarated Liz and Shira burst out of the door of the clinic, hand-in-hand.

"That was amazing," Liz said. "It really feels real now, like this is happening for real, you know?"

"Thank you so much for agreeing to do this for us."

"You're my heart, baby." Liz noticed Ben stretching out his calves absently on the sidewalk. "What happened to you?"

"Just needed some air. It was pretty intense in there."

Shira kissed Liz and then, without even attempting to wipe Liz off her lips, she kissed Ben softly on the lips. How different really was it from Ben kissing Liz, Ben wondered?

"And you, Liz, darling. I'm taking you clothes shopping—on me, of course. Let's get you styled up for the next seven and a half months."

"I don't need anything," Liz said flatly.

"You need maternity clothes, Mama."

Liz stopped short a few steps from the car. "I really don't. I'm good with what I have."

"Hey, it's on me. It's my pleasure to take you shopping for some new stuff. Your adorable body is going to be going through some serious changes. You want to look good, don't you?"

"No, obviously I want to look like a pile of shit," Liz said. "What I'm saying is, you're wasting your money on some clothing I'm only going to wear a few times."

"I'm paying," Shira said, "as a token of my appreciation for what you're doing."

"I can't even," Liz said, shaking her head.

"Don't you want to look nice?" Shira pressed.

"I can take care of myself. Give me fifteen minutes in a Goodwill and I can make myself into anything I want. I just need a size or two up. I don't need to feed the Maternity Industrial Complex."

Ben climbed into the driver seat and turned the ignition, hoping Shira and Liz would take the hint and get in the car.

"You're not shopping for maternity clothes at Goodwill."

"Oh, aren't I? What's the matter with Goodwill?"

"Come on. I'm trying to do something nice for you."

"I didn't ask for this. I don't want some suburban shopping mall cookie-cutter maternity tent. And if you think I'm going to wear elastic waistband mom jeans, you're out of your mind."

"It's not like that," Shira said. "I saw this really cute romper with skulls all over it that I'd love to see you in. There's so much cool stuff for expectant mothers now."

"I'm not your fucking Barbie doll to dress up as you like."

"Whoa. Where did that come from?"

Ben turned on the radio, hoping that the music would entice them into the car. But some crap by Aerosmith was playing so he turned the radio off and said, "Are we going?"

"One second," Shira said to Ben. Then to Liz, "Why are you so quick to assume the worst? I thought you'd like this. I thought we'd have fun shopping together. You think my kindness means I want to change you into something you're not. It's not true. I love you exactly as you are, but I want to help you when I can."

"Oh, thank you so much for your help. The fact that you think this is kindness and not some classist patronizing bullshit is all I need to know."

"Stop, please," Shira pleaded.

"You stop. It's insulting that you want to do this like I'm some piece of white trash who doesn't know how to dress themselves."

"That wasn't my intention."

"What was it then? To own me? To make me feel grateful for your generosity? Can't you see this is just another power play, flaunting your joint bank account and middle-class values?"

"You're making me sad," Shira said evenly.

"Good! Maybe you'll think twice before you pull a dick move like this again. I'm going to walk."

"Please," Shira said. "Just get in the car."

"I don't want to see you right now."

And then Liz was gone, powering down the sidewalk at an impressive clip.

"Do you want me to go after her?" Ben said.

"No," Shira said, her mouth in a pout. "Did I do something wrong there? I just don't get it."

"I think it was a nice gesture." Ben pulled into the street. "Just don't push it. Let her have a couple hours and then check in and see how she's doing. There's a lot going on right now. Hormone levels are all over the place and can affect neurotransmitters, which can cause some pretty intense mood swings."

"You read that in a book somewhere?" Shira said sharply.

"Let's just focus on what's important."

"And what is that, Ben?"

"A healthy baby is what's important."

"But I wanted to do something nice. I wanted to take her shopping."

"That's what *you* wanted," Ben said, and then Shira clued in.

"Oh, fuck. I'm such an idiot."

"You are the farthest thing from an idiot."

"Why did I do that?"

"Because you thought she'd appreciate it."

"I really did. I just don't get it."

"Please try not to let it upset you. We saw our baby today."

"We did." Shira smiled a soft smile. "Are you sure I shouldn't go after her?"

"Yep. She'll come around. I promise. Now, if you really want to go shopping I could use some new pants."

"Without pleats?" Shira smiled.

"Without pleats."

"Deal. Let's hit Nordstrom Rack."

26

Ben had just put away his new pants when Liz texted Shira to apologize for being such a terrible brat. *It was wrong how I acted. If you need me to wear a circus tent to make you happy, I'll do it, haha.*

"See?" Ben said. "Everything will be fine."

Shira thanked Liz for the apology and said there was no need; she liked the way Liz dressed.

To make up for her shopping faux pas, Shira and Ben invited Liz over for a nice Rosh HaShana dinner, and though Liz said she had plans already, she'd happily join the two of them for dinner first. "A true family dinner," Shira said to Ben.

And Ben responded, "The first of many."

The doorbell rang just after six and a freshly shaved Ben answered the door. Liz stood on the threshold clutching a bottle of red wine and a colorful spray of flowers wrapped in clear cellophane. She was dressed in a tight miniskirt and high black sheer stockings, a satiny silver shirt unbuttoned to her line of cleavage. Liz smiled sheepishly as if she was unsure if what she was wearing was appropriate for the second holiest day of the Jewish calendar. With Ben wearing his new beige khakis and a polo shirt, Liz seemed to be both overdressed and underdressed at the same time.

"Happy New Years!" Liz said with a faux-festive cry. "It smells great in here."

Shira had made her famous braided challah, and the entire condo was redolent of its warm yeasty sweetness.

Ben greeted Liz, took the wine and flowers and thanked her. Liz opened her arms for a hug, squeezing Ben and whispering in his ear. "Hey, I'm sorry about the clothing thing. I'm just super stressed. Way more than I ever thought."

"I get it. But you know, stress isn't good for the baby."

"I know," Liz said, laughing. "And that stresses me the fuck out too."

Shira appeared behind Ben, still wearing her Yiddish-lettered *Balaboosta* apron, a giant fork in her hand. "Look at you two." She laughed.

As Ben and Liz parted, Shira kissed Ben on the lips, and then, more lingeringly, Ben thought, she kissed Liz. "For a sweet year for all of us."

"Is there something I should be doing?" Liz paced across the kitchen trying to busy herself, heels clacking on the floor.

Ben was about to make a corny joke that Liz could blow the shofar, the ritual ram's horn Ben had received twenty-one years earlier for his bar mitzvah to use on Rosh HaShana and Yom Kippur, but, considering Liz had just Ubered over, any joke about blowing the shofar would sound needlessly sexual. Instead, Ben reflexively offered Liz a glass of wine.

"Just enjoy yourself," Shira said, her small hand stroking Liz's belly. And then, turning to Ben, "No wine for mama over here."

"What?" Liz said, her big kohl-lined eyes widening.

"Precious cargo," Shira said. "Can't take the risk."

"Dr Quan says one glass every once in a while won't hurt," Liz said.

"Well, better safe than sorry." Shira directed Ben with a cutting motion not to fill Liz's glass.

"Hey, it's New Year's Eve," Liz said. "I'm *going* to have a glass of wine."

"It's not New Year's Eve. It's the Jewish new year."

"I don't see the difference. It's just wine. It's not like I'm shooting junk into my veins."

"That's your argument? At least it's not heroin?"

"No. This is *your* argument, and you're being ridiculous. All I want is—"

"One small glass should be fine," Ben said, not wanting to inflame another conflict. The two of them seemed so wound up, he was afraid it would not take much to set Shira and Liz to arguing again. Ben had read in a Harvard study that small amounts of alcohol would not harm a baby and discussed this same subject with Pamela not that long ago. "I'll bet even the rabbis approve of a ritual glass of wine. You know, ceremonial—"

"Seriously?" Shira said. "I can't believe you." She popped the oven door open and ostentatiously offered Ben and Liz her back, busying herself with the brisket, stabbing it needlessly with a fork.

Liz and Ben exchanged doubtful looks, and Ben poured a touch of wine into Liz's glass as they drifted out into the dining room.

"Isn't anyone else coming?" Liz asked, circling the dining room table in her wedge heels, glass of wine in hand.

"Nope," Shira snapped, still fussing with the brisket.

"Okaaaaaay."

Fans of sliced red apple were spread out on the table beside small ceramic pots of organic honey Shira had picked up at the farmers market. Liz dipped an apple in the honey and popped it in her mouth. "Yum. This is really good."

"I get it." Shira slammed the oven closed. "The wine you brought is really good. You don't need to rub my nose in the fact you're drinking."

Ben watched helplessly as Liz's expression shifted from one of mannered forbearance to something close to atomic rage, a frightening transformation that would have had Ben ducking for cover under different circumstances. The entire misunderstanding was lamentable enough as it was, made only more tragic by the fact that Shira had eagerly practiced her speech about the cycle-of-life symbolism of the apple and the honey to Ben so that she could educate Liz and enfold her in the loving embrace of one of her favorite Jewish customs. But Shira never had the chance to say, "May your year be sweet, fruitful and filled with contentment and promise," because Liz was on fire, and Ben couldn't blame her.

"Fuck you," Liz said. "Just fuck you and your fucking attitude, telling me what I can and cannot do. You invite me to your home and you treat me like I'm some kind of addict. That shit's way behind me, okay? And this othering you're trying to pull is just not cool. If I wanted to steal your fucking silverware, I would have done it by now."

Shira had gone white when she realized her mistake, rushing across the length of the kitchen into the dining room. "Oh my god, I'm so, so sorry. I thought—"

"I'm just the dumb, fertile *shiksa* carrying your baby for you. I can't possibly understand the intricacies of your five-thousand-year-old traditions. And by the way, patriarchy is still patriarchy, no matter how you dress it up. That's why religion is poison. It does nothing more than divide us."

"No. I made a mistake, okay? I wanted so badly to do this right. I'm just nervous."

"You're more than nervous. You're unhinged."

The two of them went at it, Liz accusing Shira of treating her as a second-class citizen, of slumming with the tattooed girl. She said Shira was uptight, domineering and superior. "You like to fuck a woman because you think it's some woke act of solidarity with your downtrodden sisters." Liz got right up in Shira's face, towering over Shira in her heels, spitting her words with an intensity that almost caused Ben to jump out of his chair and physically separate them.

Shira tried to psychologize with Liz, asking what she thought was motivating such an outburst. Was she projecting? Liz called Shira a stuck up bitch and a limousine liberal. Shira said the only time she had ever ridden in a limousine was for her grandmother's funeral, to which Liz replied, "My grandmother died alone on her bathroom floor and was cremated so her ashes could be flushed down the toilet. Got it? We're different people, me and you."

Finally, Ben found the courage to interject, saying he was worried the brisket might burn. And Shira took Ben's lifeline to put a halt to the hostilities, but not before she said, "This is about us and the baby, isn't it."

Liz said nothing, dropped down into the chair intended for Shira and swallowed her entire glass of wine. "I'm just hangry. The two of us need to eat something." Liz gestured to her nonexistent belly with her beringed fingers.

"Oh, right," Shira said. "Mama needs to eat. Coming right up."

Shira served her famous brisket and a homemade kugel and her honey-glazed carrots. "Before we start," Shira said. "I just want to say how happy I am that I am able to start the Jewish new year with my two very favorite people in the world. I love and accept each of you as you are, and I hope you're able to overlook my flaws and faults. I promise to do my best to be a better person every day and to continue to help to heal the world."

"That was lovely," Ben said.

"Back at you, babe," Liz said, throwing a wink.

Shira asked Liz to light the candles, and Shira chanted the blessing in a stilted, teacherly manner. Bathed in the golden light of the candles, all the ugliness and anger and doubt seemed to have been banished, walled off into the past, another year gone. Liz's tight features had softened and, though she didn't smile, her eyes said she was open to whatever came next. Ben raised his glass and Liz and Shira followed suit. He said the blessing over the wine and they each took a grateful gulp.

The brisket was overcooked, but it didn't matter.

Ben told a story of the time one Rosh HaShana when Shira's father attempted, ostentatiously, pompously, to blow the shofar, the relentless performer in him on full display for a table of twenty, but he farted instead, and nearly died of embarrassment.

"We all had to run for cover." Shira laughed.

"It was one of the great moments of my life," Ben said.

"Stop," Shira said. "Leave the poor man alone."

"I'm pretty sure his gas attack was against the Geneva Conventions."

Shira doubled over in laughter, but Liz was not laughing, a far-away look in her eyes. "My family never did holidays. Not even Christmas, really."

"I'm sorry, babe," Shira said, the smile on her face fading.

"It means a lot that you are including me. This is special."

"Of course," Shira said. "You're family."

They talked about childhood birthdays, summer vacations and learning to ride a bike. Ben said he always preferred to run, while Liz said a bike was the first time she ever realized you can change your reality just by changing your setting. "If it wasn't for my brother's hand-me-down banana seat BMX, maybe I'd never have left."

By the time Ben got up to clear the dishes everyone was feeling good. Liz even laughed when Ben trotted out the old chestnut about the essence of every Jewish holiday: "They tried to kill us, we survived, let's eat."

"That's really kind of morbid," Liz said. "I love it."

"This is really fun," Shira said. "Having you here like this."

"I've been here before."

"Yes, I know, but it feels different now. You know what I mean?"

"I get it."

"I wish you didn't have to go so soon."

Ben knew that feeling well, that sense of loss even as you are in the presence of your beloved, because the moment cannot last and they will leave you.

"Where are you going anyway?" Ben said, sliding back into his seat at the table.

"Out," Liz said, evasively.

"That sounds kind of suspicious," Shira said.

"Please don't start," Liz said. "I don't want to spoil a lovely evening."

"Well, now you have to tell me," Shira said.

After a long pause, Liz said, "I'm going to a party, okay?" And when Shira did not respond, Liz added, "With Jeanne and Jim."

Shira's eyebrows nearly jumped off her face. "I thought you weren't seeing them anymore."

"I'm not. It's just, we've been texting a bit and they want to see me."

"You know you didn't have to say yes,"

"Maybe I wanted to see them too."

A sudden chill had entered the room, and the guttering candles flickered, causing ghastly shadows to dance across Shira's face. Ben got up to close the window.

"All right," Shira said. "And are you going to have sex with them?"

"Would it be wrong if I did?"

"You're pregnant with our child," Shira said.

"Don't even think about slut-shaming me."

"Wait," Shira said. "You're serious. You might actually sleep with them?" "I honestly have no idea. It's one night. It's not like we haven't all done it before. I promise, it's no big deal if it happens."

"Is that what you really think?"

"We never agreed we wouldn't play with other people. Whatever happens tonight does not change how I feel about you."

Shira's eyes were full of tears and she turned her face away from Liz. "Have fun then."

"That's my intention." Liz pushed back from the table. "I can see myself out."

As soon as the front door closed behind Liz, Shira broke down, throwing herself into Ben's arms, repeating over and over again, "I'm so stupid, I'm so stupid, I'm so stupid."

Ben assured Shira she was the farthest thing from stupid.

The warmth of her body pressed into Ben's, and, though the tears pouring from Shira were raw and ugly, Ben found her to be perfectly beautiful. Ben mused how easily the two of them had once found each other's bodies to be the answer to any crisis, before Liz, before Pamela, when it was just the two of them till death do them part. Could they ever return to their own private Eden, in which they were enough for each other and nothing and no one else mattered?

Ben grabbed Shira's hand. "Come on."

They stood across from each other in the yellow lamplight of the bedroom like two shy strangers, unsure what to do next, the ticking of the bedside clock audible, out of sync with the beating of Ben's pounding heart. Shira stood no more than a foot or two away from Ben, her damp eyes searching his. Ben was aware how hot his hands were, like two irons in a fire, as he pulled Shira close and kissed her fiercely.

She kissed him back, and, as if by some mysterious process, they had each gone back in time, their future as yet unimagined, just two bodies hungry for each other. They slipped out of their clothes in ardent silence, tossing them haphazardly on the floor. Ben had never felt more vulnerable standing naked in front of his wife, wanting forgiveness, redemption, a chance to start all over, to erase the last two years of pain and confusion. He wanted so much.

"I love you," Ben said.

"Just shut up and fuck me."

Afterwards Ben and Shira lay side by side on the bed, not touching, just breathing, eyes up at the ceiling.

"What are you thinking?" Shira asked at last.

"How are we going to make this all work?"

"You mean with Liz and the baby?"

"Yes."

"We'll make it work because we have to make it work."

"What if you and Liz keep fighting? I hate to see you like that. How's that going to work when the child is here?"

"I haven't shown my best self lately. I'm aware of that. But I know we'll find a way to make it work, because we have no other choice."

He couldn't stand the thought of being caught in the crossfire between Shira and Liz as they tried to raise a healthy and well-balanced child. But Ben had another choice, and that was with the baby Pamela carried, and he couldn't accept the idea that he simply would not exist in his child's life. There had to be a way to make it work in which he could be in his child's life without driving Shira away.

27

A week and a half later Ben was jarred awake by Shira frantically shaking him. He'd been dreaming of his and Pamela's child. The boy—it was a boy, only it had Ben's father's face as a middle-aged man—was trying to tell Ben something of great import, but Ben was pulled out of his dream before he could decipher the words. Ben's heart revved as he took that first conscious gasp of air, and he was wide awake in an instant. He was in his and Shira's room, lit only by her bedside lamp. It was still dark outside.

"The baby's in trouble," Shira said, hovering over Ben, her pallid face a mask of worry.

"What time is it?"

"Something's wrong with the baby."

"Wha? Which baby?" Ben said, a frigid shock of recognition shooting up the length of his spine.

"Liz is bleeding from her vagina."

Ben pulled himself up onto his pillow so he was leaning against the headboard. He glanced at the clock. It was 3:23 a.m.

"Something's wrong. Something is really wrong. Ben, I'm freaking out here." Shira's hands shook and her chin trembled as if she were about to burst into tears.

"Are you sure the baby is in trouble?"

Shira twisted her face into a hard, angry expression. "We have to go. Now. I need you to drive me. I'm too upset to get behind the wheel."

"Okay, okay." Ben dragged himself out of bed. "I'll drive."

Ben was still drowsy from sleep as their car cut through the darkness.

"Can't you go faster?" Shira said, pressing her feet to the floor as if doing so would cause the Subaru to accelerate to warp speed.

Ben did as she asked, revving the engine against the quiet night.

"I'm afraid she's having a miscarriage. I was afraid this was going to happen."

There were no cars on the road so Ben blew through a freshly turned red light.

"I know this happened because of Jeanne and Jim. It's not a coincidence. Liz is their bottom. They did this to her. They caused the miscarriage."

"We don't know that it's a miscarriage. It could be a lot of things."

"Oh yes, I do. I know how rough they can be with her. Jim is a very large man."

"Please don't go there."

Ben reached out a hand to Shira and she took it. The contrast between his large hairy-knuckled hand and her small, almost childlike one flooded Ben with a deep sense of love for his wife who needed him to assure her everything would be all right. Her hand was clammy and shook nervously. He wanted to kiss her and tell her he had no doubt that things were going to be okay—because they had each other. Instead Ben said, "Promise you won't mention this theory to Liz."

"It's not a theory."

"Do you love Liz?"

"Of course I do. You know that."

"Then don't say anything about this. Be support-ive. This isn't easy for her. This is happening in her body. No matter what happens, and I'm not saying the worst is going to happen, but if it does, there's only one thing to do and that is to be supportive."

They arrived at Brigham and Women's Hospital just after 4 a.m. Shira jumped out of the car in search of Liz, while Ben went to park the car. Moments later, Ben found Shira arguing with a woman at the recep-tion desk who would not allow Shira in to see Liz be-cause she was not family.

"Not family?" Shira screamed. "She's carrying my baby!"

Ben slipped up behind Shira and took her by the elbow, giving it a firm squeeze. "Come on. Let's have a seat."

Shira threw herself into Ben's arms. "I feel like I'm going mad. I need to do something."

Ben smiled a gentle smile, his voice softened of any edge. "I know. Try not to worry. We don't know anything yet. Maybe it's just normal spotting."

"You think?" Shira looked up at Ben, a strange, trusting look in her eyes.

"I do think."

"Okay," Shira said, her expression darkening. "But what if?"

"Let's not do 'what if?'"

Shira pulled out her phone to search for signs and symptoms of miscarriage, and Ben covered Shi-ra's hand with his own, trying to dissuade her.

"Don't," Shira said. "Just don't. I need to do something."

Seconds later the screen filled with a litany of answers.

"Sometimes," Shira said, turning Ben by the shoulders to look at her phone's tiny screen, "there can be bleeding, even blood clots. This can last for a couple of days sometimes. But," she said, raising her voice, as if pronouncing an edict, "sometimes symptoms settle down and the pregnancy carries on as normal. What do you think?"

"It's definitely possible."

But Shira knew. The way she sat with her shoulders slumped, head downturned, arms hanging loose at her sides said it all. Ben put an arm around her and kissed her on the top of her head and said he loved her.

"I'm scared," Shira said.

"I know."

Liz came out the double doors of the ER close to 6 a.m., looking drawn and pale, a blank expression on her face. Shira waited in her chair, passive and exhausted, as Liz approached.

Then Liz shook her head in a definitive no. "It's gone."

Shira cried out a single, inarticulate cry, a wrenching sound more beast than human, and buried her head between her knees. Ben stood up and approached Liz, unsure what she needed, but offering a hug nonetheless. Liz said thanks, but she didn't want to be touched after all the poking around she had just endured.

Liz dropped exhaustedly into a chair between Ben and Shira. Ben offered a sympathetic smile. Liz returned something like a smile, but looked past Ben, not in his eyes, but beyond to her reflection in the ER window. Shira lightly massaged Liz's back. "I wish I could've been there with you. You shouldn't have had to go through this alone."

"I've been through worse. Believe me."

"I know, babe, but I'm in your life now. You shouldn't have to suffer alone anymore."

"I don't see how it matters. Suffering is suffering. There's nothing you or anybody could have done. It sucks balls. That's all."

A couple appeared in the waiting room, a woman leading a man bleeding heavily from his head. He held a blood-soaked cloth against his temple as he sleepwalked towards the reception area, leaving a trail of blood behind him.

At last, after a long, demolishing silence, Liz muttered, "I'm sorry I let you down."

"Oh, baby, you didn't let me down. These things happen. I'm just glad you're okay."

Liz's head jerked as if she'd been stung. "I'm not okay. I'm pretty fucking far from okay. There was a living thing growing inside me. And now it's gone. It was more than just blood. This wasn't just a period with a heavy flow. It was—" And then Liz stopped and laughed a youthful laugh, teenagerish in its pitch and unlike anything Ben had ever heard expressed from Liz before.

"When the doctor said the fetus had no heartbeat and that it had been expelled from my body, it's like a tiny part of me died. Not some other, mysterious metastasizing being, but a part of me. Like I was going to be a mother and now I'm not. Just like that."

"Don't worry," Shira said after a heavy silence. "We can try again." After Liz did not answer, did not so much as stir, Shira amended, "Whenever you're ready. No hurry."

"Honestly," Liz said. "I'm disgusted with my body right now. The thing is, I never thought I'd be that person, a mother. It was like I had the power to create life and it was fucking awesome, like I was in awe of what I had the power to do. I mean fuck yeah! And then that power was taken away."

"It happens," Shira said. "It's not your fault. It's not uncommon for a mother to have a miscarriage on the first try, right Ben?"

Ben nodded his head in assent, but knew he should let the two of them have the space for this discussion without him weighing in. He felt a sense of dread whispering at the tiny hairs at the back of his neck that this wasn't going to go the way he and Shira wanted.

Liz, dry-lipped and pale, turned her dead eyes to Shira. "I can't."

"Can't what?" Shira urged, flapping her hands like an anxious bird.

"I can't do this again. It's just too much."

"Of course you can."

"I can't," Liz said, abruptly standing up. She tottered for a moment, and Ben rose to offer support. "I just want to go home and sleep forever."

"Babe, let's discuss this later, after you've rested. After you've recovered."

Liz stared back vacantly, her expression non-responsive, still in shock at the recent turn of events. "No. I don't ever want to talk about any of this ever again. I'm done."

Shira leapt to her feet and grabbed Liz by the shoulders. "No, no, no, no, no, no, no. This is just a minor setback. We'll get it right next time. Please don't give up on this. Please, let's try again. Just one more time. When you're ready. No hurry. But please—"

"I find you so repulsive right now," Liz said. "You need to take no as an answer. It's my body. Respect that."

What followed was almost too painful for Ben to watch: his wife dropping to her knees, clutching Liz around the waist, face pressed to Liz's empty belly, keening like a mourner as the walking wounded of the early morning emergency room waiting area looked on in numb silence.

"Won't you change your mind? Give it time?"

"Is it me you care about, or the baby you want me to give you?"

"Don't do that. Of course I care about you."

"Baby or no baby?"

"Please don't rule out trying again. Just one more time."

"I need a smoke," Liz said, pulling loose from Shira's grip. "Anyone have a cigarette?"

A construction worker nursing what looked like a dislocated shoulder slipped the hand of his functional arm into his pants' pocket and produced a crumpled pack of Newports. "Keep 'em, they're yours."

"You don't smoke anymore," Shira said, trailing after Liz, who was bee-lining for the exit with a renewed burst of energy.

"I do now."

Ben was helpless to stop Shira as she charged outside in pursuit of Liz, yanking a lit cigarette from her lips and grinding it into the sidewalk.

"I'm not done talking to you," Shira said, her face animated with righteousness. "You made a promise."

"I kept that promise. I did more to keep up my end of the bargain than you know. I've given up things, sacrificed my desires to make this happen for you."

"Don't do it," Ben was about to say. "Don't say a word."

But it was too late, and Shira went on the attack. "You didn't give up fucking Jeanne and Jim. What kind of mother goes to a fucking sex party while she's pregnant?"

"Okay." Liz nodded her head, slowly. "I see." She pulled another cigarette out of the pack and lit it, warning Shira not to touch her smoke. Liz's face darkened, features transformed into those of a dead-eyed killer. "I can do this if you really think I didn't live up to my end of the bargain. But I promise you, I will hate you forever. Whatever you choose to do, my body is off limits to you. You're not to touch me, you're not to so much as look at me with that ridiculous come-hither look in your big doe eyes. I'm done. We're finished. I'm going to call an Uber, so kindly fuck off so I can enjoy the rest of my smoke."

Ben tried to interject. "Maybe we should take some time to discuss this again later when things calm down."

Liz took her phone out and clicked around. She turned the screen toward Ben. "Tell your wife I've taken her out of my phone."

"Really?" Shira said. "You're really going to be like that?"

"Tell your wife," Liz said, refusing to look in Shira's direction, "this was all a huge mistake."

"Stop! We'll figure this out. Just please don't go."

An ambulance pulled into the driveway, its red lights flashing a dizzying crimson strobe across their faces.

"Don't even speak my name when you tell your wine-sipping book club friends about me. I'm just someone you used to fuck."

"No. No. You can't do this. We love each other. We'll find a way to make this work together. I promise I'll be better. I don't care about Jeanne and Jim. I don't care as long as you don't go."

Liz looked on impassively, her ice-blue eyes appraising Shira with a cruel coldness.

"Please don't go. Please," Shira said, and then, "Ben. Do something. Say something. She can't leave me."

Liz turned abruptly to walk away and Ben said, "Wait." But Liz continued on, not looking back. "Wait," Ben said again. But it was no use. Ben's heart broke for Shira, who stood shellshocked in the cool glow of the ambulance lights. He wanted to enfold her into a firm embrace, not just to comfort her, but to keep her from going after Liz. Shira's lip trembled, but she didn't call out as Liz disappeared behind a morning bus, and was gone.

Shira collapsed into Ben, her entire body shuddering against his.

"What do you need?" Ben said, a single hand caressing her tear-streaked cheek. "I'll do whatever you need."

"Honestly, I don't think there's anything anybody can do to make me feel better."

28

Shira slept for eleven hours without so much as stirring, and when she awoke her skin was sallow, her face creased by the pressure of her pillow against her cheek. Ben too had tried to sleep, but, lying in bed with the daylight streaming in beneath their drawn blinds, all he could think about was Shira, and the fact that once again their dream of having a child together had vanished.

"Hey," Ben said, stroking Shira's hair. "How you feeling?"

"I feel like I've been run over by a train."

"I know. I'm sorry."

"I was so stupid." Shira sat up and ran her fingers through her hair. "I knew asking Liz to carry your child put my relationship with her at risk. I knew the pressure it would put on all of us, but I did it anyway because I just wanted this child so badly."

"You're not stupid. You tried to find a way to make it work. I'd say that's pretty smart."

"I hurt you. I hurt Liz. I opened the door for Pamela and look what happened there."

Shira buried her face in Ben's chest and began to sob. "Sometimes I just hate myself so much for being broken. Billions of women all over the world are able to have a child and I can't. It's the loneliest feeling, being left out like this. Why did this have to happen to me?"

"I wish I knew. Just tell me what you need."

"What I need, apparently, is not possible."

Ben fixed himself and Shira scrambled eggs with toast—breakfast for dinner—and Shira listlessly moved the food around her plate, nibbling here and there. "I can't eat. I just feel—I don't know—hollow."

"Why don't you send Liz a message and see if she's okay."

"You think?"

"It wouldn't be inappropriate to let her know you're thinking of her."

"But she's so mad at me. I think she might actually hate me and I kinda can't blame her."

"It's worth a try anyway. Just to show you care."

Shira's face took on a determined look as she drew in a deep breath, reached for her phone and sent a quick message asking how Liz was feeling.

"Shit," Shira said, deflating. "Green. She's really blocked me. She's really fucking blocked me."

After everything that went down with Pamela, Pamela had never blocked Ben. His messages still went through blue, and he had to admit he was surprised Liz had blocked Shira.

"Now I feel even worse."

Ben reached for his phone. "Do you want to try mine?

"It's okay. I'll respect her space. I don't want to push where I'm not wanted. She's been through a lot." A vein pulsed in Shira's forehead. "I think I need to get away from everything for a while, maybe go back to Maryland and figure out how to be again. I'm gutted, Ben. This whole thing really gutted me."

"Okay." Ben understood the feeling of wanting to go back to the safety of his childhood home where you can just be taken care of as the child you once were. Sometimes Ben still wished that place existed for him. "How do you think your parents will take this?"

"Maybe in their minds there's a little of 'I told you so,' but they won't let on. They'll know I'm hurting and that's all that matters."

Ben asked Shira how long she planned on being in Bethesda.

"I have no idea. A week, maybe two. It's not running away. It's really not. It's something else." Again Shira's eyes filled with tears. "I love you so much, I can't stand the fact that I'm standing in the way of you being a father, and it eats at me, you know? I know how important this is to you."

Shira pushed her chair back from the table, went to the sink, filled a glass with water and drank it in one long gulp.

"This is not me leaving you," she said, her eyes clear and determined. "This is an act of love."

"What is?" Ben said.

A familiar expression crossed Shira's face that said she had made up her mind about something and she was not going to change it. "I won't let myself ruin your life."

"What are you talking about? You are my life."

"I'm going to fly back to Maryland and throw myself into creating art for me, not for the calendar or the publisher or for contracts with Judaica shops. I'm going to create just for me, and I'll have that space with my parents where I don't have to apologize for being selfish for a while."

"That's not selfish. You are a creator. I won't stand in your way. I promise."

"I need to do this. And I won't stand in your way with Pamela and your child."

"What?" Ben's voice could barely form the words. "Are you leaving me?"

"Of course not! I just want to give you the space to make things work with Pamela so you can be the father you've always wanted to be. See if you can make it work."

Ben leapt up from the table, his head whirling. "Stop. I love you."

"And I love you. That's why I'm doing this. I can't give you what you need. Pamela can. You deserve that chance to be a proper father."

"I want you."

"And I want you," Shira said in a tone so soft and fragile that Ben's heart nearly broke. "But I'm willing to give you the space to figure this out with Pamela."

"No. I won't let you martyr yourself like this. I don't want to do this without you. I want you. I've always wanted you."

"I know that, Ben. I really do. You show me every day how much you love me, but you have a child on the way and it needs a father. I can't deny you that opportunity. I won't deny you that."

"I won't do it."

Shira suddenly took notice of the overly bright overhead kitchen lights and padded out of the kitchen, her bare feet slapping the floor with a *plip-plip* sound. Ben followed. "We're not done talking, are we?"

"I thought being open would be good for us, to explore other people, but to always, always come back to each other. But things are different now. You're going to be a father."

"Stop this. Please. I made a mistake. I wasn't careful with Pamela. I messed up."

"We both did. We were playing with fire and didn't know it."

Shira picked up the Casey Stengel baseball on the coffee table, where it sat in a plastic-coated shell, and tossed it to Ben.

"Magic Eight Ball time."

"That's not fair. I'm not giving you up to be with Pamela."

"Just hold that ball in your hands and think about your father's grandson. Think about that life waiting for you."

"That's not fair," Ben said, his throat hitching. "I don't want to be with Pamela."

"You're saying that because you don't want to hurt me."

"Of course I don't want to hurt you."

"I'm giving you permission, if that's what you need, to try and make things work with her."

"Why would you do that?"

"Because I love you, dammit, and I hate myself for robbing you of the child you so badly want. It's my fault."

"Stop blaming yourself."

"I'm trying to find a solution, Ben. Don't you get it? Why should we both have to suffer?"

Ben slipped an arm around Shira. "Can't we just stop and talk about this tomorrow?"

"I just slept all day. You made me breakfast. Today is already tomorrow for me."

Ben hadn't slept, and he was suddenly exhausted. "You can do your art here. I'll leave you alone or we can rent you a studio. But please don't go."

"Ben, I'm not leaving you. I'm going to go see my folks, cry a bit and forget about everything that happened the past year." Shira squeezed Ben's hand in hers. "I'm just taking some space, and giving you space to figure out what you really want. You need to make that choice. I can't make it for you."

29

en dropped Shira off at Logan Airport on a Monday amid the bustle of the morning rush. Shira dragged their giant wheeled Samsonite, a hard-shelled behemoth so big that the two of them had shared it on their honeymoon in Maui. A colorful canvas carry-on was slung over her shoulder.

"Are you sure you don't want me to walk you to the gate?" Ben said, slamming the Subaru's trunk.

"I'll be fine. I've made this flight dozens of times."

"I'd like to walk you to the gate."

"You'll have to find parking and walk all the way back here. It'll take too long. I'm fine. I'm fine."

"Are you sure? You're going for a week and a half." They had never been apart that long since they had been a couple, and Ben was afraid where this new distance might lead.

"I'll call every day. I promise. Now, give me a big hug."

Ben stepped forward and leaned into a tight embrace. Shira had always given the best hugs, and Ben drew in a deep draught of her scent. God, he loved her.

Shira pulled back and kissed Ben softly on the lips. "I'd better get going."

"All right."

A car honked one short blast followed by a longer peevish blast, urging Ben to move his car.

"I'll call you," Shira said. "As soon as I land."

"I'll be waiting by the phone."

"When do you ever not have your phone with you?" Shira laughed. "Bye." And she blew Ben a kiss.

Then, serenaded by another barrage of car horns, Shira was off and through the sliding glass doors, leaving Ben alone to deal with the morning traffic.

❦

The night before Ben had headed off to college in Binghamton his father had asked Ben for one last game of catch. "My little boy is all grown up," he had said, tossing Ben his battered mitt. "Let's see what you've got."

Ben's father didn't tend towards the sentimental, but, as the two of them threw the baseball back and forth, late summer shadows lengthening around them, Ben understood, looking back across the years, that this meant more to his father than Ben was capable of understanding at the time. To Ben, this game of catch was no different than countless other times the two of them had tossed the ball back and forth in their backyard, shooting the shit about baseball stats, Ben's latest high school crush, stories from his father's childhood, rough and tumble summers in the streets of Flatbush, Ben's hopes and dreams. Ben had long since given up on replacing Derek Jeter as the Yankees' next shortstop, but he believed he had a special destiny, the way so many young people do, and that college was the first true step towards realizing himself as a successful adult.

His father still had a good arm and the ball popped into Ben's mitt like a gunshot.

"I'm not going to see you every day anymore."

Ben was puzzled by his father stating the obvious. Ben had been eager to get off to college and start being a grown up long before he was accepted at Binghamton.

"I feel like I should give you one last father/son talk."

"Last one?" Ben laughed. "I'm not going to the moon."

Ben's father chucked the ball just a little harder, nearly knocking the glove off Ben's hand.

"Smart aleck."

"What's up, Dad?"

Ben's father slipped his glove under his armpit and called Ben over to him. "Come here, kid." Then he laughed. "That may be the last time I can call you kid."

"I'll always be your kid."

"Always." His father ruffled Ben's hair. "No matter what."

Ben's father threw a heavy arm over Ben's shoulder and pulled him close. Ben could smell his father's Old Spice aftershave, a scent Ben always associated with confidence and masculinity.

"Listen, I don't care if you're rich or poor. You can be a plumber or a president, I don't care. As long as you always do what's right. Do you hear me?"

"Yeah. Okay. But how will I know what the right thing is?"

Ben's father looked Ben directly in the eyes and he was lit from behind by a nimbus cast by the setting sun, giving his words an almost holy feel. "You feel it right here." He placed his steady hand on Ben's belly. "If it feels warm, it's the right thing. If it don't, it ain't."

Driving back from the airport, Ben felt a warmth stirring in his belly. At first he thought it was just his body telling him to eat something, but then he realized he was thinking of Pamela and his child and how wrong it would be for his child to grow up without a father. Shira had planted that thought, and now he couldn't stop thinking of it. But the thought of leaving Shira behind, childless and alone, left him breathless and he had to pull over. He took out his phone and sent a text to Shira so it would be waiting for her when she landed. *You're my person. Always.*

Shira called when she landed and told Ben she loved him, and Ben managed to get through a day of work without being too distracted. But when he returned home to his and Shira's empty condo he again began to think of Pamela, pregnant with his child. He wondered whether she was having an easy pregnancy, whether she was struggling. He couldn't imagine Pamela as anything but the pale, slim woman he had so much desired, but her second trimester body would have changed by now. She would be four and a half months pregnant, and Ben had no idea how she was getting by. Was she going to doctors' appointments alone? Was anyone going to be with her when she gave birth some time in late winter? Ben assumed her WASPy parents would fly in from Philly, but they didn't sound like the warmest people on the planet.

And then what? They would leave and Pamela would be alone with Ben's infant child, trying to juggle a career she loved. This would have all happened within a year of their meeting, and Ben realized how little he actually knew Pamela. He knew that he loved her, but the more time passed he could not explain precisely why he had loved her so fervently.

He was going to have to try to see her, for closure, clarity, whatever. With a child between them they couldn't simply never speak again, could they? But Ben was afraid that seeing Pamela in real life would set off that intense need he had felt so strongly before things had turned sour. Ben had no doubt now that Shira was the person he wanted to be with, had always wanted to be with, but he also knew how hard it could be to turn away love when it was on offer. He didn't know if Pamela would even want him back at this point, but he was afraid that if she did he would take her back as well, because how do you say no to someone you love?

Ben drove to a hip little place in Harvard Square called The Sevastopol where he had taken a few women back when he was trying to date. It was a weeknight, so he had no trouble finding a seat at the bar. Perhaps a drink or two would help clarify his mind, provide him the courage to go see Pamela. He could not be with her, but he couldn't allow himself to be cut off from his child either, as if he didn't exist. Ben didn't realize how dry his throat was until he was called upon to speak by the barman, a cheery, thick-necked Abercrombie-and-Fitch type with tribal tattoos running up and down both his muscular arms.

"What can I get you, buddy?"

Ben ordered a Tanqueray and tonic because Pamela liked Tanqueray and tonic, and he liked the way it sounded coming out of his mouth. His phone sat on the bar in front of him and he picked it up periodically, composed a text to Pamela and then erased it just as soon as it was complete. Somewhere over his left shoulder Ben could hear the honeyed voices of Harvard coeds laughing. He tried to imagine the conversation he would have with Pamela, but every time he envisioned what might happen he saw the two of them in bed together, where they always seemed to end up. Their physical connection had been so strong that he was afraid he would be powerless to deny himself. But, sitting at the bar in Harvard Square, he knew that wasn't what he wanted. He and Pamela needed to negotiate the terms of their mutual surrender, Ben giving up his claim on her heart, her body, in exchange for a peace treaty in which he was allowed access to his child. But he could not imagine being in her presence and not kissing her, taking her in his arms and saying, "I love you."

Ben's drink appeared before him and the barman asked if he wanted to run a tab.

"No, no thanks. I'm going to go," and Ben tossed a $20 bill down and left his drink untouched on the bar.

Out in the chilly autumn night, a fine mist sifting across the street-lit sky, Ben slipped his phone from his pocket. He couldn't gather the courage to see Pamela, he just couldn't. What if something clicked when he saw her again and he realized in some hidden part of his heart that he wanted her, really wanted her? What if his belly warmed upon seeing Pamela again? With the child, there would be no going back, and that would be the end of him and Shira. Ben had rarely felt so alone, standing on a tightrope between two women, jagged rocks beneath, and he had an urge to hear Shira's voice, to know she was all right. Just hearing that voice in his ear would give him the strength to go back home and forget, at least for now, about trying to see Pamela.

Ben took out his phone and hit Shira's number, and right away Shira was there as if she had been waiting inside his phone for him. "Jinx," Shira said. "I was just about to call you."

Shira sounded as if she was standing right beside him, and Ben melted just to hear her voice.

"I just wanted to see how you're doing."

"Fine," Shira said.

"Really?"

"Yeah, actually. Old friends help. People from another life that never knew this version of me."

"So, you're having fun?"

"I wouldn't exactly say fun, but I'll live to see another day."

"Of course you will. I miss you."

"I know. But this time apart is important for both of us."

Ben was about to disagree when Shira said, "Have you seen Pamela yet?"

"No."

"Ben! I order you to see her. You need to figure out what you're going to do about the child."

"All right. I'm just scared."

There was a long silence on the other end of the line and Ben could hear the roar of a car engine down the street. This discussion had felt so intimate and intense, and here he was in the middle of the street. "Talk about being scared," Shira said at last. "I'm such a fucking scaredy-cat."

"What do you mean?"

"I need to ask you a favor. Fuck. I'm such a wimp."

"Of course. What do you need me to do?"

"Promise you'll do it?"

"I promise."

"Pinkie promise?"

"Just tell me."

"I packed up all the stuff Liz gave me in a box but never got around to mailing it before I left. I hate to be a jerk, but will you take it to her? I can't stand the thought of her things in our house. I need it gone before I get back. Are you mad?"

"You want me to take it to her in person?"

"Kind of. I just want to know she's okay. Will you do it for me? Please."

"Of course." But Ben had to admit, if all things were equal, he'd much rather see Liz than Pamela at that moment, even if he risked taking Liz's incoming in place of Shira.

"Great! Thank you. You're a lifesaver. I'll text you her number."

Ben put his phone away and walked around Harvard Square, looking in shop windows, feeling like he had no place to go, so, after a time, he slipped his phone out of his pocket and pulled up Liz's number.

Hi, it's Ben Seidel, he texted. *Sorry to bother you, but I was wondering if you're around tonight. I know it's last minute and you're probably busy but I have a box of your stuff Shira would like me to drop off.*

Liz's composing bubble appeared a moment later. *Keep it. I don't need it.*

Are you sure? I'll buy you a drink.

A minute passed, and then another, and then Liz's composing bubble formed a message.

Meet me at Doyle's in JP. It'll cost you more than one. See you in an hour?

I'll be there!

30

Ben drove back to his and Shira's condo, grabbed Liz's stuff and still managed to arrive early. He edged into a seat at the long wooden bar, nerves pulsing in his temples. Doyle's was one of those old-timey Irish pubs one might see in a movie, with photos of politicos of a bygone age staring down from dark, cluttered walls. A TV above the bar flashed a Bruins game. A blue plastic storage bin sat at Ben's feet, the remnants of Liz and Shira's relationship. An incredible heat seemed to be rising off the bin as if it contained kryptonite, something so potent it could melt Ben's skin off if he were to lay eyes on the contents of the container. It wasn't heavy, likely full of borrowed clothing, cheap paperback books, perhaps some token of Liz's affection—a ring, a necklace, a dream catcher, some intimate object or item of clothing he wished not to imagine.

Ben's phone buzzed on the bar top. It was Liz.

I'm in the back room.

Liz sat alone at a corner table, a dark beer and a shot of something clear and evil before her. She had chopped her hair into a short pixie cut and dyed it a bright, cotton candy blue. Her face was pale, lips painted a violent red. Liz looked beautiful, and Ben did all he could not to tell her so.

Ben settled on, "You look nice."

"Thanks," Liz said. "Slayin' lewks. That's what I do." Then, nodding towards the bin, "I assume those are my hostages."

"Yep." Ben sat opposite Liz in a hard wooden chair, the bin on the bench between them. "Yours to dispose of as you wish."

"That's all there is, huh?" Liz said, eyeing the bin. "More than a year and it all fits neatly in a little plastic coffin."

"I assume it's all there. Shira packed it up before she left for Maryland."

"Ah." Liz nodded her head knowingly. "Licking her wounds back home."

Ben didn't like the way that sounded, so he said, "Shira's really hurting."

"That's what happens at the end of love."

"How are you?"

"I'm fine," Liz said, but Ben looked in her eyes and saw a different truth.

"Really?"

"When you're poly, love comes and goes. You can't stay heartbroken if you want to stay sane. It's just the way it is. But there's always something you take away that makes you a bigger, fuller, better person."

"I'm calling bullshit on that one. You really loved her. Didn't you?"

Liz laughed. "Yeah," she said, wistfully. "I did." She reached for her beer. "I had a few serious cries, sulked for a few days, drank for a few more. But love ends. Always does."

"Let's agree to disagree on that one."

"Drink with me." Liz slid the shot towards Ben.

"What is it?"

"Pain makes you stronger, tears make you braver, heartbreak makes you wiser." Liz paused and lifted the drink with her beringed fingers, beckoning Ben to take it. "And vodka makes you forget all that self-help bullshit."

Ben tossed the vodka back and it burned his throat, stung his sinuses and filled his belly with a warm bolus of something close to courage.

Liz smiled back. "I guess I should've said *nostrovia* or *skol* or something."

"Me and Shira used to do that, say some foreign toast, some creative silly thing before we drank. It was sort of our thing, and when you were at our place the first time when you did it, it sort of ... Well, it hurt."

"I didn't know. Why?"

"It was a ritual we had going back to our days in college, and the thought that Shira had shared a private thing was like a punch in the gut."

"I am so, so sorry. I was just playing along," Liz said, raising three fingers in the air. "Scouts' honor. I take personal boundaries very seriously. I would've never appropriated your thing as my own."

Ben waved down the server and ordered two more shots of vodka, one for him and one for Liz. "Really?"

"Of course. Your relationship with Shira, quirks and all, belongs to you."

"And, your relationship with Shira belonged to you," Ben countered.

"I know. And thank you for sharing her with me. I know it wasn't always easy. It was a good thing. A really good thing. But, honestly, we pushed too hard, too fast and it flamed out. Better to burn out than to fade away, right?"

"Shira really wanted that child. More than anything in the world."

"I know. And I feel so fucking guilty for letting her down. But I just couldn't go through that again. The whole thing felt so constricting, like my life wasn't really mine anymore, and I started to resent Shira. I think deep down she just wanted the baby and I was her way to get it. I fell for it. Sue me."

"It's not like that. It never was. She loved you."

Liz fell silent, her big eyes on Ben, and his face heated under their stare. He didn't know what to do with his hands, so he picked up the empty shot glass and turned it in the light as if he were looking for some imperfection in the glass.

"How's you and her? You guys okay?" Liz tilted her head and squinted.

"I don't know. She says I owe it to myself and my child to give it a go with Pamela."

"Ahh, the three-ring circus. I almost forgot."

"You know what it's like not to have a father around. She believes that child needs a father and she doesn't want to get in the way."

"Now, I'm calling bullshit on you. Shira doesn't want you to leave her. She just wants to make sure that you *choose* her. She wants you to choose once and for all: her or Pamela."

"Shira doesn't play games like that."

"It's so obvious, I can't believe you can't see it."

"What are you talking about?"

"Shira wants to be a mother more than anything," Liz said, words flying from her mouth rapid-fire.

"She loves you and wants to be with you. She wanted you and her to raise my child because it was yours. It didn't work out. C'est la fucking vie. But you're going to have a child with another woman, and it's your child too. What's the difference if it's my child or Pamela's as long as it's yours. Don't you see it? You're going to raise that child, you and Shira and Pamela."

"What? That'll never happen. Pamela hates the very idea of Shira, and Shira—"

"Wants to be the mother of your child. Right?"

"Yes," Ben said, as the new round of shots arrived. "But."

"No buts." Liz raised a glass. "Drink."

It was hard to argue with that directive, and Ben downed his shot in an instant.

"She may not know it yet, but Shira is counting on you to make this happen. It's your child, and I'm telling you now, she would love that child as her own because she loves the fuck out of you." Liz smiled. "For whatever reason."

Ben started to object.

"Kidding. I'm kidding. Do you really think Shira would let you leave her for another woman to raise that woman's child? You can be so dense. She wants you to find a way that Pamela will share your own goddamn child with you, so the three of you can co-parent the fuck out of that kid and raise it surrounded by more love than it can stand."

"How am I supposed to make that happen?"

"That, my friend, is up to you." She tapped her shot glass with her silver skull ring. "Another round?"

"I should get going. I've got to drive." Then, after a lengthy silence in which Liz just stared at Ben as if she were trying to memorize his features for posterity, he added, "Anyway, there's your stuff."

Liz laughed. "I don't need that. I came here to see you." The expression on her face was earnest. "I told you I cared about you. I meant that. I care about Shira too, but me and her can't be around each other for a long, long, looonnng time. So, thanks for coming out and giving me the update. I appreciate it. I really do."

Ben tapped his fingers on the plastic bin. "I guess I could've just tossed it in the Charles River after all."

"Well, I don't want it. But I'm glad you came."

"Me too. So, I guess this is goodbye?"

After all they had been through, all the times Ben had wished Liz away so he could have Shira all to himself, he realized now that he was going to miss her.

A mischievous look appeared in Liz's eyes. "You're no good to drive right now. Ya lightweight! Let's Uber over to the harbor and dump this shit in. It'll be our own personal Boston Tea Party. When we get back, you'll be okay to drive."

"Are you serious?"

"Damn straight."

They arrived at Boston Fish Pier, on the south side of the main channel of Boston Harbor, with a strange solemn silence. It was a cold night, and Ben clutched the plastic bin under his arm. Ben and Liz walked along the dual yellow traffic lines flanked on either side by identical low-slung steel and concrete buildings. Their feet echoed in the silence and, for a moment, Ben felt the urge to slip an arm protectively around Liz's waist. He and Liz alone out there, without Shira, just felt wrong. "I feel kind of funny doing this."

"Because it is funny! Who would have ever imagined? But seriously, it's my stuff. It's not been blessed by a rabbi or sanctified by the Pope."

They arrived at the end of the pier, the cold air brackish in their noses, the lights of Logan Airport flickering like stars across the harbor. Liz opened the bin and tossed the plastic lid aside, where it landed beside them with a jarring crack. "You first."

Ben hesitated for a moment, uncertain if he was ready to reach his hand inside and touch the intimate belongings shared between his wife and her ex-lover.

"Tick tock," Liz said. "It's fucking freezing."

Eyes averted, Ben slipped a hand into the bin and lit upon a dog-eared paperback. Rumi, *Poems of Ecstasy and Longing*. "Are you sure you don't want this?" Ben asked, the soft, worn pages riffling between his cold fingers.

"Sadly, Shira was not the first lover I lent that book to, not by a long shot. I think it's time to retire Rumi. I don't want to become a cliché. Anyway, I've committed so much of it to memory I could recite it in my sleep."

"So, what now?"

"Toss it."

As Ben heaved back his arm to throw the book out into the harbor, Liz chanted, *"The wound is the place where the Light enters you."*

It disappeared with a quiet splash, sinking under the water in an instant.

Liz plucked out a Pixies T-shirt, the one Shira had worn to the BDSM picnic that summer.

"That was yours?" Ben said.

"Yep. I traded it for Shira's awful James Taylor concert T-shirt. Please don't tell her," Liz laughed, "but I chucked that one a long time ago. I swear I was compelled to do it by a higher power."

Ben remembered Shira returning home from Tanglewood a few summers back wearing that shirt and a huge smile on her face. She had hummed "How Sweet It Is" for weeks afterwards.

Ben pulled out a delicate bracelet and held it out to Liz for inspection. "Are you sure?"

"I bought it in a gum-ball machine for a quarter. If you think cadmium mined by children is a precious metal, by all means, keep it."

They went through several more innocuous articles of clothing: T-shirts, a black zip-up hoodie, a balled up pair of socks stitched to look as if they were wrapped in barbed wire, a few more paperbacks—Highsmith, Morrison, Marge Piercy—a Maybelline makeup kit, a hairbrush.

Liz was workmanlike in her efforts, adding a brief commentary for each object, but moving quickly until she reached the bottom of the bin.

The final object was an ink drawing on the back of a card stock menu from a restaurant called Le Paradis in the South End. Liz handed it gingerly to Ben.

Ben clutched it tightly in his raw fingers, afraid a sudden breeze would yank the picture from his hand and toss it out to sea.

"I drew this on one of our first dates. It's pretty good, isn't it?"

Shira stared back at Ben, a perfect likeness of the way she looked before she cut her hair to better complement Liz, with the odd angles and uneven layering. Shira was frozen in time right at the beginning, when the two of them had just begun being open, so much chaos yet to come. Even in black ink, her eyes glittered with warmth—that look that said Ben was the only person in the world who mattered, that look that used to be just for him. And here he was seeing it reflected back to him through the eyes of Liz.

"Are you okay?" Liz placed a hand on his shoulder.

"Wow! You must have really loved each other to have gotten to see her like this."

"We did," Liz said, holding Ben in a warm embrace. "We really, really did." She pressed her soft lips into his forehead. "Now, let's get out of here. I'm freezing my balls off!"

31

The next few days Ben did what he could to avoid dealing with the Pamela situation, but he could only put things off for so long, and, one evening, after cleaning the condo from top to bottom, answering every last one of his work emails, and running to Concord and back. Ben had run out of excuses.

Halloween was in the air, the leaves putting on their annual magic show, transforming from vibrant greens to crisp reds and yellows and golds, that sentimental smell of autumn taking Ben back to simpler times before he understood the disruptive power of love. Ben decided against texting and calling again after all his futile attempts, figuring he had better just show up and hope for the best.

Ben parked a few blocks over on a quiet side street and walked the rest of the way, allowing him a little more time to think. Pamela was going to be the mother of his child. That was a huge life event, and he had to be a part of this child's life. There was no rational argument that could possibly cut Ben out— Pamela was no heartless sociopath—but he didn't know how he would be able to convince Pamela to let him in.

He took a deep breath as he mounted the three brick steps to Pamela's garden apartment. A seasonal wreath hung on her door, and Ben noticed how elaborate it was in design, with a series of colorful grains wound together into a unified circle. The lights were on and her car was in the street. He rang the bell and waited. After a moment Ben heard Pamela moving around in the hallway.

"Who is it?"

Pamela had told him she loved him with that voice, and he knew he couldn't stand to hear that self-same voice tell him now to get lost. She asked who it was, before pulling back the curtain in the narrow vertical window beside the doorframe. Though his response was no longer necessary, Ben responded anyway. "It's me, Ben."

"What do you want?"

"Please open up. We need to talk."

"And I told you I didn't want to see you."

"You're carrying my child. Please let me in. So we can talk."

Pamela was backlit by a lamp on a table in the hallway behind her, and Ben noticed that, like Liz, she too had changed her hair, dyeing it jet black with sweeping, jagged bangs off to the side, giving it a casual windblown effect. There must have been some secret break up protocol in which hacking off one's hair was mandatory. The new style looked great against her pale skin. Her face had filled out a bit, but it was Pamela's belly that startled Ben the most. She was showing, actually showing, the curve of her belly pressing against the fabric of her shirt. He wanted to reach a hand out and touch her.

"Can I please come in?"

"Fine. But just for a few minutes. I have to work in the morning."

Ben followed her into her apartment and marveled at how much he still liked to watch her move.

"You can have a seat on the couch," Pamela said. Her voice sounded cold to Ben but he hoped that was more about him and his particular neural pathways than her intention of freezing him out. "I'm going to my bedroom to straighten myself up. Please don't follow me."

Ben nodded in assent, looking around Pamela's apartment, noticing how lived in it looked now with a stack of *New Yorkers* piled on the coffee table beside a half full bottle of Perrier, a throw blanket folded at the end of the couch, a pair of socks the color and consistency of oatmeal laid out over an arm chair.

Ordinarily when Ben came over to Pamela's place, she played music to help establish mood, but now her place was so quiet Ben could hear a dresser drawer closing in her bedroom down the hall, water rushing through the pipes from the apartment above. She returned a moment later and sat in a plush chair placed perpendicular to the couch, a good three or four feet separating the two of them.

"So?" Pamela said. "What's so important that you had to come over unannounced like this?"

Before Ben had a chance to explain, he noticed she was wearing what looked like an engagement ring. It had a sparkling band lined with small diamonds with a moderate-sized round-cut diamond, set in a raised bed that glittered as if it were filled of light. It looked expensive, really expensive. Ben wondered who had bought it for Pamela. Some Brooks Brothers Brahmin probably. Damn, she moved fast.

"That's quite a ring," Ben said, in a voice that didn't sound like his own.

"Oh, this." Pamela laughed, spinning it easily off her finger and holding it up for Ben so the light caught the diamond. "It's costume. Very *good* costume. I picked it up at E.B. Horn from their estates section. Best purchase I ever made."

"I don't understand. Why?"

"I'm showing now," Pamela said, running a hand over her belly. "Like it or not, I deal with a certain kind of donor, and they would prefer to believe I'm going to be a married mother."

"Oh. I'm sorry."

"Yeah, well. What are you going to do?"

"How are you feeling? With, you know?"

Now Pamela's face lit up and he saw the barrier between them lower just a bit. "Good, really good. Once the first trimester was behind me the nausea disappeared. Now I'm hungry all the time. But I have my energy back. I can feel her moving inside me. She kicks sometimes now, but Charlotte's a good travel companion. She goes where I go. No complaints."

"Charlotte," Ben mused.

"Yeah. Charlie for short."

Ben smiled. Charlie would be a cute name for a girl, and he knew the name held special significance for Pamela.

"I like it," Ben said. He was glad he was sitting down, because he suddenly felt lightheaded. His daughter's name was Charlie. "Wow. Can I feel?"

Pamela stiffened, and the smile melted from her face.

"I don't know. I meant it when I said we were finished. I needed a clean break for my own well-being. I really can't afford to backslide. Touching my belly is really—intimate."

"I know."

"I just don't think I'm ready for it, you touching me."

Pamela leapt to her feet and made her way across the room with a singular focus. "I've got the ultrasound images. You can see those." She disappeared into her room again, and Ben wanted nothing more than to follow her, but he knew they were both afraid of the same thing.

Pamela returned a moment later clutching a folder containing a couple pieces of paper. She thrust the folder at Ben, without even looking in his direction. "Here. They're from last week."

Ben took the black-and-white images in his hands and saw the most amazing thing he had ever seen. The ultrasound he and Shira and Liz had seen resembled a swirling hurricane with a flickering eye like one might see on a Doppler radar before a storm, but in this image there were the makings of a person, created by Ben and Pamela. It had a clearly defined head, with a nose and mouth and belly and arms and legs and hands outlined against a limitless black void, and Ben could have sworn Charlotte was waving at him, saying hello to her daddy. Ben's throat thickened and his eyes filled with tears. He had never wanted anything more than he wanted Charlotte, and he could not wait to hold her in his arms and tell her he loved her.

Eventually Ben was able to tear his eyes away from the images, and he saw that Pamela had been watching him. Head tilted in an inviting gesture, she said, "What do you think?"

"I've never seen anything so beautiful in my life."

"Really?" Pamela said, cheeks coloring.

"Yeah. I knew it was going to be something to see her, but this is something else altogether." Ben's mouth was pasty and dry, and he asked Pamela if he could have a glass of water.

"Sparkling or still?" Pamela said, rising from her seat.

"How about sparkling? Me and you. We can say a toast."

"You can be such a cornball."

"Hey, we made this together. The two of us."

Ben picked up the images again, studying the contours of Charlotte as if he were a cartographer seeking hidden treasure on a secret map. Pamela sat down beside Ben on the couch, but he was so preoccupied with the ultrasound images he barely noticed how close she was sitting to him. She handed him a long-stemmed white wine glass and clinked hers against Ben's.

"To a healthy and happy child," Ben said.

"I can't do any better than that. Healthy and happy is perfect."

They each drank their water and placed their glasses on the coffee table. What followed was an awkward stillness. This would have been the point ordinarily when they would have attacked each other, kissing as if their lives depended precisely on those kisses, before tearing each other's clothes off and stumbling into the bedroom. Up until now they had been intimate with each other every time they were together, and for a moment Ben thought maybe it wouldn't be such a bad thing to have another go. But he was going to be a parent, and that meant subverting his own desires when it came to the well-being of his daughter.

Pamela broke the silence asking, for the first time ever, how Shira was doing.

Ben told her about the miscarriage and her break-up with Liz and how she was back in Bethesda for a while but was coming back soon.

"I'm sorry to hear about the baby," Pamela said, with more empathy in her voice than she may have been able to muster just a few months earlier. "So, this will be your only child now? No other secret babies I don't know about?"

"Come on. Be nice."

Pamela was about to respond when Ben added, "How is this going to work? With Charlotte. How do we make sure she is healthy and happy and well-adjusted?"

"That's a good question. Being a single mother isn't going to be easy. I'm already freaking out about the cost of daycare and losing time at work and—there's just so much coming up it makes my head spin."

"I will help support the child. I'll do my part paying for healthcare."

"Do you think this is just about money?"

Pamela had edged over again, shifting her body over to the next cushion on the couch. "Ben, are you going to tell me why you're here?" She released a long sigh. "I needed more time. And you just show up at my place against my wishes."

"I'm sorry. This isn't easy for me either. But the sooner we figure things out, the better. We are done; I get it. But we aren't done with each other. We just can't be, right? There are things that are bigger than us now."

Pamela looked Ben directly in the eye, holding his attention with her soft green eyes. "I said some terrible things. I was petulant and angry and I'm just so embarrassed. I don't throw tantrums, but I was hurting so much and I wanted you, and I didn't want to do this alone. But I couldn't tolerate breaking up your marriage on my resume, even if that meant losing you."

"That time at the MFA, at that dreary Goya exhibit, we met for a reason. I truly believe that," Ben said. "Maybe it wasn't for the reason either of us thought." Ben picked up the ultrasound pictures, and he and Pamela marveled at them again in silence.

"Life is funny like that," Pamela said. "I mean, I knew deep down you were never going to be my knight in shining armor, but damn you were good in bed! It surprised me."

"What? Why?"

"I thought we'd sleep together a few times and things would peter out like they usually do. I just didn't think you had it in you."

"Had what?"

"I can't really describe what 'it' means exactly. It's like this weird pull or compulsion, and it's way beyond the rational brain, but I wanted you so intensely it scared me."

Ben said he understood because he too felt that intensity and need.

"I'm not trying to be insulting. You're a good looking guy, Ben, but I have been with some … really attractive men. Two or three who could have been movie stars." Pamela let out a little chuckle. "One of them, who shall remain nameless, actually was in a couple of movies you've probably seen."

"Why are you telling me this?"

"Because, Ben, you did it for me in a way none of them ever did, and I wish I knew why. It was just this thing that happened and it surprised me, and once it happened I was stuck. I just never expected to need you. I'd gone thirty-five years without ever needing anyone. I'd always been pretty self-sufficient. It was like a drug or something, and it scared me, and I wanted to run but I couldn't. I mean, you were never a cruel person taking advantage or anything, so I just kept coming back, even though I knew it was bad for me because it was going to have to end. It was always going to end. Even if you had left Shira. That level of need, it just wasn't me, and I came to hate myself for it."

Ben wished he could come up with an adequate response, but he found no words.

"It's bad policy to fall in love with a married man," Pamela said. "On that point, the advice columnists are spot on. I think one of the reasons I liked you so much is that you are free of pretension. You're not a cool guy, putting on airs and trying to impress. You didn't brag about your accomplishments, and you asked me questions and you listened, and I just let my guard down and let myself invest hope in a future for the two of us."

"But we do have a future. With her." Ben traced his fingers along the image again, wishing he could feel his daughter moving in Pamela's belly.

Pamela smiled sadly, her voice taking on a business-like tone. "We'll figure out a reasonable visitation schedule. I won't let her be a stranger to you. I promise. And I'm sorry if I gave the impression otherwise. I was wrong."

"I don't want to just visit on Wednesdays and Sundays at some pre-appointed time, dinners at Friendly's, parent-teacher conferences twice a year. Check the fatherhood box and live my life." Ben's belly felt hot, as if he had ingested a ball of fire. "I want us to share her 50/50. We'll pay half the bills, half her education, take care of her when you're not able. Half time here and half time with me and Shira."

Pamela froze, silent.

"She's my wife," Ben said.

"I know that." Her shoulders sagged, and her head dropped into her hands. "From day one she has been the bane of my existence, my absolute *bête noire*. And now you want your wife to raise my child?"

"We can all raise her. What could possibly be wrong with another person to care for Charlotte? She's my child too."

"Yes, and I'm the mother." Pamela lifted the wineglasses off the table and stood up. "You can be so terribly naïve, Ben. I know you love Shira and want to give her the chance to be a mother, but it's not my job to make that happen. Seriously, the two of us have never even met. What in the actual fuck are you thinking bringing that up with me? Don't you have any sense, or are you really that ensconced in your privilege that you really thought I might agree to such a harebrained idea?"

"Sit down," Ben said. "Please."

"Maybe you should leave."

Ben stood up and reached out a hand to comfort Pamela.

"Don't you touch me, Ben. I swear to god."

Ben drew back his hand.

"You don't understand how hard it is," she said, hands massaging her belly. "I'm doing all the work here. I carry this child everywhere I go. She's a part of me."

"And she's a part of me."

"It's not the same and you know it. Don't minimize the importance of motherhood. You can read all the books you want and take all the parenting classes money can buy, but you will never be a mother, and neither will Shira." Pamela had edged towards the kitchen to return the wineglasses, and Ben followed her. "Charlotte has one mother. That's it. And any newfangled poly-psycho arrangement you contrive is just about pleasing your wife at my expense."

"How is this at your expense?"

"Are you serious?" Pamela stood in the doorframe of her galley kitchen as if she were trying to bar his way. Her cheeks were flushed, her eyes narrowed dangerously. "This will never work. Never, never, never."

"Why? Because you loved me?"

"Because I *still* love you, and the thought of seeing you and Shira together just tears me up. Got it? It's not fair to ask this of me. You and she get everything you want—a happy marriage, a child to call your own—and what do I get?"

"You get to be a mother to a beautiful girl who will never want for love."

"And who will love me?" Her voice dropped as she muttered as much to herself as Ben. "Who's ever going to want to be with me?"

Instinctively, Ben wanted to reach out and hold Pamela in his arms, but her defensive posture kept him from doing so. "For what it's worth, I'm sure there are countless men who find you smart and beautiful and sexy."

"Oh, fuck off. You need to leave. Now."

"I'm sorry."

"Please leave."

"What would you like to happen?" Ben asked in a voice meant to be solicitous, but he was afraid it came off as wheedling and desperate.

"I don't know," Pamela said. And then, "Can I?" Before Ben could respond, she fell into his arms and began to weep.

They held each other, Pamela's chest pressed up against Ben, her heart beating wildly, tears dampening his shirt. Ben caressed her hair with the palm of his hand, fingers trailing the small of her back, and she melted deeper into him, her breathing beginning to calm. "What does Shira think about this whole thing? Was this scheme her idea?"

"She doesn't know. And it's no scheme. It's the right thing to do. She's not a villain. Shira's a good person."

"Yeah, and I'll bet she shits rainbows and gumdrops."

Ben pulled back from Pamela and looked her in the face. "Gross. That's really gross."

And then they both began to laugh, and Ben felt Pamela's stubbornness start to break. It was a small crack but enough to let the light in.

"I always had to compete for your heart, and now you want me to compete with Shira for the love of my own daughter."

"Who ever said it's a competition?"

"I don't know. What if I'm not enough?"

Ben's phone vibrated in his pocket, and Pamela asked if Ben was going to check it. He apologized and said he hated to be rude, but yes he had to get it. Shira had been checking in every few hours, and her moods fluctuated between sadness and cautious optimism. He had helped talk her down a few times, assuring her things would work out and she would feel better.

"I'm really tired," Pamela said. "This really wore me out. You should go."

Ben was about to lean in for a good night kiss when he realized that the physical phase of their life had passed and there could be no going back now.

"Okay. But I'd like to keep talking. Please think about this. I really believe it can be good for everyone."

Pamela smiled softly and led Ben to the door. She clicked on the porch light and opened the door. Ben stepped over the threshold into the cool autumn night. A neighboring house had a fire going, and the smell of woodsmoke reminded Ben that the cozy time of year was upon them and he could start wearing fleece again.

"We'll talk soon?" Ben said.

"Sure."

Ben said goodnight and turned to leave.

"Ben," Pamela said, her eyes beckoning him back.

Ben climbed the three brick steps and stood nearly nose-to-nose with Pamela. There was a twinkle in her eye, and she took his hand and placed it on her belly.

"She's awake," Pamela said. "Feel that?"

32

Ben picked Shira up at Logan Airport. Her trip back to Bethesda seemed to have energized her, and she buckled herself into the passenger seat with a big smile on her face. Her parents were great, her friends were fun and supportive, and she had an idea for a new project. Shira had only been gone ten days, but it felt to Ben as if she had been gone for months.

"I'm really glad you're home," Ben said, as they entered the O' Neill Tunnel. Traffic was light and Ben drove with a heavy foot.

"Me too," Shira said, kissing him. "And thank you for taking care of the Liz thing. I know I should have done it myself but I chickened out."

"It's okay," Ben said, testing out his Vito Corleone voice. "Someday, and that day may never come, I will call upon you to do a service for me—"

"Stop!" Shira laughed. "You are the worst Godfather."

"Honestly, it was kind of nice to see her."

"I'm glad. She's not a bad person. Just ... different ideas."

"She really loved you."

"I know. It happened. It's over. But I get to keep those experiences and take them with me wherever I go."

Pamela had loved Ben as well. It happened, it was over, but it also wasn't over, and Ben didn't know how Shira would react to that.

They passed the old Necco factory, and Ben recalled how he sometimes used to catch the sweet sugary smell if the wind was blowing right. Ben's hands gripped the steering wheel so his knuckles turned white. "I saw Pamela," he said at last, trying to catch Shira's expression in the rear-view mirror.

"And how did that go?" Shira's voice was cautious, restrained.

"It wasn't easy for either of us. But I think it was good."

"Good how?"

"Well, her name is Charlotte. Charlie."

"She named her already?" Shira said, in a voice dripping with judgment.

"Your thing is your thing, her thing is her thing. She named her, and it makes her happy, and I would never question that."

Shira sat in silence, her mood changed entirely, like the sun setting on a summer day.

"So what's going to happen now?" Shira said.

Ben saw an exit on the highway and slowed to pull off.

"What are you doing?"

"I don't want to do this while I'm driving."

"Somehow I get the feeling I'm not going to like what you have to say."

Ben pulled up in front of Kelly's Roast Beef at Revere Beach, the clouds gray and heavy out over the water. He had no trouble finding parking since they were out of season. "Are you hungry?" Ben asked.

"Not anymore." Shira climbed out of the passenger seat. "You're not thinking of leaving me for her, are you?"

"Of course not." He took Shira into his arms and just held her. "Never."

"Then what is it?" Shira furrowed her brow. "Are you going to tell me?"

Ben ordered some French fries and a couple of Cokes and they sat on the wall abutting the beach, looking out at the rolling waves.

"I saw the ultrasound," Ben said, dipping a fry in ketchup and offering it to Shira.

"No thanks. And?"

"Honestly, it was one of the most amazing things I've ever seen. That was my child."

Shira winced as if she felt a real physical pain.

"You would have been amazed too," Ben said. "You always said you wanted my child. I know that you can love Charlie."

"What are you talking about?" Shira picked up a fry, and then mindlessly tossed it aside. It was immediately attacked by a trio of hungry seagulls.

"I want us to raise my child half the time. Me and you. She's a part of me. You'll love her, right?"

"Do you know what you're asking me to do? To help raise your mistress's child."

"That's not fair. She was not my mistress. We agreed it was all okay, just like you were with Liz."

"It's not like me and Liz at all. I never said it was okay to get Pamela pregnant. Never."

"I know, and it was a mistake, but that doesn't change the fact that I'm going to be a father in a few short months. And you know how badly I want to be a father."

"Great. And where does that leave me?"

"I want us to do this together. Me and you."

"And, obviously, Pamela. Do you have any idea how crazy that sounds?"

Ben wiped his hands on a napkin and a breeze came and blew the napkin into the air. Ben asked Shira if she was cold and she just told him to go on, explain himself.

"It's not crazy. It's not any crazier than you asking me to be a donor for Liz to be our surrogate."

"It's not the same. I asked you beforehand. You're coming to me after the fact."

"What would you like me to do? Have nothing to do with my child?"

"No, of course not. You could—"

"What? Be with Pamela instead of you?" He took Shira's face in his hands, cradling her burning cheeks. "I choose you. A million times out of a million, I choose you, Shira Tziporah Seidel-Weissmann. I choose you."

"And I choose you. I hate that I ever caused you to doubt. But I do choose you. Every day I choose you, Ben."

The two of them sat in a companionable silence for a long time, taking in the fresh ocean air.

"How does Pamela feel about all this?"

Ben offered a nervous laugh. "This isn't going to be easy for her either. I still come home to you every night and wake up beside you every morning."

"She still loves you?"

"Yes."

"And you still love her," Shira said, as a statement, not a question.

"Not the way you think I do. You should never fear that love because it's a different thing than I feel for you."

"I did ask you to accept my love for Liz, and I know it wasn't easy." Shira brushed a blowing strand of hair out of her face and narrowed her eyes at Ben. "Do you still want to sleep with her?"

"No."

Shira let out a deep sigh. "So our open marriage phase is officially over?"

"Looks that way."

Shira offered Ben her pinkie. "Let's shake on it."

The two of them locked pinkies and sealed it with a kiss.

"So, you and Pamela came to this arrangement without me?"

"Um," Ben hesitated, "we didn't exactly come up with an agreement. We just agreed to keep talking."

"My parents are going to freak the fuck out. First my girlfriend is having our baby, then *your* girlfriend is having our baby. I'm afraid we'll give them whiplash."

"They love you unconditionally. They'll roll with it. I'm sure they'll find a way."

"I hope this isn't too much."

"My dad once told me after I crashed his car that there is never too much. His job was to love me no matter what, and this is pretty far from crashing my father's new car."

"But she won't be Jewish. My dad's going to freak."

"Does it really matter at this point? After all this. This is our life, not his. We will share our traditions and holidays and values, and if we do it right, they'll be right there with us."

"I guess. I can teach Charlie how to write Hebrew letters and teach her songs." And then, realizing she was getting ahead of herself again, Shira froze. "I'm going to stop talking about her right now. I won't plan, I won't project. I'll do my best just to take things as they come."

"Do you really think you can do that?"

"No." Shira laughed. "I'm already decorating her room in my mind."

Ben gave her a big hug. "Thank you for being open to this. We do what we have to do in this imperfect world."

"Yep," Shira said. "And we will do what we have to do. I promise."

33

Shira sat beside Ben in silence, a steaming mug of green tea throwing wispy ghosts into the air before them. She wouldn't look at Ben, her rigid body frozen in place, eyes alternately flicking between a dry patch of skin on the back of her left hand and the door of the coffee shop, anticipating Pamela's arrival. Ben's heart pounded, and he just wished Pamela would get there so at least the waiting and the unknowns would be behind them. It had snowed over Christmas and it was still snowing now, lending that fuzzy liminal period before the New Year, when no one seemed to know or care what day of the week it was, a quality of being outside of time. Three days of snow had made driving difficult and parking nearly impossible, with giant mounds of snow piled up everywhere, and for a moment Ben feared Pamela would take the storm as an excuse to stand them up.

Ben had spent weeks negotiating with Shira and Pamela, trying to convince them both that meeting each other was a good thing, a necessary thing even. In the end, Shira had agreed, but she had thrown her arms around Ben and squeezed as tightly as she could, saying, "You have no idea how hard this is for me."

Pamela had made no promises, except that she would meet Shira, reluctantly, and see how things went from there. Her first priority was carrying and nurturing a healthy child, she said, and anything else, well, that was just extra. She should have been on her way, and Ben still couldn't believe he was sitting with his wife in a coffee shop on Trapelo Road waiting to introduce Shira to his former lover. It wouldn't be real until she walked in the door, her third trimester belly popping.

Shira wore a thick knitted scarf around her neck as if it were protective armor, and a woolen winter hat she had knit a few years back. "Maybe she got in an accident."

"Don't do this," Ben said. Snow storms like this always set his anxiety on a hair-trigger.

"Do what?" Shira turned her full body in his direction, eyes blazing. "The roads are slippery. All I'm saying is maybe she got in an accident."

Ben squeezed Shira's hand and she apologized. "I'm just nervous, Ben. Maybe I'm not ready for this. Maybe she's not ready for this. Our lives are about to change forever. It's just ... a lot, you know?"

Ben had spoken to Pamela before she had flown back to Philadelphia for Christmas, and though she had been circumspect, she had promised to meet Shira face to face. But maybe something had changed over Christmas dinner. Maybe Pamela's parents had talked her out of sharing custody of her child. Perhaps they had convinced her to move back home where they could be hands-on grandparents—no need to involve anyone else, least of all a married Jew from Boston.

The door clanged open, and Shira swiveled her head violently, but it was just a man in a trench coat and an old-fashioned fedora. He looked like someone out of a Raymond Chandler novel except he carried a bright orange messenger bag and wore rubber galoshes on his shoes that squeaked on the wet floor.

Shira eked out a small smile, said "False alarm," and sighed. "It's not okay to be late. Not for something like this."

"Take a look outside. It's practically a blizzard."

"And yet we managed to arrive on time."

Ben slid closer to Shira and stroked her cheek with the back of his knuckles. Shira breathed in deeply, closed her eyes and molded herself into Ben so their thighs were touching beneath the right angle of the tabletop. Her muscles were clenched as hard as a marble statue, and Ben could feel the blood pounding inside her. When Shira opened her eyes they were dewy, and a tear glittered on her eyelash like a diamond.

"It's going to be okay," Ben said.

Shira drew back from Ben. "How exactly can this possibly work? I'm sure she loathes me, and I can't help but hate that it's her and not me carrying your child." Shira raised her mug to her lips but did not drink. "I'm trying to be okay with this, but it just gets crazier and crazier. Why should I expect things will ever turn out okay?"

"Because you're an optimist. That's one of the things I love most about you. You really believe anything is possible."

"Yeah, well." Shira shook her head. "I'm afraid I'll never be anything like a mother to this child, just a glorified babysitter with an empty womb and a broken heart."

"You're just scared. I'm scared too. I want us to do this together. I don't know how this is going to work, but we're going to be in her life in a major way. All I know is that we'll find a way because it has to work. It just has to because that child is going to need all the love it can get."

"Maybe this is a mistake," Shira said, shifting to get up. "I just don't know if I can—"

The front door swung open again, carrying a biting chill into the shop, and Pamela materialized out of the swirling snow, framed for an instant in the threshold, face shrouded by the fur-lined hood of an ankle-length shearling coat. She threw back the hood and there she was, pale skin, a violent slash of red lipstick painted across her lips, green eyes piercing. Pamela strode across the coffee shop with that same don't-fuck-with-me attitude she had that first time Ben had seen her at the MFA, and Ben's stomach dipped as if she had disembarked from a time machine and he was seeing her for the very first time.

Ben scuffed back his chair and stood to greet Pamela. With a kiss, a handshake, a simple wave? He caught Shira out of the corner of his eye as she looked on with a glassy stare, shoulders drooping.

Ben cleared his throat to speak, face burning, tongue as thick and useless as a wet slice of bread.

The air shifted around him, and Shira was on her feet. She'd yanked off her scarf and hat and her hair snapped with static. She reached out a hand to Pamela and said, "Hi. I'm Shira."

"I know," Pamela said, offering a stiff smile. "I'm Pamela."

"I know that too." Shira laughed nervously.

"Why don't we all have a seat?" Ben said. "Who needs a cup of Joe?"

Both women shook their heads in unison.

"Sorry I'm late," Pamela said, slipping out of her coat and draping it over a chair. "My car got plowed in and so I had a friend drive me."

There was something mischievous in Pamela's smile and the way she said *friend*.

In the two months since Ben had last seen Pamela, her belly had popped and rounded, and Ben wanted nothing more than to touch it.

Shira had taken off her coat as well, and she wore a form-fitting black turtleneck that accentuated her curves, her full breasts. Some silent combat was taking place on a frequency Ben could barely make out. The two women sat, and for a moment nobody said a word, as if the three of them were on the most awkward first date in the world. Pamela looked straight ahead, passively, completely still, hands laced on the table. Shira chewed her lower lip while Ben ransacked his mind for the right words, hot beads of flop sweat bubbling at his hairline. He hadn't prepared a script, or anything for that matter, trusting that he would rise to the occasion with the right words, but he had none.

Pamela's left hand drifted to her belly and she stroked it idly in a soft circular motion, and Ben followed Shira's eyes, a pang spiking in his chest.

Shira began to speak and then stopped herself, as if reconsidering the wisdom of her words. Then she smiled softly, took a breath and released it, and said, "*B'Sha'ah tovah*."

"Excuse me?" Pamela said.

"It's Hebrew," Shira said. "It means 'at a good hour.' It's how Jews wish an expectant mother good luck."

"Not mazal tov?" Pamela tilted her head slightly.

"Mazal tov is for after the child is born."

"So many rules," Pamela said. "I don't know how you keep them all straight."

"Not rules. Traditions."

Ben could tell how uncomfortable Pamela was by the telltale pink tinge rising at her neck and cheeks. Just a short time ago it would have been the most natural gesture in the world to lean forward and caress her hair.

"I just wanted to thank you for agreeing to meet," Ben said.

Pamela let out a dry laugh. "I'm not a monster. I'm not going to deny you access to *our* child."

Shira slumped in her seat, her hands fidgeting on the tabletop.

"I'm the mother," Pamela said, flashing a meaningful look at Shira.

"We're all scared," Shira said. "But I assure you, I have no intention of taking anything away from you."

Ben nodded. "We all want to be good to this child. How can that possibly be bad?"

"I want clarity in my life, not some never-ending melodrama. It will be a hell of a lot simpler without adding you into the equation. I never signed up for your circus."

Ben started to speak, but Pamela cut him off.

"I've spoken to a lawyer," she said, pausing long enough to let her words sink in.

Shira gripped Ben's thigh, her fingers clenching through the fabric of his pants hard enough there would be a mark the next day.

"In Massachusetts, mothers and fathers have equal rights in child custody cases. When the child is born to unwed parents, the father is required to establish paternity to assert their rights as a parent."

"But Ben is definitely the father?"

"Yeah, he is," Pamela said.

"Oh, thank God," Shira said.

"There was only Ben. But he will need to prove it to the state."

"I can't believe I'm happy my husband knocked up another woman."

"I'm not *another woman*. And that's the problem. I won't be defined as some side piece that got careless. I don't exist in relation to Ben."

"That's not what I meant," Shira said.

"This whole arrangement you're proposing is so maddeningly patronizing. You're questioning my ability to be a good mother."

"That's not what we're doing at all," Ben said. "We want to be a part of Charlie's life. She's my child as much as yours."

"That's not the way it feels to me. This child is mine; she depends *entirely* on me right now. I fail to see how you can stake an equal claim." Pamela stroked her belly. "I can ask the court for full custody and they will grant it to me if they know about your swinging, polyamorous lifestyle. Tattooed girlfriends, BDSM jamborees."

"Are you serious? You know that's not how it was," Ben said.

"Oh, really?" Pamela said.

There had to be some way to salvage the situation. He looked to Shira for an answer, and, as usual, she had one.

"I also spoke to a lawyer," Shira said. "My father is friends with the former president of the Harvard Law Review and he put me in touch with one of his colleagues who says we can counter your accusation of unfitness with our own case, and the two of us, me and Ben, with no criminal history, drug or alcohol abuse, no history of depression, a stable home with lots of money in the bank, can petition for sole custody even if there are no concerns about your fitness as a parent. They may side with us, because two parents are better than one."

Pamela stared daggers at Shira, and Ben could not believe what he was hearing. They had never discussed trying to take Pamela's child away. "Who says I'll be doing this alone? Did you ever think maybe I met someone?"

The entire world seemed to hold its breath as Ben asked, "Did you meet someone?"

"Maybe I did," Pamela said.

"Wait, what?" Ben said.

Shira leaned forward and looked Pamela confidentially in the eye. "What's his name?"

After a long pause, in which it seemed Pamela had chosen not to respond, she said at last, "Paul. His name is Paul." Then she smiled, and Ben's innards went cold. Her entire bearing changed in that instant as if she were thawing from the cold. That precise smile had once been reserved for him. She had kissed Ben with those lips and now she was kissing a man named Paul.

"And he's the friend who drove you?" Shira prompted.

"He's circling the block right now."

"I dated a guy named Paul in high school," Shira said. "He was a lot of fun. Pretty big nerd, but that worked just fine for me."

"My Paul's no nerd," Pamela said.

My Paul, Ben thought. *Already?*

The two women continued chatting as if Ben wasn't even there.

"He flies a turboprop in his spare time. Out of Hanscom Airfield."

"Oh that would scare the shit out of me," Shira said. "I'm such a chickenshit."

"I hear you," Pamela said. "But he *knows* what he's doing."

Then the two exchanged a look full of meaning, and they both began to laugh.

"Yep," Pamela said. "He sure does."

"I hate to interrupt," Ben said, so not hating to interrupt, "but shouldn't we get back to what we came here to discuss?"

"Sorry, Ben," Pamela said. Even his name sounded different out of her mouth now. "But Shira asked and I answered."

"I just have to ask one more question," Shira said.

"Go ahead."

"How did you two meet?"

Pamela's eyes sparkled, and she let out a throaty laugh. "I've actually known him for years. I manage his portfolio at my organization. We always kind of had a certain chemistry, but I never pressed it because, you know, work. The funny thing is, he was supposed to meet me at lunch at the Museum of Fine Arts but had to cancel at the last minute." Pamela turned to Ben. "That's the day we met. Talk about kismet."

It would be easy to be nostalgic about that day, knowing there really was nothing inevitable about he and Pamela meeting, and Ben was suddenly grateful to have had a chance to know her the way he did. Ben only hoped that somehow he had left Pamela a better person than he had found her.

"I'm so glad things are working out for you," Shira said.

"We're still pretty new. But I feel good about where we are."

"You look beautiful," Shira said. "You wear pregnancy well."

"You don't need to flatter me."

"I mean it. You look healthy and beautiful." Shira took a deep breath and unclenched her fingers. "Before today. Before now, right now, I never really saw you as a full human being, but rather a shadowy character on the edge of my life. Not quite a villain. I'll admit I've had my jealous moments—oh boy, have I—and I was so afraid to accept you because I know how much my husband cares about you. You were good for him during a time when he needed someone to be good to him, when I couldn't give him what he needed. So, I wanted to thank you for doing your best to be good to Ben."

"Doing my best?" Pamela said. "Ouch. What does that mean?"

"It means just that. All we can do is our best, but we're always going to hurt those we love because that love matters so damn much, and I know there's a lot of hurt around this table. We've all hurt each other. But, I promise you, neither of us want to take anything away from you. And, honestly, I never called a lawyer, and my dad doesn't know the editor of the Harvard Law Review. I was just scared and blurted out the first thing that came to my mind. It was a dick move." Shira swept her hair off her forehead and said, "I want to find a way for us to get along."

"I think we kind of do get along," Pamela said.

"There are lots of ways to build a family, and you having Ben's child makes us family in a way."

"Eskimo sisters?" Pamela laughed.

"More than that," Shira said.

Ben looked at the two loves of his life, sitting so close to each other at the battered table, and he wanted to take each of their hands in his and create the perfect circle, in which Charlie would be the center amid the safety and love of their closed loop.

"You are Charlie's mother, and Ben is her father," Shira said. "But I promise you I will care for her as if I carried her myself. What could ever be wrong with that?"

"I'm so sorry for what you've gone through," Pamela said. "I really am." Her hand drifted back to her belly, caressing it lightly, unconsciously. "I know how hard this must be for you."

"Well, I've never been much for stiff upper lip and all that. I'm extravagant in my feelings; I wear them like a Technicolor Dreamcoat."

Pamela laughed, and Shira added, "Just know how lucky you are."

"I do."

Pamela's phone buzzed on the table. She glanced at the message on her screen, her lips forming a small smile, green eyes glimmering. "I should get going. It was good to meet you."

"Ditto. We'll meet again?"

"Definitely." Pamela rose to her feet.

Ben opened the door of the coffee shop and stepped out into the wind, tangled with barbs of thick snow. Pamela followed, and then Shira. Shira slipped on some ice and grabbed hold of Ben.

"Careful," Pamela said. The fur on the hood of her shearling was dusted with a thick layer of snow.

"Where's your ride?" Ben said, not ready to say his name out loud.

"He's waiting at the corner."

Ben craned his neck to catch a glimpse of Paul's car, hazard lights flashing, but saw nothing but a row of snow-covered cars hunched like a line of sleeping sheep.

"We're going this way," Shira said. "So, goodbye?"

"For now," Pamela said, leaning in and hugging Shira.

Then she turned to Ben, a half-apologetic look on her face, as if to say, *You knew it was going to happen.*

"Is it okay to hug you?" Ben said.

"Of course."

They hugged, and, for Ben, who had never known Pamela in winter all layered up and six months pregnant, it felt as if he was holding a different person altogether.

Pamela leaned close to Ben's ear and said, "Tell me you're happy for me," in that quiet, intimate voice he had loved so much.

"I'm glad you're happy," Ben said.

"Thank you. And I hope you're happy."

She kissed him quickly on the cheek and turned towards Paul and his warm, waiting car and her new life. Pamela had never looked more beautiful than when she was walking away, and something inside Ben whispered to go after her, but Shira linked her arm in his and said, "So that was Pamela."

Ben's eyes burned in the wind, and he looked back to catch one last look at Pamela, but she had disappeared into the howling snow.

About the Author

Jonathan Papernick was born and raised in Toronto, Canada. He is the author of the acclaimed short story collections *The Ascent of Eli Israel* and Gallery of the Disappeared Men and a novel, *The Book of Stone*. Papernick has taught fiction writing at Emerson College since 2007 and serves as Senior Writer-in-Residence in the department of Writing, Literature and Publishing. He has two sons and two stepdaughters and lives outside Boston with his wife.